In 2009, she had the chance to visit Karachi and, captivated by the beauty of Pakistan and the people, she stayed for a year. *The Long Road from Kandahar* has been influenced both by army life and her time in north Pakistan.

Also by Sara MacDonald

Listening to Voices
The Sleep of Birds
Sea Music
The Hour Before Dawn
Come Away with Me
Another Life
In a Kingdom by the Sea

Sara MacDonald worked at the Theatre Royal Windsor as Assistant Stage Manager before training a place at the London Academy of Music and Dramatic Art (LAMDA). After a brief acting career, she became an army wife and travelled widely, inspiring the many settings of her novels.

Having fallen in love with Cornwall as a child, she moved there to put down her first roots and began to write. She has written seven novels, and Cornwall, in all its beauty and wildness, features in all of them.

The
Long Road
from
Kandahar

SARA MACDONALD

HarperCollins*Publishers*

HarperCollins*Publishers* Ltd
1 London Bridge Street,
London SE1 9GF

www.harpercollins.co.uk

HarperCollins*Publishers*
1st Floor, Watermarque Building, Ringsend Road
Dublin 4, Ireland

First published by HarperCollins*Publishers* 2022
1

Excerpts from *Ave Imperatrix: Complete poetry* by Oscar Wilde,
reproduced with permission of Licensor through PLSclear.

A catalogue record for this book is available from the British Library

ISBN: 978-0-00-824524-5 (PB b-format)
ISBN: 978-0-00-853256-7 (TPB)

This novel is entirely a work of fiction.
The names, characters and incidents portrayed in it are
the work of the author's imagination. Any resemblance to
actual persons, living or dead, events or localities is
entirely coincidental.

Typeset in Sabon LT Std by Palimpsest Book Production Ltd, Falkirk, Stirlingshire

Printed and bound in the UK using 100% Renewable Electricity
by CPI Group (UK) Ltd

MIX
Paper from
responsible sources
FSC
www.fsc.org   FSC® C007454

This book is produced from independently certified FSC™ paper
to ensure responsible forest management.

For more information visit: www.harpercollins.co.uk/green

To the generation of men and women who fought in Operation Herrick, Afghanistan, 2002–2014

The Breath of Sleeping Boys

Something is about to happen.

Legs are crossed fingers.

A cup falls from its handle.
A wall crumbles into the road
under the weight of a flower bed.

In their dreams
something is about to happen.

Saved and damned, saved and damned –
the breath of sleeping boys.

One wave breaks, another inhales
and something is about to happen . . .

Paul Henry

PART ONE

CHAPTER ONE

Swat Valley, Pakistan, 2007

Raza lay on his stomach on a flat rock, peering out towards the horizon where the sinking sun covered the mountains in flares of red and gold light. He held a piece of wood that he had carved into the shape of a gun and he was making soft ack-ack noises in the back of his throat as he fired.

His enemy was unseen. The invading hordes of infidel soldiers lying crouched in the shadows of the mountains were conjured and fuelled in his mind by the apocryphal but blood-curdling stories brought back from Afghanistan by his two older brothers, Ajeet and Fakir.

His father, Zamir, climbing the narrow path from the village to find him, paused at the outcrop of rocks and stood silently watching. Raza was supposed to be minding their herd of goats, but he was playing one of his endless imaginary games instead.

Smoke rose lazily from the stone houses in the valley below. The sound of the child's voice mimicking gunfire was muffled by the echoing bleat of goats.

In Zamir's imagination he heard real gunfire, saw the hardened face and gnarled hands of an older Raza, wielding a Kalashnikov with the same zeal and fanaticism as Ajeet and Fakir.

The sun began to cast shadows over the dry earth as Zamir gazed out into the dying of the day. How little had changed in his lifetime. The Russians invaded, western nations made war on the Talibs, but he was still poor, his sons were still uneducated.

Unaware of his father, Raza sat cross-legged watching the sun drop and gild the mountain peaks. The gold of sunset tinged his hair like a halo. The stillness of his small body touched Zamir. There was a yearning in him that was familiar. A longing for something the heart could not fathom; a curiosity that extended beyond his known world. It was a sensation that had no form or shape. It was a shiver that entered a man's soul, as seductive as the pull of the mountains or a woman. It was an absence in what lay before him, an intuitive thirst for something more.

Zamir turned away. He knew what he had to do. The Talibs had taken both Ajeet and Fakir as soon as they could hold a gun. He was not going to let that happen to his youngest son. He must not waver; he had made his decision. If he did not take action now, it would be too late. If Ajeet and Fakir heard of his plans they would snatch Raza while he slept.

His older sons considered Raza, and all village boys his age, as bound to the Taliban. Raza's life was theirs to mould as they wished. It was too dangerous to speak of his plans to Raza. Or prepare him for what was to come, for the boy hero-worshipped his brothers. But tonight, as they ate their meal, he must tell the boy of their trip to Rawalpindi.

Zamir let out a piercing whistle as he saw his goats beginning to wander. Raza jumped and leapt off his rock,

4

his baggy *shalwar kameez* flapping in the wind. He began to herd the goats towards his father.

Behind his beard, Zamia hid a grin. He should be angry and beat the boy for being careless with the herd, but he knew he would do no more than scold.

The sky was crimson behind Raza and the small climbing figure was etched as a dark silhouette amongst the white goats. The boy had jammed his *kufi* back on his head and iridescent threads caught the last of the light.

Zamir saw how thin Raza was. The goats and sheep were also thin. This drought was ruining the crops. Starvation was a step away. His heart ached with the loss to come, but he knew there was no other decision he could have made to secure his son's future.

As Raza reached Zamir he called out, laughing. '*Allaha'Akhabar*. God is great. All the goats are here, *Baba*.'

Zamir swiped at the boy's head. 'No thanks to you,' he muttered, pulling his turban close and wrapping his face in the thick cloth against the cold wind as night slid over the mountains.

CHAPTER TWO

Cornwall, 2009

Finn sat on the garden step of his grandparents' house in Penzance on the first day of his summer holidays. He was watching a buzzard wheeling over the trees. It was making a high mewing call as two crows tried to mug him. The large birds, weaving and soaring to avoid each other, reminded Finn of his house in Germany. The woods that surrounded the army quarters in Hohne were full of birds of prey.

He should have been flying home to Germany today, but there had been a sudden change of plan. Ben, his father, had rung to say the regiment were leaving for Afghanistan two weeks earlier than planned so his leave would begin next week.

'No point coming home for a week, Finn. Stay where you are with Delphi and Ian and help get the beach house ready for our holiday. Can't wait to get into the water with you.'

It made sense but what if Ben's leave was cancelled? It had happened before in a crisis. What if Ben had to suddenly fly off to Lashkar Gah and he did not get to see him before he left?

Finn felt the knot of anxiety begin again in his stomach. At half-term, the atmosphere between his parents, in the dark quarter surrounded by trees had disturbed him. He had felt a guilty relief in staying put with his grandparents. With Delphi and Ian, the days unfolded in a peaceful and predictable fashion. They did not constantly snap at each other.

Delphi lowered herself beside him on the step. After a bit she said, 'You know, darling, the hardest bit for you all is waiting for Ben to go. Try not to worry about your parents. I know half-term was a bit tense, but adults do bicker. Hanna and Ben both need a break and you're all going to have a wonderful, relaxed holiday together at the beach house before Ben leaves . . .'

Finn dared not tell Delphi what was in his mind. If he spoke his thoughts out loud, he might make them happen. It was true that his parents often bickered, benignly, but Finn had sensed a subtle difference in the tone of their bickering.

Hanna and Ben had taken care to smile and joke as usual in front of their children, but Finn noticed they rarely looked at one another or hugged anymore. His sister Izzy was probably too young to pick up bad vibes, but he wasn't, and his parents must think he was pretty stupid not to realize something was wrong. Finn was afraid to ask them in case it meant DIVORCE. The word filled him with dread and foreboding.

Delphi placed a small package on Finn's knees. 'I found one of my unused travel journals lurking about in a drawer. I wondered if you would like it. It's undated and the cover is rather lovely. If I'm feeling troubled about anything, I find that it helps to write my thoughts down on paper.'

7

Finn looked at his grandmother. She might be a witch. She always seemed to know how he was feeling. Delphi nudged him with her elbow to make him smile. Finn grinned. His grandmother felt solid against him; warm and safe. He began to unwrap the journal from the tissue paper. It had a blue cover with serrated edges. There were small photographs of foreign cities on each page. He could smell Delphi's scent on the paper. She must have kept it in a drawer for years. He loved it. It was a beautiful, typically Delphi present.

'Oh, cool!' He turned the pages slowly until he got to July. 'Thanks, Delphi.'

The photograph was Rome. Finn wanted to write in it straight away, but he decided he would wait until the four of them were all together again at the beach house. He would start to keep a diary of the summer. The summer before Ben left for Lashkar Gah.

That night Finn lay in bed in the room that had once been Ben's. His father's old school photos still hung on the walls. An old heavy cricket bat stood in a corner of the room. One of Ben's Iraqi service medals was pinned to a bald teddy bear on the dressing table.

Finn lay in the narrow bed, his mind constantly returning to his parents and Izzy back home in Germany. He wanted to erase the disturbing feeling he had been left with after half-term.

Hanna and Izzy had met him at Hanover Airport. Hanna was wearing a white shirt and red jeans with a large scarlet scarf wound elegantly around her shoulders. His mother was beautiful. People always turned to look at her. Her brown, shiny hair was the colour of conkers, cut sharp and straight to her chin.

Hanna had tucked his hand into her arm as they walked

8

to the car park. 'Sorry, Ben couldn't come to meet you. He is always working. He is always home late . . . You will be lucky to see much of him this half-term, I'm afraid . . .' Hanna's voice could not hide her annoyance.

Finn had said quickly. 'It's okay. Ben can't help working, Hanna. He rang and warned me . . .'

Hanna looked as if she was going to say more but concentrated instead on getting out of the airport and onto the autobahn. Silence fell as she drove. Hanna did not do small talk. Izzy fell asleep. Finn had stared out at the straight roads lined with forests flashing by. He only relaxed when Hanna turned off the autobahn to Hohne and headed into suburbia. Rows of identical army quarters lay in secure, tree-lined roads. Army wives walked black Labradors and small children under the dripping trees. Sentries guarded the gates to the barracks. Soldiers in combats yomped through the woods. They were entering a world of uniforms, military jargon, and acronyms. Finn loved it. It was a world he had grown up in, as familiar as breathing, but anathema to Hanna.

'Here we are, back home.' Hanna turned into their road and pulled up outside their quarter. For a moment she sat still without moving, as if she were putting off the moment of going inside. She unwound her scarf and shook out her dark hair so that it fell in smooth lines around her face. A sense of her loneliness, pungent and overpowering, had caught at Finn.

He stared out of the car at the dark windows of the empty quarter. The branches of trees were reflected in the glass. A strange foreboding had risen up inside him at the lack of light and warmth coming from inside. It was as if their house was suddenly devoid of life. As if his family had vanished leaving only black windows reflecting the wavering branches of trees.

Disturbed, Finn had jumped out of the car, lifted a sleepy Izzy from the back seat and swung her out with a whoop, making her giggle. It was an infectious sound and Hanna had turned and smiled at Finn as she locked the car.

'Silly of me, I should have left some lights on.'

Finn lay listening to the whoosh of the sea slapping against the promenade. He could not forget Hanna's bleak face as the trees made shadows dance in the windows of the dark house. In that second of panic, Finn had seen his home was just an empty German army quarter. Then Ben had driven up behind them gently tooting his horn. He had leapt out of his car in his combats and enfolded him in a bear hug. Hanna had gone around the house, switching all the lights on. The windows had reflected once more the lives they all led there together.

CHAPTER THREE

Peshawar, 2007

Raza was following Zamir through the crowds of the Qissa Khawani Bazaar (The Street of Storytellers). His excitement was countered by a niggling anxiety. Baba was not himself. He seemed nervous and he had made Raza pack his Friday *shalwar kameez* and fold extra clean clothes into his large bundle. His father had also taken unusual care in picking out two of his fattest sheep to sell.

'We will spend one night with your uncle Hanif in Peshawar.' Zamir told Raza as they rocked downhill in the bus packed with villagers taking fruit, vegetables, and fowl to market. Zamir's sheep were following separately in a truck containing the larger animals. 'Tomorrow, we will go on to Rawalpindi to meet your mother's cousin, Sarah, and her British husband. They are visiting from England and wish to see you, but first we must sell the sheep . . .' 'Why do they wish to see me?' Raza asked, although it explained all the clean clothes he was forced to carry. 'They have never come to 'Pindi before.'

'Cousin Sarah's British husband, he does not like her to

travel around Pakistan on her own. Usually, she stays with her relatives in Karachi. This time he has come with her . . .' Zamir turned stern eyes on Raza. 'I have told you. Your Ami and Sarah were children together in Karachi until her family left for England. Of course, she is interested in seeing you.'

They had now reached the bustle of the busy market and Zamir had tied his sheep to a post in what he hoped was a prime position by Hanif's nut stall. He did not have high expectations for his sheep, but he needed enough rupees to buy bus tickets, food, and presents for the visiting cousins from England. He gazed through the crowds. He had felt anxious as soon as they stepped off the bus. Peshawar was Ajeet and Fakir's territory; there was danger in making themselves prominent, but he needed to sell his sheep. Raza, picking up Zamir's anxiety, wondered why his Baba was selling his sheep to buy presents for these distant cousins they did not know, instead of food to fill their bellies. It had been a bad season. The ground was dry and hard from the long drought. Their crops had been poor and shrivelled from lack of rain and their sheep and goats had not put on enough weight.

The noisy market and the sound of people haggling and shouting caught at Raza in a dizzying wave of sound. He eyed the food and fruit stalls with longing but knew better than to ask for anything to eat. His stomach was never full, but he had learned to get used to the sound of it rumbling.

Uncle Hanif was sitting on a step by his hot nut stall drinking green tea. '*Assalamu alaikum.*' He beamed, showing even more gaps in his teeth. He handed Raza a cone of nuts. 'Welcome, boy. I do not see you often.'

A man in a pale turban and riding boots paused to look at the sheep. Zamir and Hanif began to extol the virtues of

12

the tenderness and taste of sheep that are grazed high on the mountains. The three men settled down to bargain over the price with tiny cups of Jasmine tea. Raza wandered away and sniffed the tantalizing smells coming from the food stalls. Cardamom tea and incense filtered into air that was laced with the smell of fresh bread. Sandalwood and tobacco infused the clothes stalls.

The smell of hot food being thrown, turned, and slapped on griddles was unbearable. The crowds thronging the narrow sidewalk jostled Raza forward like a small ship in a rough sea.

The voices of the stallholders, calling out in many dialects – Pashto, Farsi, Urdu, Punjabi, Dari – made Raza disorientated as well as hungry.

He turned and let himself be carried back on a wave of people to Baba and Uncle Hanif. They were still haggling over the sheep. Raza sat on the kerb by the monsoon drain and ate his nuts slowly to make them last.

The Pathan wanted lamb for his daughter's wedding and he and Baba were arguing about how many people the two sheep would feed. Not many, Raza thought.

The last time Raza had come down from the mountains he had been with Ajeet and Fakir. They had not come into the town but headed straight for the Kohat Valley, for Darra Adamkhel, about forty kilometres away. Raza felt excited even thinking about Darra. The valley was a mass of gun shops and factories manufacturing and selling arms. Every gun known to man could be made or copied in Darra. It was a thrilling place. Once Raza had held a gun as small as a pen that could fire a .22 bullet.

Craftsmen, as young as Raza and as old as Zamir worked in the factories, often designing their own guns. They were adept at replicating English Lee Enfields, .303 rifles, revolvers, and Sten guns.

Ajeet and Fakir stroked and handled the guns lovingly and placed them in Raza's hands so that he could feel the weight and heft between his palms. Inside the factories and workshops, he watched copies of Russian Kalashnikov automatic rifles and guns being made for the Pakistani army. Every weapon of any description changed hands here, for a price.

The atmosphere was heady with tension and intent. To a Pashtun, the choice of a gun was a serious matter, a way of life. Crouched with his brothers on the floor of a gun shop, beside fierce men bartering for a beautifully crafted gun laid lovingly across their knees, made Raza feel part of their world.

Restless with the relentless roll of each day and constantly hungry, Raza knew he only had to wait a few more years before he could join Ajeet and Fakir and carry his own gun across his shoulders. Raza also knew that his Baba wanted him to have an education.

The first school he had attended had been blown up. The second school, even further away, had closed after a month. The teacher, threatened by the local Taliban, had been too frightened to return.

Zamir had been taught to read in a *Madrassa*. He was patiently teaching Raza to read with the aid of old local newspapers. He also taught him Urdu, his mother's language, and the little English he knew.

Raza was quick to learn, but fidgety. Zamir did not have books to keep him interested and Raza quickly grew bored, longing to escape to the mountains and into his imagination; to run with his sheep and goats and play *Mujahideen*.

Zamir was respected in the village *Jirga* for his wisdom in settling disputes. Women especially came to him for advice. He had treated his wives well and never beaten them. Some of the other elders, however, remembering how zealous Zamir had once been in seeing off the Russians, believed he had grown soft with age.

To protect Raza, Zamir was careful of what he said out loud and what he taught his son. He never admitted his reverence for books and learning, especially not to his eldest sons.

Raza finished his bag of nuts. Baba and the turbaned Pathan were now gesticulating loudly, both pretending to be insulted by offer and counteroffer. Uncle Hanif joined in defending family honour. Raza sighed, scratching the bites on his legs. This could go on for ages and he would die of hunger.

Raza noticed how his Baba's eyes kept darting through the crowds. Was Baba afraid that his brothers might suddenly appear to interfere in the selling of his sheep or stop their journey to Rawalpindi?

His brothers grumbled endlessly about how the old man had lost his fire, was growing senile. It was true Baba no longer wanted to hear about killing infidels. Nor was he interested in admiring the devices and weapons his brothers carried. Baba's face would close at their boasts. He would walk away from them to be alone or go to the mosque to pray.

Once, his father had turned on Ajeet angrily. 'Don't you ever wish for an end to all this bloodshed and death? Don't you crave a better life for your sons and daughters? A place where they can be educated and enjoy all that Allah has blessed us with?' Zamir had waved his arms at the snow-capped mountains and the orchards that lay in blossom in the valley below.

Raza remembered the contemptuous look Ajeet had given Baba. He had accused him of growing old and treacherous. If the Taliban did not fight for the people, who would? Did the old man want them all just to sit back and let the

Pakistani army force them out of their homes? Drive them out of the Tribal Areas and down into the cities?

Raza hated it when either of his brothers showed disrespect for Baba. He would have liked to defend his father, but he was not brave enough to risk his brothers' anger.

The deal with the sheep was abruptly sealed. Hands were clasped. Zamir looked pleased. Uncle Hanif produced tiny cups of black tea and the brothers crouched on their haunches sealing their bargain and indulging in local gossip.

Raza was about to wander off in the hope of some generous stallholder when he was alerted by his uncle's lowered voice whispering his name. Raza turned and caught both men watching him. He felt a sudden shiver of dread. There was indeed something strange about this visit to relations in Rawalpindi.

CHAPTER FOUR

Cornwall, 2009

The night before Ben and Hanna arrived in Cornwall the evening was glorious. Silvery and mild and the surf clean. Finn took his board out and surfed for a couple of hours with local boys he saw each summer.

The shabby and much loved beach house was ready for everyone. It lay at the end of a long sandy track, the last chalet on the curve of a long surfing beach.

Finn had helped Delphi sweep the sandy floorboards, tidied his small bedroom with the two built-in bunk beds and chucked out a load of his old books so there was enough room to accommodate Izzy's toys.

Delphi stuffed the fridge with food and Ian set up a new barbecue as the old one had rusted away. He was so keen to try out his new toy that they decided to get the sleeping bags out of the car and stay the night. They picnicked on sausages, burgers and rolls and Delphi, watching Finn's face glowing from the sea, saw him begin to relax. All that was needed now was a united Ben and Hanna, good weather, lovely friends, and two weeks of fun for the four of them.

17

Delphi was glad the Applebys had been able to change their holiday plans to still join Ben and Hanna. They always brought fun and laughter. Fergus and Ben had been at Sandhurst together, joined the same regiment and served together in Iraq. Mary and Hanna had become unlikely but good friends.

Looking out into the dark where the water swelled and rippled, Delphi thought she should be used to Ben heading for war zones by now, but she wasn't. In fact, it got worse with age, and grandchildren.

She made some hot chocolate and took it in to Finn. He was sitting up in his sleeping bag on the bottom bunk bed turning the pages of the journal she had given him.

'When did you get this journal, Delphi?' he asked. 'Why did you never write in it?'

Delphi placed his mug on the old stool beside him and sat awkwardly on the edge of the bunk. 'I bought it on a long weekend in Rome, a hundred years ago. Ian booked the trip as a surprise. You can see the pages are slightly yellow, even though I've had it wrapped in tissue paper in a box . . .'

Finn looked at her. It must have been special if Delphi had kept it so carefully all these years. Why had she suddenly decided to take it out and give it to him?

'But you always write in your diaries. Every year. You must have bought it so you could write in it,' he persisted.

'I did,' Delphi said. 'But somehow, I could not commit any of my feelings to paper at the time. I would often get the journal out to look at the photos, to remind myself of that time and the places I travelled though. Then, when I had no need to be reminded, I tucked it away for the right person to fill its pages. And that's you!' Delphi laughed but Finn caught the edge of regret in her voice.

He examined his grandmother's face. 'Perhaps you were afraid to write things down in case they really happened?'

Delphi thought, *I bought a beautiful journal I was unable to deface with my treacherous feelings at the time. Yet, this treasured little book has stood, all these years, for hope and the power of love.*

'You know, darling,' she said brightly, 'writing your fears down doesn't make them come true, it just makes you face them. Putting them on paper somehow makes them seem smaller and more manageable. Those empty pages need filling with little episodes of your life, all your happy, funny, and anxious thoughts. We don't want the journal to crumble away sad and unused . . .'

Finn smiled and nodded. 'Okay. I'm going to start tomorrow . . .'

'Good. Go to sleep now. You'll need your energy for that little sister of yours.'

Finn groaned. 'Izzy will have had thirteen hours in a car, Delphi!'

'Don't!' Delphi laughed as she went out of the door. Finn's little sister may not have been planned, but what a wonderful difference she and boarding school had made to the solemn little boy Finn had become with Ben away so often. Hanna had been initially distraught at finding herself pregnant again, in a way inexplicable to Delphi.

Izzy, Delphi thought, has brought much-needed laughter and noise into that little family.

CHAPTER FIVE

Peshawar, 2007

Before they left Peshawar, Zamir, Raza and Hanif went to the mosque for prayers. As Raza knelt on his prayer mat between his father and uncle a shaft of sunlight slanted out of a high window across the floor reaching the fingers of his left hand.

He was struck by the luminous quality of the thin ray of light that caught the dust moats and made the edges of his fingers translucent. He was used to the beauty of sunrise and sunset over the mountains but kneeling, secure, between his father and uncle, this light seemed unreal and very bright, like a dream he should remember.

The wonder of it was followed by a sharp premonition of loss. Raza pressed his head into the prayer mat so that he could connect with the earth under him. He was conscious of the body heat of the two men each side of him. He bowed and prayed to the familiar rhythm of prayer until the moment passed.

*

Raza and Zamir sat on their bundles as they waited for the bus to Rawalpindi. The bus eventually swayed into sight, packed with people inside, on the roof, and hanging off the side windows. Raza stared as he always did, in awe and admiration. This particular bus was exceptionally ornamental. There was a bright red background on the sides with inlaid blue and green peacocks. There were gold moons and inlay over the cab. Swirling flowers covered the wheel hubs and silver beads swung from the front bumpers. There were little coloured glass shards on the back of the wing mirrors and carved bird's wings over the windscreen.

As a small boy Raza had never been content with just looking at the decorations on the buses, he needed to touch and examine the vibrant colours and delicate artwork. Zamir had explained that the Mughal queens used peacock feathers to adorn their bodies. Peacocks represented pride, which was why so many featured on the buses and trucks.

Two old women behind Zamir and Raza began to push and shove as the bus began to disgorge its incoming passengers. Raza said, 'You go inside, Baba. I will sit on the roof with the luggage.'

Zamir shook his head. He knew that Raza could not bear a long journey inside with so many people. 'I will travel on the roof with you. I am not too old to climb the side of a bus yet.'

Raza clambered nimbly onto the roof of the bus and bent down for their bundles. Zamir followed more slowly holding onto the bag with water and food for their journey. They sat on their bedrolls against the ornate rail at the front of the cab. Raza wound a length of cloth round his head to hide himself from the sun. Zamir was shielded by turban and scarf that he held across his face against the dust that would rise from the parched earth of the valley.

After what seemed hours, groaning and puffing dark

smoke, the bus turned awkwardly with the sheer weight of people aboard and swung like an elephant down the steep road towards the Kohat Valley.

As they passed through the flat plains housing the gun factories Zamir watched his son sit up and take interest. He was aware Ajeet and Fakir brought Raza here behind his back. It had been one more reason to feel uneasy; one more reason to make the decision he had.

Ajeet and Fakir had shown an increasing interest in the boy this past year. Zamir knew they would have no compulsion in grabbing Raza from him. Once he had been a fierce fighter with the *Mujahideen*. Now, he was an old man without power, and they had no need to treat him with respect.

Zamir could not tell Raza his plans for him. Despite his promises to Sarah, it was too dangerous. And how do you tell your son you are going to send him away? When he thought about Raza's bewilderment and his blind trust in him, Zamir's mouth dried and his heart beat painfully with the looming loss to come.

For a second, he wondered if he was giving himself room to change his mind at the last moment. Zamir shook his head violently against his own weakness and Raza turned. 'What is it Baba?'

'Nothing. Sleep. I will see you do not fall.'

Raza smiled and closed his eyes. How could he fall swamped by luggage and bodies? He yawned. Last night he had slept on a charpoy under the trees of a Peshawar street and it had been noisy. By the time the bus had left the valley and began to climb uphill Raza was slumped against his father fast asleep.

The rocking of the bus was soporific. Zamir dozed and daydreamed of his past. With his hands idle, memories filled his mind. At Raza's age his father had sent him to a Madrassa before he joined the *Mujahideen* to fight the Russians.

It was in the Madrassa that Zamir had his first glimpse of a world outside his own village and beyond his own country. His encounter with Mullah Rafi was the beginning of an inner life; a life where he allowed himself to privately reason, to form opinions and views he had to keep to himself.

Mullah Rafi had been educated in Lahore and then gone on to England to study. He was regarded suspiciously by the other mullahs. He had books, both in English and Urdu with pictures and stories. The boys were supposed to spend endless hours learning passages from the Koran by rote, but unlike the other mullahs in the Madrassa, Mullah Rafi was neither a religious fanatic, nor militant.

Outside, under the trees, in the cool of the courtyard, he quietly told his ragbag circle of boys, that in the west the law allowed every child, girl or boy, to go to school and receive an education. It was their right. No one was executed for opening a school or teaching in it. No one was put to death for belonging to a different tribe, for having a differing belief or religion.

Mullah Rafi told the listening boys that it was not true that all *goras* were evil. Pakistan was a sovereign country, her borders must be protected from invasion from east or west, but many foreigners came to Pakistan to do good. They helped build schools and health centres for the poor and Pakistan desperately needed these things.

He explained that in England, Islam thrived, mostly peacefully, among many other religions. Islam is a gentle religion, Mullah Rafi told the boys, and this has been forgotten. Allah did not want them to breed hate in their hearts for all *gorahs,* but to be educated and compassionate in order to understand a world outside Pakistan. Education is for both boys and girls, he told them firmly. Every single village in Pakistan should have a school.

The old mullah's words had wafted uneasily over the boys like an incomprehensible and dangerous foreign language. Zamir had listened and stored the essence and power of the alarmingly traitorous words until they were burnt into the fabric of his memory like an indelible tattoo.

As the mullah talked within the outer walls of the Madrassa the children could hear the endless chant of prayers and the terrifying rant of the head mullah with the older boys inside.

An instinctive frisson of fear shimmered through the listening boys. The only school left within one hundred miles had been blown up two weeks ago and celebrated by the mullahs here.

The leaves on the branches of dusty trees had rustled like a collective sigh as Mullah Rafi bent closer. 'Ignorance,' he whispered, is the enemy. This is how people in power want to keep you young boys, in ignorance. The answer to conflict is not in holding a gun and killing but by learning the nature and heart of your enemy. This is how you win wars and find resolution. Remember this . . .'

Zamir had remembered, but not necessarily for the right reasons. Mullah Rafi had been beheaded two days later for being a spy, a western puppet, a traitor to Islam. His severed head had been placed on a spiked gatepost, for all the boys to see the consequences of deviating from the word of Allah; of becoming contaminated by western influence and opposing *Jihad*.

All the boys received a beating for listening to the old mullah's words. For Zamir, nothing could expunge the shock at first hearing anyone openly express a veiled admiration for *infidels*.

24

When he was older, Zamir realized that the mullah must have known he would be put to death. He had sacrificed his life trying to implant a flicker of knowledge, a glimpse of hope for a less violent world in the hearts of indoctrinated boys. Zamir felt a fragment of comfort in the memory of Mullah Rafi. He had been unable to change the fate of his older sons, but it was in his power to change Raza's life.

Zamir sighed. From the time he could walk, Raza had hero-worshipped his older brothers. He had been proudly waiting to join them in *Jihad*. No conversation could prepare him for what Zamir was going to do.

Zamir understood Raza's longing to hold a gun, to fight. He was a *Pashtun*. When he had been Raza's age, he too had believed in the *Mujahideen,* Taliban, or anyone who helped fight off the Russian invaders of Afghanistan.

Fighting *Jihad* had been a way of life but the relentless death and destruction, the endless punitive laws and wanton cruelty to their own people had turned Zamir's stomach. He had come to see that it did not matter who was in power or who invaded. Taliban promises of recompense, electricity, land, drinking water, or a better life, were never kept. Your sons were lost to you. They died or were turned into men who had no compassion, even for their own families. Zamir had once stopped Ajeet beating his wife to death for dropping a bowl of rice in her terror of him.

He heard the echo of Mullah Rafi's voice as if his life had come a full circle with his youngest son. *Ignorance is the enemy. This is how they want to keep young boys. Ignorant. Uneducated. The answer is not in hate, in holding a gun and killing, but by understanding the nature and heart of your enemy. This is how you win wars.*

Zamir looked down at the sleeping face of the son he loved and shivered. Raza was not yet safe.

CHAPTER SIX

Cornwall, 2009

Hanna, Ben and Izzy arrived at the beach house in the late afternoon, frazzled by the ferry and a long drive with a small child. The hot August day still held warmth and their spirits soared as they looked out at the sea dancing with reflected light.

Finn stood grinning, happy and relieved to see them. Delphi and Ian had left Finn to greet them, knowing they would all be tired, and Hanna would prefer it. Finn knew that his grandmother irritated Hanna. He wasn't sure why, but her voice would change when she spoke Delphi's name. He had quickly realized, when he started boarding school, that it was better not to talk to Hanna about what he did with Delphi in term time.

Izzy rushed at him like a small tornado. Finn groaned as she threw herself at him. 'My God,' Hanna said, laughing, as she hugged Finn. 'Stop growing, Finn! You are only twelve and nearly as tall as me . . .'

Finn grinned. 'Not very hard to be as tall as you, is it?'

'Don't be rude,' Hanna said, her eyes on the glittering sea. 'Or I will make you call me Mother . . .'

Finn laughed. Hanna would hate to be called Mother. It was different with Izzy, but when he had been a baby, Ben and Hanna had never referred to themselves as Mummy and Daddy. Like Ben, he had always called his parents by their Christian names . . .

'I have to get into the water before the sun goes . . .' Hanna turned and ran into the beach house to change.

Ben pulled Finn to him. 'Great to see you, old thing.' They followed Hanna in with the bags. 'Do you know where your swimming things are?' Ben asked his daughter.

'In the top of her case,' Hanna called.

'I'll help Izzy. Go and get changed,' Finn told Ben.

'My new swimming thing is pink,' Izzy told Finn while she hopped up and down.

'Gosh! That's a surprise,' Finn said. 'Who would have thought it?'

Izzy looked at Finn sharply as she stepped into the neon pink swimming costume. 'Not a surprise, Finn. You know I like pink.'

Hanna came into the room. 'Finn's teasing. Come on, let's get into the water. We can unpack later.'

Ben hoisted Izzy onto his shoulders, and they set off down the beach past the clusters of families packing up for the day. Hanna dropped her towel in a heap and ran from them, ploughing into a sea alight from the dropping sun.

Ben stood watching her as she swam away from them with strong, confident strokes out to sea. Hanna was an exceptionally good swimmer, but her lack of fear of either strong currents or tides unnerved him.

Finn, squinting into the sun, saw his mother dive and disappear from view. She swam underwater for what seemed

27

an eternity. Then, up she came for air like a sleek seal, with the sea glinting and glittering all around her.

Ben let out his breath and pulled Izzy's armbands up over her wrists. She wriggled away and took off into the shallows with Finn and Ben close behind her.

The tide was on the turn and Ben still had his eye on Hanna as he played in the shallows with Izzy. Hanna lay on her back in the sea floating, oblivious, staring up at the sky. Finn longed to swim out to her, but some instinct told him that she needed to float peacefully on that shimmering sea on her own.

Hanna turned upright as if she had suddenly remembered them. She waved and smiled. 'Go on, go and swim with Hanna, I'll watch Izzy,' Finn said. He wanted them to be happy. He wanted them to be happy with each other.

'Good lad! Thank you . . .' Ben ran through the shallows and swam fast and effortlessly out to Hanna. When he reached her, he dived under her making her squeal. Then they both swam side by side in a silvery pathway made by the setting sun.

His mother was fearless in water. Like a mermaid, which is what Ben often called her. Hanna had grown up in Oulu, Southwest Finland, out in the wilderness, beside lakes and forests. 'My father was a forester,' she told Finn in the days before Izzy. 'He taught me to swim before I could walk . . .'

It was why Hanna didn't mind seaweed. She was used to diving off trees into weedy lakes with the water so cold and deep it nearly stopped her breath. 'You never knew what was down there,' she whispered to Finn. 'Lurking in the depths of a smooth dark lake . . .'

She would tell Finn stories of a private world so un-inhabited that a fish jumping would sound like a gunshot. A voice echoing over the water would sound like a hundred voices, making the birds on the lake fly upwards in wavering, filigree clouds.

'When the trees and earth were thick with snow,' Hanna whispered to Finn. 'The suffocating silence would swallow me whole. Make me feel tiny. Make me feel a little black dot in an infinite white landscape . . .'

She told Finn she was so often alone in the wilderness she formed vivid images of the water, sky, and trees dizzily encircling her. She felt at one with their roots centred deep in the earth. 'I did not need friends. I had the wild.'

'You are still wild!' Ben would joke. But Hanna had lost her wild place at 13 when her mother got unexpectedly pregnant again with twins. Her parents moved to the city to retrain, became different people. Had a new family, a new life. 'I never forgave them,' Hanna joked, smiling.

'I was a cuckoo in the nest . . .' But her smile never reached her eyes and Finn thought it was probably true.

Hanna and Ben were swimming back to shore in the dark, deep blue, their heads close together. The last of the sun was blinding, reflecting in dancing sparks off the water.

Finn felt a surge of joy as Izzy reached up and took his hand. *It was going to be all right.* He and Izzy ran along the shoreline kicking and jumping the curl of small waves.

'How about fish and chips in the café tonight?' Ben called, scooping Izzy out of the shallows and throwing her up in the air, making her squeal.

Ben knew that Delphi would have put supper for them in the fridge. He also knew that his mother would have loved to be here to meet them. She had learned to stand back and wait to be invited to her own beach house so Hanna would not feel encroached on.

Ben felt the familiar ache of guilt, knowing all Delphi and Ian did for them. He should override Hanna, but it had become easier, as the years went by, just to let it go, to convince himself Hanna was right to want the beach house to herself. It was a small thing. But, not to Ben. This year, particularly, he would have loved to have Delphi and Ian waiting for him.

As if he had read Ben's thoughts, Finn said, as they walked up the beach. 'We could ring Delphi and Ian to come, couldn't we?'

'Yus! It's a party. Tell 'em to come.' Izzy clapped her hands.

'Why don't you?' Hanna asked, glowing from her swim. 'Ask them to join us for fish and chips if they are not doing anything . . . it's a good idea to meet up before the Applebys arrive tomorrow . . .'

Ben smiled. 'Okay, I'll do that now . . .' He put Izzy on the ground and dug out his mobile. He was well aware that Hanna would make it politely clear to Delphi that, after tonight, they would be very busy with the Applebys. Ben also knew that Fergus and Mary, having spent countless holidays in Cornwall at the beach house, would automatically include Delphi and Ian, as a matter of course. 'Oh God,' he had complained to Fergus once, at a narrowly avoided family rift. 'I wish my mother and my wife could just try to get on. Delphi goes overboard on all things and Hanna withdraws into one of her icy silences.' Fergus had laughed. 'They are two strong women of a different generation and culture and the only thing they have in common is you, poor bugger!'

Ben pressed his parents' number. When Delphi answered he said, 'I have people here clamouring for you both to head over and have fish and chip with us . . . Please.'

Happiness is so easy, so fragile, Ben thought, hearing Delphi's happy laugh. He stood listening to Hanna and Izzy in the shower. He watched Finn unpacking her soft toys and placing them onto the bottom bunk. *He was home.*

30

He let out his breath, feeling the tension begin to leave his shoulders. Ten days of leave shimmered enticingly in front of him.

He went to the fridge and pinged open a beer. Outside the beach was nearly empty. The sun had dropped below the horizon leaving a trail of scarlet vapours spreading across the sky. Ben stood on the wooden veranda watching. He did not need to imprint a scene so familiar, but he consciously did so. A shadow flitted over him at the thought of what lay ahead. Not all of his boys would come home. Or back in one piece. Ben shook his melancholy away, letting the crimson sky and the soft murmur of the sea envelope him. This is what he would remember. This is what would sustain him in the months ahead.

CHAPTER SEVEN

Rawalpindi, 2007

Rawalpindi hovered in the shadows of its tribal past. It had been destroyed and then rebuilt by the Mughals in the fourteenth century. In the nineteenth century, the British guarding the North-West Frontier had turned it into a garrison town. It stood on the ancient Grand Trunk Road and was still a garrison town and the headquarters of the Pakistani army.

At the bus station Uncle Maldi was waiting to greet them.

Raza's head throbbed with the bus fumes and the noise and chaos of people looking for their luggage. He felt an urge to take off to the green hills he could see in the distance. Cities made him dizzy.

As they walked to Uncle Maldi's flat carrying their bundles, Raza looked about him. Baba used to tell him stories of Rawalpindi. In winter, snow fell softly from the Himalayas. In summer rich people from Lahore and Karachi passed through to go to Muree to escape the heat. Once upon a time, his father said, climbers and walkers from all over the world flocked to the mountains, now it was no longer safe.

In the middle of the cascade of army lorries, motorbikes and hooting cars a *Pathan* dressed in a turban and leather waistcoat rode a large, black horse. The man's head was high and his back ramrod straight. Raza stopped and stared in admiration. He and his horse seemed oblivious to the danger that rushed past them as they made their stately progress across the wide intersection.

Uncle Maldi smiled. 'That, my son, is one of our feudal lords. No one would dare to knock him off his horse! Come, let's get you home. Your aunt is waiting. Are you hungry?'

Zamir snorted. 'Of course. He is a boy. He is always hungry.'

'And you, brother?'

'I too am hungry.'

'Sarah has arrived,' Uncle Maldi said. 'She's staying at the Pearl Continental. She will come to eat with us tonight.'

'Alone? What about, Chinir, her husband?'

'Chinir, he has to go to a conference meeting this evening . . .' Maldi lowered his voice. 'Maybe, Sarah thought it better to meet Raza for the first time on her own.'

Zamir grunted and Maldi said, 'Don't worry, you will meet Chinir tomorrow.'

'It is important that Chinir likes the boy,' Zamir said quietly.

Raza, walking behind his father and uncle said, 'Why? I don't care, Baba.'

Zamir turned. 'Those big ears of yours will get you into trouble one of these days.'

Maldi was caretaker for a block of apartments. He had a tiny ground-floor flat on site with two small rooms and an outside lean-to with washbasin, hose, and a lavatory.

The kitchen was in a tiny, covered yard leading from the main room and consisted of a gas stove, a small table, shelves and an old, cracked sink.

Aunt Jalar was waiting at the door to greet them. '*Assalamu alaikum*, Raza . . . Zamir,' she cried and enfolded Raza to her ample frame. She had Jasmine tea and sweet cakes ready and Raza eyed them greedily. The two men, however, made him go outside with them to wash before prayers.

When they were over, Raza squatted on the ground beside Zamir. Aunt Jalar handed him a small plastic plate with one of the cakes and a bottle of water. Raza drank the water thirstily then picked the cake up and opened his watering mouth wide. Zamir jabbed him with his elbow, hard. Irritated, Raza turned and saw his father glaring at him. 'What, Baba?' he whispered crossly.

'Do not embarrass me by stuffing the whole cake into your mouth as if you are a starving dog,' Zamir hissed.

Raza looked down at the second cake. What was Baba's problem?

They were quite small enough to go into his mouth in one go.

He bit a delicate piece off. Then desperate to have his mouth full of sweetness pushed the rest of the cake in and closed his eyes in happiness.

Sarah Ali arrived from her hotel that evening in a shiny grey car with a uniformed driver. Raza thought she was probably the most beautiful woman he had ever seen. She had a mass of thick dark hair and eyes like water pools. She wore a shimmery grey *shalwar kameez* so delicate it shivered in the slightest draught. Her hair was so shiny that her *dupatta* kept slipping off no matter how many times she pulled it up around her head.

Raza tried not to stare. He felt shy but fascinated. Why

34

would someone so rich and beautiful come all the way from England to see him and Baba? Sarah held him gently by the arms looking at him closely. When she smiled it was like the sun coming up over the mountains to warm him. 'I haven't seen you since you were a baby, Raza. What a fine boy you've grown into. Did you know you have your mother, Samia's eyes?'

Raza shook his head. Zamir was silent. His beautiful, pale bride, Samia had been buried by nightfall on the day she died. Her parents were dead. There had been no one but him and his newborn baby to mourn her passing. Sarah and her parents had come as soon as they could to pay their respects. Now, here Sarah was to take that child. Raza would be safe. Zamir trembled with anxiety, so much could still go wrong.

Jalar sat them in a circle round a thick, heavy tablecloth laid on the ground in the main room. She hurried in and out of the kitchen laying dishes on the cloth, helped by her niece, Basma.

Sarah noticed Zamir's nervousness. He was sweating, Raza noticed too, wondering if his Baba was ill as he repeatedly wiped his forehead with his fringed scarf.

Sarah watched Raza eyeing the food ravenously, uncertain how much to put on his plate. She leant forward and placed a small portion of everything onto his plate with some rice.

'There is plenty, Raza,' she whispered. 'Eat slowly to enjoy.'

Raza tried, but it was hard not to eat fast when you were so hungry. He kept his eyes firmly on the tablecloth in case the feast should disappear, and he would wake up from this beautiful dream.

Zamir sat, withdrawn and silent next to Sarah, cross-legged with his eyes downcast. He was the last to put food on his plate. Aunt Jalar kept jumping up and down and running back and forth to refill bowls of white rice and green curry. She was conscious of how important this meeting with Sarah was.

Uncle Maldi, who was as good-natured and cheerful as Zamir was silent and monosyllabic, kept the conversation going. 'Well now,' he said to Sarah. 'What do you think of our Mrs Bhutto returning to Pakistan at last. Is this not a wonderful thing?'

'Yes,' Sarah said carefully. 'It is. I just wish I had known she was going to have a rally here in Rawalpindi tomorrow. The traffic is going to be terrible in the morning.'

'Jalar and I are thinking we might attend the rally. There is a special bus that has been arranged from this district . . .'

Zamir looked at his brother sharply. 'It will be chaos out there.'

Maldi spread his hands out. 'To have the honour of Benazir Bhutto coming here to speak to us is worth the inconvenience.'

'I was not thinking of inconvenience,' Zamir said. 'I was thinking of Mrs Bhutto's enemies who will also be there.'

'Please. No politics this evening . . .' Aunt Jalar interrupted quickly. 'You two brothers can argue later . . . Sarah, please . . . eat.'

Jalar's food was turning to dust in Zamir's mouth. All his life he had managed to keep a sense of pride in himself, in his standing, in the village, in the home he had built himself from the stones of the mountains. He felt achievement in owning his small fields and his herd of sheep and goats. He had been proud of his three dead wives and of his profligacy in having sons.

Yet, watching Raza pushing food into his mouth, Zamir was overcome. The boy looked small, vulnerable. He was innocently unaware of what this meal represented to him, or to the whole family.

Shame filled Zamir. Shame and a bruised ego. He was not able to give his son enough to eat. He had not even had the courage to tell him the truth about their journey here.

Zamir stared at Raza as if he already belonged to someone else and what he saw was not *a fine boy,* but a skinny, undernourished child who was too small for his age. Zamir saw his life through Sarah Ali's eyes. They would hold pity if he could bear to look into them. Sitting in the warmth of his family, Zamir found his confidence in himself, in his plans for Raza's future, wavering.

He looked up and met Raza's anxious gaze. 'Eat, *Baba.* Are you ill?'

Zamir shook his head exaggeratedly from side to side to reassure him. 'No. No. I will eat. I just cannot eat as fast or as much as you.'

Everyone laughed and the tension in the group round the table eased. Raza had been conscious of Sarah Ali watching him from under lowered eyes. When she spoke to him, he tore his eyes away from his food and looked up to find her smiling at him. 'Raza, will you come and meet Chinir tomorrow? He had to work tonight, but he is looking forward to meeting you.'

'Is Chinir my uncle?' Raza asked. 'Aunt Jalar says I must call you auntie, but Baba tells me you are my ammi's cousin.'

Sarah smiled. 'Chinir is not your uncle and I am not your auntie. Your aunt Jalar is being polite. I am indeed your ammi's cousin.'

'Then what do I call you?'

Sarah hesitated, glancing at Zamir. 'For now, Raza, just call us by our names. Sarah and Chinir. Okay?'

Raza looked unsure. Was this respectful? 'Okay,' he said.

Sarah smiled. 'My driver will come for you and your Baba tomorrow morning. We'll go sightseeing together. We'll eat some more lovely food and have fun. How does that sound?'

Raza looked at his father. Zamir nodded. 'Okay,' he said again.

Sarah Ali's car slid into view outside the window. She was about to offer her hand to Zamir and Maldi when she remembered she was in Pakistan. She embraced Aunt Jalar. Clasped Raza in a waft of heady perfume. Closed her palms to the two men. Then with a rustle, she disappeared into the dark to the car and was swished away into the night.

Raza stood with Zamir and watched the place where the car had been. 'So,' Zamir asked. 'Did you like Sarah Ali?'

Raza nodded and hopped up and down. 'She is beautiful.' He looked excited. 'Where will we go in that car tomorrow, Baba?'

Zamir placed his hand on his son's head. 'You will have to wait and see. It's late. Time to sleep. I will get your mat for the *charpoy*.'

'I don't want to sleep under the tree, Baba. Something might drop on me.'

'Whatever dropped on you, my son, you would eat it,' Zamir said drily.

CHAPTER EIGHT

Cornwall, 2009

Finn's Diary

The Applebys arrived at lunchtime in a new cool Range Rover. Ben said, 'Oh, my God, how the rich live!' Fergus laughed and told Ben he needed something big enough to pull yachts for his business.

Hanna and Ben are always happy when the Applebys are around. Mary is Irish and a bit mad. Fergus is my Godfather. He used to be in the army with Ben, but now he runs a yacht hire business. He and Ben are still best friends. They both drink a lot of beer and get noisy and competitive and Hanna and Mary roll their eyes.

There have been scenes and musical beds here. Izzy is now sleeping in the bottom bunk next door with Zoe. Zoe yelled that if she had to share a bedroom with Harry, she would drown herself, so Harry is now in my room in Izzy's bunk. Harry is thirteen. He is usually good fun, but he is a bit moody this holiday.

He is quite rude to Fergus and he and Zoe argue all the time. Zoe is fourteen and really sarcastic, but Izzy loves her and follows her everywhere. Izzy is the only person Zoe is nice to, and that's because Zoe secretly loves being worshipped.

Most days have been really hot. Me and Ben and Harry and Fergus have been out surfing nearly every day. In the evenings we've all played really noisy rounders. Everyone cheats, especially Ben and Fergus when they are drinking beer. Zoe takes it seriously and shouts at them and Harry tells her not to be a drama queen. Mary can hit a ball like no one I've ever seen. When she has the bat, Fergus yells 'Be afraid. Be very afraid!'

Last night we went to an exhibition of Delphi's paintings in a gallery in Penzance. It was really good, there were lots of people there. And lots of red dots appeared on her paintings which means they are sold. There was a painting with a little girl with Izzy's face in a garden. Mary bought it.

Afterwards we went to the Thai restaurant and stuffed ourselves and the grown-ups got drunk and toasted Delphi who had sold a lot of paintings. Ben said he was proud of her. Hanna told her she thought it was a fantastic exhibition. I could tell she meant it and Delphi was pleased. She told us that all of us being there had made her day. Then she turned to Ian and said that she couldn't do what she did without him. Everyone was happy. Ben had his arm round Hanna and Delphi. Ian and Fergus were going on about fishing. Harry and Zoe were not arguing, and Izzy sat on Mary's knee until she fell asleep. We left the car and got a taxi home. Mary and Fergus sang Irish ballads all the way back to the beach house.

Harry and Zoe hid their faces. It was embarrassing and funny at the same time.

It's great surfing with Ben. I will never be as good as him. When he was my age, he won loads of competitions and stuff. It's like when you are in the water with your board, nothing else matters. I get why it makes Ben so happy.

I wish the days were not going so fast. Delphi and Ian came at lunchtime and brought a picnic. Ian took Ben and Fergus off fishing at the reservoir. Last night we all went to St Ives for a last dinner together because the Applebys leave tomorrow.

It has been fun being a crowd of us on holiday, even if Harry and Zoe are moody and stuff. I don't want this holiday to end. I want Hanna and Ben to go on laughing. When they're with Mary and Fergus, they are happy, and they like each other again. I want them to go on being happy when the summer is over. I want that feeling to last forever.

On the day before the Applebys were due to leave, Finn woke to the pattering sound of rain. After days of sunshine, it sounded melancholy. Outside, seagulls screamed and floated on thermals and the smell of wet earth filtered in through the shutters. The wooden floors of the old beach house creaked and expanded as the temperature changed. It felt as if the beach house was breathing quietly around him.

Finn sensed that Harry was awake too, but neither spoke nor broke the spell. Finn wondered if everyone was silently lying awake in their beds listening to the rain that heralded the end of the holiday.

After breakfast Hanna and Mary set off for Newlyn to buy fresh fish for their last supper together. The sun miraculously came out and everyone else had gone down to swim. Finn stayed behind. He wanted peace to finish his book. He lay on the wooden veranda outside his room on an inflatable bed, hidden from the beach and the rest of the house by drying towels on the veranda rails. He had his earphones plugged in, book propped up, iced drink by his side.

He was absorbed in his book and only vaguely conscious of the car coming back and Hanna and Mary moving about in the kitchen at the back of the villa. He did not call out to them. He was enjoying being invisible.

Mary and Hanna came out and sat on the sand just outside the beach house. The ice in their cold drinks clinked as they settled in the sun loungers. Finn pulled his earphones out. He should get up and show himself. Let them know he was lying just behind them, but he did not move. He was annoyed. Why couldn't they have just gone down the beach to find the others so he could be on his own for a bit?

Finn quietly reached out for his book and turned the page. Mary said, obviously carrying on a conversation they had been having inside, 'Have you talked to Ben about how you feel, Hanna? Does he realize how depressed you've been?'

'I've tried,' Hanna said. 'He just says, "I'm in the army, Hanna, this is my job. I have to put in these hours to make sure the regiment is ready to deploy at the end of the month . . ." He's too busy and preoccupied to want to know how I'm feeling . . .'

Mary said, 'I do remember that being an army wife is bloody hard, Han. Fergus did Bosnia and Iraq and being left in German army quarters with two bickering infants wasn't fun. So, I do understand, but it's tough for the guys too. I'm sure it's got worse since Fergus came out. With so many defence cuts, life seems to have got much harder with impossible hours and conditions. So much is now expected of them. I don't think Fergus worked the hours Ben does. He thought Ben seemed pretty stressed out when we first arrived . . .'

Hanna said almost angrily. 'I'm going back to Finland, Mary. I've made up my mind.'

Finn froze. There was a long silence. Mary said in a shocked voice. 'What do you mean, Hanna? That you're leaving Ben or that you're going back to Finland while he's Afghanistan?'

'I'm not sure yet.'

Mary swivelled round in her chair. 'Hanna, for God's sake! Ben is about to go off to a war zone. You can't spring this on him. It's cruel. He's going to have enough to contend with. You have to support him while he's in Afghanistan.'

Hanna said quietly. 'Who supports me, Mary? I'm tired of it all. I've been on my own with Izzy for months at a time. My life has been on hold for years and I want it back. I can support Ben from Finland. I don't have to sit in an army quarter in Germany.'

Finn didn't want to hear any more, but it was too late to run away. Mary's voice was low. 'Of course, go and visit your family in Finland while Ben is away, Hanna, but that army quarter in Germany is your home, the family base. The children need that security while Ben's away fighting. Ben needs to know you are all safe together. Why haven't you talked to him about this? I can't believe you would wait until he is about to leave to drop this bombshell on him. Please, tell me you don't mean it.'

'I do mean it. I wanted us all to have a lovely summer holiday together and then I would tell Ben.'

'What about Finn and Izzy?'

'Finn will be at boarding school here. I will take Izzy with me.'

43

'Hanna, for goodness' sake, think. Finn and Izzy will lose their home while their father is in one of the most dangerous places on earth. You will tear your little family apart . . .'

Hanna's chair creaked as she swivelled round to face Mary. 'You think I'm selfish, that I am not thinking about anyone but myself. I thought you might understand, Mary. If I go under, so do my children.'

Mary sighed. 'Oh, Han, I can see you're unhappy and depressed. Please, before you do anything, talk to someone professional. Because you're not thinking straight, really, you're not. You've lost sight of all the good things in your life. Ben adores you. You have two fantastic children. You knew what Ben did before you married him. You chose an army life and all that it entailed. The good and the bad bits. Ben spelled it all out to you before you married and you *chose* it, Hanna.'

Finn lay motionless, his eyes riveted to the two heads glimpsed between the towels. Mary said more gently, 'When you get back to Germany go and talk to your doctor. This isn't you talking. It isn't that Ben doesn't understand your loneliness or boredom. He just can't do anything about it at the moment. He has a responsibility to his men. He's taking them into a war zone, and he knows that however well he's trained them, some will be severely injured or not come home at all. Just imagine how that must feel, Hanna. You can't pile more stress on him. You can't do that to him. I'm sorry, darling, but you need to dig deep and find resources to cope. You need to stay positive and strong, for Ben, and for your children . . .'

Hanna got up from her chair. Her voice was cold. 'Mary, what you are telling me to do is to sacrifice my life for Ben's. Sorry, I've had enough of it. I won't stay in Germany while Ben is in Afghanistan. I can't see any further than

44

that at the moment. It's not as big a deal as you are making it. Ben won't like it, but he won't see it as you do . . . that I am walking out on him.'

Mary said in a voice equally cool, 'This is me you are talking to, Hanna. We both know that this is a very big deal. Let's go and join the others, they will be wondering where we are. Let's also make this last day together as fun as possible, for the children.'

When they had gone, Finn realized he was trembling. He got up. It served him right. He had listened to a conversation he was not meant to hear. He could have moved away or shown himself at any point and he had not.

He went to find his wet suit and body board. He pelted across the beach and straight into the sea where the waves were small and cold and slapped at him like a punishment. He pummelled his back legs until he was far out from the sound of voices from the shore. He wept as he swam. Like Mary, he knew that if Hanna went home to Finland she might never come back, and she was going to take Izzy with her. He thought of the autumn term at school, of the grey Cornish skies and the mists that closed in as winter came. Ben would be in Lashkar Gah. Hanna and Izzy would be somewhere in Helsinki. The quarter in Germany, the only centre that bound their lives together, would lie empty leaving the ghosts of them all wandering from room to room looking for each other.

CHAPTER NINE

Rawalpindi, 2007

It was early. The morning was cool. Small purple bougain-villea blooms blew down into the yard. A faint mist lay around the hills muffling sound. The roads were exceptionally quiet. Raza stood with Zamir, Aunt Jalar and Uncle Maldi outside waiting for Sarah Ali's car to arrive.

Raza was wearing a spotless new *shalwar kameez* and brand new plastic sandals. The folds in the material where the *shalwar kameez* had been folded were still visible, making Raza look like a small, waifish mannequin. He wanted to scratch the stiff material that felt itchy and uncomfortable against his skin.

Zamir too had dressed carefully. He had still said nothing to Raza. He told himself he was right to wait; he would see how Chinir behaved with his son before he told the boy anything. It would be easier to explain things when Raza had met both Sarah and her husband.

The big black car came into sight and slid to a stop. Zamir turned to Maldi. 'If you go to the Bhutto rally, take care. Especially if you take Jalar with you.'

'I am undecided,' Maldi said. 'I have heard rumours of busloads of troublemakers making their way there to disrupt her speeches. If I go, I will go alone.'

The driver jumped out to open the car door for Sarah and Chinir. '*Assalamu alaikum!*' they both called, as they emerged smiling. There was polite handshaking, then Chinir bent and put his hands on Raza's shoulders. 'So, you are Raza. I have heard a lot about you. All of it good.'

Raza regarded Chinir solemnly and tried not to laugh. The tall man's *Pashto* was terrible. He could not think of anything to say, so he nodded.

Chinir turned to Zamir. 'Our hotel is packed with politicians. The roads are going to get busy today so we thought we might drive to the hills for a few hours of peace.'

'Salim, our driver suggested Damen-e-Koh,' Sarah said. 'I've never been, but I gather there is a beautiful terraced garden where we can see all of Islamabad spread below us . . .'

Zamir closed his palms and inclined his head. '*Shukriya.* That sounds like a good programme.'

Raza was eyeing the car. It was shiny and spotless with pale leather seats. Surely there would not be enough room in the back for all of them . . .

'Would you like to go in the front with Salim?' Sarah asked, laughing. Raza nodded, wondering if Sarah could read his mind. Salim opened the front passenger door for him with a little flourish and Raza jumped in. Zamir, Sarah, and Chinir climbed into the back. Salim slammed the doors and Raza excitedly strapped himself in. Grinning, he waved grandly to his uncle and aunt as the cars slid, noiselessly, down the road.

The low hum of conversation floated to him from the back of the car, but Raza could not hear what anyone was actually saying because of the sound of the engine. He sat upright feeling proud and important as Salim drove towards Islamabad.

He pretended he was the son of a warlord. He practised looking down his nose at the beggars at the traffic lights and the little boys who ran to clean the windscreen. Then he caught Salim grinning at him and felt foolish. The driver winked at him. 'Nice car, huh?'

Raza nodded vigorously. It would be nice to wear a smart uniform and drive a big powerful car like this . . . if he had not been destined to join his brothers in *Jihad* . . .

'Mr and Mrs Ali are very good people,' Salim said, glancing at him. Raza nodded silently. 'Do you have a voice, small boy from Peshawar?'

Raza turned his green eyes upon him. 'Of course, I have a voice when there is something to say.'

Salim laughed. 'Good. You'll need that spirit where you're going, boy.'

Raza had no idea what Salim was talking about. He looked out at the swathe of trees that surrounded the city and at the houses nestled into the shelter of the hills.

Salim eased the car onto the dual carriageway. The traffic going the other way, from Islamabad into Rawalpindi was heavy. Overflowing buses rattled past in flashes of colour, bejewelled arms hanging out of the windows. Police hurtled down the middle of the road pushing vehicles aside, using their horns. The dense traffic began to thin as they turned north and left the outskirts of the city.

Damen-e-Koh lay 25000 feet above sea level and the gardens, both natural and man-made, were formed into terraces that lay against the fertile range of the Margalla Hills. As they turned into the entrance Raza grinned as he spotted monkeys swinging away into the trees.

'Stay here and wait for us, please, Salim,' Chinir said, in English, when they had parked.

'I no go anywhere, Boss. Roads too busy. Anyway, it is nice here,' Salim said.

It is beautiful, Sarah thought, as they got out of the car. The air was cool, the atmosphere tranquil. Islamabad lay below them in a great sweeping map of colours and architecture.

They stood in a small, silent group by the curving safety rail lined with pots of red flowers and gazed down at the city of golden mosques and old colonial government buildings. Zamir felt awe at the beauty of the white Shah Faisal Mosque crouched beneath them. Its four minarets reached up to a sky, so blue it seemed purple.

Raza liked the feeling of being high above the world. He loved the space and the trees. He shielded his eyes against the sun and watched children rushing about hiding from each other among flowerbeds of yellow flowers and leafy hedges that lined the paths.

He felt a strange surge of joy in this unexpected day. He had been cooped up for hours in Uncle Maldi's house being polite. Now, he fought an urge to run and disappear into the darkness of trees. He wanted to be himself again, against the soft shadow of hills.

He moved back to the rails of the lookout and gazed down at Rawal Lake and across the flat plains towards Bhurban. Home lay somewhere beyond. He thought of faded old Miah, who cared for him and Baba, but could not speak. He thought of the small stone house where he and Baba lived and the thin, starved puppy he had been secretly sharing his bread with. He thought of the tame goat he had reared who ran to him when he whistled. They would be missing him. Unease sprang at him again, pricking his skin. He turned to find Sarah's eyes on him. 'You were a long way away. What were you thinking of, Raza?'

Confused, Raza could not answer. He wanted to stay

here, in these beautiful gardens with Sarah and Chinir, but he also felt a strange urge to be home, safe in his own place on the mountain. Where he could daydream and plan his adventures.

He turned to look at Baba, but his father was gazing fascinated at all that lay below him. Sarah said, 'Let's take a walk. We can stop somewhere for a drink or an ice cream.'

Chinir called to him. 'Hey Raza, come and look at this. I can show you exactly where we are . . .'

Raza, Sarah, and Chinir bent and traced with their fingers the sweeping geography of Islamabad carved in stone. Zamir, standing apart, felt his heart flutter as he stood watching the three heads framed close together against the purple sky.

CHAPTER TEN

Cornwall, 2009

Even Izzy caught the general air of melancholy that rose, tangible in the afternoon, as the Applebys' car disappeared down the track, onto the coast road and away.

The laughter, banter, and noise of people all talking at once disappeared with the family, leaving a heavy silence, the feeling of being left behind when the party moves on.

There were three days left of the holiday, but the weather was breaking. Bruise-like clouds hovered over a sullen sea. Ben and Hanna took the opportunity to start to tidy and pack up the beach house. The air of gloom lingered over the darkening day. No one wanted the holiday to be over. No one wanted to head back to Germany.

Ben and Finn tidied up outside. Finn hosed down the surfboards and wet suits and hung them at the back of the beach house. Ben swept the porch and put the wooden chairs away in case a storm blew them away. Izzy played quietly with her dolls. Hanna cleaned the fridge and endlessly wiped the ageing kitchen surfaces. Nobody said much.

Finn, watching his silent parents, wondered if Hanna

had told Ben about wanting to go back to Finland. Ben was quiet and preoccupied, but he often was before he had to go away. At lunch Hanna was moody and she suddenly snapped at Izzy, making her bottom lip wobble. Finn glared at her. Ben picked Izzy up and took her out onto the balcony and sat in the wooden rocking chair looking out to sea. Finn could hear him beginning a story. Hanna sat rigid. Finn stood up, scraping his chair. 'Don't take your temper out on Izzy,' he said, marching to his room.

The rain came slanting sideways in a huge burst of wind that hit the beach house head on. Ben and Izzy ran in from the balcony laughing. Hanna got up and pulled on her mac and went out into it without saying a word. Ben called after her. 'Hanna you are going to get soaked . . .' But Hanna did not even turn.

Ben watched her for a moment and then said, 'Come on, get your waterproofs. We'll go over to Penzance and see if Delphi and Ian can cheer us up.'

They carried the atmosphere of post-holiday blues into Salubrious House with them. 'Hanna needed a bit of peace,' Ben said lightly. Delphi looked at her subdued grandchildren and got out Snap. The rain eventually stopped, and Delphi and Izzy made messy scones which they ate in the garden. Ben watched as Ian showed Finn his new binoculars. His children were happy. He closed his eyes. The scent of roses after rain was pungent. He felt a mixture of sadness, love, and dread; the fear of leaving his children without a father. Slowly, he let Delphi, Ian, and the garden lure him back to a peaceful frame of mind. He looked up to find Delphi watching him. He smiled. 'We've had a lovely holiday, thanks for everything, Delphi.'

'Please take care in Afghanistan, my darling.'

'Sorry we were all a bit grumpy when we arrived. It's just, you know, my going away is hanging over us all . . .'

'Of course, it is. You are all coping wonderfully . . .'

Ben stood up. 'Time to go,' he called to Finn and Izzy.

He hugged Delphi. 'Don't worry about me. I'll be back before you know it . . .'

'Shall we come out to say goodbye to you all tomorrow, Ben?'

Ben hesitated. 'Let's say goodbye now, in case we leave early or . . .' He met Delphi's eyes. 'Hanna does not seem in a good place at the moment . . .'

'Understood, darling. Do give her our love . . .'

Delphi waved until the car was out of sight. She felt an unnerving sense of doom. She stood in the drive looking after them until Ian came and put his arm around her and guided her inside.

CHAPTER ELEVEN

Marghalla Hills, 2007

Raza ate his ice cream slowly, eyeing the families laden with picnics walking up the steep road that led up into the misty hills. Small children charged ahead, their laughter floating back on the wind. Raza felt a longing to run after them, melt away from the expectations of adults into the cool darkness of trees.

Chinir, noticing his restlessness, said to Sarah. 'Why don't we gather some snacks together for a picnic and take a short hike up the path towards Pir Sohawa?'

'That's a great idea, Chinir,' Sarah said, then, seeing Zamir's face fall, she said quickly. 'Would you prefer to stay here in the gardens, Zamir?

'*Shukriya*, Sarah. I will be happy in these gardens until you return. I will not move far from this point. You take the boy.'

They left Zamir in the shade and made their way uphill past beds of fragrant roses. Raza began to relax as they climbed the path upwards into the trees. Carpets of worn grass wound into secret shady areas where the wind whispered and wavered through the branches of firs.

'Come on, Raza!' Chinir called, laughing and leaping away into the trees, 'Let's explore!' Startled, Raza grinned at Sarah, then took off after him.

'Don't get lost!' Sarah called. 'I'm going to stop at the next picnic place. Meet me there . . .'

The pungent smell of fir cones filled Raza's nostrils as he ran after Chinir. The pine needles were soft and gave beneath his new sandals. He felt free again, like he did at home, and he and marvelled at this strange man who played like a child.

All was suddenly quiet. Chinir had stopped running. Raza could no longer hear him puffing. There was no sound but the branches of the trees swaying and creaking. Chinir was hiding. Raza moved stealthily forward placing his feet on the ground in a way that made no sound, like his brothers had taught him. Every so often he stopped and listened, scanning the trees ahead of him for Chinir.

Instinct drew him to the right, and he crept towards a group of firs with broken lower branches. Here there was cover. Within the shadows he caught a flash of Chinir's shirt. Raza circled round. Twigs cracked as Chinir shifted his weight. He was as noisy as an elephant. Raza closed in. Chinir was crouching, peering round the tree ready to run. Raza, grinning to himself moved stealthily up behind him and leapt out at Chinir with a blood-curdling yell.

Chinir swung round with a terrified yelp. The fear in his eyes startled Raza making him jump back. Spooked, they stared at each other wide-eyed. Then Chinir began to shake with laughter, his whole body convulsed. It was so infectious that Raza collapsed on the ground giggling beside him. They both laughed hysterically until they ached, and tears ran down their faces.

When they joined Sarah at the picnic table, they were still setting each other off in little spurts of laughter. Amused,

Sarah said, 'What's so funny?' Raza and Chinir shook their heads. Neither could sensibly tell her. Sarah did not mind. She was elated by Raza's face transformed by laughter.

Zamir had tucked himself into a small corner of the garden and was praying, his thin body bent to the earth. Sadness caught at Sarah. How alone this old man was going to be without Raza. The bond between the two of them was obvious.

When Chinir and Raza disappeared to search for a lavatory and Zamir had finished praying, Sarah went over to him. Zamir turned his solemn face to her. 'I hope my son behaved.'

'Of course, he did,' Sarah said. 'It's a joy to spend time with him . . .' She took a deep breath, already anticipating the old man's response. 'Zamir, you promised you would prepare Raza, but he doesn't know why we are here, does he? Chinir and I cannot just carry him off. He needs to understand why you've made this decision for him and he needs to trust us. Zamir, I want him to feel safe with us . . .'

Zamir held up his hand. His face was closed and implacable. 'Raza is ten years old. He is a child. He cannot make the right decisions for his future, only I can do that. I decide what is best for my son, Sarah. He will abide by my decision. Raza indeed will leave with you when you return to England . . .' He stopped. 'Are there more hold-ups? Is everything in order? I understood you have all the correct legal papers for him to enter England with you?'

'Legally, there is nothing to prevent Raza leaving Pakistan with us, Zamir. We have all the relevant documents we need,' Sarah said.

'Then perhaps you have changed your mind? Maybe, now you and your husband have met Raza, you do you not wish to take him back with you into your life in England?'

Zamir's fierce green eyes held Sarah's. He reminded her of her terrifying Karachi grandfather.

'We haven't changed our minds, Zamir, far from it. Our only reservation is, if this is the right time to take Raza back with us.'

Zamir stared at her. 'There will never be a right time, Sarah. You live in the west. You will never understand the risk of my talking to the boy before I left my village. With each day that passes it is more difficult for me to keep Raza safe . . .'

Chinir called anxiously, 'Sarah! Come on! We have to leave. We need to start back now before Bhutto's rally ends. Salim is anxious about the traffic . . .'

Salim had turned the car and had the engine running and they all hastily clambered in. Raza nipped into the front seat again before anybody could object and they headed back towards Rawalpindi in silence.

As they neared the outskirts of the city the traffic grew heavy and congested. Chinir leant forward and was about to say something to Salim when the sky ahead of them erupted into flames. Seconds later came the explosion, followed by rapid gunfire. In the distance black smoke shot into the sky. The world shimmered and stopped. Traffic ground to a halt like a silent slow-motion film. Men clinging to the outside of the crowded bus ahead of them seemed suspended against the violent sky like a held breath.

Zamir whispered, 'Benazir Bhutto. They got to Mrs Bhutto . . .'

Young men began to yell and jump off the bus shrieking wildly. 'Oh, my God!' Chinir dug, frantically, into his pocket for his phone, as if he could somehow dial 999.

'We can't possibly know that yet, Zamir. Don't jump to conclusions.'

'Please, God, let it not be true,' Sarah whispered, terrified.

Zamir closed his eyes. The inevitability of violence today made him weary beyond hope. Bhutto had returned to Pakistan, but her enemies were never going to let her live in peace to win an election. Never.

The crowd of men who had jumped off the stationary bus were now screaming and wailing and tearing at their clothes. Cars were beginning to edge around the bus and Salim let out the clutch. 'Boss, we need to get out of here. Whatever it is that has happened, it is going to get violent.'

'We should have started back sooner. I should have watched the time,' Chinir said, angry with himself. 'Can you get off the dual carriageway, Salim?'

There was the sickening sound of sirens behind them and cavalcades of armed trucks packed with Rangers and police hurtled down the middle of the road pushing traffic aside, using their horns.

Salim said, 'I don't know, Boss.' He was sweating. He glanced in the driving mirror at Sarah. 'It is not great idea to take side streets either, with all this anger. This big car draw attention and we have Mem. If Mrs Bhutto dies, things going to get very bad. People do not care who they attack in grief, but I will try to find a way out of here . . .'

Raza, wild-eyed, turned to look at his father in the back of the car. Zamir had an overpowering desire to reach out, grab his son and pull him over the front seat to keep him safe.

Salim did a three-point turn, the engine screamed, and they flew down the dual carriageway the wrong way. Other frantic drivers were doing the same. Sarah closed her eyes and prayed. At the next junction Salim shot across the oncoming traffic and exited.

They crawled into the side streets of Rawalpindi as Salim searched to find a road that would lead them back to Uncle Maldi's house.

They found themselves near the bus station as a mass of people poured from the buses out into the streets. It was clear the crowds were out of control, yelling hysterically as they ran. Large groups of men were waving sticks, their faces contorted with rage and grief. They screamed Bhutto's name over and over, breaking the windows of parked vehicles as they ran.

Raza pressed down in his seat. Salim said softly, 'It's okay, boy. Keep down. Don't meet their eyes . . .'

Salim checked the window and door locks and kept the car moving slowly forward. Suddenly a youth with wild eyes and broken teeth noticed the sleek black car sliding away and began to run towards it. He pushed his face against the front passenger window hurling obscenities. Raza shrunk back. He heard Sarah whimper with fear behind him. In moments the car was surrounded, and the crowd were pushing at it in a fury. Salim let out the clutch and the car leapt forward. Two boys fell off the bonnet. Salim swerved to avoid them, jammed his hand on the horn as the car gathered speed. Furious faces fell behind them as people jumped out of the way. There was a sickening thump as the wing of the car hit someone. Sarah gasped.

'Don't stop, Salim. Keep going . . .' Chinir cried urgently. 'Keep going. Good man. Good man.'

Salim navigated the speeding car deftly through side streets until the sound of the rioters were long behind them. He slowed down and they drove two blocks in silence. Zamir, full of foreboding, prayed, *Inshallah, Maldi and Jalar stayed home. Inshallah, they did not go to the rally.*

'Stop here, Salim,' he said suddenly, leaning forward. 'Raza and I will walk the rest of the way. It is not far, and it is safer. Raza and I can go unnoticed. This car cannot. You must get Mem back to the hotel, it is dangerous for her here in these streets. Go left, straight back to the main roads where the traffic flows.'

Sarah tried to prevent Zamir and Raza getting out of the car. 'Zamir, please, please, come back to the hotel with us . . .'

Zamir turned his piercing eyes on Chinir. 'It is your duty to look after your wife, Chinir. Get her out of here. It is mine to find my brother. Raza and I will be all right, but it is no longer safe for you out here. Go straight back to your hotel now.'

Chinir nodded. Zamir got out of the car and opened the front passenger door and beckoned Raza. '*Inshallah*, you will get safely home, Peshawar boy,' Salim said.

They watched the car slide away. Zamir took Raza's hand and keeping to the shadows they began to walk in the direction of Maldi and Jalar's flat. In the distance they could still hear shouts and gunfire. Wafts of tear gas reached them on the wind making their eyes sting and water. The air was alive with tension, but the few people still on the streets were hurrying, like Zamir and Raza, to the safety of their homes.

When they turned the corner of the road where Maldi's apartment block stood, Zamir could see that Maldi's windows and doors were closed and shuttered. The flat was in darkness. No one was home. Zamir's stomach lurched with fear.

CHAPTER TWELVE

Cornwall, 2009

Finn's Diary

The beach house was empty when we got back from Penzance. Hanna wasn't here. It's raining hard again, and Ben looked worried. He asked me to get Izzy in her pyjamas while he went out to look for her. I watched him go out into the rain, all hunched up against the wind. Hanna wouldn't have stayed out in this weather all this time. I bet she is drinking tea in the café.

Izzy is grizzly so I put her in the old half bath with some toys. Izzy gets engrossed in her own little world really easily. I almost wish I could be 4 again. You don't understand much, and the world is safe. The sea is crashing about out there. I feel like there is a storm coming in or something. I wish Ben did not always feel like he has to please Hanna and get her out of her moods . . .

Finn sighed and put his diary down. He remembered that night, at half-term, when Ben came home really late from training his men. When Finn had run down from his bedroom, Ben had been standing in the kitchen doorway in his combats swaying with exhaustion. Hanna was saying, 'Can you go straight upstairs and say goodnight to Izzy before she forgets what her father looks like, please?'

As if Ben stayed out late, on purpose, to annoy her.

Ben had turned to hug Finn, smelling of sweat and outdoors. 'Sorry, old thing, I'll try to take some time off for a bike ride in the woods with you, tomorrow . . .'

'Actually,' Hanna said, 'surprisingly, we all do manage to entertain ourselves when you're not around, Ben. We've had enough practice.'

Finn flinched at the memory. Why did Hanna do that? Why did his mother have to be sarcastic when she knew Ben was only doing his job? He was the boss. He was responsible for all his soldiers.

Finn heard Hanna and Ben's voices and ran to check Izzy in the bath. She was ready to come out and he quickly wrapped her in a towel, and she ran out to Hanna and Ben. Neither of them were looking at each other. Ben was soaked, Hanna was relatively dry.

'Were you in the café?' Finn asked accusingly.

'I was in the café,' Hanna replied. 'I hear you had a good afternoon . . .'

Hanna bent to the fridge, got out a bottle of wine and poured herself a glass. Ben scooped Izzy up. 'Come on, Pumpkin, let's find your pyjamas.'

Furious, Finn walked into the kitchen, reached past Hanna and got another glass out of the cupboard. 'Pour one for Ben,' he said, rudely. Hanna shot him a look but poured the wine.

Ben had tucked Izzy into bed and was in the bathroom

getting out of his wet clothes. He climbed into the tiny bath and turned the hot tap on to warm up Izzy's water. His knees were folded to his chin. He looked ridiculous. Finn began to laugh. Ben grinned and eyed the wine. 'For me, I hope?'

'Yeah.' Finn handed him the glass of wine with a flourish.

'What a nice boy you are,' Ben said. 'Stay and talk to me. You might have to help me get out . . .'

They both listened to Hanna reading to Izzy. Ben said softly. 'The days before I leave are always hard and Hanna's dreading going back to Germany. Things will be easier back home when the regiment leaves, for all the wives. No one can settle until we've gone . . . We're still here, but never around. Normal family life is suspended . . .'

He smiled at Finn. 'Once my tour is over, I'm due for a posting. I've put in for a job back here in the UK. Hanna has got that to look forward to . . .'

Finn stared at Ben. So, Hanna had not said anything to him about going back to Finland. Ben wasn't looking at him. He had closed his eyes. Finn hesitated. Should he say something? Should he tell Ben about the conversation he had heard with Mary?

'Bliss!' Ben said, holding up his glass of wine. 'Or it would be if this was a proper bath . . .'

Hanna might not have meant what she said to Mary. It might have been just a mood. He must not say anything. Ben was so still Finn thought he had fallen asleep, crouched awkwardly in the stupid bath.

'Do you ever get, like, scared about going to Afghanistan and fighting the Taliban?' he asked suddenly.

Ben opened his eyes. Finn could see him thinking carefully about his answer. 'A degree of trepidation is normal, but not something to dwell on. We train so hard, Finn, that all the strategies for staying safe are in built by the time we deploy. It is why I've hardly seen my family this year. Some of my young soldiers think Afghanistan is going to be an exciting game, like PlayStation. It's been hard to make this conflict real to boys who have never been out of an inner city. We just have to make sure they're so well trained and prepared by the time we land that they react automatically to any threat. It's the difference between living and dying . . .'

Ben shut his eyes again as if to shut out what was coming.

Finn whispered, '*Please* don't get killed, Dad.'

Ben's eyes flew open as if he had only just realized he was talking aloud.

'Me!' he scoffed. 'I'm extremely good at taking care of myself. I'm going to be stuck in an operations room. You don't need to worry about me.'

Finn said, 'Good thing we got to have our holiday. It was fun, until the Applebys left, wasn't it?'

'It was a great holiday. Brilliant weather, lovely company, and good surfing . . .' Ben grinned at Finn. 'Today was a little post-holiday, anti-climactic, blip. It always happens when those Applebys leave, you know . . .'

Ben emptied his wine glass. 'I shall think of all this every day I'm away. I'm going to be a long way from the sea . . . Come on, help your old man out of this bath and I will make you scrambled eggs . . .'

CHAPTER THIRTEEN

Rawalpindi, 2007

'Aunt and Uncle are not home.' Raza's voice was small and anxious. Zamir reached under the wheel of Maldi's old motorbike for the key and they pulled the shutters open and went inside. The air smelled damp and stale and they stood in the dark empty room not knowing what to do.

'Come, we will wash and then pray, Raza,' Zamir said. They went out into the yard and used the thin hose. Raza shivered as the cold water sliced over his body.

They were drying themselves in the yard when they heard a shuffling noise coming slowly down the road. Two bent figures, leaning on each other limped towards the gate. Maldi was supporting Jalar, who looked as if she was about to collapse. As Zamir rushed out to help them, Raza saw, with horror, that both Maldi and Jalar were covered in blood. *Thanks be to God they are alive*, Zamir thought. He took hold of Jalar and he and Maldi helped her inside.

'Where are you hurt, Jalar?' Zamir asked. 'Raza, quickly, get drinking water for your aunt.'

Raza stood frozen by the sight of so much blood. Maldi

said quickly, 'This is not our blood. It is not our blood, boy. Your aunt Jalar is not injured. She is in shock . . .'

They placed Jalar on her bed and she sat on the side and began a pitiful wailing, rocking herself backwards and forwards. Raza ran to the rusty fridge for the boiled drinking water and Maldi pressed the bottle to Jalar's lips.

She drank thirstily and Maldi whispered to Raza to go around the back of the building and fetch Jalar's niece, Basma from flat number three.

'Hurry, she will calm your aunt and help her out of these clothes . . .'

He pushed Raza gently towards the door, but Jalar cried, 'No. No. If Raza goes for Basma my whole family will run here. I will not be able to breathe . . . wait a moment, I will be all right . . .'

Raza stared in fascinated horror at the congealing blood that covered his uncle and aunt's hands. Did all this blood belong to someone else?

Jalar began a low anguished prayer that Mrs Bhutto might live. Maldi turned to Zamir; his face was grey with shock. 'They shot her in cold blood. They shot her and then the bomb went off. Bhutto had no chance . . .' He lifted his arms in despair. 'There were so many people dead and injured, brother. You were right. I should never have taken Jalar. No woman should see what she has seen today . . .'

He pointed to his blood-drenched clothes. 'A little nearer and we would also be dead. This is the blood of the two boys in front of us . . .'

Jalar was staring down at her hands that had been unable to stem the bleeding of a dying young boy. She said tonelessly, 'Pakistan will never change. Never. The bloodshed will never end. You are right, Zamir. You are right to send the boy to a better life . . .'

She started wailing again and Zamir walked Raza to the door. 'Run and get your cousin. Do not say why. Just bring her.'

Benazir Bhutto died that evening, causing three days of riots. The hospital where she died became a focus point and under siege. Crowds of her supporters ran amok, venting their anger and grief in more violence. Gangs of Sunni pitted against Shia roamed the city ransacking cars and property, terrorizing a shocked population, causing all normal life to shudder to a halt.

Sarah and Chinir were trapped in the Pearl Continental Hotel in Rawalpindi. A shaken Chinir spent his time trying to get a flight back to London. He wanted Sarah out of Islamabad, out of Pakistan.

Zamir and Raza were trapped in Uncle Maldi's tiny flat by the endless curfews. Transport anywhere was erratic and dangerous. The violence over Bhutto's death was spreading like wildfire and had reached Peshawar too.

It was no longer safe to sleep outside in Uncle Maldi's yard at night where it was cooler, and Raza began to feel like a caged animal. He was not used to being cooped up at night with three other people in one small room. In the early hours of the third day, he was so claustrophobic inside the house that he crept out to the yard and sat under the tree where he usually slept in his *charpoy*. He looked up at the stars and thought of Sarah and Chinir and remembered their afternoon in the gardens. It seemed like a dream now. The ice cream, the game of hide and seek. He smiled, remembering the way he and Chinir could not stop laughing because they had made each other jump. That day had been good.

He knew from Maldi, who had a mobile phone, that Sarah and Chinir were anxious to fly back to England as soon as possible. He would not see them again. He could not even say goodbye.

Aunt Jalar's words kept going through his head. *You are right. You are right, Zamir, to send the boy to a better life.* He heard a movement in the dark.

'Raza?' Zamir whispered.

'I am here, under the tree, Baba.'

Zamir sat beside Raza in the damp early morning air watching the sky lighten. 'Will it be safe to go home today, Baba?'

Zamir cleared his throat but seemed unable to form words.

After a moment, Raza said, 'Baba? Were you going to send me away with Sarah and Chinir?'

'Yes.'

'For how long?'

'For as long as it takes to get an education.'

'You did not tell me.'

'It is hard to tell your son that you are sending him away, even though it is for his own good.'

'Baba, everyone knows you must have passport and papers to go to England. I do not have them.'

'Sarah and Chinir, they have your passport and papers.'

Raza felt a jolt of fear. 'Sarah and Chinir will have gone back home to England by now. It is too dangerous here for people like them.'

'They are still here,' Zamir said gently. 'They rang your uncle's mobile phone this morning. They have not been able to leave their hotel.'

Raza said firmly, 'Maybe, when I am older, Baba, I will go and visit them in the UK. They are very nice people. Now, I think it is time to go back to our sheep and goats, they will be missing us . . . It is not good in Rawalpindi. I want to get the bus to Peshawar and then we will soon be back home in our village.'

'It is not safe in Peshawar either, Raza. That's why I want

you to go to England with Sarah and Chinir. If you stay in Pakistan bloodshed will rule your life. You have been offered a chance and we will take it.'

Raza's voice rose. 'No Baba! I will fight this violence with my brothers. I will . . .'

Zamir laughed bitterly. 'Your brothers, they are part of this violence, as I once was, as my father and his father were. You too will become trapped by it, if you stay. I want more for you, my youngest son. I want you to change the pattern of things, to be educated . . .'

'Ajeet and Fakir . . .'

'Ajeet and Fakir were not offered the chance you have been offered. They know only how to fight. They had no choice. When I was younger, I too had no choice. You do. Sarah and Chinir have no children. They will care for you as their own.'

Raza took a deep breath. 'Baba, thank you, but I cannot go to England with them. You need me to help you with the goats and the sheep. They are used to me. I am used to them. I will come home with you. You need me . . .'

Zamir placed his hand firmly on Raza's shoulder. 'I need you to make me proud, to work hard to educate yourself. I need you to have a different life to me, and to your brothers. I do not care what you become, a doctor, a teacher, a businessman. When you return to me here in Pakistan, I will die a happy man.'

Raza stared at his father. Baba was old. All this education would take a long time. Baba could die before he returned. He might get ill and he, Raza, would not be here to take care of him. Zamir guessed what was going through Raza's mind.

'I'm getting old. Yes, I might die while you are away, but I will die content. If you stay with me, I will have failed you. You have seen the blood of boys like you spilled over the clothes of your aunt and uncle. You have this one chance of a different life. If that opportunity had been offered to me, at your age, I would have taken it with both my hands . . .' Zamir's eyes held the zeal of a long-held dream. 'Raza, you will have schooling, books, a whole world will open to you . . .'

'I will not have you, Baba,' Raza whispered. He had never heard or seen his father like this. Inside the Baba he knew, lay a stranger he did not know.

'You will always have me.' Zamir pressed Raza's hand to his chest. 'I am not sending you to the ends of the earth. We are a plane ride apart. I will travel into Peshawar so you can talk to me by phone . . .' Zamir grinned a rare black-toothed grin. 'Why, you will probably have one of those new phones, like Chinir.'

Raza gently removed his hand. He had experienced unexpected happiness with Sarah and Chinir. They had seemed young after Baba. He was used to the long silences of his father and the isolation of the mountains. For a moment, just for a moment, watching other children running and playing in those gardens, he had wondered what it would be like to have Sarah and Chinir as his parents. Now he was paying for this betrayal. God was punishing him.

Zamir said, 'When it is safe to drive into the city, I will take you to the Pearl Continental Hotel and you will leave on the plane to England with Sarah and Chinir. They have booked three tickets. There is no more to be said on this matter . . .'

Raza shivered. Baba's face was stern and shut. There was indeed no more to be said. Zamir had only beaten Raza once in his life, for disobeying him, for getting lost on the mountains after sunset. Zamir had wept as he beat him. Baba's tears had hurt Raza more than the stick.

*

Zamir stood beside Salim, his face impassive. Raza looked small and afraid amongst the thousands of noisy, milling people all intent on leaving Islamabad. *This must be done quickly.* Zamir took Raza by the shoulders, kissed the boy's forehead, then held him firmly away from him before stepping back, out of reach.

For a second, Zamir thought Raza would run to him. His eyes blazed as he held his son's gaze. *You are a brave Pashtun!* Raza faltered, then he turned without another word and followed Sarah and Chinir into departures. Long after he had disappeared, Zamir stood frozen to the spot. Eventually, Salim touched him gently and the old man turned, and they made their way through the crowds to the waiting car.

CHAPTER FOURTEEN

Cornwall, 2009

Finn woke in the night to the sound of Hanna and Ben arguing. Even above the wind he could hear them. It began as a low thrum and started to build to a slow-burning anger. Their muffled voices, rising and falling, reverberated round the wooden beach house, sliding under the doors and through the cracks. There was no place for anger to hide here. No way not to hear the recriminations or desperation in Hanna and Ben's voices. Finn lay tense, waiting for his parents to remember their children were lying next door. Waiting for it to stop. But it went on and grew in a frightening crescendo.

In the bunk bed below him Izzy began whimpering. 'It's okay, Izzy,' Finn whispered, climbing down to her. By her night light he saw she was lying rigid with her hands over her ears. Finn marched to his parents' bedroom and banged on the door. He opened it a crack, not wanting to see them, and hissed. 'Stop it! You're upsetting Izzy . . .'

There was a startled silence as Finn banged their door

shut again. Izzy was sitting up in bed looking small and tearful. Finn knelt and placed her rabbit back into her arms and got her to lie down.

'Go back to sleep,' he whispered, tucking her into her duvet. He saw her lip wobble.

'Mummy and Daddy are shouting. Can I come in your bunk, Finn?'

'No, you might fall out. I'll stay here until you fall asleep, okay?'

Izzy nodded. 'Don't like it when Mummy and Daddy shout.'

'Do they sometimes shout at home?'

Izzy nodded. 'Mostly Mummy. But not as loud as this . . .'

'All grown-ups argue sometimes,' Finn said. 'Go back to sleep now, Izz.'

Finn lay down beside her on top of her rosebud bed. She clutched rabbit and turned towards him and closed her eyes. Finn heard the sound of the fly door to the balcony as Hanna and Ben went outside. Their voices were now a dull, relentless hum, but Izzy slept.

This was it, then. Hanna must have told Ben she wanted to go back to Finland.

Finn looked down at Izzy sleeping and felt such a fierce and protective love for her that tears came to his eyes. He knew in that moment he would always feel like this about Izzy, even when they were adults.

He must have fallen asleep for he woke feeling cold. Ben was bending over him. 'Finn, you're frozen,' he whispered. 'Izzy's fast asleep now. Come on, hop up to your own bed. You need to warm up.'

Ben kissed the top of Finn's head and heaved him up into his own bed.

'Sorry you heard us arguing,' he whispered. 'We'll talk tomorrow.'

Finn reached out suddenly and held on to Ben. Misery caught at both of them like spiderwebs.

Ben whispered, 'Sleep now. I promise I'll talk to you in the morning. Okay?' Finn nodded and the next minute was asleep.

CHAPTER FIFTEEN

Islamabad, 2007

The plane rose and circled over Islamabad. Raza sat in the window seat, his face closed, staring out. Sarah had tried to persuade him to change into western clothes in the hotel, but he had refused.

She explained that it was winter in England and it would be very cold when they landed. Raza stubbornly pulled on the small leather jerkin that Zamir had made him from goatskin over his *shalwar kameez*. Sarah sighed and put shoes, socks, and a coat into her hand luggage.

Zamir, knowing that Raza would initially refuse to wear western clothes, had handed him a huge, checked shawl as big as a tablecloth to wrap round him. When the aircraft engines started up Raza clutched the cloth to him, his face white and pinched with helplessness.

In an effort to distract him, Chinir tried pointing out the films he could watch on the small screen in front of him. Raza turned away, closed his eyes, unable to focus on anything but his terror of leaving Baba.

When the plane doors finally clunked shut, a wild look

passed over his face. As they taxied along the runway he bent and pressed his face to the window to see the last of the airport buildings, where he imagined his father still stood. Disbelief crossed his face as he watched the green hills of Islamabad disappear below him.

Once airborne, Raza refused to speak or eat. When the lights were dimmed Chinir showed him how to tip his seat back into a bed. With a small sigh Raza wrapped the huge shawl around him like a shroud and disappeared, head and body underneath it.

Chinir and Sarah looked at each other, traumatized. Sarah whispered. 'It is all like a horrible nightmare. I did not want taking Raza home with us to be like this . . . I still can't believe that Benazir Bhutto is dead, that it really happened, that we were caught up in it, Chinir.'

'After this, I never want to come back to Pakistan,' Chinir muttered. 'I've had it with this bloody country. Nothing changes, it all just gets worse.'

When Sarah closed her eyes, she could still hear breaking glass and screams. She could see faces full of wild, pointless rage. She never wanted to witness such violence again. She knew Raza too was in shock, but at least he was safe. He was safe with her and Chinir now.

Raza struggled up suddenly and lifted the window blind. He stared intently down at the stark, blurry mountains of Afghanistan. His fingers splayed across the porthole window as if he could trace his way back home. Then, he turned to them, frantically, throwing his blanket off and trying to get out of his seat.

Chinir put out a hand to restrain him. Sarah said quickly in Pashto. 'Raza, It's okay. You can pray on an aeroplane. Calm down. Go first with Chinir to wash.'

People were staring. Sarah bent to Chinir. 'We should have thought of this and taken him to the prayer room before take-off. There's a *Qibla* up in front. Let him wash, then show him where it is, or he is going to get more agitated and cause a scene . . .'

Sarah found Raza's embroidered *kufi* and prayer mat and gave them to Chinir. When Raza emerged from the lavatory, he placed the *kufi* on his head and clutched his prayer mat.

Chinir was embarrassed, and ashamed of his embarrassment. They were in business class, where people washed and prayed privately, if they prayed at all.

He showed Raza where to kneel. Oblivious to all but the need to pray, Raza rolled out his mat and bent his head to the ground. He rocked back and forth, eyes closed, lips moving. A clear image of Baba also praying comforted him.

Chinir watched the small boy in his baggy *shalwar kameez* for a moment then went back to his seat. He and Sarah stared at each other. Had they made a huge misjudgement? The subtle divisions that separated them from their own culture and comfort zone in Pakistan could not have been more apparent at this moment. They had made themselves responsible for this frightened, rigidly devout little boy. They were all he had.

Raza came padding back on small bare feet. He squeezed past them, eyes averted. He wrapped himself up in his shawl, tipped his seat back and disappeared back under it to the dark oblivion of sleep.

CHAPTER SIXTEEN

Cornwall, 2009

Finn woke late the next morning. He remembered Hanna and Ben's raised voices with a sick lurch. The rain and wind had stopped. The day felt eerily calm and silent. Izzy's bunk was empty. Finn could hear her talking to Hanna. He got dressed and went out to the kitchen. Hanna was giving Izzy breakfast. His mother was puffy-eyed and still in her pyjamas. She nodded at Finn but did not meet his eyes.

'Where's Ben?' he asked.

'He's gone for a run,' Hanna said. 'Could you keep an eye on Izzy while I get dressed? She did not have supper last night and I want her to eat that egg.'

Hanna hardly glanced at him before she disappeared into the bedroom.

Finn poured himself a bowl of cornflakes feeling abruptly angry. Of all Hanna's moods he hated being made invisible. This is what his mother did when she was away in some other place in her head. She blanked him out. He thought of all the times he had wondered what he had done when he was little.

Finn helped Izzy get dressed and then sat on the floor while she played with her doll's house. She was very quiet today. He wished Ben would come back. The day felt fragile and unreal. He heard Hanna on the phone talking in Finnish. Was Hanna going to say anything to him? Tell *him* she was returning to Finland? Finn's resentment and fear grew.

Hanna eventually came out of her bedroom and said, 'Finn, I need to go to Truro for some things. Would you mind staying with Izzy until Ben gets back?'

Finn felt a wave of misery and fury engulf him. It was as if he did not exist or something. 'Why don't you take Izzy with you? It's like you take it for granted that I will always look after her, even though you've hardly spoken one single word to me this morning. NOT ONE WORD . . . It's like I'm invisible or something . . .' Finn's voice cracked. Hanna stood, startled, staring at Finn as if coming from a long way away.

Ben suddenly appeared on the balcony steps. 'Daddy!' Izzy cried and ran to him. Ben scooped her up. The air was alive with tension. It was as if neither of his parents could bear to look at each other.

Finn's heart beat painfully. If he did not get outside, he would suffocate.

Hanna was still looking at him. She started to say something, then stopped. Tears formed in the corner of her eyes, before she turned and walked back into the bedroom.

Finn turned and fled out onto the balcony, past Ben and Izzy and down the wooden steps onto the beach. He kept running for the rocks at the far end, putting as much space between himself and his parents as possible. He pushed himself until his legs ached. When he reached the rocks, he clambered over and waded through the outgoing tide to the long space of empty beach. It was spewed with seaweed and debris from the storm. His stomach felt as if he had eaten stones. When he reached the shelter of sand dunes, he threw himself down and closed his eyes, listened to his aching heart racing.

He did not know how long he lay there before he heard Ben call out, 'There you are!' Finn didn't say anything. He didn't sit up or open his eyes. He wished he had brought a bottle of water. His throat was dry. He dreaded what was coming.

Ben threw himself down beside him and said softly, 'I don't like you wading round before the tide is out. It's dangerous, as you know. Will you sit up and look at me, old thing? I need to talk to you.'

Finn did not move. He didn't want to hear it. Ben said quietly, 'Don't make this any harder.'

Finn opened his eyes and sat up. Ben's face was a grey colour under his tan. He handed Finn a bottle of water and a sandwich. 'I'll eat half if you do.'

Finn, despite himself, was hungry. Ben had made his favourite: bacon and apple. He handed half to Ben and drank deeply from the bottle of water. Then he bit into his sandwich.

'After last night you have the right to be angry with both of us,' Ben said. 'I'm so sorry you had to hear that, Finn.'

'Hanna's going back to Finland, isn't she?'

Ben looked surprised. 'She's told you?'

'No, she's hardly spoken to me this morning. I heard her talking to Mary at the beach house. Mary was angry with her.' Ben did not say anything. 'If Hanna goes back to Finland does that mean you are going to split up?'

'I don't know, Finn. I don't think Hanna really knows what she wants, apart from not wanting to be in Germany while I'm in Afghanistan. She says she has to get away, go back home.'

'You mean for a long holiday while you are away?' Finn said hopefully. 'That wouldn't be too bad, would it. If Hanna just went back to Finland, for a few weeks?'

Ben sighed. 'Finn, Hanna doesn't want to be in Germany at all, that is the problem.'

'But what about Izzy? All Izzy's friends are there, and her playgroup and stuff. Germany is our home. It's all she knows. Maybe, if you say that Hanna can go for like a month, or as long as she likes, she'll feel better.'

Ben smiled. 'Finn, it's not a question of my giving Hanna permission. Your mother can take off and visit her family any time she likes, she knows that. She just doesn't want to come back. She wants to leave Germany and our quarter for good . . .'

Ben reached out to touch Finn and his misery was apparent. 'It's been a really hard and lonely year for Hanna. We've got to try to understand how she must be feeling, Finn . . .' Ben paused and cleared his throat. Finn saw that his hands were shaking. 'Hanna has booked two tickets for her and Izzy to fly to Helsinki tomorrow . . . That's it. She will not be coming back to Germany with me . . .'

Finn felt sick. 'What about all her clothes and things? What about Izzy's toys and stuff?'

Ben shrugged. 'She says she will buy what she needs when she gets to Helsinki. She will go back to the quarter in Germany at some point to pick up her stuff . . .'

Finn had gone so pale, Ben said quickly, 'Finn, Hanna's made it very clear that she feels wretched about leaving you. If she could, she would take you to Helsinki to be with her too . . .'

Finn stared at Ben, horrified. 'There is no way I'm going to Finland with Hanna. Why didn't she tell me? You wouldn't let me go, would you? You won't let her take Izzy?'

Ben sighed. 'Of course, I wouldn't have you uprooted from your school here, Finn. It's totally impractical, Hanna knows this, but Izzy is a little girl, she needs her mother. My hands are tied . . .'

Ben let out his breath in a little explosion of regret. 'I had not realized how bad . . . how depressed Hanna was . . . She's seemed so happy while we've been here. Let's just pray when she's spent time back home with her family, she will see things are not as bleak as she imagines . . . She will feel better . . .'

Ben ended lamely as if he did not quite believe his own words.

'Let's get back to the house, Finn. We need to all sit down together . . . I'm so sorry this is happening.'

'There is nothing to say is there? Hanna never talks to us. It's not your fault, it's hers!' Finn shouted, jumping up. 'Why is she spoiling our lives? She's selfish . . . I hate her.'

'No, you don't,' Ben said. 'Your mother's not selfish, just terribly unhappy. She's had enough of army life . . .'

'Well, if you think Hanna's not selfish why were you shouting last night?'

Ben stood looking down at Finn. Finn's precociousness stung sometimes, but it was a reasonable question and he needed to be honest.

'I was angry because Hanna must have thought about going back to Finland for quite some time, yet she did not say a word to me. It affects us all as a family and she has given us no warning. No time to get used to or understand her decision. No time to even respect it . . .'

Ben's voice was low, but Finn could hear the anger creeping back into him.

'I was angry, because Hanna walked out into the rain without saying a word about her intentions. While we were in Penzance to give her some space, your mother marched to the beach café and booked tickets for her and my daughter to fly off to Helsinki tomorrow. Hanna did not think to discuss any of this with me first. So yes, Finn, I was very angry indeed . . .'

82

Ben turned and looked at the sea. 'But I shouldn't have lost my temper and shouted at her, Finn. Nothing gives me that right . . .' He smiled at Finn. 'Losing it achieves nothing. Remember that . . .'

They trudged back along the beach in silence. As they rounded the rocks over the wet sand, a seal popped up out of the water and they stopped to watch him. Finn slipped his hand into Ben's and whispered, as they got near the beach house, 'I want Izzy and me to go to Delphi and Ian's tonight, please.'

Ben squeezed his hand. 'Give Delphi a ring. I'll go on in.' Finn's hands trembled as he dialled Delphi's mobile. When Delphi answered with a pleased 'Hello, darling!' Finn burst into tears. 'Please come, Delphi. Please come quickly. Hanna is going to leave Ben and fly back to Finland and take Izzy with her . . . They had a terrible row . . .' Finn stopped, incoherent.

There was a second of shocked silence from Delphi. Then, 'Finn, darling, where are you?'

'At the beach house.'

'Are both Hanna and Ben there?'

'Yes inside. Please come . . .' Finn begged.

'I'm putting the phone down and getting straight in the car. I'll be with you in half an hour. I know you can hold on in there until I get there can't you?'

Finn nodded. 'Yeah.'

'Good boy. Go inside now and be with Izzy and I'll be there before you know it . . .'

Delphi flew into the hall for her car keys and found Ian talking to Ben. He put his hand over the receiver. 'Crisis, old thing. Ben trying to explain . . . he's worried about the children . . .'

'Tell him I'm on my way.' Delphi said, flying out of the front door to her yellow Beetle.

CHAPTER SEVENTEEN

London, 2007

England was a shock from which Raza thought he would never recover. The cold bit into his feet as soon as the plane doors opened, numbing them. The damp air swooped, making his bones ache, seeped into his skin like an extra undergarment, adding to his misery.

The sky was grey. The world was grey. Raza shivered uncontrollably, despite wearing Zamir's sheepskin jerkin and winding his huge shawl around him.

Sarah saw that Raza's chattering teeth were due to fear as well as cold. She pleaded for him to put on the warm clothes she had bought for him, but he steadfastly refused. She wanted to clutch the frightened boy to her and reassure him, but his eyes warned her off.

Sarah's parents, Liyana and Daniyal, were waiting at Heathrow to meet the plane. They welcomed Raza warmly but were horrified to see Raza barefoot in sandals. Raza had placed his *kufi* on his head and was clutching his huge trailing shawl around him like a shroud.

Daniyal put his arm round Raza and led him through

the airport. The boy seemed catatonic and Daniyal glanced at Chinir. Raza had been Sarah's obsession and Chinir had gone along with it. He hoped it was not going to spectacularly backfire. This little boy was not a city boy but a tribal child from the mountains.

Raza passed into Sarah and Chinir's house impassively. On being shown his room Raza remained expressionless. He eyed his bed with the expensive coverlet and laid his bundle of belongings firmly on the floor by the window. He dug out his prayer mat and began to wander around the room looking from door to window to try to get his bearings.

Chinir pointed to the ceiling where he had painted a small *Qibla* in indelible paint so that Raza knew in which direction to pray. Raza nodded. He felt numb. He longed to curl up and sleep, but his stomach growled.

Sarah took him down to the kitchen, where Liyana had prepared a meal for them all. Raza ate ravenously, stuffing biryani into his mouth with his fingers. 'He didn't eat anything on the plane,' Sarah and Chinir explained protectively. 'No wonder he's hungry.'

Liyana smiled at Raza encouragingly. 'Let him eat as much as he can, he has some growing to do.'

After he had eaten, Chinir showed Raza the intricacies of the modern power shower. Suspicious at first, Raza became fascinated at the strength of the jets, and for the first time became animated as he stood under the warm water. Chinir had to pull him out after twenty minutes and wrap him in a towel, wondering what on earth his water bill was going to be like.

Sarah had placed a clean *shalwar kameez* on his bed and Raza pulled them on, relieved. When Sarah opened the duvet for him to climb in, he shook his head and smoothed out his shawl on the floor.

Sarah, shaky with weariness, bit her lip in exasperation. Chinir pulled the single mattress off the bed and placed it by the window. He rearranged the duvet over it with Raza's shawl over the top instead of the coverlet. Raza climbed straight in.

'Go to bed,' Chinir whispered to Sarah. 'You're exhausted. I'll stay with him until he sleeps.'

'Raza knows perfectly well what a bed is for,' Sarah said tightly, near tears.

'Of course, he does, Sarah, but he doesn't want to sleep in one. He wants to hang onto what he knows. Let him pretend he is sleeping on *a charpoy*, if it comforts him.'

As Raza lay under the duvet, clean and warm and full of good food, he began to feel fractionally better. He waited for Chinir to join him on the wide mattress, but Chinir just went on sitting in the armchair, so eventually Raza indicated that there was plenty of room beside him. Chinir smiled, touched. He lay beside the thin boy on the mattress. In minutes Raza was asleep and it dawned on Chinir that Raza had probably never slept alone in his life.

Raza woke in the night and could not remember where he was. At first, he thought he was dreaming, then the small night-light revealed Chinir beside him in a strange and silent room, where he could neither hear the wind through the trees, nor the faint scrabbling of animal noises coming from outside. The only sound was the thick tick of a clock somewhere in the house.

As his journey to this place flooded back, Raza wept in the dark for Baba, for the cold air of early morning penetrating through the curtain covering the door, for the sound of his goats and chickens. He wept for the particular, comforting smell of Zamir and the sound of him snoring. For the familiar sounds and smells that meant he was safe home in his village.

When dawn filtered through the window curtains Raza slipped out of bed. He went and splashed water over himself, placed his mat in front of the *Qibla* and prayed. He prayed with all his heart to Allah that Baba would realize he had made a very big mistake and recall him home immediately.

CHAPTER EIGHTEEN

Cornwall, 2009

Somehow, Delphi had persuaded everyone out of the cold cheerless beach house back to the warmth of Salubrious House. In truth, it had not taken much. She had taken one look at Hanna and Ben's pale and haggard faces and bundled Finn and Izzy into her car. She had gone back into the cold, draughty beach house to collect the children's night things and instructed Ben and Hanna to pack up their things and follow her to Penzance. 'The children need a united front, whatever happens next, and that is what we are going to have,' she said firmly.

Neither Ben nor Hanna put up the least resistance. Delphi saw they were both emotionally drained and needed to be organized into some semblance of order.

It was only September, but so damp and miserable that Ian had lit a fire. Delphi sat both children in front of it watching a DVD of *Frozen*. Both children sat like little zombies watching it. In the kitchen Ian was heating up a vast bowl of stew he had found in the freezer and defrosted. Every now and then he popped his head into the sitting room to talk to the children, fearful of what was coming next. *What timing,* he thought. *What timing.*

Delphi was checking the bedrooms, pulling out the day bed in Ben's old room so Izzy could sleep with Finn. She put the electric blanket on in the double bed in the spare room and switched the immersion heater on for extra baths.

As she did all these things, Delphi felt sorrow build up between her ribs. *This has been coming for so long.* She glanced at her Buddha and prayed for strength. She must try to do and say all the right things. It was vital she wasn't partisan. Vital that she listened to Hanna.

She heard Ben's car park in the drive and went down to help them bring in their things. She took one look at an ashen Hanna and took her straight upstairs and ran her a bath. She poured liberal amounts of lavender in and placed a big fluffy bathrobe on a hook of the door. Hanna sat awkwardly on the bed. 'Thank you, Delphi,' she whispered. 'I'm so tired . . .'

'You're exhausted. Have a sleep after your bath. I'll make sure no one disturbs you. Are you going to be safe in hot water? I don't want you to faint.'

Hanna smiled. 'I won't faint, Delphi. Thank you for having us here . . . I . . .'

'Go and have your bath,' Delphi said quickly. 'We can all talk later. I'll bring you up a cup of tea.'

Hanna nodded thanks. For the first time in her marriage, she was grateful for Delphi being Delphi.

Delphi found Ben sitting between his children watching the end of *Frozen*. 'Hanna is having a bath and a nap. Come on, we're all going to have an early supper. Ian's done a stew and baked potatoes. What we all need are . . .'

'Carbohydrates!' Ben and Finn chimed together. It was Delphi's answer to everything. Finn was suddenly starving. Even Izzy ate everything on her plate.

Ben said, 'That was lovely, thank you, both of you.'

'There is plenty for Hanna when she comes down,' Delphi said. 'Why don't you and Ian play a game with Izzy before bed. Finn will help me clear up, won't you darling?'

Finn nodded. Delphi shut the kitchen door and Finn told Delphi what he had overheard Hanna telling Mary about going back to Finland. About the terrible row that had erupted last night. Delphi stopped washing up and went very still as she listened. She didn't say anything for what seemed a long time. Then she said:

'I'll talk to Ben, and Hanna when she's up. I promise I won't keep anything from you. We will sit down and try to sort things out. Try not to worry . . . Now, darling, will you take a cup of tea up to Hanna and see if she is awake?'

Finn reluctantly carried the mug of tea upstairs. Hanna seemed to be asleep, so Finn left it on her bedside table. He looked down at her open suitcase and saw for the first time how much stuff she had packed. She had filled a large case and Hanna was good at travelling light. It looked as if Hanna had never been planning to go back to Germany, only she forgot to tell them.

He left the room and shut the door behind him. He stood on the dusky landing and thought about going back in and waking Hanna up and asking her if it was really true. To hear her say out loud to him she was really leaving. But he went into his bedroom, picked up his diary and started to write.

Half an hour later Hanna knocked on Finn's closed bedroom door.

'Can I come in, Finn?' Hanna had had a bath and smelled of flowers and was wearing Delphi's big spare dressing gown which made her look tiny. She sat on Finn's bed.

'Is Izzy all right? Has she had supper yet?'

'We all have,' Finn said. 'Delphi saved some for you.'

'That's kind,' Hanna said carefully. 'I better go down.' She did not move, and Finn knew she was dreading going downstairs.

Hanna looked at her feet and whispered. 'What about you, Finn? How are you?'

Finn felt unable to breathe in the small bedroom full of Hanna's scent. No words came. He felt sweaty and angry. How did she think he was? She didn't really care about him, or Ben. Or Izzy really. Just herself. There was nothing to say. All her stuff was packed in the spare room. She had been planning it for ages. It was like she was half gone already.

'Finn . . .' Hanna reached out to touch him. 'I'm sorry. I know it must seem like I'm deserting you, but I can't stay. I need to go home. I love you and I would take you too, if it were possible . . .'

Hanna stopped. Finn would not look at her. His face was stony. Hanna said miserably, 'I wish I could make you understand . . .'

Finn looked at Hanna then. 'You haven't even tried. You never talk to me. You never said anything about leaving us, about not coming back to Germany, all the time we've been here on holiday together. Like it was a secret that didn't affect anyone but you. It's like you think I'm too stupid to see anything is wrong. Or I don't matter because I'm mostly at school, not home with you all the time . . .' He stopped, words choking him.

'Finn, of course you matter. I never wanted you to go to boarding school in the first place, but it is the English way. I missed you . . . That is why I was planning to go back to work before Izzy came along . . .'

'But Izzy did come along and now you're going to disrupt her whole life too. Nothing is going to stop you, is it? Nothing matters except *you.*'

Hanna stood up. 'I am sorry, Finn, I can't cope with this now. I know it is bad timing to make such a decision, but you are happy and settled here in school. Ben is going to be away doing the job he loves and is trained for, but I am stuck in a life that is completely foreign to me . . .'

'What does that mean?' Finn said, staring at her. 'Suddenly, you can't bear to be, like, an army wife, anymore?

'It means,' Hanna said tiredly, 'I'm sick of sleepwalking through my life. I love Izzy but doing nothing but look after her is driving me crazy. This is not good for her or me. There is no reason for me to stay in a German army quarter on my own with a small child while Ben is in Afghanistan. I wish you and your father could see that. Finn? Please . . . try to understand.'

'All the other army wives are staying together. They don't go back to their parents. It's no fun for them either,' Finn said obstinately. 'Why is it different for you? You can go to Finland as much as you like, you don't need to live there. Mummo and Pappa could go to Germany and stay with you . . .'

'I don't want to ever live in that quarter in Germany again, Finn,' Hanna repeated quietly. 'I don't want to be there.'

Finn stood up. He was not going to let her see him cry. 'Go back to Finland then . . . I don't care.'

Hanna stood up too. She had two red spots on her cheeks like someone had slapped her. She whispered, 'Finn, I'm not saying that this will be forever . . . but I do need to go away and think about my life for a while . . .'

'Bugger off then.' Finn was furious because now he was crying.

'Finn!' Delphi stood in the doorway. 'Please go and make me some coffee. I'll be down in a moment . . .'

Finn went downstairs. He heard Delphi and Hanna both

cross the landing and go into the spare room and shut the door.

He put the kettle on and looked out at the camellia trees at the bottom of the garden. There was nothing out there that wasn't grey. He opened the back door and listened to the sea crash onto the prom on a high tide. Summer and sunlight were gone, and he shivered. It felt like his life and everything safe and familiar was being pulled relentlessly from underneath him.

Finn's Diary

8 p.m. Izzy insisted on getting into my bed, so I let her. Ben, Hanna, Delphi, and Ian are in the sitting room with the door shut. Izzy keeps watching me anxiously. She's only little and she doesn't really understand what's happening.

I've got this weird feeling in my chest, like a cat is sitting on it. Hanna is going to take Izzy away from us, and everything she knows. I won't be there for her. Ben won't be there for her. I can't even remember what life was like before Izzy . . . I can hardly remember before she was born . . .

'Story, Finn . . .' Izzy pleaded. Her eyes kept closing but she was trying to stay awake. Finn put his journal aside and lay beside her and closed his eyes.

'Once upon a time,' he whispered. 'There was this naughty little mermaid who sat on the rocks and combed her hair and sang the most beautiful songs. Her voice was extremely loud for a little girl . . .'

'Like me?' Izzy took her thumb out and smiled.

'Just like you. Her voice was so loud and so enchanting that all the fisher boys in their boats could not help steering towards the rocks where she was sit—'

93

'What's enchanting?'

'Bewitching. Lovely—'

'Like me! Go on. Did they crash?'

'Yep. The fisher boys hit those rocks with a sickening crash and the cruel, jagged rocks made holes in their shiny, expensive fishing boats and slowly all the boats began to sink beneath the sea. The fisher boys managed to jump into the waves and climb up on the rocks, but they could not find the naughty little mermaid. She was hiding, but they heard her giggling as she swam away in the dark blue sea and they thought they saw the wave of her hand bedecked in seaweed bracelets and her long hair disappearing into the foamy waves . . .' Finn stopped breathless.

'Did the fisher boys drownded? Did the fisher boys' daddies come and save them?'

'Clever girl. That's exactly what happened. But the fisher daddies were very cross with the fisher boys. "We've told you time and again about those naughty mermaids. You must close your ears or plug your iPods in—"'

'Don't be ridicleus, fisher boys don't have iPods.'

'How do you know? Anyway, the fisher daddies said, "You have been very silly fisher boys and you have damaged our expensive boats so you will have to come home right now and work very hard to mend them—"'

'And no ice cream?'

'Definitely no ice cream.'

'What happened to the naughty little mermaid?'

'She went home to her mummy and pretended she had been to school all day, but her mummy was suspicious because her packed lunch was still in her school bag and she was very tired from all the singing . . . She went to bed and straight to sleep . . . just like you.'

'No . . . more! I want more stories about the naughty little mermaid.'

'No more, Izzy. Go to sleep, then I might let you stay in my bed all night.'

'Okay.' Izzy knew when she had a good deal. She pulled rabbit to her and closed her eyes. Five minutes later when Finn turned to look from his diary, she was asleep.

Hanna stood outside the door of Finn's room, hovering. She wanted to go in to her children. She wanted to . . . what? Make things better? Tell Finn things would come right, when she did not really believe they could. She stood in the dark shivering, daring to face herself for the first time with the truth. If Kai had not got back in touch after all these years. If he were not back in Helsinki, would she be leaving, now, at this precise moment in all their lives? Kai had emailed last summer to say that his wife, Sigrid had left him. They were locked in a battle over the children and he needed a friend. He and Hanna began to email each other regularly. He was sad. Hanna was sad. Each knew the other so well it was like falling into warm water. They both began to rely on each other for support, despite how it had ended between them, twice. After they left art college Hanna had taken off travelling. Kai had grown tired of waiting for her and had shocked her by marrying Sigrid.

Years later, still enthralled by Hanna, he had in a weak moment employed her in his interior design firm. A married man who had been unable, in the end, to walk away from his wife and young child. A decent man who had called time. Hanna's misery, then and now, coloured everything, affected every decision she made.

Listening to the soft voices of her two children on the other side of the door made the enormity of what she was doing stark. Hanna reached for the door handle when the voices ceased. She would try once more to reach Finn. As she did so, two things happened. The reflection of her pale face framed in the landing window caught at her; another house accentuating her otherness, her isolation and loss of self. And Ben and Delphi's voices rose up from below. Companionable. Complicit. Together. Something in Hanna hardened. She did not have to justify anything to anyone here. This family would still go on turning without her. She was taking back control of her own life. She was not leaving Ben for Kai. Kai was as adrift as she was. He had just been the catalyst, pulling her back to the life she once had; the person she had once been. Hanna was still not quite honest enough to acknowledge that just the presence of Kai on the edges of her life had been enough to give her wings. She moved away across the dark landing, into the spare room where her packed cases lay waiting on the floor.

CHAPTER NINETEEN

London, 2007

Sarah woke early the next day to a message from Maldi. She had briefed him on the difficulty she was having in persuading Raza to wear warm clothes or sleep in a bed. The bed did not matter but Raza's insistence on wearing his *shalwar kameez* at all times would have consequences. It wasn't just the cold. When he started school Raza would stand out if he refused to wear school uniform. Sarah was frightened he would make himself an immediate target for bullies.

Maldi told her this had made Zamir anxious. He did not want to return to Peshawar until he had spoken to Raza. With the help of his nephew, who had Internet connection, Maldi told Sarah he could set up a Skype call. Raza and Zamir could talk when convenient.

Sarah felt relieved. 'I think Zamir is the only person Raza will listen to at the moment,' she told Maldi.

Maldi agreed. 'Raza, he needs to see his Baba. Zamir, he needs to see his son. Let us try to link up in one hour. Then all will proceed well, Sarah.' Sarah wished she had Maldi's optimism. She went upstairs to ask Chinir to wake Raza.

When she got back to the kitchen Liyana and Daniyal were making tea. Daniyal, an eye surgeon, was catching an early train back to Derby. Liyana, who taught English as a second language, was staying on to help Sarah settle Raza and to teach him basic English vocabulary. The more English Raza could learn before the Christmas term started the easier it was going to be for him.

In the nature of Pakistani families, Liyana was eager to talk to Zamir.

'Ami,' Sarah said, irritated, 'this is not a social call. The whole point of this Skype call is for Zamir to reassure Raza about our western ways . . .'

Liyana smiled at her daughter benignly. 'Sarah, I need to establish how much English Zamir managed to teach Raza, and how quickly the boy picks things up. Zamir also needs to be reassured that Raza is in safe hands . . .'

Daniyal said quickly, trying to avert a mother and daughter clash, 'Liyana, the link to Rawalpindi will no doubt be tenuous. Zamir knows Raza is in good hands, he handed him to our daughter . . .'

Sarah laughed. 'Thank you, Aba.' She switched on the computer. 'Here goes. I hope we can link up without a hitch . . .'

Miraculously, Maldi and Zamir's anxious faces appeared on screen.

'*Assalamu alaikum,* Zamir.'

'*Wa alaykumu as-salam,* Sarah. How is my son?'

'Raza is fine, but he needs to wear warm clothes. It is very cold here.'

Zamir shook his head in sympathy. 'Sarah, I am sorry for the worry. I will speak to my son. He must do as he is told. Do not be anxious, the mountains too are cold. He is accustomed to the cold. Sarah . . .'

'It is a different, damp cold here. It eats into your

bones . . . If you could reassure Raza that he is not betraying Islam if he becomes a little westernized to fit in, it might help . . .'

Zamir smiled. 'I can. After all it is I who sent him to the west. Sarah, Raza can be obstinate, but he learns quickly.'

Sarah went to call Raza. Liyana took her chance to greet Zamir and explain that she was a language teacher and would be on hand for a few weeks to help and encourage Raza and to teach him English. Zamir gave Liyana a rare and relieved gap-toothed smile. He had done the right thing. Raza was in a good place. Already, the boy's education was beginning . . .

Raza burst into the kitchen and his eyes widened as he saw Zamir on the screen. *Baba on a computer.*

'*Assalamu alaikum*, Baba.' Raza grinned widely.

'*Wa alaykumu as-salam*, Raza.' Zamir leant forward to peer at his son on a screen thousands of miles away. This was indeed a magical thing to see and hear from so far away.

The Ali family slid out of the kitchen to leave Raza and Zamir to talk on their own. Raza burst into a torrent of Pashto. Baba had not returned to Peshawar without him. This was good. Baba would understand . . . Raza began to explain the strangeness of the west. The Ali's lived with so many empty rooms. There was no hose to clean yourself before prayer in this house of Sarah and Chinir. 'Baba, I have not even heard the call to prayer from the mosques that they tell me are here—'

'Raza,' Zamir interrupted sternly. 'Hear my words and keep them in your heart. You have had no time to learn anything yet. Observe. Listen. Do not judge until you understand. I have entrusted you to good people. Their ways are different. Learn them. There is no disgrace in wearing western clothes. You know perfectly well that many devout Muslims here do so. When you start school you must, of course, wear the English school uniform to make me proud. NOT over your *shalwar kameez*. It is a respect to the school and to the teachers. You must wear warm clothes when it is cold and when Sarah tells you to. When you are at home or at leisure, you may wear your *shalwar kameez*. You will not forget to be a good Muslim, or a Pakistani, because you wear different clothes. Inside you are the same. Neither do you need to pray five times a day to be devout. In school it may not be possible. You know in your heart that you did not always pray five times a day out on the mountains with the goats. If you wish, you can think about Allah five times a day. Are you listening to me, Raza?'

'Yes, Baba, I am listening,' Raza said patiently. He had never before heard his Baba talk so much. 'But I wish to come home now. I think this education is a mistake. Pakistan is best place for me.'

At that moment, Zamir loved Raza so much he was overcome. When he could speak, he said, 'Pakistan is indeed the best and most beautiful place. That is why you must learn all you can in England. Work hard. Make me proud of my son, the doctor, the teacher . . . the educated man who will come back to Pakistan and do great things in the country he loves . . .'

Raza stared at his father. He was beginning to pixelate into small squares that jumped. 'Trust Sarah and Chinir . . . trust Daniyal and Liyana. They are your family, until you return to me . . .'

Zamir's words began to distort, then with a little blip his face disappeared. Chinir came into the kitchen. He tried to get Zamir back, but the link was gone. Raza sat staring at the dark screen where the face of Baba had been. He stayed rigid with hope for ten minutes without moving a muscle in case Zamir reappeared. Then, he walked out

100

of the room and up the stairs and shut the door of his bedroom. He knelt on his prayer mat and rocked until the pain eased. He must accept his fate here in this place. Baba wished it. With Allah's help, *Peace be with Him*, he must accept his fate.

CHAPTER TWENTY

Cornwall, 2009

They stood in a small group at Newquay Airport. Izzy was clutching the handle of her pink bag, excited because she thought she was going on another holiday. Hanna's nervous excitement, her anxiety to be on the plane was tangible. Finn looked at Ben. His face was drawn as he too stared down at Hanna's bulging case. *It might be a short time. It might be forever.*

Finn picked Izzy up and she clasped him round his neck. Her fair curls covered his face. She smelled of shampoo and little girl. Finn held her tight and prayed that she would be all right, that she would not be too homesick and lonely for him and Ben.

Ben took Izzy from him and carried her to the check-in desk. He wanted to hold her until the last minute too. He helped Hanna lift the cases to be weighed. As soon as they disappeared, Hanna said, 'Izzy and I will go through now, Ben, get security over . . .'

Ben nodded. He rocked Izzy and buried his nose in her hair. He looked at Hanna over her head. 'Have a safe journey. Let me know when you get to your parents.' He placed Izzy gently on the ground and kissed Hanna on the cheek. 'Take care of yourself. Try to be happy . . .'

Hanna held her cheek against Ben's for a second. 'You take care. Stay safe. Concentrate on what you have to do out there, Ben. Izzy, Finn, and I will be all fine and stay in touch with each other. Don't worry about us. Promise?'

'I'll try,' Ben said. 'I'll try.'

Hanna turned to Finn and wrapped her arms around him, but Finn froze, keeping his hands to his sides. He was trying to hang onto something frightening inside him that threatened to escape. Hanna touched his face. 'I will email you every day.'

Ben and Finn stood and watched Hanna and Izzy walk away. Izzy's curls bounced. She turned once, her footsteps faltering. Her lower lip trembling. Then they were gone through to security.

Finn stared at the spot as if he could make them reappear. Ben touched his arm. 'Let's go.' But Finn could not move. He felt himself slipping away to the ground. He heard someone howl like an animal and it scared him. It was only when Ben was holding him hard against his chest Finn realized the sound had come from him.

'Ssh. Ssh . . . old thing . . . It's okay. It's okay . . .' Ben hoisted him up and carried him out of the airport and back to the car. He made him breathe air deep into his lungs and held him tight. 'You know what they say. If you let the people you love fly free, they fly back . . .' Ben said.

'Who said that?' Finn asked.

'I have no idea,' Ben said, smiling, making Finn smile.

Delphi had made them a Thermos of tea and they sat in silence drinking it until Finn felt better. Ben turned to him. 'How do you feel about checking out Fistral Beach and watching some serious surfing? Be silly not to while we're here, wouldn't it?'

Finn nodded. 'Yeah, silly not to.'

Both of them had forgotten how awful it would be in season. Fistral Beach was heaving with surfers, surf school, and tourists. Ben and Finn walked along the beach and sat huddled on the sand among the crowds watching the professionals with awe. The surf was clean and there were a lot of people in the water. 'Makes you realize what average surfers we are, doesn't it?' Ben said.

'I'm average. You're good,' Finn replied. 'I'll never have your stamina.' He looked down at Ben's brown legs in his shorts, taut with exercise and then at his own skinny legs. He longed to fill out, instead he just grew upward like a beanpole and he was still smaller than some of his friends.

'Rubbish,' Ben said, getting up suddenly. 'Stamina is something that comes with age and training your body. I was as skinny as you at twelve . . . Come on, I've had enough. Too many people. Let's just see if we can find Ian's fishing tackle shop before we head back. I'd like to buy him something. I'm going to miss his birthday.'

Newquay was an ugly town full of pubs and games arcades. They found the fishing shop and brought Ian vivid new fishing lures, more for the colour than anything else. On the way back to the car they saw a tiny jewellery shop that sold expensive pens. Ben bought them both sleek silver fountain pens. 'For writing blueys. Now we can write to each other with identical pens.'

'Thanks, Ben,' Finn said, delighted. He had always wanted an old-fashioned fountain pen. He could use it to write his diary too.

Nothing feels quite real, today. Finn thought. It was as if he and Ben were floating underwater. Like they were in a weird dream in this crowded tourist town. In a moment they would both wake up and Hanna and Izzy would be coming out of a shop and Izzy would fly towards them holding up something pink . . .

Driving back to Penzance, Finn knew Ben wanted to say comforting and reassuring things to him but was too tired. He didn't have the energy. Finn held the box with his new pen close to his chest and hoped Ben knew he didn't need to say anything; that it was okay just to sit in the car together in silence.

Finn lay in bed. His diary and new pen lay on the bedside beside him. He could hear the comforting murmur of voices downstairs. Hanna would be in Helsinki by now. Izzy would be in a strange bed. He thought about going downstairs to ask Ben if Hanna had left a message on his phone. He wanted to know if Izzy was okay. But he sensed he should not interrupt the conversation going on in the kitchen. His eyes prickled with tiredness. The thought of Ben leaving him here and going back to Germany alone made him sad. He knew he could not go with him. Ben would be off to Lashkar Gah in a few days.

The holiday had come to such an abrupt end that Finn felt as if he had been hit by an unseen wave. He knew even Delphi could not make miracles happen. He closed his eyes thinking he wouldn't be able to sleep, but darkness came swiftly to end the strange day.

Finn woke in the dark and crept into Ben's bed. Ben was snoring gently. There was grey light coming from behind the curtains. Finn curled up in Ben's warmth waiting for Ben's phone alarm to buzz. They had said their goodbyes last night. Ben wanted to creep out first thing in the morning without waking anyone, but Finn was determined to see him off.

When Finn next woke it was light and the bed was empty. Ben was gone. Finn moaned and rolled into the dip where Ben had been. He thought of Ben driving onto the ferry, speeding up the autobahn. He thought of their quarter, which he had not even seen this holiday, and his room and the woods where he and Ben ran on Wednesday afternoons together . . .

Finn's phone bleeped. *Just stopped at Exeter Services for a coffee. Did not want to wake you. I've booked you in for some surfing competitions at Sennen. Thought it might be fun! Ring you tonight when I'm home.* Xx

At ten, Ian put his head round the door. 'Fancy getting up and having some breakfast, old thing?' Finn did not think he did, but then he smelled bacon and changed his mind. He got dressed reluctantly and went downstairs.

'I'm going to drive over and check the beach house,' Ian said to Delphi. 'Make sure Ben locked everything up. He was distracted.'

'Good idea,' Delphi said. 'Finn and I will come with you. I need to come and gather up sheets and towels.'

Finn wasn't sure he wanted to go back to the beach house just yet, but Delphi said she would be grateful for some help. As soon as they arrived, Delphi lit little candles in front of her Buddhas. Finn caught her wafting what looked like an incense burner full of herbs or flowers or something, around all the rooms.

'Delphi, what are you doing?' he asked, incredulous.

'I'm expunging bad vibes from the house and welcoming back my happy spirits . . .'

Finn glanced at Ian, but he just rolled his eyes. Finn laughed and went to check the surfboards were securely slotted and locked together under the house. It occurred to him that Delphi's little charade might have been for him, but you could never be sure with Delphi.

PART TWO

CHAPTER TWENTY-ONE

Cornwall, 2009

Delphi drove Finn back to school on Sunday afternoon. They travelled in companionable silence as Finn made the mental adjustment from one life to another.

The Causeway was Finn's imaginary border, a bridge between his grandparents and school. He gazed across the mudflats where egret and curlew waded among the samphire, his eyes following the aquamarine shimmer of sea beyond the land.

He wound his car window down and took a deep, shivering breath like a condemned prisoner on the way back to his cell. He did this each term and Delphi normally smiled, knowing that Finn was perfectly happy and secure at school. This term was different. As soon as Ben had flown out to Afghanistan, Finn had withdrawn. The only time his face lit up was when he spoke to Izzy on the phone. He had teased her gently, made an effort to be funny for her, but he was monosyllabic with Hanna. Finn made it clear to Delphi and Ian that he did not want to talk about his mother. Ian had taken him to the surfing competitions that Ben had booked at Sennen to distract him, and it had. Finn was competitive and enjoyed pitting himself against some serious surfers.

Delphi had rung the school and spoken, briefly, to both Ed and Mercy Dominic, who ran St Michael's School. At 12, Finn was approaching an awkward age and Delphi did not want him to grow stroppy, stop working, or retreat into himself.

As Delphi drove through the school gates and up to St Trelawney, Finn's boarding house, she said, 'Darling, please try not to worry, things will work out . . .' She nudged him. 'Try and do my Buddhist thing . . .'

Finn smiled. 'Oh yeah, chanting at dawn will make me really popular . . .'

Delphi smiled back. 'You've got your stash of blueys so you can write to Ben as often as you like. When you're back for weekends we'll pack off parcels to him. Will you make a list of the things you think he might like?'

Finn nodded. Delphi hesitated, knowing his face would close.

'Finn, please, email and keep in touch with Hanna. It's important. None of us really knows how she's feeling.'

'I'll leave messages for Izzy. I've got nothing to say to Hanna.' Finn climbed out of the car and went to the boot and hauled out his case, groaning at the weight of it.

Ed and Mercy Dominic came out of Trelawney House and greeted them both as if by accident. Delphi waved, instantly cheered by Mercy's pink-striped hair. Ed was a young, enlightened head who had taken over the school six years ago. Meeting and marrying Mercy had been an instinctive stroke of genius. Together they were slowly trying to change the stuffy ethos of an English public school into something less rigid and hidebound by tradition. Mercy, a Canadian psychologist, shared Ed's vision for St Michael's.

The school, even in Ben's day, had always been unapologetically academic. Under Ed's headship there was no longer any privilege, patronage, or parental donations. Two scholarships a year were awarded. The school welcomed both difficult and gifted children from diverse or tricky backgrounds, but they all had to go through an entrance exam and interview. Places were won on merit and they were like gold dust.

Ed smiled at Finn. 'Someone's had a holiday like a seal, by the colour of you . . .'

Mercy said, 'Delphi, lovely to see you, we loved your last exhibition . . . have you time for a cup of tea . . .'

'Love to,' Delphi said briskly. Finn looked at her suspiciously. Delphi never stopped for tea with Mr and Mrs Dominic.

Ed Dominic said, 'Let's get your case inside, Finn . . . Good heavens, what have you got in here . . .'

Between them they pulled the heavy case with its squeaking wheels down the corridor and into the four-bedroom dormitory Finn shared with three other boys.

'You've got the same bed and the same roommates as last term except for one new boy,' Mr Dominic said, indicating the bed by the window opposite Finn. 'His name is Raza Ali. He's from Pakistan. I'd be grateful if you would keep an eye on him, make sure he settles in with us? I gather he had a tough time at his London school . . .'

Finn sat on his bed. The last thing he wanted to do was look after anyone else. Ed Dominic, watching the normally affable Finn, wished he did not have to constantly see the bloody fall-out of parental selfishness. Delphi had not said much on the phone, but enough to alert him. The boy's father leaving for Afghanistan was enough without his mother taking off as well.

'Raza couldn't speak a word of English when he was

brought to the UK two years ago by members of his British Pakistani family. Despite that, he managed to pass the entrance exam here. No mean feat. According to his family he's not thriving in England. He's homesick. He does not want to be here. I'd like to change that. I'd like you to help make sure that he feels welcome at this school, Finn.'

'Why me, sir?' Usually, Mr Dominic picked up on boys' moods. Mr Dominic held Finn's eyes. 'Raza Ali grew up in north Pakistan, not so far from where your father is now on the Afghan side of the border. Both of you have your hearts and minds turned in the same direction at this moment, to the fathers you love. Is that enough for me to choose *you* to try to be a friend to him?'

Finn looked at him. 'Yes, sir.'

'Good.' Mr Dominic put his hand on Finn's shoulder. 'I know life can be tough, Finn. Come and chat to Mercy or me anytime. Okay?'

Finn nodded. 'I'll see you next door in five minutes. Mrs Dominic has made a cake and you can say goodbye to your grandmother . . .'

CHAPTER TWENTY-TWO

Cornwall, 2009

Driving Raza to a boarding school was hard for Sarah. Despite Raza winning a scholarship it felt like a personal failure, a form of defeat. She and Chinir had been unable to make Raza feel happy or secure.

On the drive Chinir had opted for relentless cheer, exclaiming at the beauty of the school buildings and grounds. When the car stopped outside the front door, the startling Mercy Dominic came out to welcome them. Sarah had liked her at Raza's interview. She exuded an air of warmth and humour. Mercy showed them to the dormitory where Raza would be sleeping.

'I suggest you don't prolong your goodbyes,' Mercy said to Sarah quietly. 'I promise you we'll keep a close eye. Come through the green door on the right of the stairs and find me when you are ready.'

The boys slept in small dormitories of four, in separate 'houses' named after saints or Cornishmen. Each house was run by a different housemaster and helped by young trainee teachers or post-graduate students, called housemothers. It was an unknown world to Sarah and Chinir.

'I think life will be easier for you, here, Raza . . .' Sarah said, not knowing if this was true. She was trying to hide her anxiety as they stood round Raza's bed, trying to cram more and more things into his locker. 'This school is much smaller than your London school. I am sure you will be happier . . .'

'We'll phone you regularly to see how you're getting on,' Chinir said, suddenly having cold feet about what they were doing. 'This school will be very different, and you will be with other scholarship boys. You won't be bullied here for wanting to work hard. I think you will find schoolwork *mandatory* . . .'

Raza smiled. Having heard the word and taken a liking to the positive sound of the syllables, he had used it indiscriminately.

'Thank you, I will work exceedingly hard . . .'

'We'd also like you to be happy, make friends, have fun . . .' Chinir said gently.

Raza stared back at Chinir solemnly. 'Thank you,' he said, again, politely.

'If you can't settle, if you're unhappy, you must let us know . . .'

Raza put his palms together. 'Please do not worry, Sarah. I have passed the exam. I have liked the teachers. You both have given me this chance to come here. Thank you. I will be okay.' It was obvious he wanted them to leave.

As Raza walked out to the car with Sarah and Chinir he saw a boy saying goodbye to a silver-haired woman in brightly coloured clothes getting into a yellow Volkswagen Beetle car.

As her car turned in the drive outside the house and drove away the boy looked miserable. He raised his hand

and then took off abruptly, running down some steps to the playing fields.

Chinir turned his car around too and he and Sarah waved and waved until they disappeared out of sight round the bend. Panic rose in Raza. He stood rooted, looking down the drive after them. Mercy Dominic appeared by his side. 'Raza, would you like to come and have some tea and cake with me? Or would you rather have a bit of time to sort your things out and come along later?'

Raza thanked her but said he would like to put his things away.

'A good idea. Make the most of the peace. Finn, the boy in the bed opposite you, is here. You'll meet him soon, but the other two boys won't be back in school until tomorrow.'

CHAPTER TWENTY-THREE

Raza sat cross-legged on the bed in the small dormitory gazing out of the window at the clouds. His fingers lay on his knees as if he was meditating, which he was in a way. He had learnt that if he sat still in reflective position people tended to leave him alone.

He had begun to cloud-watch in London. In the midst of buildings and rooftops, the sky, with its endless movement and sweep of clouds seemed the biggest space there was to expand and float away.

In Pakistan, he had watched violet storm clouds roll down the valley in an instant to close it from the outside world. He had watched sunrise tinge the clouds golden like the edge of a sari. In England, clouds were his private escape. A place he could breathe and still be Raza Ali.

The empty room felt peaceful. He thought of Liyana and Daniyal back in Derby. They had spent most of the summer in Cornwall helping Chinir and Sarah settle in the rented house Chinir had found. Preparing him for this school.

Raza suspected that Sarah and Chinir had only decided to transfer from London to Cornish hospitals so that he could go to this school. They had both denied this; they had solemnly sworn that they had been thinking about moving out of London for years because of the cost of living.

There had been endless days buying a school uniform and ticking off the list of things he would need. How the Alis loved to shop. It was a Pakistani pastime. Raza found it exhausting. Liyana and Sarah were constantly hopping around for a bargain and constantly at odds over what constituted one. Daniyal raised his eyes heavenward and patiently carried the bags.

Before they went back to Derby and their jobs, Liyana and Daniyal had given Raza a red leather-bound Koran in a black satin cover. Raza stroked the silky material. It was his treasure.

He had alternated between relief at leaving London and a school he hated, and the dread of another unknown. He was afraid of failing in his studies in this new place. He was afraid of letting Baba and his family down.

He gazed out of the window and marvelled at the beauty of a huge tree on the lawn. Its trunk was turning a silvery colour as the day faded.

The boy he had seen earlier came back into the room. Raza closed his eyes and stayed still. The boy did not speak.

Outside, there were the sounds of boys returning to other dormitories. They called out to one another. There was the sound of laughter; late arrivals banged their cases down in the hall. The boy in the next bed rummaged around in his locker then sat on his bed. When Raza turned his head a fraction to glance over at him, he saw that he was absorbed in writing in a book. Raza returned to his clouds.

Later that evening, having checked all returning boys were safely inside Trelawney House, Ed Dominic walked back down the corridor towards his own green door. Most of the boys were making toast, tea, or hot chocolate in the kitchen. Finn and Raza Ali had been sitting on their beds studiously appearing to ignore each other.

His instinct to put both boys together could radically backfire. He had taken a risk. The invidious Afghan–Pakistani border was a thin, invisible line. Raza Ali, with his startling green eyes, came from a village near Peshawar in the Tribal Areas. Who knew where his sympathies and family allegiance lay? Finn had the shaken look of a boy whose life had suddenly come apart.

All Ed Dominic knew for sure was that he had two unhappy youths on his hands, both separated from their fathers by roughly the same war.

CHAPTER TWENTY-FOUR

Finn had hated Delphi leaving. He had not felt this way for years, not since he was little. He knew why, but he was still angry with himself. He stomped off to the pitches where he could glimpse the sea, then around the little wood and back. He dreaded having to exchange holiday boasts with his friends, pretend everything was okay, when it wasn't.

Taking a deep breath, Finn peered into the games room where there were a few early boarders playing table tennis. He played a couple of matches and they all had a half-hearted moan at being back at school, competing loudly for who had the most lush and expensive summer holiday.

Finn had a sudden memory of Ben throwing Izzy up in the air as they stood in the shallows of an aquamarine sea. He threw his table tennis bat down on the table. 'Got to go . . . Just remembered I'm supposed to be looking after a new boy . . .'

He ran out into the late afternoon, jumping down the steep stone steps and across the lawn to Trelawney House. Breathless, he leaned against the trunk of the old fir and fought an overpowering sense of loss.

As he walked across the lawn to the front door of the house

119

a small, disembodied face seemed to hover in the window of the dormitory. As he got nearer, he saw the Pakistani boy sitting cross-legged on his bed facing the window.

When he entered the room, Finn decided not to disturb the still figure. Delphi meditated each morning, and no one ever interrupted her. He got out his diary and began to write.

Somehow, the words would not come. He knew he was self-consciously watching himself, trying to pull emotion from a place that was dry. He put the diary down and glanced over at the boy. He could sit spookily still.

Finn looked out of the window. The sun was caught behind cloud but shafts of light like swords blazed earthward like a biblical scene.

If he felt small and alone in the face of that sky, what must the Pakistani boy be feeling? Without turning from the sky, Finn said, 'I'm Finn.'

After a moment Raza said, 'My name, it is Raza Ali.'

He turned to look at Finn, and Finn, taking his eyes from the sky, saw that Raza Ali had extraordinary, pale green eyes.

The two boys stared at each other slowly, taking the other in. When they glanced back at the sky it was already fading into sunset. Raza uncrossed his legs and got off the bed and stretched them. Finn saw that he was small for his age.

'Are you hungry?' he asked. 'I'm going to the kitchen to make toast.'

'I am hungry, yes,' Raza said. 'But first, I must wash and pray.'

'Do you want the prayer room, or will you pray here? Isa Okafor prays here . . .' Finn pointed up at the eye on the ceiling.

'I will pray here. Thank you,' Raza said, bending and pulling his prayer mat from his bedside locker.

'I'll be in the kitchen, across the corridor. I'll put some toast on for you, okay?'

'Okay. Thank you,' Raza said, hurrying to the bathrooms to wash. He was very hungry. Of all western food, toast from a machine with butter was the most delectable.

Finn and Raza sat on bar stools in the tiny kitchen munching toast. Neither boy felt like talking. Apart from Finn's, 'Marmite?' To which Raza had shuddered, making Finn grin and point to Nutella or marmalade, there was silence. The silence felt fine. The two boys munched and eyed each other surreptitiously. Raza could hear the voices of other boys calling to each other outside the kitchen in the corridors. He could hear Mrs Dominic reassuring a parent. Suddenly, Raza felt a rush of overwhelming displacement and fear. He gripped his mug. What was he doing here in this place? It would be worse than the London school. He could not even go home at the end of the day. Finn looked up, startled by the sudden misery and fear in Raza's luminous eyes. He cast about for something to say.

'The first night in school is always bad,' he said gruffly. 'But it gets better once you get into a routine and make friends and stuff . . .'

Raza's unnerving eyes were fixed on him. Finn could see the shadow of himself within them. 'I still hate the first night back, too. Don't worry, everyone feels the same, they just don't let on . . .'

Raza nodded but could not speak, his eyes mirroring gratitude. 'Tomorrow, I'll show you around. We'll find out what classes you are in and everything . . .'

'Indeed. Thank you,' Raza finally managed in a small voice.

Finn smiled. 'Another piece of toast?'

Raza smiled back. 'Yes, please.'

121

CHAPTER TWENTY-FIVE

Before lights out Finn got out the one bluey he had received from Ben and read it for the umpteenth time. Ben's large distinctive writing comforted him.

Hi Finn,

I have, at last, arrived in Camp Bastion. The plane, predictably, broke down in Dubai, so spent a few uncomfortable hours there with restless soldiers. I will spend a couple of nights here in Bastion. Then RSO1-Reception Staging and Onward integration update training on arrival in Lashkar Gah where I take over and begin my job. I'm thinking of you. I'll write and email when I can, but don't worry when you don't hear, it just means I'm very busy. You are back at school next week. Have a good term. Keep cheerful and don't worry.

Love you lots,
Ben

Finn grinned. Ben always used army acronyms that no one understood. He picked up his phone and sent a text:

Hi Ben,
It is the first night back at school. I hope you are okay.
Write when you can and stay safe. It is nearly lights out
so can't write much. Love you lots, Finn xx

Finn switched off his phone and put it into his locker for
the night. Raza was lying still with his light off.

It seemed odd to be sleeping with two empty beds. Mr
Dominic had said there was trouble with the Paddington
to Penzance train, so Peter Chan was stuck with his
mother in London and Isa Okafor was stuck somewhere
in Nigeria, unable to reach the airport because of some
coup. 'Our dormitory is a bit like the United Nations,
sir.'

'Very good, Finn.' Mr Dominic had grinned. 'Let's hope
you can all keep the peace in here . . .'

As Finn switched his light out Mercy Dominic put her
head round the door. 'Goodnight, boys. Sleep well.'

Her footsteps retreated down the corridor. Silence slowly
descended from the other rooms. Light filtered in from the
hall through the glass on the top of the door. Finn had
always found it comforting.

Later, Mercy or Mr Dominic would do a last check of
the rooms before they went to bed. Finn felt for his iPod
under the pillow. He might need his music for sleep to come
and blank out the places his mind might wander to. He
imagined Ben travelling across a barren Afghan landscape
to Lashkar Gah. Would he go by land or by helicopter?
Why didn't he know this?

Finn turned on his side and hunched up the duvet. He
thought of Izzy always losing rabbit in the night . . . or
waking suddenly not knowing where she was. Missing him.
Missing Ben.

He glanced over at Raza Ali. 'Good night,' he whispered. That boy had an unnerving ability to seem invisible.

'Goodnight, Finn,' Raza replied.

The house creaked. There was the odd footstep on the stairs but otherwise the house slipped into a heavy silence. A silence that was full of people. Raza turned on his back. A half-moon filtered through the crack in the curtains. He would have liked to leave the curtains open, but he did not know if the other boy, Finn, would mind. He was glad he was not alone in this room. He had never enjoyed sleeping alone. Never got used to it. In the London house when the terror of being alone in the dark got too much, he would throw the thick curtains open to let the streetlight in and sit watching the angle of houses and rooftops against the sky. Glimpses of people moving past lighted windows of neighbouring houses made Raza feel he was not the only person alive and sleepless.

When he arrived in England the longing for Baba, for home, for Pakistan had been unbearable. As he closed his eyes at night Raza would imagine himself back in that small stone house. He would conjure the prickly feel of his blanket, the smell of wood smoke, curry and goats or the warmth emanating from Baba's familiar body.

With his father beside him Raza knew nothing bad could happen. Without him, there were so many possibilities for getting things wrong. Sarah and Chinir were kind and patient with him, but Raza was conscious of their surprise at all he did not know about British life.

He learned quickly, but it had been hard sometimes to accept things he could not grasp the point of or found distinctly unhygienic. The lavatory, for instance. There were no hoses to wash your private parts. You had to use paper and flush everything away and your hands would then be unclean. Raza had been appalled. Chinir and Daniyal had found his horror amusing but they had been inflexible about his habits in the bathroom.

Raza had no problem with showering. He loved all Sarah's little bottles lying on the shelf. He tried each in turn. Chinir eventually had to tell him he took too long in the shower and left an alarm clock in the bathroom. He would set it when Raza got in the shower and when it rang ten minutes later, he was supposed to get out and turn off the water.

After a while, Raza could time himself to the minute and the clock disappeared, with, he noticed, many of Sarah's little bottles which had smelled like flowers. 'Expensive flowers, dear Raza. Look, I have bought you your very own shampoo and shower gels. See,' Sarah said.

After two years, as he approached puberty, Chinir and Sarah had installed a shower room for him in what had once been a small dressing room off the landing. Chinir had made a joke about it, rolled his eyes, and explained that women were quite fussy and did not like pools of water and wet towels in their bathroom.

By this time Raza had begun to recognize irony. *He was not tidy enough to use Sarah's bathroom.* He thought how much had changed for him in two years. He had gone from outside tap, hose, and plastic bowl. From a pit with bucket that had to be emptied, to his own shower room. How shocked Baba would be if he saw how much comfort Raza lived in now. He was a bit shocked himself at how quickly he had become used to these things.

When they returned to England with Raza, Chinir, an orthopaedic surgeon, had to go straight back to work. Sarah, an anaesthetist, was not due back at her job until after Christmas, but her hospital was short-staffed, and she was frequently called out in an emergency.

For the first two months Raza had spent most of his time with Liyana, a specialist teacher. She had patiently sat and taught him English each morning. She had taken him out into a London full of Christmas shoppers and made him practise what they had learnt as they moved through the crowds.

Raza had been petrified and Liyana had held his hand tight. It was tough love, as she tried to familiarize him with the parts of London he would need to travel when he started school. She had negotiated a leave of absence from her school in Derby to help him settle and acclimatize.

Raza had been bewildered by all he must learn. He had shrunk away from the noise of the traffic and the thundering speed of the tube trains rushing underground through dark tunnels towards him. He had closed his eyes against the thousands of people pushing and shoving as they rushed to work. He had fought the damp cold as well as the over-heated stores. He had felt so miserable he thought he would die of heartache.

He had obeyed Zamir and worn European clothes while he was out, but as soon as he was back inside the house he changed into his own clothes. He was convinced that at any moment he would disappear and become someone else. He would be Raza Ali no longer and he would never be able to return home to his village.

Zamir could not have had many books to teach Raza English, so Liyana had been surprised at how many English words Raza had picked up and understood. He was a fast learner. Within weeks he was writing and grasping the meaning of simple sentences. Within a month, by listening to the family speaking only English at meals, Raza could answer them hesitantly.

Raza's reverence for books, all books, made Liyana realize that, unschooled as he was, he had a ferocious curiosity and observance to detail. She suspected that Zamir, who had never had the chance to exercise his own intellect, had recognized this.

Raza also proved extremely competitive and he loved the quizzes Liyana set. She got Raza and Chinir to challenge each other with English and Pashto words. Raza hated to lose, but so did Chinir.

With patience and encouragement, Liyana worked exhaustively to prepare Raza for the life he would have to lead in England.

Raza thought about Liyana as he lay in a strange bed in the dark dormitory. Without Liyana, he would not have got a scholarship. He would not be here now. He listened to the silence outside. No traffic, no horns, just the sound of the wind in the big tree outside the window. If he closed his eyes tight, he could almost pretend he was home in his beautiful Swat Valley. Raza turned on his side, shakily unsure he really wanted to be here in this school. And yet . . . He thought of the boy, Finn, in the other bed. The boy who had made him toast, who was going to show him around. A tiny flicker of warmth curled around Raza's heart. He had never before had a friend.

CHAPTER TWENTY-SIX

Raza woke to a startling sound coming from Finn's bed. He sat up, the hairs prickling on the back of his neck. The sound was a rising wail of loss. Raza recognized it. He padded over to Finn's bed. The boy slept, thrashing around, his cries muffled, rising and falling like a refrain. He was having a bad night dream. Raza reached out and shook Finn cautiously. Finn jumped and sat upright, and Raza leapt back.

It took Finn a moment to fully wake up. Then his eyes cleared, and the two boys stared at each other.

'You were having bad night dream,' Raza said.

'Ahh . . . Yes.' Finn shook his head to banish it. He could still remember the horror of the dream. Raza went to his locker and found a bottle of water. He unscrewed the top and handed the bottle to Finn. Finn drank thirstily.

'Sorry I woke you up.' Finn handed the water back.

'It is all right,' Raza said. 'I too have bad night dreams sometimes.'

He put the bottle of water back in his locker and got back into bed. His feet were cold. Finn whispered unsteadily, 'I dreamt my father was dead.'

Raza stared at Finn across the room. 'That is a very bad night dream . . . but it is not real. You are awake. It is gone.'

Finn slid down the bed. 'I hope it doesn't come back.'

Raza was silent. Then he said, 'Before I leave Pakistan, I never have bad night dreams. When first I came to England, I have many bad dreams I have to wake myself up.'

'Yeah, like . . . Just now . . . I knew I was dreaming but I couldn't wake myself up.'

An owl hooted somewhere out in the night and Raza shivered at the sound. 'It's just an owl,' Finn said. 'They are beautiful night birds of prey. You don't often hear them because they are becoming extinct.'

'Extinct?'

'They are dying out because we are destroying their habitat – the places they live and the small mice and stuff they eat.'

'At home we too have birds of prey. They can swoop to take a newborn lamb or goat. They fly away in a quick moment, before I can even feel the shadow of them on my face.'

Finn turned on his side. 'Tell me about where you live.'

'You mean where I live in Pakistan, not England?'

'Yes. Where you live in Pakistan.'

'I live in small village in Swat Valley in north Pakistan. It is situated on edge of mountains about three hours from Peshawar. I live there with my father and with our goats and sheep. We grow vegetables and have apricot trees and fruits. It is quite small piece of land and when the rains do not come the land gets dry and all our vegetables die. All day I would be on the mountain caring for my sheep or goats. Until the sun goes behind the mountain and my father comes to help me take our animals to lower ground . . .'

Raza's voice was growing thick and soft and sad and then it petered out. 'I didn't mean to make you homesick,' Finn said. 'It sounds a beautiful place, the place where you live. Very different.'

'Yes, it is most beautiful, and it is most different. I will sleep now.'

'Good night, Raza.'

'Good night.' It was the first time anyone had asked Raza about his Pakistani home.

'I miss Ba— I miss my father,' he whispered.

Finn sat up. 'Your father is in Pakistan. My dad is in Afghanistan. They are nearer to each other than to us at the moment. Isn't that sort of weird, when we are here in the same room?'

Raza thought about it. 'It is a strange thing, indeed. Is your father a soldier?'

'Yes.'

'*Inshallah*, both our fathers will stay strong and well . . .'

'*Inshallah?*'

'It means, if God wills it. God willing.'

'Okay,' Finn said. 'Goodnight, Raza.'

'Goodnight, Finn. *Inshallah*, we now sleep peacefully without bad night dreams . . .' Raza said, smiling.

Finn grinned into the dark. '*Inshallah*, to that.'

CHAPTER TWENTY-SEVEN

Hi Ben,

Thanks for your email. I'm glad you're okay and settling in and stuff. I am in the same dorm with Isa Okafor and Peter Chan, again, but neither of them are back in school yet. Mr Dominic asked me to look after a new Pakistani boy. He is in the bed opposite me. He is a bit strange. I've never seen anyone who can sit for so long without moving a muscle and he has these really green eyes even though he is a Pakistani. He's cool, though.

Dad, I have to go, it's prep. Write and tell me what you are doing and don't get hurt. I will write you a bluey soon.

Lots of love,
Finn

Finn's Diary

The first two weeks are nearly over. I hate the beginning of term because we are not allowed to go home for the first weekend. It is supposed to help everyone settle back into school, but I think this rule should just be kept for new boys who get homesick.

Peter Chan turned up two days late, as usual, with the latest gadgets from Singapore. That city is IT heaven! He has the latest iPhone 3 or 4 or something. I tried to pretend I wasn't interested, but everyone is jealous. I suppose if Isa does not make it back from Nigeria, we will have someone new to fill his bed. I hope he is okay. A coup in Nigeria is a bit difficult to imagine in Cornwall.

Not sure what Raza Ali makes of the school. He hardly says anything in class, but he certainly takes things in. I think it must be true that he had a hard time at his London school because he seems really wary of other boys, even when they are trying to be friendly. It is as if he is sizing people up to see who might cause him trouble. The only boy he should not trust is Chatto.

We are in most of the same classes, English, maths, and sciences but Raza is also having a lot of extra tutoring in English grammar, history, and geography. He is brilliant at maths.

Boys from all religions have to attend School Assembly each morning, but they are allowed to come in after Christian prayers are finished. Every day someone has to read a poem or prayer or inspiring quote of their choice to end assembly.

I think Raza is a stricter Muslim than Isa. Isa often forgets to pray, or he slopes off to the prayer room when he wants to get out of something. Peter Chang is a Christian. Consumerism is his god.

I ought to warn Raza about David Chatto. He's not in Trelawney House, but he will definitely have a go at Raza. Chatto is one of those bullies who takes *his time to strike, like a snake. He's clever, but nasty. He waits until he spots someone's weak point and then goes in for the kill. His father is a politician, and his mother is a fashion designer or something, so he seems to think he is more important than everyone else. They live mostly in London, but they have a big second home here, too. Delphi thinks I should feel sorry for him as his parents rarely turn up for any school events. I don't feel sorry for him at all.*

After prep this evening Raza went off to pray. The prayer room is next to the school chapel and I hung around waiting for him. Not sure why, maybe instinct or something. I opened the chapel door a crack. Someone was practising on the organ. I looked inside. I thought about Ben. I didn't go inside or actually pray, I just thought about him, for God to keep him safe.

When I turned around, there was Chatto, making me jump. 'Surprised you aren't in the mosque praying with your new little Muslim mate.'

He was sneering as usual. I ignored him and he slapped his hand to his forehead. 'Of course! I forgot. Granny is a Buddhist.'

I held the chapel door open. 'You must be down here to pray, Chatto. Don't let me stop you.'

He looked a bit caught out, so I knew he had deliberately come down the corridor to hassle Raza. Raza came out of the prayer room at that moment and I moved towards him and we both walked back down the corridor without saying anything. Raza turned to look back at Chatto, then at my face, but he did not say anything. Delphi says bullies are unhappy and miserable people who don't like themselves. All I can say is they like making other people miserable.

I'm in bed now. Peter Chang is showing Raza the wonders of his new iPhone. Peter Chang is as different to Chatto as it's possible to be. He doesn't care where people come from. He either likes them or he doesn't. He's from Singapore and loads of different cultures live together. Chatto on the other hand is a prat.

Lights out now. Raza goes to his own bed and pulls the curtain back a bit so he can see the sky. He always does that. His pyjamas are too big, and he looks small and skinny. I suddenly feel a bit like I feel about Izzy sometimes. Like, I need to look out for him, and I really don't want to have to worry about anyone else. I have to warn Raza about Chatto, but I don't want to scare him. Chatto will pick up on that faster than a cobra strikes.

CHAPTER TWENTY-EIGHT

Swat Valley, 2009

After Raza left for England, Zamir would compose letters to him in his head. Once a month, when he travelled down to the market in Peshawar, he would close his eyes and dictate these thoughts to Ameena, Maldi's daughter-in-law, married to Asif, his nephew. Ameena would copy it into an email and send it on to Raza.

Occasionally, Zamir got fed up with Ameena's helpful suggestions in what were supposed to be private letters to his son, and he would buy a thin blue airmail letter and fill it with neat Pashto and post it with a prayer, hoping Raza would find comfort in the familiar language of home. The letters took a long time to arrive in England and sometimes got lost in the post.

Raza treasured these letters. He would read the words slowly and feel the heat, the smell, the colour, and warmth of Pakistan flow over him like a cloak. When Raza had been in his new Cornish school three weeks, Miah, the shadowy woman who had looked after Zamir and Raza, since his birth, died. Faded back into the dry earth in her sleep. Zamir and Samia had never known her true age or her real name.

They had taken her when she turned up brutally beaten one day, staggering on all fours up the mountain to his house. Zamir suspected she had been beaten or raped and then turned out by her family for dishonouring them. But she could also have been a runaway from an abusive husband or her in-laws.

Samia, heavily pregnant with Raza, had nursed her back to health, but Miah's mind had flown to another place. She could never tell them what had happened or where she came from. She never spoke and remained mute.

It became obvious within weeks that she was pregnant. Zamir had been worried when Samia told him. Tribal honour was unflinching. He waited each day for a vengeful father or husband to demand his property back. He dreaded she might belong to a local Talib. But no one ever came for the girl and if anyone in the village knew about her, they did not say.

Miah still had the thin body of an adolescent and her small, malnourished body had little strength to expel her baby when her time came. After a long torturous labour, the tiny child died within minutes of her birth. Miah showed no emotion except shame, dragging herself outside the house so that she did not dirty it. Samia, perhaps with some premonition of her own death, had wept for the damaged little child-woman. She brought Miah back into the house and nursed her. Her body was covered in welts and old scars. She flinched if anyone moved too quickly towards her. Samia and Zamir never knew why she had sought them out for shelter or how she knew she would be safe with them.

Two weeks later Samia started labour. Raza was breech. The women in the village summoned the doctor from Peshawar, who had a roving clinic, but he arrived too late.

Raza was saved by a rapid Caesarean, but Samia bled to death.

Raza would have died too had it not been for Miah. With her breasts full of milk, she clamped the baby to her as she wept for Samia.

Zamir knew then that, Allah, blessed be to him in his mercy, had sent Miah to them, but it was ten days before he could bear to look at Raza.

As the years went by Miah was merely a faint presence in their lives. Neither Zamir nor Raza were ever unkind to her. They greeted her each morning and said goodnight each evening as she left for her tiny shack next door. Zamir respected the girl's need to be invisible, but he had no real idea of her character or emotions, and he gave them little thought.

Miah looked after them devotedly and expected nothing in return except food and somewhere to sleep. She never wanted to accompany them down on the trucks or bus to Peshawar. When her chores were done, she would sit for hours, quite still, facing the mountain. When times were hard for Zamir, Miah went without food to feed Raza.

When her clothes became colourless and worn Zamir would choose a new *shalwar kameez* for her in the markets or roadside stalls. Miah would bow her thanks and stroke the material with pride but her old *shalwar kameez* would have to fall to pieces before she would wear the new one.

When Zamir wrote to tell Raza that Miah was dead Raza felt a rush of unsuspected emotion. Miah had always been there, like his goats or sheep were always there. He had never considered that he, Raza, had been the centre of her life, perhaps her only reason for living. But now, he felt a visceral shock at the loss of her, her shadowy figure gaining a haunting power in death that she had never had in her neglected and stunted life.

137

CHAPTER TWENTY-NINE

Cornwall, 2009

Raza and Finn were walking back to Trelawney House through the school grounds after prep. Raza was especially quiet and preoccupied.

'Are you okay?' Finn asked.

'Yes,' Raza replied. 'Thank you.' And was silent again. Finn wondered if he was homesick. 'You're allowed home this weekend. I bet you can't wait.'

'I can wait,' Raza said. 'I have to go to this wedding. Pakistani weddings, they go on for days and I do not even know the people getting married. They are people Sarah works with in the hospital. It is bad luck that they marry on my first weekend out of school. Most inconsiderate.' He grinned at Finn.

'Is that why you're fed up?'

'No, I am not fed up. It is something else. My uncle in Pakistan send me email with message from my father. It make me sad. Someone . . . who look after me since the day I am born. She die. Someone I never say goodbye to.'

'Oh,' Finn said. 'Sorry . . .' He did not know what else

to say. 'Really sorry,' he repeated. They walked a little way in silence then Finn asked, 'Do you have to go home this weekend?

'No. Sarah and Chinir, they are feeling guilty about this wedding on my first weekend home. But I do not want to stay in school, you will not be here. You are going home . . .'

'You could come home with me and go to your family next weekend . . . if you wanted.'

Raza turned to Finn. 'Your family, they would have me?'

'Yeah, of course. I go to Delphi, my grandmother's. She's cool about me bringing friends back. So is Ian, my grandpa.'

Raza looked confused. 'Why do you call your grandparents by their names?' He was a little shocked by this disrespect to the old.

Finn laughed. 'Ben, my dad, always called my grandparents by their Christian names when he was a child and I guess I caught it. My grandpa isn't actually my dad's real dad, so maybe . . . calling them both by their names had something to do with that. Dunno really . . .' Finn said watching Raza's puzzled face.

The English are indeed strange, Raza thought. *And complicated.*

'Yes!' he said, cheering up as he suddenly saw an escape from the wedding. 'I would like to come to your home. Indeed, that would be very good. But I will have to ask Chinir and Sarah first.'

'Sure,' Finn said. 'I'll ring Delphi. If you like she could ring and talk to them.'

Mr Dominic passed them in the gloom going the other way, towards the school buildings. 'If you two don't stop gossiping like a couple of old women and get a move on you're going to be too late to make toast . . .' he called. Both boys started to sprint, and Ed Dominic grinned to himself.

*

139

Sarah hid her surprise when Raza rang her to ask if he could go to stay with Finn that weekend. He had never in all his time in England asked to go anywhere. She felt a surge of joy. It looked like Raza might have made a friend.

When Delphi rang her, Sarah was more than reassured. She gave a little whoop as she put the phone down.

Chinir eyed her wryly, thinking of the terrible year just behind them. 'It's early days,' he said, 'but let's pray this is a breakthrough . . .' He sighed. 'Honestly, Sarah, couldn't you have got us out of this wedding? I wanted to hear how Raza is getting on . . .'

'They are my colleagues. They are trying to make us feel welcome in Cornwall,' Sarah said. 'I could not refuse without hurting them. Oh, Chinir, I feel hope. It would be so wonderful if Raza could be happy and make friends at last . . .'

Hi Ben,

*We were making toast when I heard the news
that two soldiers died today on patrol in Helmand.
I know you will be in lock-down now and will not
be able to even phone or email for twenty-four
hours. I hope you are safe. I am trying not to
worry. Mrs Dominic says that if you had been hurt,
we would have heard before the news went out, but
it seems ages since I heard from you. Please be
careful and don't worry about any of us. We are all
okay.*

*I probably won't be able to fill all this bluey
because of lights out and also not much happens in
school. I lead a very boring life . . .*

*I will stop worrying now! Mrs Dominic just
came in to tell me that Delphi rang to say you got
through to her before the news blackouts and you
are safe. She even says I can finish this bluey to
you . . . Just quickly I'll tell you about this
weekend. Raza, the Pakistani boy in my dorm, is
coming home with me tomorrow. Delphi is picking
us up. We'll go straight to the beach house if the
weather is okay. Got to go Ben. PLEASE keep safe.*

Love you, tons, Finn xxxxx

CHAPTER THIRTY

Delphi picked the boys up on Friday afternoon in her yellow VW. It was a beautiful late September afternoon, the leaves turning, the light mellow and golden on land and sea.

Finn and Raza were waiting by the door of Trelawney House, Raza nervously clutching his small bag. Delphi climbed out of the car and called, '*Assalamu alaikum*, Raza,' and enveloped both boys.

'*Wa alaykumu as-salam* . . . Mem,' Raza replied, startled, as Delphi ushered them into the car. Finn grinned at Raza's face as they squeezed into the VW.

Raza, overawed, insisted on sitting in the back. As they shot off down the drive, he wished he had asked Finn what respectful name he should call this grandmother. After their confusing conversation he was anxious to be correct.

'Straight to the beach house?' Finn asked Delphi, hoping to avoid a food shopping trip.

'Straight to the beach house. Ian's already there. This weather is too glorious to miss . . . but I don't think it will last.'

Delphi eyed Raza in the mirror. He was looking out of the window, his body held stiffly. She thought, *I mustn't overwhelm him. Ask him too many questions.* She talked over her shoulder to include him. Explaining about their shabby beach house where they spent their summers and where Finn and Ben surfed all year round.

Raza had only been in Cornwall two months. Most of that time had been taken up settling into the new house. Listening to Liyana and Sarah argue companionably about where the furniture should go or discovering the nearest shops. Daniyal and Chinir, on the excuse of networking, had made for the nearest golf club, so Chinir could put his name down.

Chinir and Sarah were city people not actively drawn to the sea. So far, they had walked beside a creek near Truro, and glimpsed, from the safety of the car, the wild sea hitting the sea wall in great spouting waves as they passed through Penzance. Liyana had shuddered when she looked at the sheer power of the water flying up in the air and splattering over the car and onto the road.

Raza had felt exhilarated. However, the concept of surfing on top of those waves remained incomprehensible to him. He looked out of the car window with interest as Delphi turned onto the coast road and wove through a small village that seemed deserted, past a church, and then bumped down a sandy road towards the sea and the beach chalets. Finally, they turned onto a smaller track, past a café full of surfers until they reached the last beach house sitting on its own, squarely facing the sea. Raza felt dizzy with so much sea and sky.

Ian was outside setting up his barbecue. He came over to the car and greeted the boys. 'Good to have you, Raza. Only ankle-snappers today, I'm afraid,' he said to Finn. 'But I got your wetsuit out in case you wanted to go in anyway.'

Raza saw two horrible black rubber things lying over the balcony rail like empty bodies. They were like the outfits

143

rich young Pakistani girls wore to cover their modesty when they swam in the lakes at home or in hotel swimming pools.

'Ankle-snappers just means small waves,' Delphi explained to Raza.

Raza was horrified at any expectation that he might have to get into one of those rubber things and go into the water. A Pakistani wedding suddenly seemed preferable. He turned to look at the sea. It was not a wild sea but the waves breaking seemed big enough to him.

Delphi, who was watching him, said, 'You probably don't swim, Raza?'

He shook his head. 'Indeed, I do not swim, Mem.'

'Come on, let's take your things inside. I'll show you where you and Finn are sleeping. I'm afraid the house is old and creaky. There are only bunk beds, but I hope you'll be comfortable.'

'Thank you,' Raza said. 'I will be most comfortable.'

The room was small, and the wood painted white to keep it light. The window did not look out to the sea but towards high sand dunes. The bunk beds had bright duvets on. There were small paintings on the walls of things Raza could not quite make out. As Finn dropped his bag, he saw that Delphi had painted a small *Qibla* up on a beam so Raza would know which way was east.

Raza saw it too and, in the instant that he saw it, like a sign from Allah, he knew that all would be well with these strangers. Delphi smiled.

'I also put one on the corner of the veranda, Raza, in case you prefer to pray outside. It is particularly lovely when the sun sets, it's my favourite place to meditate . . . Finn, darling, if you're going into the water, do it now while Ian gets the barbecue going . . .'

'Will you be okay if I go in and surf for a bit?' Finn asked Raza.

Raza nodded. 'Indeed. I will unpack. I will wash, I will pray. Then I will come to watch you on your board . . .'

'The bathroom is just across the corridor, Raza,' Delphi said. 'We will be outside.'

Raza prayed inside the house. He liked the simplicity of it. Liked the bare floorboards and panelled walls. The house smelled of wood and varnish and of the outside. Sand particles clung to his bare feet as he crossed to the bathroom. Distant sounds drifted into the house. Laughter, voices, the whishing roar the sea made. He put on clean clothes, a kurta, and baggy trousers and laid out his prayer mat. This evening, the prayers came easily. He thought of Baba and felt near to him in this simple house. There was a peace here that penetrated the walls and filled the rooms.

The house creaked softly as if it was sighing. Raza realized he was smiling. He put his mat away and went outside through glass door that led onto a long veranda that surrounded the front of the house. Standing in one corner there was a small shrine with a Buddha. In front of the Buddha there was a small bowl of flowers with stones and shells all around him like an offering.

Raza looked up and saw Delphi in the distance sitting on the sand watching Finn in his black suit wading out into the waves. To the side of the house, Finn's grandfather was bent blowing at the barbecue and humming softly to himself.

Raza kicked his sandals off and walked down the wooden steps onto the sand. When he reached Delphi, he sat cross-legged beside her.

Delphi turned and smiled. They both sat silently watching Finn catch snappers as the sun sunk lower and lower into the sea until they could hardly see him. He had become part of the path of gold that stretched across the water.

Raza stood up as Finn started to wade in to shore. He

145

wanted to be inside that gold halo too. He hitched his baggy trousers up but when his toes hit the water, he recoiled in shock. 'It is indeed as cold as the lakes in Swat Valley in winter,' he yelped.

'No, it's not!' Finn said. 'Just stand still, let your feet grow used to the water and you'll find it's actually quite warm. It's September so the sea has had all summer to warm up.'

Raza doubted it, but pride made him stand still beside Finn. Ian wandered down the beach with a glass of wine for Delphi and sat down beside her. 'What incredible eyes that boy has.'

'He's a *Pashtun* from north Pakistan,' Delphi said. 'You find those amazing green eyes all over India . . . I'd love to paint the pair of them standing there in the last of the evening sun.'

Ian smiled. 'For a new friendship they seem remarkably easy together. Clever Ed. Come on, I'd better start to cook the sausages before the temperature drops.'

Delphi got to her feet and called 'Finn! Go and get in the shower, Ian's about to cook . . .'

Delphi took Ian's arm as they walked back across the sand. 'I was sitting watching Finn and thinking how Ben would love this evening. Ian, it's so sad. Izzy and Hanna could be here with us too, having fun before the summer ends . . . I could have cossetted them both before they returned to Germany.'

Finn and Raza ran past them over the sand. Ian said, 'Are you going to talk to Finn about Hanna this weekend? Or is it going to be tricky with Raza here.'

'I must try to get him to talk to her. Hanna is hoping to Skype him before he goes back to school.'

'Leave it until tomorrow. Go and meditate while the boys shower and come back your old jolly self.'

Delphi laughed. 'Quite right. Pour me another glass of wine and I'll be straight back.'

'Wow! Those sausages smell great.' Finn ran down the steps, hair wet from the shower, with Raza following tentatively behind him.

'Beef sausages and lamb cutlets. I hope you're hungry, Raza?' Ian said. 'I might have bought too much food.'

'I am always hungry, sir,' Raza said smiling. 'Indeed, my family they comment on this.'

Ian laughed. 'Good. I'm glad to hear it. There are drinks in the fridge. Help yourself, both of you. Then you can butter some rolls for me . . .'

They sat muffled up in sweaters at the small table on the veranda.

There were old rugs on all the chairs and bobble hats on hooks inside the kitchen door. The last of a pomegranate sun slipped silently into the sea turning the world ochre.

'It gets very cold as soon as the sun goes down at this time of year,' Delphi said to Raza, who was munching burgers and sausages with relish. Finn too had a full plate, but he was quiet, looking out to the waves that had faded to nothing but smooth glass. *He's missing Ben*, Delphi thought.

Raza, gazing seaward, was captivated. This light, this sudden change in the texture and movement of sea seemed to him nearly as mysterious as the violet shadows that flew swiftly across the mountains at home. Sea and mountains made Raza feel small and insignificant in a landscape that dwarfed yet excited him. He would tell Baba that there were, after all, beautiful, wild, and lonely places in England that must be blessed by Allah to stir his heart.

CHAPTER THIRTY-ONE

On Saturday morning the weather changed. The day was sullen and shut in by mist and grey clouds. Delphi and Ian left the boys sleeping, knowing it would be near lunchtime before they emerged. She heard Raza get up and wash before he prayed, then all had been silent again. A northeast wind flung itself round the house, blowing under the doors and through the cracks in the windows and chilling the house.

Ian lit the wood burner and Delphi delved into the cupboard under the bookshelf looking for Ben's atlas. She found it and took it to one end of the kitchen table with a cup of coffee and opened it up. *Pakistan. Afghanistan.* With her finger she found Helmand Province and within it in smaller letters *Lashkar Gah*. She left her finger there. Sat in the sleepy house that creaked around her and offered up her own prayers.

Finn and Raza sprung into the kitchen in pyjama bottoms and T-shirts, hungry for tea and toast. Delphi smiled. '*Assalamu alaikum!*'

'*Wa alaykumu as-salam!*' they both crowed in unison, folding their hands together and making her a little bow, very pleased with themselves.

Finn switched the kettle on and went over to the table. 'What are you looking at, Delphi?'

'Ben's atlas. I couldn't find it in Penzance. I wanted to see exactly where Lashkar Gah was, and I thought Raza might show us where he lives in Pakistan.'

Both boys came over and leaned over the heavy book. Delphi pointed.

'Look, this is where Ben is based, in Lashkar Gah in Helmand Province.'

Finn stared at the tiny name in italics written on the enormous map.

Lashkar Gah. He imagined dusty buildings and high walls with sandbags on the top. And holes in the walls where soldiers could fire through. He could see camp beds in makeshift rooms, but he found it hard to visualize army cooks in kitchens, or long tables where soldiers ate together doing normal things. In his head, Ben, all soldiers, were on perpetual patrol in a barren landscape.

'Camp Bastion must be somewhere there, in Helmand Province, mustn't it?' he asked. 'Dad goes there quite often. It's huge, like a big city.'

'This is an old atlas. Camp Bastion won't be on it. Current maps will all show it, of course. It has such significance at the moment. Although it will probably fade back into the sand once British and American soldiers leave.'

Finn stared down at the map. 'Why will it fade back into the sand? The Afghans could use it for themselves. Keep everything as it is. It's sort of weird, a strange camp like a city in the middle of nowhere. With canteens and gyms and workshops and stuff. With planes taking off and landing all the time and a huge hospital with tons of doctors . . . Ben told me, lots of lives have been saved in the hospital there, Delphi. He says that Afghan children and civilians are rescued and treated when they've been blown up by IEDs, or they get sick. They don't treat just soldiers. They treat injured Taliban too, you know . . .'

Delphi smiled. 'Yes, darling, I do know.'

Delphi saw Raza shift uncomfortably from one foot to the other.

'Raza, can you show us where you live in Pakistan? This thick purple line is the Afghan–Pakistani border . . . Look Finn . . .' She replaced her finger on *Lashkar Gah* and measured about an inch, crossways, to the purple line. 'This is how near to the Pakistani border Ben is.'

Raza leant nearer and peered at the English map. Familiar names from Afghan on the lips of his brothers leapt up at him. *Kandahar, Oruzgan, Kabul, Kohat, Khyber Pass . . . 'This is Khyber Pakhtunkwa. It run along Safed Koh Mountains, and passes through the Afghan–Pakistan border . . .'*

Raza placed his finger on the purple line and moved it over into Pakistan. *Peshawar, (Darra Adamkhel). Waziristan. North-West Frontier Province. Swat Valley. Home . . .*

Finn bent close to the map, fascinated. 'You are right!' he said to Delphi. 'Look how close Lashkar Gah is to Peshawar . . . on a map, anyway.'

Raza also peered closer at the tiny, familiar names on the map above Peshawar, as if he might see the name of his village, but there was just a vast, brown mountain range. 'Somewhere, here, high above Peshawar is my village . . .' He pointed vaguely at the brown mass. 'It is not on map.'

Finn stared at Raza's finger, hypnotized. *North-West Frontier Province* the map stated in large letters. And just above his finger *Waziristan Tribal Areas*.

Delphi smiled at Raza. 'Small villages won't be depicted on maps of this scale. How far from Peshawar do you live, do you think?'

Raza thought. 'In the bus or truck, it will take maybe three hours if no one break down. In winter it is much longer. In snow or rockfall, the road it cannot be passed . . .'

'Goodness,' Delphi said, staring at the map. 'Your father still lives there?'

'Yes. My father, he lives still in our small village. We grow vegetables and apricots and pomegranates in the valley. It is a very beautiful place, Mem, with orchards full of blossom and deep lakes in shadow of mountains . . .'

Raza broke off, sick, suddenly, for the smell of almond blossom and his mouth full of sweet apricots; for the sound of sheep pulling at the grass and the cries of goats as they leapt from rock to rock.

Delphi put her hand on his arm. 'Your home is one of the loveliest areas in the world, Raza. I spent some of my childhood in Kashmir . . .'

Delphi's finger traced upwards and right until she reached the disputed border of broken lines. India. Pakistan. *Kashmir.* 'I still have dreams of this magical place. I still have a secret longing to return, so I know how you must feel so far from home and from your father . . .'

'I didn't know about your childhood in Kashmir. I thought you had just gone for a holiday,' Finn said, a note of accusation in his voice.

'Come on.' Delphi got up from the table. 'You must both be hungry. Let's get you a late breakfast. I'll make tea. You make toast, Finn, or get the cereal out. It's too near lunch to do a cooked breakfast.'

'Why have you never told me about your childhood in Kashmir?' Finn, affronted, could not let it go. Delphi took a deep breath.

'Because,' she said quietly, 'my father was killed out there, so I find it hard to talk about.'

The smell of toast filled the kitchen as Delphi poured tea into big white mugs. 'Sorry,' Finn said. He was sorry but he was also curious. 'I didn't know.'

Raza looked solemn. 'I too am most sorry.'

Delphi smiled. 'It's a long time ago, darlings. Come on, let's plan our day . . .'

By midday the wind had dropped and turned into a stiff breeze. Delphi wanted to get a parcel off to Ben before the post office closed. Finn was anxious to add items of his own to the parcel so they both went off to the village leaving Raza with Ian. Raza explained to Delphi that since coming to England he had learned to dread the word *shopping*. 'Pakistani women, they love to shop. They will shop all day. They never cease to tire of shopping.'

Delphi laughed. 'There are quite a few English women like that too, Raza. We won't be long.'

Ian, who had already been out playing a round of golf, thought they might take down his rods for a spot of sea fishing. 'He rarely catches anything,' Finn whispered to Raza. 'He just finds fishing peaceful after a week with my whirlwind grandmother.'

He made a whirling motion with his finger and Raza grinned. Ian set off with Raza to the far side of the beach in companionable silence. After a while Ian asked, 'How are you settling into school in Cornwall?'

'I like this school better than the school in London.'

'That's good. London school big, was it?'

'Noisy, sir. There are many of us in one class. I do not speak good English. To learn quickly, to study many subjects, is hard.'

'It must have been. You must be a bright boy, though. Finn says you won a scholarship.'

'Since I came from Pakistan, I have many extra lessons

152

after school and in holidays when Sarah and Chinir are working at hospital.'

Ian looked down at Raza. How diligently he must have worked. How strange and frightening London must have seemed after his village. There was an air of aloneness about the boy; in the dignified way he carried himself; in the way he held himself in, arms wrapped about his thin body. Contained, Ian thought. Carefully contained.

They stopped near the rocks at the far end of the beach and Ian began to assemble his rods and set up his frame for fishing. Raza watched. Men fished in the lakes at home but with simpler rods. Much patience was needed to fish. In Pakistan, Raza never had enough patience to sit still for long periods of time. There had been too many other things he always wanted to do. In England it was different. Time stretched like elastic before him with no end. He had learned to retreat inside his head, to be still.

He gazed towards the rocks and thought he would like to climb them. Ian saw him looking and smiled. 'Go ahead. Go and explore, Raza. The beach carries on the other side of the rocks. Just be careful. The tide's going out, but you need to keep well away from the rocks near the sea. The waves have a long reach and can swipe you off your feet . . . I don't want to lose you.'

Raza grinned. 'I too do not want to lose me. I will keep very much away from the sea. I will climb these rocks to the other side and then I will come back.'

Ian watched him springing from rock to rock with perfect balance and expertise. As sure as a little goat. He stopped worrying and turned to concentrate on his fishing.

Raza, clambering and jumping up boulders, smiled and described the scene for Baba in his head. The rocks were worn smooth by constant pounding and were pleasing to his bare feet. Small pools were left in crevices filled with slimy coloured seaweed and, sometimes, tiny starfish. There were few people about. Everyone seemed to stay at the surfing end of the beach where there was a café and shop.

Raza reached the top of the rocks and looked down on an almost deserted white beach. The mist had lifted but was hanging in the distance like fallen clouds. The sea sparked in soft silver light. Raza drew in his breath at the perfection of a place with no people.

He climbed quickly down the other side of the rocks and planted his feet in the sand and stared ahead of him, exhilarated. Then he took off, running faster and faster until his chest felt it would burst. He laughed as he ran, laughed for the sheer pleasure of being alive.

'Ahh! Ahh! Ahh!' Raza yelled as he ran. 'Ahh! Ahh! Ahh!' There was no one to hear him except the seagulls and his voice was drowned out by their cries. He felt at one with the opaque and changeable sky, with the wind whipping his hair, with the crushed shells beneath his feet.

He was hardly aware of his laughter turning to tears as the pain burst inside him. He kept on running until his legs gave away and he collapsed onto the sand and faced the swollen sea. The waves crashed wild and windblown, full of a mysterious force that thrilled and terrified him. He felt the salt spray of them on his cheeks. He felt something in his heart that he had not felt since he left Pakistan. Happiness.

As they drove into the village Delphi said to Finn. 'I think the weather is going to close in. We'll go back to Penzance tonight. Ben knows you're home this weekend so he will ring if he can.' She paused. 'Hanna is going to Skype later. Izzy is dying to talk to you.'

Delphi watched Finn's expression change. 'I'll talk to Izzy,' he muttered. Delphi changed gear, shot up the hill, past the church and parked in the village hall car park and turned to him.

'I know you're still angry and upset, darling, but it's important you keep talking to Hanna, Finn. We need to support her while Ben's away. We need to be kind. We need to make her feel she can come home to us anytime and all will be well.'

Finn sniffed and said nothing, his hand on the door handle of the car. 'Whatever you think, Hanna is unhappy and fragile, or she would not have taken off like that. Do you really want to make the situation worse, darling?'

Delphi put a hand on Finn's arm, aware of her own struggle to come to terms with what Hanna was putting her children through.

'You love your mother, and she loves you, Finn. It doesn't have to be a long conversation. Believe me it will make you feel better.'

Finn sat silent in the small car looking straight ahead. Delphi opened her car door. 'Come on, let's buy a few more things to put in this parcel and post it in the last village post office in rural England . . .'

Finn and Delphi sat at the top of the Penzance house on Delphi's huge computer waiting for Hanna's Skype call. Finn remained stony-faced, but as Hanna and Izzy blipped into view and he heard Izzy's excited voice calling his name, he was awash with conflicting emotions. Hanna looked as immaculate as ever. Her hair was a little shorter but still a shiny, sharp cut.

Finn grinned at Izzy. 'Hi Titchet!' he called, grinning at her. 'What have you been up to?'

Izzy laughed and put her face right up to the screen. 'Not Titchet! Naughty boy! Finn, Finn, Finn . . .' She repeated his name over and over like she used to when he got back for holidays and Finn saw she was near to tears with missing him.

'Hey, Izz!' he said quickly. 'I'm doing some mermaid stories for you, with little paintings. I'll put them in the post as soon as they are finished. Okay?'

Izzy nodded, her hair bouncing. Her eyes were brimming but she was trying to smile. Finn wanted to grab her and hold her tight. Beside him he felt Delphi take in a deep breath and say brightly. 'Izzy, darling, what a lovely dress you're wearing. Is it new?'

'Yeth,' Izzy said. 'To thow Finn.'

Finn said, 'Wow! You remembered my favourite colour. You look cool in red, Izz.'

Hanna said, 'Finn?' Her voice was tentative. Finn met her eyes. She smiled. 'You look well. I had forgotten how brown you were from the summer.'

Finn had tried to push from his mind how beautiful Hanna was, or how soft and husky her voice. He did not know what to say to his mother, but he could not take his eyes off her.

'Finn,' she said, 'I thought Izzy and I might come to England for Christmas. I have sent Ben an email. I wondered if his halfway leave might be around Christmas. Would you like that?'

'Yeth! Yeth! Yeth!' Izzy shouted.

Finn wanted to shout. *Do you mean you might come home for Christmas and never go back? Do you?*

But he said, 'Yeah . . . be good.' He looked away from Hanna to Izzy. 'What's with this yeth, yeth, yeth?'

'I've loft a tooth.'

'At Christmas, I'll tickle you until all your baby teeth fall out, then you can grow new ones . . .'

'No, no!' Izzy giggled. 'I'll wet mythelf.' Finn and Delphi laughed.

Hanna said, 'Are you're sure you could cope with us all, Delphi?'

'Of course, I can cope with you all. I'll be in my element, you know me, Hanna. What a lovely thing to look forward too. Will you help me do the tree, Izzy?'

'Yeth, I'll help. Wait for me to come.'

'I certainly will.'

Hanna said, 'Is all well at school Finn?'

'Yeah, thanks,' Finn said. 'I'll have to go now. I've got a friend staying.'

'Who?' Izzy demanded.

'No one you know, nosy knickers. His name is Raza.'

'No one hath a name like that. Let me thee.'

'Who, Raza?'

'Yeth. You're making him up.'

'No, I'm not.' Finn went to the door and called out, 'Raza!'

Raza's head appeared at the bottom of the stairs. 'Could you come up and prove to my little sister that you exist?'

Raza climbed the stairs. 'I think I do.'

Finn grinned. 'Please say hi to my sister, Izzy, who thinks I'm making you up.'

Raza moved to the computer shyly and stared at a little girl in a red dress and a woman with a lovely face. '*Assalamu alaikum*,' he said, bowing slightly to the screen. The little girl stared back at him with a solemn face. Raza smiled at her. 'Hello, how are you?'

Izzy leant against Hanna and was mesmerized by Raza's flashing smile and his strange green eyes.

'Say hello to Raza, Izzy,' Hanna said, nudging her gently.

'In my country we say *Assalamu alaikum*. In England you say, hello, how are you,' Raza said, with an English inflection, still smiling at the little girl. Izzy, curious, leaned away from Hanna.

'Where ith your country?' she asked.

'It is Pakistan.'

'Why are you in England, not at home."

'I am at school with Finn.'

'Why . . .'

'Izzy . . .' Finn said quickly, knowing Izzy's questions would run on and on. 'There! I was telling you the truth. I was not making Raza up.'

'Well, it'th a funny name,' Izzy said.

'So is yours,' Delphi retorted, and Izzy giggled.

Hanna said, 'We must say goodbye and let you all get on with your evening. Raza, it is nice to meet you.'

'Goodbye, Mem,' Raza said. 'Goodbye, Izzy.' He bowed to the screen and slid to the door. Izzy called. *Thlam! Ekum! Raza.'* Raza laughed as he went down the stairs.

'Bye then,' Finn said to Hanna. 'Speak to you soon, Izzy-busy, okay?' Izzy nodded but her smile was gone. 'I'll send you emails and mermaid stories . . .'

'Promith?'

'I promise.'

Hanna said, 'Have a good rest of the weekend, Finn. I'll email.'

Finn nodded and left the room and clattered down the attic stairs to his room. Raza was sitting on the edge of the spare bed not quite knowing what to do with himself.

'Sorry about my sister,' Finn said. 'She's a bit precocious.'

'Why are you sorry?' Raza asked. 'She is nice little girl.'

'Yeah,' Finn said. 'She is.'

Raza looked at him. The atmosphere in the upstairs room had been full of unsaid things. He wanted to ask why Finn's mother and sister were not in England with Finn. He could see Finn was miserable. 'Would you like to play computer game?' he asked.

'Yeah. Good idea. Angry Birds?'

'Very hard,' Raza moaned. 'Let's do it!'

That night Raza lay in the bed beside Finn in the Penzance house full of beautiful things and bright paintings. It was a strange house with many stairs. Delphi had her studio at the top of the house. She could see the sea from the top windows and also from the bedroom below where she and Ian slept.

On the first floor there were four more bedrooms. Finn's room, the smallest and sunniest, lay on the other side of the house from the sea, overlooking the garden. Two beds, a desk with Delphi's old computer and the childhood things Finn had grown out of lay around the room. Downstairs there was a big kitchen and breakfast room. There was a sitting room, full of photographs with French windows that led out onto a small, secluded garden. Raza felt overawed by the sheer size of the house and bewildered why anyone would need two houses, or even one house with so many rooms.

He preferred the beach house. He had never stayed in an English person's house before. Daniyal and Liyana's house in Derby was large, but it was always bursting with visiting relations. Every space was used. Beds were rarely empty. Sarah and Chinir's house in London had been big by Raza's standard but was in fact a small, compact terraced house.

Beside him in the dark Finn tossed and turned and eventually got up and stood looking out of the window into the dark. Raza had been conscious of Finn's unhappiness all evening. Ever since he had spoken to his mother and sister. He had hardly eaten any supper.

Raza propped himself on one elbow and whispered. 'What is your trouble, Finn?'

Finn did not turn around immediately, but he left the window and got back into bed. 'Sorry. Did I wake you up?'

'I have not slept.'

Finn sighed. 'Me neither.'

Raza waited.

'My mother is in Finland with my little sister.'

'Yes,' Raza said carefully. 'I do not know this place.'

'It is in Scandinavia. I'll show you on a map tomorrow. It's a small, cold place with a lot of snow in winter.'

'You are called after this place?

'In a way. It began as a joke between my parents, then they began to like it. My mother is Finnish, but my dad did not want me to have an unpronounceable Finnish name.'

'Oh, I see,' Raza said, not sure that he did. 'Your mother she has gone home to visit her family.'

'Yeah,' Finn said abruptly.

After a moment Raza said, 'She is away until Christmas and this makes you sad?'

Finn lay down on his back and put his arms under his head. 'She should be in Germany with Izzy, at our army house. Where we all live. It's where I go in the holidays. It's where Izzy goes to school. It's our home. When my dad went to Afghanistan my mother suddenly decided she wanted to go back to Finland. She took Izzy and I don't really know whether she will want to come back. She hates Germany.'

Finn's voice cracked. Raza felt a great sadness. Finn's mother had abandoned him in England. He did not know what to say. After a while, not sure whether Finn had fallen asleep, he said, 'My mother, she died when I was born. I never know her, but I had a happy life with my father and visiting my uncles in Peshawar. When I was ten, my father, he take me to Islamabad. I believe we are going to visit relations of my dead mother from England. Instead, my father he give me to Sarah and Chinir. They are good people, but he did not say one word to me of his plans for me. He just tell me that I must leave all the troubles in Pakistan and go with them for education in the west. The next day he put me on a plane to England with these relations. They speak only English and Urdu. I do not speak English or good Urdu. I am *Pashtun*. I speak Pashto. I could not believe my father would send me away, but he believe it is the best for me. I have been very sad, very angry, and unhappy in England, Finn. This is why I work so hard, to make my father proud, then I can return to Pakistan . . .'

Finn sat up. 'Bloody hell! You had to get on a plane with strangers?'

'Family. But strangers, yes. They have been very kind to me, but I hate the school in London. I don't want to be there. Last year one of my brothers, Fakir, he was killed in Waziristan by American drone. My father, he tell me that I cannot return home to mourn him because it is too dangerous. Our dead must be buried by nightfall, but still, I want to go back to Pakistan to respect my dead brother. So, I went a little mad and I broke things in the house in London because I was so angry. I told Sarah and Chinir that I hate this life. I hate London and my school and if I could not return to Pakistan, I would run away . . .'

'Did you?' Finn asked, swinging his legs over the side of the bed. 'Did you, run away?'

'No. Sarah and Chinir were shocked because I am never before so angry. I think I hide my anger too long. I am ashamed. I make them very sad. They look for different jobs out of London. When they find job in West Country, they look for another school for me. Then they hear about your school and put me in for the scholarship. All this they did for me. They tell me, if you are still unhappy in one year, we will take you back to Pakistan.'

161

Finn stared across in the dark, trying to imagine being put on a plane to another country and leaving his family, his whole life, behind him. Having to learn a different language and live in another culture with strangers.

'Do you still wish you were back in Pakistan, Raza?'

Raza lay back in his bed. He had never spoken to anyone about his feelings before. 'Today,' he said, thinking back to the deserted beach, 'with your family, I feel that I might be happy in England, for a little while, in this place by the sea.'

Finn smiled across at him in the dark. 'Good. You can come home with me anytime, you know. Delphi is definitely going to make you into another grandson.'

'That will be indeed excellent,' Raza said solemnly.

Delphi put her head round the door. 'What are you two doing, still awake? I'm going to make myself a hot chocolate. Any takers?'

'Any chance of a piece of toast too?' Finn asked, suddenly hungry.

Raza swung his legs out of the bed happily. Toast solved everything.

'Come downstairs then,' Delphi said. 'Honestly, you two must have hollow legs . . .'

CHAPTER THIRTY-TWO

Ben rang on Sunday morning. Delphi heard the husky weariness in his voice, the slight deadness of tone. He put on a cheerful act for Finn, assuring him he was fine. When Finn asked about Christmas, Ben told him he had to be with his men for Christmas, but there was a chance he would have to come back for a briefing in London early in the New Year. Finn hid his disappointment and Delphi was proud of him. She did not think Finn was fooled by Ben's upbeat tone. She heard him telling Ben he had spoken to Izzy and Hanna, knowing this would make Ben happy.

When Delphi took the phone back to say goodbye, Ben sounded less tense. She walked away and stood by the French windows in the sitting room.

'Tough week?' she asked quietly.

'Yes. Relentless for my soldiers. One of my sergeants was killed this week. He had only been married a few months. His baby is due next week . . .'

'Oh, Ben, how tragic,' Delphi said under her breath in case Finn could hear.

'Yes, it is . . . Anyway, I'm okay. Don't worry. Luckily, I don't get much time to think. Better go, Delphi, I have to keep these calls brief. I want to try to catch Hanna, speak to Izzy . . .'

'Good. Finn and I have just posted a parcel to you. Please take care, darling.'

'I will. Thanks for everything, Mum.' And he was gone.

Delphi stood looking down onto the garden. A thrush was bathing noisily and with sweet abandon in the birdbath. Ben only ever called her *Mum* when he was subconsciously in need of the comfort that word brought.

It did not matter how much pre-deployment training you had, Delphi thought, nothing on God's earth could help you accept the death or terrible injury to your soldiers. The unforgivable waste of life. A young widow left bereft. A child who would never know his father. Delphi closed her eyes against the black fear that hovered like a shadowy presence.

She walked back into the kitchen where Finn and Raza were surfing cartoons on the television. Ian had wisely escaped to his workshop at the bottom of the garden.

'It's a lovely morning,' she said, 'How about a walk and a pub lunch before I take you guys back to school?'

CHAPTER THIRTY-THREE

Swat Valley, 2009

One morning Zamir received a shock. Emerging from his house in the half-light he saw Hasan, the young boy who helped him with his goats, running with some urgency up the track from the village. His father, Jamel, had sent him ahead to tell Zamir that Fakir, far from being dead, had walked into the village the previous night with another Talib and gone straight to his empty house. His wife, Nadira, believing him dead, had been forced to go back to live with her eldest son in Rawalpindi, taking their only daughter with her. No woman was safe living alone, especially with a young daughter.

Zamir, staring down at the breathless child, felt dismay. *May Allah, in his goodness, forgive me. I feel no joy in my son being alive.* Fakir's return could only mean one thing, and everyone knew it. Fakir was recruiting. He would put pressure on families with young sons to relinquish them to him. They would take simple boys like Hasan off to a Madrassa to brainwash them, turn them into fanatical boy soldiers with a deep hatred of the west. They would be trained and deployed for military operations, used in planting and detonating IEDs.

Hasan's father, Jamel, desperate and sweating, clambered up the mountain after his son, begging Zamir for help. His other sons were too young, but Hasan was eight and vulnerable, being small and a little simple.

Both Zamir and Jamel knew Hasan was ideal for the purposes of the Talibs. He was a docile, biddable boy; the kind easily persuaded to strap an explosive waistcoat around his thin chest before being sent out to maim, kill, and die a martyr's death.

It was becoming increasingly common for the Talibs to take small boys over the border to do their dirty work. Children were rarely stopped by military patrols or checkpoints; it was too divisive. These young boys barely understood the concept of their own deaths. They were blinded by fear, as well as an innocent fervour, a belief in a better world waiting for them.

'Has Fakir seen Hasan?' Zamir asked.

Jamel shook his head. 'Fakir and the stranger walked into the village late last night. They went straight to Fakir's house. They still sleep.'

'Go back and tell your neighbours to swear Hasan died of some disease or a fall from rocks last year. Stick to your story. Quick, go and do it. Make a cairn of stones on the mountainside. Tell them that is where Hasan is buried. I will take him to the caves. I will tell him what will happen to him if he comes out. Go . . .'

Zamir found naan bread, water, a large shawl and together, as the sun rose, he and Hasan climbed upwards with the goats to a group of hidden caves buried into the mountain.

As a child Zamir had taken refuge with his father and uncles in these caves during tribal wars. They had hidden weapons from the Russians here. Boundaries and disputes changed with the years, but the caves remained, impenetrable and dangerous for those who did not know the complicated layout of passages into the mountain.

Zamir, having terrified the boy into staying hidden, left him with a tame goat kid for company and told him to sleep. This was one thing the child excelled at, even when he was supposed to be minding the goats. Zamir promised him someone would come for him before nightfall then he made his way back to the pasture above his house.

Jamel had sent two small daughters to mind his goats and Zamir, now exhausted from his climb, made his way back to his house. After he had washed and prayed, Deeba, the old widow next door, brought his breakfast. Zamir sat in front of his house and waited.

Fakir arrived alone. He was limping badly and had two fingers missing from his left hand. He looked older. '*Assalamu alaikum, Fakir.*'

'*Wa alaykumu as-salam,* Baba,' Fakir said. 'I see word has already come. You are not surprised to see me.'

'You are certainly no ghost, Fakir,' Zamir said drily. 'Was news of your death a mistake or did you need to disappear?'

Fakir opened his mouth in a semblance of a smile that did not reach his eyes. Zamir saw his missing and black teeth. Fakir touched his chest. 'I was wounded. Better to stay dead.'

'Not for your wife. Could you not have sent word to Nadira? She could not stay here, a woman alone. She returned to Rawalpindi to find Aneel.'

Fakir shrugged. 'I did not trust her. I can find a new wife.'

When the widow had brought Fakir refreshment he said, 'This valley is growing empty of people, of the young. It is becoming a place of ghosts.'

'What do you expect? People are afraid. They are caught between Talibs, military sweeps, and American drones. They have no choice but to flee to the cities.'

'Where they will starve on the streets instead of fighting our enemies.'

'In the cities they have a chance of staying alive. The Taliban promise much and deliver little. You take their sons, promise land, water, electricity, and the hope of something better. None of which is in your power to give. Why have you returned here, to this village, Fakir? Not to see me, I think.'

Fakir's watching eyes reminded Zamir of one of his sheep. They held not a glimmer of light or warmth.

'This is my village, Baba. The place I grew up. I know the families who have boys the right age for *Jihad*. Men that I once played with as a child. Many of these men fight with us. Others, willingly, in Allah's name, offer their sons when they become of age. It should be the duty of all men and women to sacrifice their children for Islam, to glory in death . . . after which, naturally, comes their blessed reward in heaven.'

His expression chilled Zamir. There was an edge, a cynicism in his voice that Zamir had never before heard. As if Fakir no longer believed in all the virgins waiting for him in heaven.

Just as Zamir was thinking, *My son has become disillusioned?* Fakir said under his breath, 'It is foolish for any man to try to hide their sons or to send them away, Baba. This will only bring trouble upon them.'

Zamir met Fakir's eyes. 'Raza is not in hiding. Or gone from us. He is being educated. Only by education will this country prosper, Fakir.'

'You tricked my little brother. You betrayed him. If you wanted him educated, we, his family, would have found him a Madrassa . . . Raza's life was here with us, his brothers, his family. We taught him well. He was a fast learner. He could dismantle a gun and clean it quicker than anyone I know. Raza never forgot what he was taught . . . His mind was quick. He would have become a leader of men – a *Jihadi*. His destiny was with *us*,' Fakir repeated angrily.

'If that were true, Allah would have prevented my son leaving Pakistan. The Madrassas are full of mullahs who have hate in their hearts, but little education or true knowledge of the Koran, just the love of power. You say Raza could have been a leader. You mean fighting with the Talibs and dying with the Talibs. In a few years Raza will return to Pakistan an educated man and he will work for his country another way. There have to be other ways, Fakir. Invading forces come and go. At some point you *Jihadis* will have to sit around a table and do business with governments, men not of your persuasion or liking . . . Look at our tribal history, look at our changing world. . .'

As Zamir was speaking he became aware of Fakir listening closely and of some underlying anxiety in him. Fakir was no longer a young man. His body had taken a battering. He did not move so fast or so surely. He did not have the charisma of Ajeet or the intelligence of Raza. His power came from where it always came in the insecure: in brutality, in terrifying those under him who might undermine him. There were constant power battles within Taliban groups. Fakir, now vulnerable, could well be fighting to hold onto his position.

He must see, as he passed through villages, fighting men left with terrible injuries, shattered limbs. Men who could no longer fight their cause were discarded and forgotten. They were left with the nightmare of violence that went on and on unreeling in their heads, along with their abandoned or dead wives and children.

As if he had caught his father's thoughts from a fleeting expression of pity or a relaxation in Zamir's stern face, fury seemed to erupt from Fakir, although he kept his tone low.

'Have you forgotten your duty in your worship of the west? Have you forgotten how you once were, Baba, noble and proud to be a *Pashtun?* I remember how you used to be when I was a child. You were prepared to fight any threat to our country. You were brave and brought honour on our family . . . Now . . .'

Zamir froze him with a look. Fakir stopped, suddenly aware of Zamir's anger and also of his father's position and respect in the village. To impugn his father's honour would have consequences.

This village was not a Taliban stronghold; there were few Taliban sympathizers here. His uncles would happily shoot him in the head in the name of family reputation if he could not hold his tongue. Fakir had the power to have his father killed, if he so wished, but tribal honour and pride still ran deep in his veins.

He said quickly, 'Baba, I believe you thought you were doing the right thing for Raza, but you did not think of the consequences of sending him to the west. He will absorb into him their values. He will be influenced by their freedoms, but he will never be accepted. I hear that he is not happy in their country. When Raza returns to Pakistan, he will not be happy or accepted here either. He will never be trusted. He will be a danger and in danger. This is what you have done to your youngest son . . . You have taken from him his home and his country forever.'

Fakir's last words struck such fear in Zamir's heart that they suffocated all other emotion, even anger.

Zamir finally made himself look at Fakir. 'I am pleased that you are finally learning to think for yourself as well as killing the innocent and spouting a selective version of the Koran. This is progress, for you must be getting an education of sorts from the people you are with who cannot all be stupid or unaware. Words, however, should be used carefully. Words can be as powerful as the gun and just as dangerous. Never question my honour again.'

Fakir's body registered resentment. Eventually, resigned, he got to his feet.

'They say the boy, Hasan, is dead.'

Zamir nodded. 'He was a simple boy but loved by his family.'

Fakir was sure Hasan was very much alive, but he turned away. He was not going to battle with this stubborn old man any longer. He had had enough. He nodded at his father and started back down the track to the village.

His bones ached. There were suddenly many questions in his mind. When he and Ajeet had been young their father had been away fighting the Russians. Like Raza, all he and his brother had thought about was joining their father in *Jihad* as soon as they were old enough. Their mother had been a silent woman; her life taken up with surviving and feeding them while Zamir was away. She died abruptly carrying a load of wood, collapsing into the dry earth as the dust wind whirled and whipped around her fallen body. The hundred-day wind had almost buried her before she took her last grateful breath.

Zamir had changed over the last decade. The father Raza had grown up with was not the same father that he and Ajeet had known. Zamir had been feared and respected by his elder sons, but not loved. When Zamir had put his gun down and settled down to village life with a new young wife, he had grown soft.

For a moment, Fakir let himself imagine how his life might have been. Educated men from Europe, the Middle

East, from all over the world had slowly been joining the Taliban in bigger numbers to fight the American and British forces in Afghanistan. Fakir, listening to their fervour, their ability to express intent and inspire confidence, had, for the first time, grasped the importance of learning. To plan, to have a strategy, limit casualties against a superior firepower. To outwit an enemy on the ground or in the air, to cheat them of victory. Most of all, to have the confidence and the knowledge to implement a coherent plan against a vast invasion force, was an enviable skill.

Fakir's own expertise was incendiary devices. He had started out at 10 making crude bombs, but over the years he had been shown by experts how small, how sophisticated an incendiary device could be; easier to place in the most unexpected places. These devices were the most powerful and lethal weapons they had had to injure and kill in large numbers.

Fakir had learned new bomb-making skills quickly. He never forgot once taught. He never fumbled, lost his nerve, or made a mistake. But he realized that, if he had only learned to read, he could have experimented, practised making his own variations of bombs. Relying on memory was not enough anymore. Sophisticated bombs meant absolute precision. You had to get the mix exactly right or blow yourself up in the process. He was unable to write things down and his memory was now beginning to fail him.

He understood why the mullahs needed young boys uneducated, unquestioning, and fervent, as he and his brother had once been, but at 40 years old he began to question the wisdom of this. He had lost three fingers as well as more serious injury to his body. His bomb-making days were over.

Afghans and Pakistani Talibs of his age who could read, as well as experts from foreign countries, were teaching younger Talibs, from complicated plans downloaded from the Internet. Crude bombs were still widely used and could be assembled by children if necessary, but Fakir wanted to trigger bombs using mobile phones as radios. He wanted to master a more sophisticated and precisely timed bomb to defeat the foreign soldiers.

If he could only understand and identify captured foreign equipment, he could adapt it. He was getting left behind because he was illiterate and could not follow written instructions.

His father had offered to teach him to read as a young adult, but Fakir had not wanted to feel diminished, had been too proud to accept. Zamir would never know how bitterly Fakir regretted this now.

CHAPTER THIRTY-FOUR

Cornwall, 2009

Finn lay in the dark after lights out thinking of Ben in Lashkar Gah. Missing him was always worse at night. He hoped Ben wasn't too lonely without them all. He squeezed his eyes tight shut and prayed he was safe. He had not had a bluey for a while. He thought about the day Ben had been issued with his army kit for Afghanistan. It had been half-term and Ben had been anxious to pack it away before Hanna and Izzy got home.

'Can I help?' Finn had asked.

'Sure, you can,' Ben said. 'We'll go through the packing list together.' Ben had got out the black bag and Bergan and laid all his kit out on the sitting room floor. There was a lot of it. He looked at the itinerary that charted clearly what each item was.

'Boy Scout's dream,' Ben said, picking up a holster, blast goggles, glasses, desert boots, and flip-flops and lining them up.

Finn had admired body armour with pouches for grenades and knives and a blast-proof helmet. There were underpants, socks, foot powder . . .

Finn had put his hand under Ben's bulletproof waistcoat and placed his fingers over Ben's heart to make sure it would be protected.

'What about your legs and arms, Ben?'

'I need my arms to shoot and my legs to run, old thing. Can't fight in armour . . .'

Ben had glanced at his watch and begun to fold his kit up neatly and quickly and put it back in his Bergan. He did not want Hanna and Izzy coming in and seeing his weapons lying on the floor.

The memory lay, indelible, in Finn's mind. The sudden, visual understanding that Ben was not going away on exercise. These weapons were not a game but a glimpse of war.

CHAPTER THIRTY-FIVE

Ed Dominic stood in front of his class and shuffled the papers in front of him. 'Last week I asked you all for an essay on "vanished lives". I told you it could be about anything. A tribe, a species, a country, or merely a way of life, although I did suggest you refrain from endless prose about vanished Cornish tin mines. I asked for the writing to be a personal account or something that touched you or had affected your own life and not merely a list of facts.

'I expected some pretty good essays from you all but you have exceeded my expectations. I've been humbled by the standard of some of your writing. Well done. I've got four essays that I would like to be read out in class . . .'

Mr Dominic pushed back his hair that had a tendency to flop over his eyes. 'Raza, I was especially impressed by your essay. Well done. It fulfilled everything I asked for in "vanished lives". I wonder if you would mind reading it out to the class?'

Raza was horrified. The essay had taken him hours. He had lost himself in the writing, but he still found English punctuation baffling. In the end he had given up and just let the stories Baba told him flow.

'Sir, I cannot. My English is not good enough. Indeed, it is very poor still.'

Ed Dominic laughed. 'Do you think any of us here in this room could write a long essay in Pashto, Urdu, or any other language for that matter? Raza, this is a fascinating glimpse of a life we don't know. Please don't deprive us . . . You are the only one who can make your world come alive.'

Raza's friends banged their desks. 'Come on, Raz, let's hear it . . .'

Finn, sitting next to him, said under his breath. 'It's okay. Mr Dominic would not ask you to read it out unless it was brilliant.'

'You said I forget my prepositions . . .' Raza hissed. 'You laughed at my full stops. Indeed, you said they were like little faces I put everywhere that stops a sentence in its tracks . . .'

Finn grinned. 'Well, no one is going to see your full stops, are they?'

Mr Dominic smiled. 'We're not here to judge your English grammar, Raza, just to hear your story. Please?'

Vanished Lives by Raza Ali

In days of my grandfather many tribes who lived in North of Pakistan near borders of Afghanistan roam free. In summer they live among mountains. Women make small fields for vegetables. These tribal peoples they pick fruit and nuts from the trees in the valleys and store their harvests to sell in the harsh winters when they must feed all of themselves.

When winter draws near leaders of the tribes they must judge when it is time to leave the mountains. It takes many days to prepare their long camel trains for their journey. There are hundreds of women and childrens with their tents and provisions, their flocks of goats and sheeps.

The long journeys back and forth from the mountains down to the plains and valleys are dangerous. Indeed, harsh winds can blow red dust for many days. Mountain passes can freeze, and mists descend to trap peoples into the mountains. Indeed, they have many things to fear. The different tribes sometimes fight each other for what they have harvested all summer.

In a poor country it is said that some tribes believe that no man is thief; that each man has duty look after himself and his family. It is also said that no man must dishonour or steal from his own tribe. Every tribe that roams and crosses the borders of Afghan and Pakistan they have their own ways and different customs.

The Wazir and the Mahsud tribes they can live happily side by side. The Wazir hunt in packs but the Mahsud they will hunt alone. My father, he tell me of these many tribes who wandered the earth freely, even in the days of his childhood and growing up, but I do not remember them all.

Once there were the Siahpads from Killa Kund. There were Mangals, which are a Brahui tribe of Baluchistan. A Baluch tribesman he was very fierce. There were also the 'foot' people, the Pawindahs.

The largest tribe was the Kharot tribe. They numbered millions. They travel in huge caravans of sheeps and herds of camels. These are restless peoples who never cease moving from place to place to find work and sweet grazing for their cattle. As soon as grazing is finished, they move on to another place.

My father, he tell me this story. With the coming of one spring a huge caravan of peoples of the Kharot tribe start back for the highlands. The caravans they are piled with food and provisions that the peoples had brought with money from working and trading. The men, women, and childrens of this tribe are happy because they have bought bright cloth and small jewels for themselves. Indeed, it has been a good summer for them.

In those old gone days the roaming tribal people do not think or know of other worlds. The tribes are so many the earth seem to belong to them. They harm no one and keep to their own customs and rules. These peoples have lived same life for centuries.

But when the Britisher Empire comes to end this flow of peoples through international borders begin to be questioned by the government. First. It is the Pawindah tribe, the' foot' people. They are challenged one day as they cross the Afghan/Pakistan border. The government do not want the tribes to be free, to only answer to themselves. They see the flow of tribes across the borders as defiance and threat. They wish all tribes now to be answerable to government called The State.

179

This day my father speak of, the Kharot tribe start moving from the highlands same as always. But they hear a rumour from a friendly soldier from one of the outlying forts. This rumour it begin to spread like a whisper in the grass. No tribes will be able to pass over the Afghan/Pakistan border without papers of identity.

No one believe this thing is true and the Kharot tribe make for Kakar Khorasan, the same point that they always cross the border.

There are thousands of them all travelling together but they are broken into Kirri or Clans, like in Scotland. Each have their own a leader. Wives, chickens, child-rens, tents, dogs, flocks of sheeps, many hundreds of camels.

On second day of march the tribe stop to rest. They peg black tents into the ground and sit around their fires. Smoke rises into night air. The women are anxious about these rumours spreading everywhere.

The men they talk among themselves. It is impossible for them to produce papers. How can they do this thing? They never have no birth certificates, no papers, no identity, just belonging to their tribe. They never go inside any government building to say who they are. They are roaming peoples.

Next morning the tribe move onwards, and they are meet by friendly soldiers from the fort. The soldiers tell them to please not to proceed but to go back for they have orders not to let any tribe to cross the border. But the Kharot peoples cannot go back. These hundreds of people cannot return to the mountains, winter is upon them and they will all die.

They do not listen to soldiers. They move on believing in strength of numbers. Indeed, they are bewildered that any persons could truly wish to stop them to cross to safe valleys. Besides, they have no choice with their long caravans full of their womens and childrens.

More soldiers meet them at the Kakar Khorasan crossing. Again, they are warned to go back. Soldiers tell them if they try to cross border they will have to shoot because they cannot disobey orders.

The soldiers beg the Kharots please to turn their caravan round and warn those coming behind that they can no longer cross the border. These soldiers they do not want to shoot the Kharot peoples.

But the first Kirri of the caravan of Kharots stand firm. The men of tribe come to decision. Everyman women and childrens will hold the Holy Koran aloft above their heads and storm the border. They are great in number and Allah will protect them.

They rush forward, all these thousands of peoples, believing all will be well and they will safely reach the other side. The soldiers open fire on the Kharot tribe. All are mown down in moments from the fierce fire of the soldiers who must obey their orders. All die. Scattered across the dry earth. Many hundreds of bodies of men, womens, childrens and beasts. It is massacre. They say the soldiers weep.

Every tribe coming after see or hear of this terrible thing. It is end of Nomad tribes of Pakistan and Afghanistan. All borders are patrolled forever more. No tribe is free to roam the earth as he will. No man can travel freely in their own lands again.

Today, many peoples still cross Afghan/Pakistan border back and forth, secretly. But for old tribes of West Frontier their lives of freedom and much happiness far away from all governments and rulers end forever. Their roaming way of life it vanish.

While Raza read, the whole class listened in hushed silence. No one shuffled or moved. Raza held the room. When he finished there was an intake of breath, a pause, then Mr Dominic and the whole class held their hands up and clapped him. Raza looked up, startled, to find a sea of smiling faces. He glanced at Finn. 'Wow! Raz, brilliant!' Finn looked as pleased as if he had written the piece himself.

As Raza stood, a small, embarrassed figure in front of his class, he suddenly thought how proud Baba would be of him at this moment. His school friends had listened enrapt to a world they had not known even existed. For a moment, he had brought the roaming tribes of Pakistan alive and made the tragedy of their end, live again. He had wept as he wrote, for the vanished tribes, for his lost home. Standing in front of his classmates, Raza hoped they might understand that his beautiful country held much more than constant violence. Perhaps, now, they would see mountains and lakes, apricot orchards and almond blossom scattering the dry land where ordinary people prayed for peace.

Raza sat down abruptly. It was his first taste of acceptance; of being good enough; of being part of this world whilst staying firmly bound to his own.

Dearest Finn,

It is the early hours of the morning and I have just come off guard duty. (Officers have to do guard duty out here!) I spend these nights in a Sangar – a concrete tower with firing windows. I look out over the main road that is clustered by buildings and a graveyard full of small fluttering green flags on poles.

I like this quiet time as it gives me time away from the hub of darkened rooms and computer screens to think. I watch the locals waking up and heading for work through binoculars.

It has been raining here so the Pashtuns are wrapped up in thin blanket cloaks, all in natural colours. Their way of life and their clothes in this part of the world can have hardly changed in 200 years . . .

It was good to speak to you this weekend. Glad you were able to talk to Hanna and Izzy. They sound fine, don't they? I managed to speak to them both. Izzy is the same bouncy little girl she ever was!

As soon as my leave is confirmed I will let you know. I'm sorry I can't be back for Christmas, but I need to stay with the boys. All being well we will be together for New Year, but you know enough about army life to understand nothing is a given. I must finish for now; the sun is coming up and I will celebrate one day closer to coming home with a flask of tea. Delphi says you are being amazing considering the circumstances and upheavals of our lives at the moment. I am very proud of you, Finn.

You take care. More soon.

Love you lots, Ben xxx

CHAPTER THIRTY-SIX

It was Remembrance Sunday. It was the one time of the year that Delphi accompanied Ian and Finn to church. The death toll of soldiers in Afghanistan was relentless and the sermon reflected the sombre mood of the country. The visiting priest had been an army padre and he spoke movingly about fear and the sacrifice of war. At the church door Delphi thanked him. She had been touched by his account of his war in the Falklands. Delphi told him she had a son out in Afghanistan. The priest had taken her hand and said quietly, 'The difference, my dear, is that your son is in a war where the enemy is unseen and everywhere . . . We at least knew who and where our enemy lay . . .'

As Ian, Delphi, and Finn followed the possession to the Cenotaph on the prom, a cruel wind whipped at them from an icy, leaden sea. The silence was followed by a lone bugler playing out of tune. Finn stood shivering as the priest's voice was whipped away to the screech of seagulls. Ian guided them both home; his arms firmly around their shoulders, instilling, as only he could, his quiet, reassuring presence in their lives.

They stumbled gratefully inside the house to where the smell of roast lamb wafted to them from the kitchen. Finn ran straight upstairs for his phone to see if Ben had messaged him. Delphi went to the kitchen.

Ian poured her a drink. Delphi was sleeping badly. Ian heard her wandering the house or climbing upstairs to her studio at night. Ben had had many difficult postings and dangerous moments, especially in Iraq, but Delphi had weathered these with outward calm and pragmatism.

This time the relentless parade of coffins returning from Afghanistan and passing through a hushed English Wootton Bassett village was affecting the whole country and unnerving Delphi. The added stress of Hanna leaving when she was most needed by Finn had upset her more than she admitted.

Ian was unable to banish the creeping feeling that Ben had done more than his bit in violent conflicts. It was time he left the army, before his luck began to run out.

He was concerned about Finn too. The boy said little about his anxiety for Ben when he came home at the weekends, but he watched every news bulletin with obsessional concentration. As the weeks passed, he had begun to develop an unhealthy compulsion to check the news for anything on the war in Afghanistan. It was like a talisman for him, if he watched the breaking news, nothing bad could happen to Ben.

When Delphi told Finn that she would rather he did not repeatedly watch news items about dead or injured soldiers, Finn had got upset.

He told her that he could not watch the news at school because he was doing prep at 6 p.m. The 10 p.m. news was too late, and Mr Dominic monitored the television in the games room.

'I need to know what's going on, Delphi. It's my dad out

there and Mr Dominic restricts the use of our computers and what we can watch at school . . .'

And so he should. Delphi thought. The war in Afghanistan was becoming a morbid obsession and Delphi and Ian tried to engineer it so that they were playing games or eating at main news bulletins. Ian had developed an avid interest in watching rugby or football or searching for old films that could deflect Finn.

That evening when Ian drove Finn back to school, Delphi sat at her desk with its cracked jars filled with paintbrushes and stared at her painting of birds in an exotic garden of her imagination. Something was off-kilter. Something was missing. She sighed and looked away at her Christmas list. Her next exhibition was at the end of the month. After that she would concentrate single-mindedly on Christmas.

She tried to banish the notion that this family Christmas was pivotal, that everyone's happiness depended on her. She knew that she could only facilitate, not take responsibility for Ben or Hanna's lives.

Each morning she meditated, trying to relinquish attachment or hope to an outcome that she had no control to determine. But the little nag of anxiety would not leave her. In theory, it all sounded wonderful. Hanna, Izzy, and Finn, all here together under one roof with the dazzle and excitement of Christmas for the children. But Hanna was not the easiest person to be closeted up with. Even if Ben did make it for New Year, he would be unable to leave the grimness of Afghanistan entirely behind him. He would still be locked in with his men, impatient of trivia, preoccupied, and often unapproachable. He would have an insatiable need to go off on his own, or to fish silently with Ian. He and Hanna would have to play out their difficulties here, in view of children and parents, and it wasn't ideal. Delphi knew that Ben wanted, with all his heart, to fly into a big happy family New Year with those he loved; for everything to be hunky-dory, for all to be well. But she was afraid that his expectations of himself, and his ability to cope with so much hope and good will, might not be sustainable.

When Ben phoned her there was a creeping disillusion in his voice she had never heard before. With Hanna so far away, in every sense, he wrote Delphi more blueys than he had for a long time. He had lost four soldiers to death or injury in a month and his distress was evident. He would write to her in the early hours of the morning when he came off guard duty.

Vivid letters of a world glimpsed through a Sangar window as he watched a red, dusty morning in Afghanistan begin; his binoculars scanning a deceptively bucolic scene while a heavy and light machine gun lay by his side.

Afghans are a beautiful warrior race, he wrote. *The men are striking, bearded, and angular. They ride to work early on their bicycles, eight to ten people on a tricycle, motorbike, even tractors. We have to keep a beady eye on what they carry. Even an innocent black umbrella needs closer scrutiny. In a way, guard duty is the most peaceful part of my day, as I get time to reflect . . .*

Finn, Delphi knew, also had high expectations of Christmas. It was obvious that he longed to see Izzy again and to have his parents together in this house, with her and Ian as safe referees. And Hanna, what were her plans now she was back in Finland? What decisions might Hanna have come to in Ben's absence? A brief New Year together was too short, and beautiful Hanna had the power to wound both Ben and Finn and deprive one little girl of growing up with a father and brother she adored . . .

Delphi stood up abruptly and lit a candle in front of her Buddha. She must stop these negative thoughts. They were affecting Ian, her work, her very being. Natural fear was one thing, giving in to morbid, self-defeating thoughts were quite another. The future was impossible to determine or predict and it was pointless of her to even try.

Finn lay in the dark as Raza and the other boys in the room slept.

On Remembrance Sunday in Germany the army church was always packed with people. A lone bugler would play 'The Last Post' and 'Reveille' from a balcony. It used to make him shiver. Everyone would go on to the mess for a Families Curry Lunch. It would last for hours. There would be a roaring log fire and they would stay on and play games with neighbouring families. Finn liked those lunches and the feeling of being part of something.

In the dark, after lights out, Finn would take himself back to the empty army quarter in Germany. He thought of the house just as they had left it, as it was when they all lived there. He walked through the rooms still full of their possessions. Full of the four of them who were no longer there. The fridge still had those stupid magnets on the door. Scattered mail lay on the kitchen table with the blue china salt and pepper and Izzy's colouring books.

The plants on the windowsill drooped, like they always did when they were away. The folding doors between the dining and sitting room lay open. The big dark table and heavy dining chairs lay one end. The silver regimental statue stood in the middle, with the silver candlestick that had once been Delphi's.

Silver and glass were still on the sideboard. Finn loved to see the table formally laid for dinner parties, glowing with silver cutlery and glass and candles, especially at Christmas.

Hanna could make the house look like fairyland. In

188

Finland they put ice candles on the top of gateways so people could find their way home in the winter. She used to put them on their gatepost and light them and everyone would stop and admire their flickering light.

Finn wandered through the house in his head noticing things he never bothered about when he lived there. The sitting room always had to be tidy in case people came, but behind the sofa was a plastic box of Izzy's toys and dolls. The sofa and chairs were not army furniture. They were Hanna's choice, Scandinavian and made of light wood. The sitting room and the dining room always looked as if they belonged to two different worlds. Hanna's world. Ben's world.

Finn floated himself upstairs and down the long corridor. Hanna and Ben's room. He looked through the door. The bed was neatly made. Hanna had left small pots of stuff on her dressing table. The wardrobe was slightly open, and Finn could see the edge of her red dress, the one he really liked. The one that made Ben say 'Wow!' when she wore it. The edge of her red dress made him sad. Would she come back for it? Ben's cufflinks and his old gold watch were still there on the chest of drawers. Finn closed the door and crossed the landing into Izzy's room.

It was as if she had left the room for just a minute. Toys and dolls were scattered across the floor. Her bed lay crumpled from her sitting and jumping on it. The fairy lights round her bed were still lit. Her doll's house lay open and her tiny towelling dressing gown still hung on a hook on the door. Finn could hear the sound of her laughing, smell her hair and the baby soap on her skin . . .

He had a powerful feeling that if he could only concentrate hard on everyone being back in this house, he could change things back to how they once were.

He walked slowly to his own room and stopped at the

door. For some reason he was afraid to go in. His bed, his desk, his books and games lay just as he'd left them. Finn stood looking in, longing to step inside and be the boy who lived here with Ben and Hanna and Izzy. But he could not take himself over the threshold. His imagination refused to let him back. Like in a dream, when your legs are moving but you are staying in the same place. Finn, troubled, half dreaming, believed that if he moved back inside his room in that silent and empty army quarter, he might be trapped there alone in a time that had passed. He would cease to be the Finn he was now, lying next to Raz in this bed in a school dormitory.

Raza was not sleeping either. He was listening to Finn toss and turn. Finn had come back to school unusually quiet. He had not joined in with the Sunday evening chat and toast and hot cocoa with Mr and Mrs Dominic. Raza saw Finn was sad, but he did not know how to best comfort him. Finn was away somewhere in his head with his Baba. Raza knew what that felt like. He sat up and felt for the huge shawl Zamir had given him that lay over his bed. He padded across the cold floor and placed it like an eiderdown gently over Finn, smoothing it over him. Finn stopped tossing and turning and was still. Raza kept his hand for a moment on Finn's shoulder, then went back to bed and lay in the dark listening out for Finn until he heard him breathing deeply in sleep.

Ian lay on his back listening to Delphi moving about in her studio above him. He wished he could say, 'Come on, old thing, everything's going to be fine.' But he could not. Ian did not believe in any particular god, certainly not the humourless, thunderous, droning Scottish Presbyterian God of his childhood. He had not however ruled out some higher power akin to Delphi's belief in Karma.

However, benign detachment from situations you had no power to influence seemed difficult to sustain full time. Certainly, that wonderful trust and calm that usually lit up Delphi's world and infused her paintings was failing her at the moment.

He alone knew Delphi's early battles with stark fear that turned into depression. She had been a much loved, joyous child. Her colonial childhood in India had been snatched away by the brutal murder of her father. Everything in Delphi's benign, safe, and happy life ended abruptly. Within its seamless security her father had been hacked to death by a loved and long-serving member of the household. There was no safety anywhere, so a traumatized Delphi, sent off to a cold English boarding school, slowly discarded all remnants of a middle-class existence that had betrayed her. She resolved to leap into the unknown. The worst thing possible had happened. She had nothing more to fear or to lose.

She became the charismatic art student rebel. Outrageous and popular. Careless of any consequences of her actions, she found herself pregnant by a man she hardly knew. A kind and decent lecturer called Alastair Benn. He had supported her emotionally and financially but had died of cancer ten months after Ben was born.

In the dark of Remembrance Sunday, Ian sighed. He had been Alastair's GP. This was how he had met Delphi. He watched and loved her from a distance, living the rackety life of a gypsy, trailing Ben behind her, until he could bear it no longer. He had no illusions. He offered Delphi a home for Ben and a love that did not have to be returned. Delphi accepted. Ian was a good friend and she needed stability for her child . . .

Ian sat up and put the bedside light on. He thought he would go and make Delphi tea and take it up. He did not want to dwell on those first years with her, they had been hell. But he and Ben had formed an unbreakable bond. A deep love and trust that had never faltered. This had taken longer with Delphi. He had almost given up. But it had come together, their life, it had all come together in the end. Ian held onto the bannister as he went downstairs. He still needed to protect Delphi as he had when she was a young art student. He still wanted to keep Ben safe, and he could do neither of these things. All he could do was be there.

Delphi, up in her studio, listened to Ian going downstairs. She knew he would make her tea. His steps were heavy and careful on the steep stairs. A feeling of overwhelming love hit Delphi. Ian was nearly 80, fifteen years older than her. How diminished her life would be without him. Her love. Her beloved rock.

She had married the hard-working, gentle Scottish doctor for all the wrong reasons. Security, a safe roof for her and Ben. The knowledge that Ian was a good man. She had felt soothed by the lilting accent of the Western Isles. She had never deserved him. She had treated him so badly, that even now, it physically hurt to remember.

She had taken so carelessly all Ian had offered her. Then, feeling like a butterfly with clipped wings, she would take off with other artists to paint, to sleep around, tempting and goading Ian into leaving her.

Ian remained steadfast. Ben needed him. For years he endured Delphi's selfishness and neglectful parenting. He had known that she had never wanted a cosy, safe, existence, but he had thought motherhood might tame her relentless search for danger and an alternative lifestyle. For something always just beyond her reach.

One day after a particularly long absence of weeks,

Delphi came home and found the house empty. Ian had taken Ben away to Scotland for the summer. Delphi had not even realized it was the summer holidays. She wandered through the rooms and saw how ordered they were. Ben's clothes neatly folded on his chair. The house clean. Her studio untouched as she insisted. She looked at the calendar and saw the date in July circled, a little smiley face on the top. *Fishing holiday for Ian and Ben.* This time there was no note telling her there was food in the freezer. No telephone number where she could contact him and Ben.

Delphi had opened the French windows to sunlight that felt abruptly feverish. The house behind her lay still and empty. She could smell a stranger on her clothes and felt a terrible rush of hot shame.

She thought of Ian, an overworked GP, driving all the way to Scotland with *her* son so that they could have a summer holiday, and she, his mother, had no idea where they were. She knew with a sickening jolt that Ian had come to the end of his endurance. He had had enough.

Delphi was immobilized by her terror of losing him, of losing them both. She knew that Ian's rare ability to love her without judgement had been because he wanted to keep her somewhere in his life. He had promised her freedom to be herself within their marriage and she had abused it. He had finally realized she was not going to change; he was just giving her permission to carry on a feckless lifestyle.

Delphi sat for hours on the step long after the sun had gone. She understood for the first time all that Ian had so generously given her and Ben. Unconditional and unwavering love. She felt sick at the thought of what she had thrown away. All that she had lost. She did not think she could face life without him, the prospect terrified her. He was the only person who recognized the frightened child in her, terrified of letting happiness in, in case it was snatched away. Ian had been patiently waiting for her to grow up and she had refused to. On the cold stone step Delphi recognized what love meant. She did not think she had ever, once, told Ian she loved him.

She found them, her husband and child, huddled by a cold river near Fife, singing to keep warm. She called out and they turned as one, their faces lighting up her life . . .

Delphi began to search for a religion, a belief, that would change her self-absorption but would give her freedom to explore another way of living, a renewed trust in the order of things, a strength that would protect her from the random, the sudden and the brutal, or at least the acceptance of these things. She chose Buddhism; turned and viewed her life from an altered perspective, fought for a form of happiness each and every day. Because of Ian and Ben, she began to believe in herself and paint seriously.

Delphi became a woman with a natural instinct to make people happy, but it had been hard won. Ian was often, jokingly, referred to by their friends as hen-pecked, unable to get a word in edgeways. She was perceived as the strong character, yet without Ian, she knew she would have wobbled her way through life. Ian was the quiet centre of her and Ben's world. He was the rock on which they had built their lives.

A thought hit Delphi with some force. She had once been as selfish as Hanna. Self-centred Hanna, selfishly leaving Ben and her family when they had most need of her. Knowing she was inflicting hurt and doing it anyway. It was a shock for Delphi to recognize that she and Hanna were not so different. She too had been monstrously selfish and self-absorbed when Ben had been a little boy. How could she gauge the harm she herself had done? Perhaps Ben had married the cool and distant Hanna because her unavailability was familiar and resonated with him from childhood.

As Delphi sat cross-legged before her Buddha, she pushed these thoughts away and listened to the faint thrum of the sea. Of Ian slowly coming back up the stairs to her. She caught sight of her painting of birds and saw immediately what was missing. There was no sense of flight or joy. No fluidity of movement or essence of life. All the positive energy people loved in her work was missing. She would have to begin again, fill the canvas with life and hope. She must capture her imaginary birds, wings spread to the light, flying free and safe into the eternal blue of the unknown.

CHAPTER THIRTY-SEVEN

Raza took up running, partly to keep warm and partly for the peace it bought him. On sports afternoons, he took the path through the school grounds, down to the bottom gate that led across fields.

After a few miles he reached an inlet or small creek. In winter there were only a few people walking dogs. He liked the dank, still water and the dripping, leafless trees. He liked the feeling of age and stillness and the huge heron birds that erupted out of small trees to stand patiently on one leg in the mud. Curlews warbled over the mudflats and stabbed with their small, curved beaks.

Running helped Raza think. He knew that in three years he had changed, and he was sometimes afraid of the thoughts that came sliding into his head. Baba had always been his compass and Raza wondered if his constantly changing views on this new life made him a bad Muslim.

Chinir and Sarah were not devout. They prayed randomly, celebrated Eid and mostly kept to Ramadan. They would not have understood his fear of becoming westernized or his guilt about thoroughly enjoying the luxuries that had come to him.

196

The school in London had taught him about being an outsider. Despite, or perhaps because of a large Asian population, he had quickly picked up the undercurrent of prejudice that ran through Britain. It had been useful because it prepared him for boys like Chatto, who muttered 'little Taliban' at him whenever they passed in the corridors.

Friends of Chatto would sometimes call him 'LT' but without real malice. More of a trying to be clever catchphrase, though never in front of Finn.

It was nothing to the taunts Raza had had to endure in London and he saw, with surprise that many boys in this boarding school had to put up with rude nicknames and it did not seem to offend anyone's honour.

Finn's friends had taken Raza into their circle in a casual, accepting way, without question. They had not been particularly curious about his way of life in Pakistan until after he had read his essay out in class. His story had triggered a curiosity about his country and an interest in the tribes Raza had written about. That he was a *Pashtun*, spoke Pashto, not Urdu and came from the Swat Valley in the North-West Frontier, dangerously close to the borders with Afghanistan fascinated his classmates. These were the names and the regions they saw on the news and in the papers.

Mr Dominic had shown them a large map of all the different states in Pakistan. He asked Raza if he could explain where the vanished tribes had originated from. David Chatto had immediately stabbed his finger up on the North-West Frontier. 'Taliban Country, isn't it, sir? This is where my father says the insurgents flow across the border into Afghanistan to kill and mutilate British and American soldiers and the Pakistani government just turn a blind eye . . .'

The class had shuffled in front of the map in embarrassment. Their eyes slanted away from Raza. To Raza it had seemed a long silence, but Mr Dominic said, eyeing Chatto coldly, and pointing at the map, 'As I understand it, Chatto, up in the Northern Province, thousands and thousands of people fled *from* the Taliban down into the cities to safety. They were displaced and forced to live on the streets unless they had relatives or family to help them. From what I have read, the Pakistani military now consider it safe for people to filter back to their homes in the north, but many will never go back to their lands because of their fear of the Taliban. Am I right, Raza?'

'You are very right, sir. Many of our villages lie empty. Many people they have long gone to cities. My father, he stay,' Raza said, feeling a great surge of gratitude and respect for Mr Dominic.

Running along the empty creeks, with the eerie cries of strange birds reminded Raza a little of the lake rising up from his mountains at home. The peace of still water.

'Are you homesick?' Finn had asked. 'I'll run with you if you like.'

Raza had placed his hand across his chest. 'Thank you. I think I will run with my thoughts in this peaceful place to make senses of things.'

'Okay,' Finn had said. 'Cool.'

As Raza ran along the muddy path, he thought what troubled him most was the one thing he could never talk to Finn about. Three years ago, when his father had made him leave Pakistan, Raza had only one aim, to return to his village and continue his life as if there had been no interruption. He would find Ajeet and Fakir and go with them to fight. He would resume a life he had always intended to follow.

In the London school he had fed his secret anger of boys who taunted him and of older girls who were immodest and loud. He had hated everything about England, although he liked and respected Sarah and Chinir. But when Liyana and Daniyal had taken him to stay in their house in Derby in the school holidays, he had learned to love them. Like grandparents, they generously gave him their time and when he was with them, he relaxed and felt secure. He never stopped longing for Baba and home. But slowly, through study and quiet places in parks, libraries, and museums, he discovered an escape and an appetite to learn. As his English improved, he discovered a love of reading English books. He became conscious of the small kindnesses of good people. He discovered ball games, the cinema, the Internet. Toast.

When he was interviewed for a scholarship to the small Cornish school, he was surprised to find the teachers genuinely interested in him. They congratulated him on his English and were amazed at all he had achieved in a short time. When he was awarded a scholarship, it had made him feel proud, but best of all he had made his Baba so proud that he had travelled to Peshawar just to talk to him on a computer.

There was an order and discipline that Raza understood in this Cornish school. The classes were smaller. The teachers were welcoming. But it was the moment he met Finn that Raza's world was changed by friendship. For the first time since he arrived in England, his life seemed to have a meaning and spring open in a way he never dreamed possible. He loved and felt comfortable with Finn's grandparents. He was accepted by Finn's friends. They all called him Raz. Raz, a self he hardly recognized, but rather liked.

There would always be boys like David Chatto. He must ignore them. Yet, he felt shame for the instinct Chatto had for his lie. For is not silence a lie? If he had spoken up in that classroom, told everyone that Fakir and Ajeet, his two brothers, were indeed both Talibs, what then could Mr Dominic have said?

He might also have added that he too would probably be fighting with the Talibs, if Baba had not sent him to the UK. His words would have been the truth, but it was also true that Baba was made angry by his elder sons and loathed the way they lived their lives.

To the undulating call of seabirds, Raza remembered that Fakir was dead. He realized how influenced he had been by the brothers he hero-worshipped. He could still hear their voices in his head. *Raza, do not listen to an old man talking. Baba was a proud fighter like us when he was younger man. He grows senile* . . .

Raza had seen Finn writing thin blue letters to his Baba in Afghanistan. He had seen his face light up when he spoke to his father on the phone. He had seen the photo of a smiling man in uniform on Finn's computer, and in the silver photograph frames in the grandparents' house.

These grandparents were the kindest people Raza had ever met and he could never feel proud that Ajeet and Fakir were making bombs and killing soldiers like Finn's Baba.

Raza was troubled that he could never tell Finn the truth. He felt his lack of honour like a huge weight upon him. He had begun to read articles, online, written by academic, informed Pakistanis, writing about their own country with brutal honesty. He googled sites on Pakistan politics and history, and he began to realize what a wise man his father was.

He, Raza, had been ignorant of everything except a love of guns and make-believe. His only excuse was that he had been a small boy at that time. Yet he felt conflicted; he still loved his brothers, and he was afraid of becoming a bad Muslim who would forget his prayers and his own ways, in this new world he was beginning to fit into.

His loyalty and honour should lie with his own family, his own country, and his brothers. Yet, Finn, with whom he could talk about many things, felt more of a brother to him now than Ajeet and Fakir.

Raza could not remember any conversation with them that did not include hatred for the west or guns and stories of killings. Like a veil lifting, he now saw them for what they were: uneducated men. This made him sad and guilty. It felt a terrible betrayal. It made his heart thump with pain.

Raza resolved to write to Baba of his troubled thoughts. His father's beliefs had changed in his lifetime too. He had lost faith in *Jihad*, in relentless violence, but he was vehemently against the automatic right of foreigners to invade Afghanistan or meddle in countries that did not belong to them.

Was his friendship with Finn, a western boy, a non-Muslim, whose father was fighting with the invaders, a betrayal? Raza knew it was not. Finn was the most honourable boy he had ever met. He increased his pace. He would stop thinking now and concentrate only on running. On his feet moving over the damp path and his breath pumping out air against the backdrop of birds calling one to another across the mudflats.

CHAPTER THIRTY-EIGHT

Christmas lights were beginning to spring up all over town, but the weather was grey and oppressive. The Christmas term slid to an end.

After two weeks of silence Finn was relieved to hear from Ben. There had been a surge of soldiers killed or injured in an increased use of IED attacks on British Forces. The immediate news blackout, until relatives could be informed, always unnerved Finn.

One Sunday evening Raza, Finn, Peter Chan, and Isa Okafor, who had finally returned from Abuja at half-term, were in Ed Dominic's sitting room watching television, when there was a sudden news flash.

Two soldiers had been killed and four injured by a roadside bomb while out on patrol in Lashkar Gah. One of the dead men was thought to be an officer although this had still to be verified.

Finn froze, felt sick. It would be hours before the names of the dead and injured would be announced. Mercy snapped the television off and knelt beside him.

'Finn? Look at me. If your dad had been involved in that incident, we would have heard before the news flash . . .'

Watching Finn's face drain of colour, Mercy took his icy fingers between her own, far from sure of this. Ed said, reaching for the house phone. 'Finn, let's ring your grandparents . . .'

At that moment the phone in his hand rang. It was Delphi. Someone from the regiment had managed to contact Hanna in the seconds before the news blackout. 'Ben is shocked but unhurt. Please tell his family . . .'

Delphi sounded shaky. 'Ed? Ben must have been out on that patrol with his soldiers, but I would rather Finn did not know that at the moment. I think things are grim out there right now. I just wanted to tell him Ben is safe, and I'd be grateful if you could keep him away from the television . . . if you can . . .'

'Delphi, of course,' Ed Dominic said. 'All of the above. I'll hand you to Finn.'

'Thank you.'

But Finn heard the tremble in Delphi's voice when she reassured him Ben was safe. It increased his anxiety. 'Delphi, do you know if the soldiers were from our regiment? On the news it said a cavalry regiment. Were they Ben's soldiers?'

'I don't know, darling, but I think they probably were . . .' Delphi lied.

'You're sure Ben's all right?'

'I'm absolutely sure, Finn. He specifically wanted to reassure us.'

Finn shivered, wondering who had died on that patrol. Which of their neighbours on the patch in Germany would have to go through the dreaded knock on the door. 'If any of his soldiers died, Ben will be gutted, Delphi,' he whispered. 'We all know each other.'

'I know, darling. I know. It's horrible, but everyone in the regiment will support each other . . . try not to dwell.

Let's keep busy. Christmas soon, and then Ben will be back with us for New Year.'

Mercy made hot chocolate for everyone and Finn's friends sat trying to comfort and distract him. Ed was impressed by the kindness and maturity of the boys. They were careful of the words they used to reassure Finn. Not one of them muttered clichés.

Iso said, 'When there was a coup by government rebels at home in Abuja my father was arrested by the opposition. I thought he was going to be killed. It is a very bad feeling, but my father was okay, Finn. He was frightened. I was very frightened, but he was okay.'

'My grandfather,' Peter Chan said, 'thinks that nobody learns from history anymore. There are some places on this earth no one can conquer . . .'

He glanced at Raza. Raza was so much one of them now that they tended to forget he might have a totally different view. 'What do you think, Raz?'

Raza had been aware of Finn's anxiety all term. As the numbers of soldiers killed in Afghanistan grew, so had Finn's fear for his Baba.

'It is very bad when soldiers and Afghan people die,' he said cautiously. 'When American and British government send soldiers to Muslim countries, Muslims want to defend his country from foreign invasion. Many Afghan peoples do not like Taliban, but many do not trust foreign soldiers either. They think they bring more troubles and violence. Ordinary peoples are caught in middle. Foreign soldiers, they invade Afghanistan, and then they leave, they go back to their own countries. But problems in country do not leave with them . . . Ordinary peoples who help or work for foreign forces, even if to do good, they are punished by Taliban, they can never live safe again . . .'

Raza looked at Finn, his face anxious. 'This is what I

think, but I am very sorry for death of British soldiers who go to help Afghan people fight against Talibs . . .'

Finn said, 'It's okay, Raz. I'm not convinced our soldiers should be in Afghanistan either, but the Afghan army are being trained for when the British and Americans pull out, you know. My dad says that the Afghan government would actually like us to remain longer, because of the Taliban . . .'

Finn glanced at Mr Dominic, who had sat down and was listening.

'At home in Germany, our regiment collects money so schools in Afghanistan can re-open, and the Royal Engineers, they are, like, building water stations and bridges over rivers to connect people who are cut off in isolated communities. My dad says they are trying to help make life for Afghans suffering under the Taliban, like, better, you know . . . especially for women and girls.'

He looked at Raza's face, 'Maybe, you think that it's not really possible for soldiers to change anything in Afghanistan. I wish my dad wasn't out there fighting the Taliban, but I'm proud that he is.'

Raza looked at Finn with his vivid green eyes, trying to find the right words. 'It is not that Afghan people do not wish for progress, Finn. It is that the Taliban have too much power to lose if you educate boys like me. If you build schools. If you give people voices and hope of better life, the Talibs will lose their power. I know nothing about politics before I come to Britain and read books, before I can use Internet. Before England, I only know what mullah preaches in mosque. What my Baba tells me . . . I do not fully understand how Islam religion can be used by ignorant men to ferment violence . . .'

Ed and Mercy Dominic were listening fascinated to this exchange between the boys. Ed had the feeling that Raza and Finn had had this sort of conversation before, and he was touched at the trust the two boys had built between them in so short a time.

Finn grinned. 'Educating boys like you, Raz, is a fearful thing. You're even brilliant at maths.'

'Yeah,' the other two groaned in agreement. 'You're even good at maths.'

Raza shook his head. 'No. It is my father who is clever. He want me educated, so I see with different eyes out of more than one window . . .'

'The trouble is all governments in the world have both eyes focused on what's in it for them,' Peter Chan said, portentously.

'Comes down to power again,' Iso said, yawning. 'Power and corruption.'

Ed Dominic laughed. He could see that Finn was slowly restored.

'I think we'll end this impressive philosophizing for tonight, boys. Bed, please. Mercy or I will be in to turn lights out in twenty-five minutes.'

Before the ten o'clock news came on Ed Dominic rang Delphi to reassure her that Finn had settled. Delphi had always seemed an ageless, joyful woman, but the years of worrying about Ben going off to violent places was beginning to take its toll. Hanna disappearing back to Finland and leaving Finn in Cornwall could not have helped either. He hugged Mercy suddenly, startling her. She laughed. 'What brought this on?'

'Just counting my blessings,' Ed said, kissing the top of her head.

CHAPTER THIRTY-NINE

Finn and Raza headed into town to do some Christmas shopping on the last Wednesday afternoon before school broke up. Raza was delighted as it was normally sports afternoon. He loathed sports afternoons on the freezing, windy, rugby pitch. He enjoyed ball games but not in this temperature. Not unless he was wrapped up in a huge shawl from nose to feet.

'Do Sarah and Chinir celebrate Christmas?' Finn asked as they headed for the centre. 'I don't mean the Christian side of it. I mean the food and present bit.'

Raza grinned. 'You joking? Pakistanis, they never miss a festival or chance of a party. Sarah and Chinir, they are British, remember. We have many decorations in the house and a big meal on the day of Christmas, but we do not eat the bird.'

'Turkey.'

'No, we do not have that. We go to Derby this year to Sarah's parents. They are very nice. Liyana, she teach . . . taught me English when I first come to England. Now, I must find Christmas presents for them. It is very hard.'

'Tell me about it!' Finn said.

Sarah and Chinir had driven over to the house in Penzance to pick up Raza one weekend after they had been to an engagement party of a colleague. Sarah had been wearing a stunning scarlet and gold *shalwar kameez* and Chinir an embroidered *sherwani* in heavy brocade.

Finn had stared, fascinated at a glimpse into Raza's exotic world. He thought Sarah amazing with her long, glossy hair and beautiful clothes.

'Normally, Sarah, she is wearing jeans,' Raza said, amused at Finn's open mouth. 'Or a white coat and spectacles. She does not go to hospital dressed in *shalwar kameez*.'

'I know that!' Finn said, embarrassed. 'But she looks a lot better than you in your *shalwar kameez*.'

He wondered what Raza must have thought about the clothes girls wore in England when he first arrived. At school it was still boys only, except for the sixth form. Finn had noticed that Raza seemed shy or uneasy around girls and never looked directly at them. Once, he had asked Raza how he had found having girls in the same class in his London school and Raza's face had closed. He had shrugged without answering.

In fact, Raza had been appalled at the way English girls showed their bodies when he first arrived. He had not expected them to be veiled or dressed like Pakistani women at home, but he was astonished that their fathers and brothers allowed them to show themselves in this way.

He was not a city boy or used to seeing many westerners and the ones he had seen had been mostly aid workers who dressed modestly. It had been a shock. Most of the Pakistani and Asian girls in his class in London had dressed modestly, but they behaved like the English girls they were. They challenged Raza contemptuously with their eyes, seeing his disdain and knowing instinctively that he stood for a way

208

of life their parents had left behind, but would still try to make them adhere to.

Chinir had told Raza he must take care to hide his feelings. Western women might not always dress modestly, but that did not mean they were immodest. He was living in a different culture here. In England it was not a sin to show your legs and arms or wear short skirts. Women liked to do that. They considered it their right. It did not mean they were bad or not respectable.

'But,' Raza asked, mystified, 'why do their husbands and fathers permit them to dress this way? Why do they allow it?'

'Come on, Raza,' Chinir had said, irritated by a glimpse of Raza's religious, circumscribed life. 'You must have watched films or TV in Peshawar. You know that western women do not dress like girls in north Pakistan, nor, indeed, like Muslim women in the cities who always carry a *dupatta* to cover themselves.'

Raza had been miserably silent. He had not watched films and TV except at Uncle Maldi's house in 'Pindi occasionally and they had been loud Indian musicals. Music had been forbidden by the Taliban in his village. In Peshawar he had glimpsed western news flashes and seen TV adverts through shop windows and on hoardings. Strange hybrid versions of women, advertising local products with American or English accents while dressed in *shalwar kameez*.

Zamir's family were devout, unlike Chinir. It was strange, Raza was sure that Zamir would never have allowed him to watch western movies, yet he had happily sent him to the west.

Sarah had understood. 'It's hard for you, Raza. I wish we'd had more time to prepare you for life here, but you have to understand England is very different from Pakistan. It is not a Muslim country. The same rules do not apply.

209

Women, in theory, are equal, treated the same way as a man. They are not required to hide themselves away. They are, more or less, free to dress as they please, and they do. Whether, as Muslims, we agree with it, is not the point. This is British culture, and we have to take the best of it and reject what we do not wish for ourselves . . .'

She had touched Raza's arm, wary. 'British people here are just as shocked by the fact that Pakistani girls are hidden away, veiled, forbidden education in many places, and then married off at fourteen to work like a beast for their husbands and in-laws for the rest of their lives. They find this just as disturbing as you do to see them airing their arms and legs . . .'

Raza had got up from the table and gone to his room. He had thrown himself in misery and confusion onto the bed. Baba had given him to these people. He, Raza, had travelled all this way with them to this country that Baba appeared to think was a nice place. He knew Sarah and Chinir were good people, but he also saw clearly that they did not condemn the ways of women here. He heard in Sarah's voice and the words she did not say that she did not agree with women staying hidden or veiled or under the protection of their fathers until marriage.

To Raza, in his first months in England, Sarah and Chinir were Pakistanis who lived in England. He could not accept that they were British, and Pakistanis of a different generation to his father. Their freedoms had been very different to his own.

Now, nearing his third Christmas in England, Raza, pushing through the crowds of Christmas shoppers with Finn, could smile at English girls and even joke with them occasionally. He did not meet their eyes, for he could not believe this was respectful, but he understood that the sexes mixed freely. He also saw that Finn and his school friends

210

were nearly as awkward and embarrassed around girls as he was.

'Oh God! I hate crowds,' Finn moaned. 'How many presents have you got to find?'

'Three. If you think this is a crowd, Finn, you should come to Peshawar at *Eid Al Adha*.'

'No, thanks,' Finn said, concentrating on Izzy's present because she was the easiest to buy for. They ended up in Waterstones poring over books they had no intention of buying. Peter Chan spotted them coming out. 'There you are! Come with me. We will go to my uncle's for tea. It will restore us.'

They ploughed their way through the Christmas shoppers to the Jasmine Restaurant where Teddy Chan, a jovial, bespectacled man, sat them at a corner table of the empty restaurant and brought them Jasmine tea and small bowls of left-over egg fried rice and spring rolls. Isa joined them, packages jutting out of his knapsack. 'I had to get seaside things to take back for my little sisters,' he said, collapsing.

'I thought you weren't going back to Nigeria for Christmas,' Finn said.

'Change of plan. Now I am flying with my mother to my aunt's house in Abuja, where my sisters stay. We are not going back to our home in Lagos. We hope my father can join us.'

Peter Chan smiled smugly. 'No shopping for me. Singapore has the best shopping in the world, so no point . . .'

Finn and Raza made a face at him, their mouths full of his uncle's fried rice.

Back at school Raza and Finn threw their packages on the bed.

'What will you do for the holiday?' Finn asked Raza.

'I will eat much. The house of my family will be full of Pakistani friends of Liyana and lonely people that she and

211

Danyial work with. Also, I think they make programme for a party. Chinir, he must come back to hospital for duty two days after Christmas Day. Liyana and Sarah, they will shop in Derby all day in the sales, and talk . . . talk . . . I will grow bored and read and study my English grammar and feel I am shut inside box . . .'

Finn laughed. 'Typical English Christmas then! Ring me when you're back in Cornwall.'

'You will be very busy with your father and your family.'

'Yeah, but I'd like you to meet my dad.'

'Thank you,' Raza said politely, unsure of this. His experience of the military in Pakistan had not made him want to spend time with them. 'Okay. I will ring you when I am back.'

'My dad is not a scary military man. My mother is more likely to scare you, actually.'

'Oh dear,' Raza said worriedly.

'I'm not serious, Raz.' Finn sat on the bed. 'Can you never go home for holidays, to see your father?'

Raza shook his head. 'My Baba, he tell me where we live is dangerous just now. Many people are getting kidnapped, sometimes killed. Also, it is much money to go home to Pakistan.'

'Can you Skype your father. See him that way?'

'My father does not have computer. I do not think about going home. Christmas is not Muslim festival, Finn. Indeed, at the house of Liyana and Danyial there will be much food and jollity.'

Finn laughed. 'You'll be fine, then. I'm going to check my emails to see if there is one from my dad . . .'

Finn fished his laptop out of his cupboard, trying to rein in his excitement. Ben had rung to say he was going to be home for Christmas after all. He had to attend a military defence conference in London on the twenty-ninth of December. 'Oh no!' He cried, staring at the screen.

'What?' Raza asked, startled.

'I've got a message from my dad. The weather's closed in. No planes can fly out of Afghanistan at the moment. Everyone's stuck, so the soldiers who should be flying back home on leave now, will have to fly out when my dad should be flying home, so he might not make it for Christmas Day, unless they increase the flights back to the UK . . .'

'It is winter in Afghanistan,' Raza told him. 'Weather is very bad this time of year, Finn. But it change quickly. Clouds open and shut. *Inshallah*, your Baba will get home in time. I will go and pray that you will all be together for your festival day.'

Alone, Finn sat and looked out of the window. The weather was closing in here as well, shutting the school in mist. Hanna and Izzy were arriving on the twenty-second of December, in one week's time. Finn wondered how he would bear Christmas if Ben did not make it home.

CHAPTER FORTY

There was a small window in the weather. Ben made it from Lashkar Gah to Camp Bastion on the twenty-first of December for the flight back to the UK the following morning. He prayed the weather would hold because he had fought for a seat on this particular aircraft. The weather held, but the ageing military aircraft did not. Before the trouble in the engine was fixed, Ben spent a long night in Dubai with hundreds of tired soldiers desperate to be home.

He landed at Brize Norton and dashed for a taxi to Reading to pick up the Cornish Riviera to Penzance. Delphi had sent him the train times but warned him there were limited trains over the Christmas period. In case he flew in too late for the last train on Christmas Eve, she had arranged for a driver to be on stand-by to drive Ben down to Penzance. Delphi was leaving nothing to chance, but at Paddington Ben managed to struggle onto a packed afternoon train to Penzance.

He was still in combats and rocking on his feet with exhaustion. He knew it was unlikely he would find anywhere to sit without having booked. He edged through the first carriage with his rucksack searching for a place. As soon as they saw his uniform people moved their coats and papers and looked around them to locate a spare seat. An old man ushered him into his seat by the window and moved into the next seat. Touched, Ben stowed his rucksack and collapsed into the seat gratefully.

Doors slammed, the train slid out of the station and Ben closed his eyes against the dizzying wave of people around him. Immediately he was back in Lashkar Gah, the dust blowing and sticking into every crease of his skin. He saw the curving shrine of names written on planks of wood; the small white crosses burnt behind his eyelids. He had five hours to concentrate on getting his head away from those images of death and blood and gore before he reached Penzance.

He opened his eyes and a young woman smiled at him and placed a cup of coffee in front of him. The youth opposite, sporting a *Help for Heroes* wristband, split his beer cans and handed Ben one with an embarrassed grin. The old man who had given him his seat, turned his paper and pushed it gently Ben's way.

Ben could not speak. He was overwhelmed by unexpected kindness. This normality, this sense of order, of being safe, felt surreal. Instilled guilt. He was back, but he could feel no excitement, just a wave of nothingness. He put his head back on the seat rest and looked out of the window at lush green fields and cattle. Dust itched his eyes and the inside of his combats. He felt dirty and unwashed and he had no idea what he looked like. The old man leaned towards him. 'Afghanistan?'

Ben nodded, praying he wasn't going to start asking questions. The man murmured. 'You rest. You look done in, son.'

Ben closed his eyes again and slept.

*

Hanna too was having trouble with her flights. She had planned to be in the UK by the nineteenth of December so she could be in Cornwall with Finn when Ben arrived the following day. When Ben told her that he would be delayed by weather she had changed her flight to the twenty-first. She could not stand too many days with Delphi on her own if Ben did not make it for Christmas.

Hanna's Finnair flight had then been delayed and she had endured hours at Helsinki Airport with a bored and over-excited 4-year old.

She missed her booked flight on to Newquay where Delphi was going to meet her and had to stay in London for the night. Eventually, she got on a flight to Newquay the following day, feeling tense and unprepared for a reunion with Finn or with Ben.

When she saw Finn's sweet, anxious face scanning everyone coming off the plane, searching for her and Izzy, Hanna felt the enormity of what she had done, what she had taken from him.

Izzy made a sound like a small bird, a cry of almost pain as she glimpsed Finn. She let go of Hanna's hand and flew at Finn, throwing herself up into his arms and clinging, crushing his neck with her arms.

Finn turned his back on Hanna and Delphi, holding Izzy tight to him. Neither spoke. They swayed together for a long time, eyes tightly closed, clutching each other, oblivious to all around them.

Delphi wanted to cry. Hanna had frozen. Delphi moved and kissed her on both cheeks. 'So glad you made it . . . my dear girl.'

She willed Finn to turn and greet Hanna. Her daughter-in-law looked as coolly beautiful as ever; but stricken. Eventually Finn turned and Hanna moved to kiss him. He lifted his flushed face to her, but he did not move his hands from his side.

'Right, darlings, come on. Ian is waiting with the car . . .'

Izzy slipped her hand into Delphi's and Delphi held it firmly. Izzy sighed and gave a cheerful little skip then a hop.

When Ben woke the train had reached Plymouth. All the people in the carriage had changed apart from the old man, who was sleeping. Ben listened to the rise and fall of inconsequential conversation going on around him. It drew him into the comfort of small concerns, trivia, shallow, familiar repetitions. He let the collective sound flow over him, needless words scattered like pointless confetti to pass a journey. He felt himself relaxing as he slowly came back down into his own world.

A different, middle-aged woman, sitting next to the old man said, 'I'm going for a cup of tea, love. Like one? You've slept a long time.'

Ben nodded gratefully, realizing how thirsty he was. He felt drugged with unaccustomed sleep and incapable of movement.

The old man woke, yawned and shook himself like a dog aroused from sleep. Ben wondered if he ought to do the same in an effort to banish torpor. The woman returned with his tea, refusing to let him pay her for it. She told him she had just been to Plymouth to see her daughter and son-in-law, who was in the Marines, so she knew what service life was like.

'On leave, love?' she asked.

'Yes. Just home for Christmas.'

'Where is home?' the old man asked.

'Penzance,' Ben said. The old man told him he used to have a picture-framing shop in the town for many years,

217

although he was now retired and living in Camborne with his daughter.

'I bet my mother knew you. She's an artist,' Ben said. 'Delphi Charles, but she paints under her family name, Tregonning.'

The old man' s face lit up. 'Delphi Tregonning! Of course, I know her, everyone does. Wonderful woman. Years ago, I used to frame all her paintings . . .' He peered at Ben. 'I met you when you were a little boy. How strange. You did seem somehow familiar.'

Ben laughed. How bizarre. How typically, beautifully Cornish to sit opposite someone who knew someone you knew, or were related to, or lived next door to, or went to school with.

When the woman left the train at Truro, Ben went and washed his hands and face. He stared in the mirror at his bloodshot eyes. *I am nearly home.*

The old man was getting out at Camborne. 'My daughter works in the town and this is where we share a house, but I miss Penzance. I miss walking on the prom. I miss watching the *Scillonian* sail to Scilly at exactly nine-twenty. Remember me to Delphi, won't you? Tell her Bill Rowe sends his regards.'

'I will,' Ben said. 'She'll be amused we met on the train. Thank you for your company, Bill.'

The old man smiled and gathered up his things and Ben got up to help him. 'I can manage, only a rucksack. You take care, son. You take care of yourself.' He held out his hand. 'Happy Christmas.'

'Happy Christmas, Bill . . .'

The train was almost empty, the carriage silent. Black sea glinted on his left. St Michael's Mount rose up, lights in the castle dulled by mist. The train slid into Penzance station. On the platform a group of familiar figures stood, the smallest one in pink. Their hair blew about in a stiff wind from the sea. All eyes were riveted on the train. Waiting for him.

CHAPTER FORTY-ONE

Finn's Diary

Delphi has really gone mad with the decorations this Christmas. The whole house looks lush, but my room, the one I'm sharing with Izzy, looks like fairyland. It's way over the top and I'm glad no one at school can see it! I helped Delphi fix the fairy lights over the window when I broke up from school. Delphi made a sort of canopy of silver stars on midnight blue over Izzy's bed and she even painted one of the walls with small pink fairies.

Ian and I picked a tree last weekend. We always have one with roots on and it's got a really nice shape. We decorated the upper branches but left the lower ones for Izzy to do. Decorating the tree is the one thing I can't bear to miss, even if I am too old, really.

When Hanna and Izzy arrived, we took Izzy upstairs and made her close her eyes until we were in the bedroom. Her mouth fell open and her eyes bulged with astonishment. For once she could not speak! She just circled the room in wonder taking everything in.

For a moment I thought Delphi might cry. I think it's because Izzy won't be little forever. She will stop believing in Father Christmas and then things will never be quite so magical again. Although, if anyone can make us believe in fairies, it is Delphi.

When Delphi and Izzy were examining the luminous silver stars over the bed, I saw Hanna's face. She looked suddenly cross, like she does when Delphi has gone over the top. Then she quickly smiled and said, 'Goodness, this is . . . amazing, Delphi. You have worked your usual magic. What do you say, Izzy?'

'I don't want a thank you. Just enjoy, darling,' Delphi said as Izzy hugged her in a tired, grateful way.

Delphi has put Ben and Hanna on the top floor, in the room next to her studio, the place she sleeps when she is painting, or she does not want to disturb Ian. She told Hanna that she and Ben would have a bit more private space at the top of the house. It won't be so easy for Izzy to jump into their bed in the morning, anyway.

I keep thinking of Hanna standing among the fairy lights. Was it like, because she did not want Izzy to be happy here, when Hanna probably wants to stay in Finland forever and make her life there? I'm trying not to think about it because it's Christmas.

When we were all waiting for the London train to come into the station with Ben, Hanna took my hand. I could feel she was shaking. I held her hand tight and we did not say anything, but it felt okay. Then suddenly the train was in the distance all lit up, and I felt really excited, but also terrified my dad would not be on that train. But he was. Ben jumped out in his combats and huge kitbag and it was like he had never been away. Izzy and I pelted down the platform

221

yelling like lunatics and Ben scooped us both up. Yep, me too! People getting off the train laughed and called out. 'Have a wonderful Christmas!' Then Ben put us down. He reached out for Hanna and she ran and hugged him, and I wanted to cry with a great happiness and relief. A crowd of men, who were probably a bit drunk, cheered and wolf-whistled, and we all laughed, but I was a bit embarrassed. Then Ben hugged Delphi and I saw him close his eyes for a moment because he had made it home.

CHAPTER FORTY-TWO

Finn's Diary

Christmas Eve

Today we have all been busy with present wrapping and shopping, collecting the turkey and carting loads of vegetables and drink into the house. Ben was up early. He insisted upon going off on his own to the shops to buy us all presents, even though we told him not to bother. Hanna and Delphi told him they had Christmas shopped for him, but he said that even Penzance was exciting after Helmand Province.

But, later, as I bicycled to get something for Delphi, I saw him on the prom, just leaning over the rail watching the sea. He wasn't shopping at all, so I guess he just wanted to be on his own. When I asked Ian if he thought Ben was okay, he said that he was just getting his bearings. Finding a compass point. That what's important to you changes when you see people killed or injured. Like, here we all are, busy getting ready to celebrate, and Ben's thoughts are still with

*his soldiers who died, with their families, because their
Christmases will never be the same again. Ian told me
to give Ben time to ease back to our world.*

*What Ian says is true. I am writing this on Christmas
Eve on my bed by the light of hundreds of fairy lights.
It is like being trapped in a fairy grotto. I am going
to turn them out in a minute, or I won't get to sleep.
Izzy is asleep, at last. I can now give Ben the signal
for Father Christmas as he is dying to go to bed.*

*Tonight was good. It was really Christmassy. Hanna
and Ben seemed happy and I saw them holding hands.
Then they went off with Ian to Midnight Mass at ten
o'clock. I've signalled Ben, now I've got to pretend
to be asleep too because I still get a stocking and it's
childishly fun to squint at my dad in his red hood
and feel the rustle of crackers by my feet at the end
of the bed. Tomorrow is going to be the best Christmas
ever.*

*

Hanna breathed deeply as they walked to church through
the town. The smell of the sea was reassuring, briny, wild
and uncontained. It felt guiltily good to be out of that warm,
beautifully decorated, claustrophobic house for a while. Pubs
were overflowing and parties of the underdressed and silly,
still benign, fell out of pub doorways. She felt Ben beside
her, smiling; saw he was beginning to relax. She had been
shocked at his weight loss, at the stress etched into his face.
She had a glimpse of how he would look when he was older,
when the lines were permanently etched in that familiar,
attractive face. That easy smile of his was not so quick to
come, nor was his attention so fixed on her or the children
or Delphi. She knew that a piece of Ben was still in Lashkar

Gah with his soldiers. Hanna wondered if Christmas might have been easier for him if he had stayed with 'his boys'. Family Christmases had so many expectations. It was often the exchange of irreverent banter and crude humour that got men through a rough tour; the familiarity of staying in army combats, the shelter of an army base; church services conducted by a military padre who had comforted and buried their mates. *Getting their heads down. Getting on with it,* had a strong pull against fatigue, and the demands of trying to seem normal and jolly with families at home.

Away from pressure from an outside world that male bonding held men in as firm a grip of fellowship, loyalty, and pride as family. Sometimes, more so. Hanna knew to her cost. When men were in war zones the regiment replaced family. Wives shimmered on the outside of a bond they could neither compete with, nor wholly understand. Soldiers experienced horror together and that was exclusive. With his fellow officers Ben did not have to explain his moods. Men drank together to forget, not to be convivial.

Hanna, escaping from an army environment for the first time in thirteen years, felt as if blinds had fallen from her eyes; she was suddenly an outsider looking in. In Helsinki, with Izzy, away from the apron of army life, she had, at times, felt vulnerable and unprotected. There was no telephone number to ring if something went wrong. No umbrella of a department. No officer on duty to talk to if Ben was away. No medical centre where you knew the doctor by first name.

This flash of understanding of her subconscious dependency made Hanna furious with herself, as if somehow, she had let herself become infantilized. It was ironic, if illuminating. She had wanted to flee from that dark army quarter and her circumscribed military life, only to find that life had melded itself securely around her like a safety belt without her realizing. Within it, she had often felt an outsider. Outside it, she felt the insecurity and loneliness of the real world.

Ian, Hanna and Ben walked up the steps and entered the candlelit church. Hanna sat between them as the pews rapidly filled up. Ian moved away to speak to someone, and Ben picked up Hanna's hand.

'Okay?' he asked.

'Yes. What about you?'

'I'm fine, Han. I do realize Christmas at Delphi's can make you claustrophobic.'

'Delphi has waved a magic wand and created fairyland for the kids. I feel grateful to her, Ben. You and I cannot do this for them at the moment and it is exactly what they need.'

Ben looked down at her. Hanna had changed in some indefinable way in the time they had been apart, but Ben could not say what it was that was different. He smiled. 'Maybe we too need Delphi's magical Christmas. There's something intensely comforting in seeing all the little traditions still going on at home year in year out. All the ancient decorations coming out . . .'

Hanna squeezed his hand. 'Happy then?'

'I am,' Ben said as the choir filed in behind the vicar. Hanna relaxed. Ben was in the right place, after all. She felt relief, for she would not have returned to spend Christmas with him in Germany. She could not bear to go back. Not ever. The thought of it filled her with the terrible, suffocating grey ennui that had coloured her days in that quarter.

Hanna sat in the packed church between Ben and Ian and felt a fleeting wistfulness for what might have been, for what they might have had together, if he had not been in the army. She closed her eyes. If she had not been attracted to Ben's uniform and a need to put Kai out of her mind

226

she would not be here now. *She would not have Finn and Izzy.* She shivered. She could never regret her children.

Beside her, Ben and Ian sang familiar carols and Hanna had a flash, a fleeting glimpse in her mind's eye, of the photograph of herself, on Ben's desk, being torn slowly down the middle with a little ripping sound.

Feeling the warmth of Ben's arm touching hers, Hanna felt the old sexual pull of his sheer physicality. She thought back to their first meeting. She had been drinking wine by the Serpentine with Annalisa, when Ben and an army friend asked if they could share their table. It was an early evening in summer and the café was packed.

Ben had been based in north London. Hanna was in London for six months, banished by Kai to help his sister, Annalisa, set up a branch of their interior design business. Minimalist Scandinavian interiors had been all the rage at the time. Despite her wounded heart, Hanna was having a great time advising the wealthy on how to update the inside of their houses.

Ben couldn't take his eyes off her and Hanna had been amused. He was tall, fit, and attractive, but not really her usual type. She liked her men Bohemian and arty, but there was an electric sexual chemistry between them. Hanna had no doubt they would end up in bed together.

She set out to seduce an already smitten Ben. Hanna knew that he would probably not have slept with her on their first meeting. She had made all the running. They had gone to bed that Friday evening and hardly left until Sunday lunchtime when Ben was on duty. Hanna was surprised how good sex was with him. She had only heard derogatory stories about English men.

In the next few weeks while she was having fun and a little distraction, Ben had been falling in love with her. He told her he had to keep pinching himself. He was an uncomplicated, happy man, the military had great parties and she and Annalisa had been impressed, but she had never intended to end up with him . . .

Ian leant towards her and whispered, 'I'm surprised the candles don't ignite the alcohol fumes wafting around this church, aren't you?'

Hanna laughed and as she sang a carol, she remembered how shamefully she had behaved when Ben had driven her down to Cornwall to meet his parents for the first time. Ben's excitement in wanting to show her where he had grown up and spent his youth surfing had piqued her interest.

She had not been in the least interested in his parents, did not want to get that involved. But she had needed to get out of London, swim in the sea, walk by water again.

Hanna had found Delphi interesting and not at all how she had imagined. She liked Delphi's paintings, recognized her talent, but found her overpowering. Too effortlessly courteous, too English, too interested in her and in Ben, her only child. Ian, the quiet husband she liked a lot, but their large, cluttered, three-storied Cornish house made her feel trapped. Hanna had slipped away without telling anyone, walking on her own on the prom, swimming in her underclothes from the sea wall, leaving Ben to make excuses for her rudeness.

The truth was, she could not be bothered to be polite. She would never see them again, so she did not see why she should subject herself to Delphi's scrutiny. She cared little if Ben's parents approved of her or not. She had rung Kai's home number from the prom, and he had been furious. 'Hanna, you really don't care who you hurt, do you? Grow up. Face life as it is. I love you, but I won't hurt Sigrid again. Before I was married, you didn't want me. You decided you were too young and buggered off travelling. I married Sigrid, who did want me. I was wrong to let you come and work for me. I was wrong to sleep with you. You and I are not going to happen, Hanna, it is too late. Sigrid is pregnant again and my life is with her . . .'

Ben had driven her back to London in a stony and angry silence. Hanna, miserable and stung by the finality of Kai's words, knew she had stepped over a line, broken a social code. He had wanted his parents to like her and instead he had subjected them to her bewildering rudeness.

Ben had gone off on some army course without ringing her. Perversely, or perhaps, because of Kai's brush-off, Hanna found she missed him. 'Don't fuck him about,' Annalisa told her. 'Ben's a nice guy, why hurt him? You're hardly a camp follower. Your affair with him has no future. Sleep around with someone else, Hanna. Preferably with someone who doesn't give a damn, like you . . .'

But Hanna had rung Ben and apologized for her behaviour and asked if they could meet. She told him about Kai, confessed she was on the rebound, asked if they could still be friends. Ben had laughed politely and said no, he didn't think so. He flew off to the Congo with the UN.

Hanna, reading how volatile the country was, sent him postcards with pictures of London or Helsinki to his regiment. She signed each one, *Your friend, Hanna* and hoped they reached him.

If she had taken Annalisa's advice, she would not be sitting here in this candlelit church, hurting Ben once again.

Coming out into the cold air, Hanna surprised both Ian and Ben by taking their arms as they walked home. She felt abruptly grateful that her children were together tonight, sleeping in a warm, safe house waiting for Father Christmas in Delphi's Fairyland.

Delphi breathed deeply in her kitchen and fought exhaustion. Finn and Izzy were upstairs. They had been wrapping presents together, but now the giggling and running about had stopped, and Delphi hoped Izzy was finally asleep. She poured herself a glass of wine and opened her front door and gazed out at the sea glinting in front of her, lit by the string of lights along the prom. The pubs were emptying, and bursts of drunken laughter issued out into the night air.

Delphi breathed in the raw dampness. She let the rare moment of being alone settle in a form of thanks. They were all here, together, under one roof. So precious. Yet, it hurt her to see the change in Ben. The same Ben, but something missing. He was safe home for Christmas, but Delphi caught glimpses of fatigue that was beginning to settle like the dust of Afghanistan into the pores of his skin. There was nothing she could do but be here and let him be. She longed for his quick, easy laugh, his lost happiness in Hanna. She longed to reassure him that his little family were fine, all waiting for him to return, but only Hanna could do that.

Ben moved downstairs in the dark avoiding the stairs that creaked. He could smell the resinous tang of fir and see the glint of baubles on the Christmas tree by the light of a lamp Delphi always left on. He stood in the large open-plan room remembering the pull of his childhood and that Christmassy feel of anticipation that faded with age.

He stood gazing at the tree as the decorations moved gently in the air. Around him the house sighed to the breathing of the sleeping people he loved. He stood listening to the steady tick of the kitchen clock. He stood in the silence of the hushed house thinking of Hanna asleep in the bed he had just left.

She was mercurial, like quicksilver, like water slipping between his fingers. He could not hold onto her. She eluded him. He had just made love to her, and there she was solid in his arms, but the essence of her dissolved as he held her to him. She was inexplicably absent, the spirit of her else-where. It felt as lonely and as disturbing as sex with a stranger.

Ben knew he had to draw back from introspection. It was too dangerous tonight, on Christmas Eve. He was bone-tired. He needed all his enthusiasm for his children, for the coming day. Hanna and Izzy were here with Finn, let him be grateful for that and not want more. He switched the kettle on and put hot chocolate in a mug and then went to the cupboard and got out the brandy bottle and added a slug to the mug. He sat in the dark room drinking it, drawing strength from the power of this house with Delphi and Ian at the heart of it.

He was afraid to fall asleep. Like a slow-motion reel of film, that morning would unroll behind his eyelids, unfurl like the snap of a green flag. The Jackal armoured vehicle in front of him avoiding the dead dog; the flash, the impact of the IED that flipped the vehicle over and blew the two soldiers manning the machine guns into the red dust.

The shocked, split-second silence. His own driver fran-tically reversing to a safe distance in the wheel tracks they had already made. His voice yelling into the phone for the medics. Trying to keep his voice calm and reassuring; reminding the boys of strict procedure, the need to wait. The endless minutes ticking by while a safe lane was secured to the injured. The slow moving forward with a mine prodder; the careful marking of their passage forward. Sweat and fear blinding them, horror driving them forward to get to the injured men. The smell of blood, the body parts, the terrified face of Lance Corporal Buckley with his arm blown clean away. Comforting him with meaningless words as Corporal Parton, known as Dolly, the team medic, tried to stem the bleeding and the boy cried out for his mum. Checking the injured while

Dolly's beautiful Welsh voice kept up a professional, reassuring flow of words to contain the shock and horror of the rest of his very young team.

Hearing at last the blessed sound of helicopter blades. Watching the Medical Emergency Response team assessing, working fast and professionally, running with the injured, with Buckley aged 23 and four days, towards the yawning mouth of the MERT helicopter. Watching it lift and clatter away into a clear blue sky. Within eight minutes Buckley had been in hospital receiving life-saving treatment. He, Ben, had escaped without a scratch, it was not his blood on his combats. The guilt that he was untouched, while young soldiers were mutilated, haunted him. His job was directing from the centre. He did not go out on regular patrols, but he had trained these men. He had needed to see the danger he was directing them into.

Christ! Here he was sitting worrying about Hanna seeming a little distant. She was always distant, for God's sake. He had a wife. He had a life. He had lived to see this Christmas. Finn and Izzy had a father . . .

Ben heard a movement above him and then the slow stiff steps of Ian coming downstairs. Ian searched Ben's face and, smelling the brandy, said, 'What a good idea.' He got out a whisky glass and poured a tot into it and sat in the chair by the window.

Ben's breathing was loud and uneven in the room. Ian started to talk. His voice still held the soft hint of a highland inflection. He talked about fish; the beauty of a new mayfly he had added to his collection; the flash of kingfishers and of river trout jumping in crystal clear rivers. He spoke of the peace of the loch where he fished last summer, so silent that a leaf dropping sounded like a footstep.

His words flowed like warm waves over Ben and when Ian stopped talking, they sat in silence for a while. Then

Ben got up and placed his hand on Ian's thin shoulder and left it there a moment. 'Thank you. Night-night, Ian.'

'Night-night, old thing. God bless.'

Ben lay beside Hanna and remembered all the times when he was a child that Ian had opened his magic box of fishing flies to distract him with their mysterious delicacy and vibrant colours. To enthral and comfort him when nothing, and no one else, could.

CHAPTER FORTY-THREE

On Christmas morning Izzy and Finn carried their stockings up to Hanna and Ben's room. Finn had managed to keep Izzy out of their room until 7.30, which he considered noble. They crammed into the bed together and disappeared under a mountain of Christmas paper as Izzy dived into her stocking. Delphi had even made little stockings for Hanna and Ben. 'You think of everything. Thank you,' Hanna said, when Delphi brought them up tea in bed.

The stockings were Izzy's bit of the day, Finn thought. She always grew excited about every tiny wrapped present or orange. Delphi stood for a moment taking a photograph of them all sitting together buried in tinsel, paper, and oranges.

Izzy and Finn went off to church with Ben and Ian, but Hanna stayed behind to help Delphi. When they got home there was a delicious smell of stuffing and turkey filling the house, mingling with the brandy Delphi was pouring over the Christmas pudding. Ian poured drinks for everyone while Izzy bounced about desperate to open her presents.

Finn felt a surge of happiness and expectation.

Christmas at Delphi and Ian's was like a ritual they always followed. He loved the adherence to it. Everyone held their glasses up and said 'Happy Christmas' to each other before the Opening Ceremony.

Hanna's mobile suddenly started in her bag and she jumped up to answer it. Finn thought it must be Mummo and Uki, his Finnish grandparents, but Hanna didn't call him or Izzy to talk to them. She turned her back on the room and walked over to the French windows and spoke softly into the phone.

Ben looked annoyed. Finn could see that Hanna seemed rude, but she was trying hard to get off the phone. She was well aware that present-opening time was sacrosanct.

Ben called. 'Hanna! Can't you ring whoever it is, back?'

Hanna quickly muttered something into the phone and ended the call. Her face was hot, and Finn thought she looked sort of guilty or embarrassed when she turned around. He heard Delphi whisper to Ben. 'Darling, please . . . leave it.' But Ben couldn't.

'Was that your parents? Didn't they want to speak to Finn and Izzy, Hanna?'

'It wasn't my parents. Just a friend from Finland wishing me Happy Christmas . . .'

'Right,' Delphi said. 'Everyone got a drink? Come on, then, Izzy-busy is bursting to open her presents . . .'

When Izzy was tearing her first big present open, Finn heard Ben say to Hanna, 'What friend? Why not ring her back later? Why look so furtive?'

'Ben, you don't know them. Does it matter? I'm sorry they rang at the wrong time . . .'

Ben said after a minute, 'Sorry.' He went and sat on the floor next to Izzy and handed Finn a small parcel. 'This is from us all. Hanna, me, Delphi, and Ian. We all think you deserve it . . .'

It was a small parcel wrapped in scarlet and gold paper. When Finn opened it, he found an iPhone. He stared down at it, speechless. This cost serious money and Ben and Hanna did not believe in big presents.

'It's why there are not quite so many parcels under the tree for you this year . . .' Hanna said. 'With a smart phone you will have no excuse not to ring or email me . . . everyone . . .'

'Thanks. Thanks. Wow!' Finn said, pink with excitement. 'I really, really, wanted one. Some of the boys have them at school now . . . I can't wait to tell Raz. He got an iPhone when he moved to Cornwall.' Finn got up to hug both his parents, feeling overwhelmed.

Ian and Finn spent the next hour helping Izzy put together a little house for her collection of woodland creatures. Ben went into the kitchen to help Delphi. Hanna disappeared upstairs.

When Finn ran up to his room to find his old mobile, he found her sitting on Izzy's bed texting on her phone. Hanna jumped when she saw him. Really jumped. She said, 'Oh, Finn! You startled me. I'm just seeing if I can get hold of Mummo and Uki so you and Izzy can wish them a happy Christmas.'

'Are you homesick?' Finn asked. Hanna had always missed having Christmas Eve with her family. She smiled, 'No, Finn, I'm fine.'

She patted the bed, and he went to sit beside her. 'Ben won't mind you ringing them,' Finn told her. 'You don't have to hide upstairs. I think he's still a bit stressed out.'

Hanna nodded but did not say anything. Then she said, 'Are we okay, you and I, Finn?'

Finn didn't know what to say. It was hard to stay angry with Hanna when she was in front of him, yet he instinctively sensed her secretiveness. He longed to ask her if or when she was coming home, but he didn't want to hear the wrong answer.

236

'Okay, for now, anyway?' she whispered, nudging him hard. Finn smiled.

'We're okay,' he told her because he wanted it to be true.

'You better go back down,' Hanna said. 'I'll be just behind you . . .'

Then she suddenly said, wistfully, 'I always wanted you to call me Hanna, but just lately I've had a yearning to be Mum. When you were little, you used to swap between the two. But now you never call me Mum and I miss it . . .'

Finn stared at her. Oh, the irony. She leaves him, then wants him to call her Mum, from a distance. 'It's a bit late to ask me to change what I call you, Hanna,' he said. 'I call Dad Ben. He doesn't mind.'

'Ah, but you call him Dad too, when you are sad or anxious, without knowing it, because it's instinct.' She smiled. 'I know I am not making any sense.'

Finn didn't know what Hanna wanted him to say. He stood awkwardly by the door wanting to go downstairs. Hanna said, 'I guess, I just wondered if you were still angry with me, inside?'

'I'm not angry with you,' Finn told her, not knowing if this was strictly true. He didn't say that she was totally confusing him. He did not say, *What the hell do you expect? You left me and Ben.* He did not say any of the things that kept him awake at night, because Hanna seemed sad and it was Christmas.

Downstairs Delphi was basting an enormous turkey. When she realized that she had forgotten her apricot and herb stuffing, she got it out of the fridge and was fussing about it cooking in time. Suddenly, Ben snapped, 'Oh, for goodness sake, Delphi, what does it matter? How many different stuffings do we need?'

There was a silence and Izzy looked up from her toys.

Ian got himself up from the floor and moved towards the kitchen.

Delphi said, 'You are quite right, darling, it doesn't matter a jot . . . Stick this back in the oven for me will you, it's enormously heavy.'

Ben put the turkey back in the oven. 'I'm going to have a cigarette in the garden,' he said. He opened the back door and went out and down the steps. Hanna had come down the stairs and she moved towards the door to go after him. Ian said, 'I think it might be a good idea to let Ben have space for a moment or two, Hanna.'

Finn had never heard Ben snap like that at Delphi. He went and sat with Izzy. When Ben came back inside, he grinned at everyone. 'Sorry I'm a grumpy sod,' he said and went and hugged Delphi.

'What's a grumpy sod?' Izzy asked, quick as lightning.

'A lump of earth,' Finn told her, and everyone laughed. She got up and ran to Ben and grabbed his legs. 'You are a grumpy lump of earth . . .'

By the time they all sat down to Delphi's huge lunch, Christmas cheer was restored. Afterwards they pulled on coats and blew along the prom to Newlyn so Izzy could try out her new scooter. Then everyone collapsed in front of the telly.

By the evening the grown-ups had drunk too much and got silly. They played stupid games and ate leftovers. Like every Christmas, Finn thought happily as he watched Ben and Hanna fooling about tickling each other. He felt pretty sure they wouldn't do that if they were going to split up. He went up to bed and sat up amidst Izzy's fairy lights jotting down the day in his diary so he would not forget it.

Finn listened to Izzy's breathing. It had been a happy day, but now he was writing it down and thinking about everyone, it kind of changed to something different. He kept remembering things that did not seem important at the time but were still there in his head.

Finn did not believe Hanna was ringing her parents when she was upstairs. He always knew when she was lying. She had left her phone upstairs when Ben got cross, but he could hear constant texts coming in and every so often Hanna would run upstairs to check, as if they might be important. It seemed odd and he knew Ben had noticed it too.

Finn heard him say, jokingly, to her, 'Why don't you bring your phone downstairs, Hanna, instead of running up and down checking it all the time? Have you got an illicit lover texting you or something?'

Hanna had laughed. 'Oh, I have several. It is extremely difficult to choose . . .' She had put her hand on his arm. 'My phone constantly bleeping annoys me, as well. I haven't got hold of my parents yet and I asked them to get back to me. There are also a couple of old college friends I've recently caught up with and they keep drunkenly texting me . . .'

Ben had put his drink down and put his arm round her. 'Why shouldn't they, darling? I'm not checking up on you. Sorry I was irritable this morning. Bring the phone down or we might miss your parents . . .'

Finn put his diary away and started to check out some of the functions on his new iPhone. He texted Raz and told him he was bloated with too much food and all the adults had had too much wine. Raza texted back to say he was buried under Pakistani relatives he had never heard of, and he might never see Finn again . . .

Finn woke in the early hours of Boxing Day when he heard Ben coming slowly down the stairs from his room

239

in the dark. He passed his bedroom door and trod on the creaky floorboard on the top stair as he went downstairs. Finn looked at his watch and saw it was only 4 a.m. He got out of bed and went onto the landing and looked down. Ben had a torch and was shining it into the bowl on the hall table, looking for car keys. Finn opened his mouth to whisper down the stairs that he wanted to go with him. Then he remembered Ian telling him that Ben needed space, so stayed silent. Ben found Ian's lumpy bunch of keys at the bottom of the bowl and opened the front door. After a moment Finn heard the old Land Rover fire up and drive away.

He went back to his room and pulled the duvet back over Izzy and got into bed. He could hear his heart thumping loudly in the dark. Everyone was sleeping. No one but him knew that Ben had left the house. Finn knew he would be heading out to the beach house, but he didn't like the fact that Ben was sleepless, that he might be worrying about his soldiers back in Lashkar Gah. Or anxious about Hanna.

Finn couldn't get back to sleep. He lay thinking about Christmas Day and how things seem one thing and then turn into another when you go back over them. He wished Hanna and Ben would not try so hard around him and Izzy. They were used to them bickering and contradicting each other all the time. It did not feel normal when they were like this, like they were sort of strangers to each other, so polite and careful and stuff. The only one who really sailed through Christmas Day was Izzy with her obscene amounts of presents . . .

He texted Raza even though he would still be asleep. *When are you back in Cornwall?*

Raza was not asleep and texted back straight away. *Driving back with Chinir to Cornwall tonight. Too much women talk, talk and shop, shop! I will have Cornish house to self all day. It will be very good!*

Cool! Why are you awake too? At this moment I can't imagine house to self . . . Finn looked up. He realized, that is what Ben needed, a house to self for a bit . . .

CHAPTER FORTY-FOUR

Raza sat beside Chinir in the car flying through the night back to Cornwall. It had been good to see Liyana and Daniyal again, but the house had been bursting with their relatives and friends. Children fell asleep all over the house and in his bed. Adults sat around at the big kitchen table, in the sitting room, on the floor, talking, talking, talking Urdu, Pashto, Sindhi, English. All happy, all in a festive mood.

Raza thought his head would burst with the clamorous noise of it all.

Sarah had teased him. 'Oh, you are no longer a Pashtun, but a little English gentleman who cannot cope with the noisy excesses of Pakistani people partying.'

Raza had denied it hotly, but the truth was that he had lived quietly with Zamir most of his life except for village weddings, or Eid, and celebrating the end of Ramadan.

'I am not English. I am Pashtun from rural village used to peace and quiet!' he had retorted with a grin.

Sarah had seemed to him especially glowing and relaxed this Christmas. It made Raza feel he was not such a disappointment to her, for he knew they had not been as close as Sarah had hoped.

On Christmas Day she announced to everybody the reason for her newfound radiance. She was pregnant. Against all the odds and after all this time, she had conceived. Raza, watching Chinir's proud face, slipped out of the room and up to the top landing. He prayed to Allah to watch over Sarah and her baby. He prayed also that this child might be the girl that Sarah longed for.

He loved the peace of travelling by night beside Chinir. Liked the feeling of speeding towards an empty house, to his room full of his books and work and private belongings. Was he growing English in his need for privacy?

Chinir yawned and stretched. 'We'll stop soon and eat. Oh, isn't it wonderfully quiet? I can hear myself think . . .' He grinned at Raza. 'I love Sarah's family, but oh my God, two days are quite enough.'

Raza laughed. 'I am sure every year there are more and more people.'

'Liyana and Daniyal collect people together like pebbles. It is exhausting. It is why I volunteer to work each Christmas.'

Raza looked shocked. 'But each year you say. "I don't believe it! I am on duty again."'

'Ah, but I also say to Sarah, "You know it's only fair that I work at this time when other doctors want to celebrate Christmas with their families." We have our Muslim festivals, Eid-ul-Fitr holiday, Kashmir Day, Labour Day and endless Pakistani weddings, for which I am obliged to attend.'

'Okay,' Raza said. 'This is true, but they are not holidays, here . . .'

'I am a doctor in the overworked NHS . . .' Chinir did not add, that as he did not strictly observe Ramadan, he was hardly deserving of celebrating the end of it.

'Does Sarah know that you tell small untruth?'

Chinir laughed. 'Of course, she knows. It is a dignified device we have without spelling out that I prefer to come home to peace and let Sarah and her parents have a happy time together without me at Christmas. Are you okay to forage for yourself in an empty house when I'm at the hospital, Raza? I am on long shifts. Will you be seeing Finn?'

'I love an empty house.' Raza turned to look at Chinir as he drew into the motorway services. 'Finn, he has asked me to meet his father, but I do not think I will go.'

Chinir switched the engine off. 'Why?' When Raza did not answer, Chinir said, 'The Pakistani army and the British army are very different things, Raza. I understand your fear of uniforms, but Finn's father will not be in uniform with an officious moustache. Don't be afraid of meeting him. He is not going to shout at you. I am sure he will be a gentle and thoughtful person, like your friend.'

Raza poked at a hole in his jeans. 'He . . . he is also fighting in Afghanistan.'

Chinir said, 'Come on, let's go and get something to eat.'

He pinged the car locked and as they walked across the car park to the garishly lit entrance, he asked. 'How do you feel when Finn talks to you as a friend? When he's worrying about his father being injured?'

'I feel sorry. I do not want for Finn's father to be hurt. I try to explain what many Afghans feel about foreign soldiers in their country. I do not say all foreign soldiers should never be in Afghanistan. I do not say that indeed, my two brothers they are Talibs, Chinir.'

Chinir threw his arm around Raza's shoulders. 'I'm not sure what to say to you. You are caught in a culture clash and it's difficult for you to feel . . .'

'To be honest,' Raza said quickly.

Chinir smiled. 'You know, Raza, what I have learnt from you since you came to us?'

Raza shook his head and Chinir said, 'I have learnt that you are one of the most honest people I have ever met. Never think you are dishonest by not declaring all your feelings. No one does. Just go on as you are, being a good friend to Finn. Understand how he feels because you love your own Baba. Sarah and I are very proud of you. We made many mistakes with you at the beginning . . . I've never said that I am sorry, Raza, for your first unhappy years with us. All you have achieved is entirely down to you . . .'

They pushed through the heavy glass doors to a rush of noise. As they were queuing for food, Raza said, 'Chinir, it is true that I was at first unhappy and angry with you and with Baba. I did not want to be here in England, and I was lonely and ungrateful, but now . . . now, I thank you for all that I have . . .'

Chinir smiled. 'You have your first good friend here. Trust Finn. If he says he wants to see you, then he does. You will have to meet his father sometime, won't you?'

Raza shrugged. 'Yeah. Yeah . . .' He stared at the vats of food across the counter. 'Can I have chips?'

'Chips! Typical English boy,' Chinir said, raising his eyebrows.

'What is it that you are having, then?' Raza demanded.

'Curry and chips because I have no wife here and I can,' Chinir said.

CHAPTER FORTY-FIVE

The sun felt warm as Finn and Ben ran through the park. The trees dripped rain flurries on their heads and the tarmac paths steamed. A blackbird sang and squirrels shot in front of their legs and up the trees. It felt like spring, but it was a benign trick.

Finn, running beside Ben, felt as if a weight had fallen from him. They ran past the tennis courts, keeping to the paths, past the small adventure playground Izzy loved and out round the wide roads of large, heavy Victorian houses, mostly bed and breakfast now, or split into flats.

They crossed the main road onto the promenade and ran on to Newlyn catching their breath on the bridge. 'Come on, let's have breakfast at the Fishermen's Mission,' Ben said. 'It must be years since I went inside.'

It was an old-fashioned building with a large room with a billiard table, newspapers, games, and a small canteen to cater for fishermen coming off the boats or working in the warehouses. It was open to the public and popular for its cheap breakfasts. They pushed open the doors onto a noisy hub of gossip. There were tables of burly fishermen playing cards and the language made Finn giggle.

As they queued for their bacon and eggs, an older fisherman suddenly recognized Ben. Wandering over, he greeted him and winked at Finn. 'Your dad told you 'bout the time he fancied being a fisherman, has ee? Never seen anyone so sick in all me life. Sick as a dog and never came out to sea again, did ee?'

Ben looked embarrassed and the old man gave Finn a wink. 'Put him off the navy and sent him to the trenches, it did, young man.'

'I'm cavalry!' Ben said, laughing. 'I see you haven't given up your storytelling, Tom. Though it's true to say I've never been so sick or so scared in my life . . .'

Finn, who thought Ben's life had begun with his birth, was fascinated. As they sat down at a table, he asked, 'You really thought about being a fisherman?'

'No! I was just bored and full of myself, waiting to see if I had got into Sandhurst . . . I've never been allowed to forget I was hideously seasick . . .' Ben looked down at his plate. 'We've successfully defeated the point of the run . . .' He grinned at Finn. 'It's not the best breakfast in the world but it is strangely comforting to see this place never changes. Everyone goes on doing the same things . . .'

'What's the food like out there?'

'Pretty good. Meals are important for morale. Food is usually the highlight of the day for the men.'

'But you're thinner.'

Ben was thinner and there were dark shadows under his eyes.

'Long hours, that's all. Come on, we'll be in the doghouse if we don't get back.'

As they wandered home Finn bent and picked two flat, round stones from the beach. Delphi edged her garden with them. Fishing boats were sliding out of Newlyn in a calm sea that glinted in winter light. 'This is what I think about when I'm on duty,' Ben said. 'Days like this.'

'Wish you didn't have to go back,' Finn said, his mood abruptly swinging round.

'Ah, but I'm more than halfway through now. Just think, by spring I'll be home. We'll have the whole summer together. I'll have leave and we'll come down here and surf, just you and me, for hours . . .'

'But where will we be, Dad? Where will we be living when you're home again?'

'Germany. I'll have a couple of months to hand over my job but obviously I haven't got my next posting yet, Finn.'

There was a change in Ben's tone of voice and Finn caught it.

'Will Hanna be going back to Germany?'

'Not until I'm home, Finn. Izzy has settled into a nursery school in Helsinki. Hanna doesn't want her to have too many moves. We'll wait to see where I'm posted.'

Finn said, 'That's rubbish. Izzy doesn't particularly like Finland. She gets muddled. Sometimes she thinks you and I are still in Germany and she and Hanna are on a little holiday. She would settle back into her school in Germany quick as anything . . .'

'But your mother wouldn't,' Ben said tightly. 'That's the point, Finn. All the reasons she did not want to stay alone in Germany, still stand.'

'Nothing's changed, then?'

'Nothing's changed.' Ben's voice was clipped, resigned.

'So, will she be back in the quarter when you come home?'

'I'm sure she will, Finn,' Ben said. But Finn knew he was far from sure.

'If she isn't back home in Germany, will you come here, Dad? Will you come to Cornwall, so Delphi, Ian, and I can see you?'

'You bet I will.' Ben threw an arm around Finn. 'But I

think it's all going to be fine. Your mother looks much better and happier. She's seeing a lot of your grandparents and her old friends in Helsinki. You wait, in a few months she'll be ready to come back to the quarter knowing it's only for a short time. I've specifically asked for a UK posting, so try not to worry. All will come right, Finn, just be patient. Okay?'

Finn nodded, wanting to believe him. But he couldn't forget Hanna's secrecy. All those texts and phone calls pulling her somewhere else. . . .

As they left the prom and crossed the main road home, Ben said, 'I know it's hard, but don't ever think Hanna doesn't love you, because that's a given. Let's give her space to be with her family so that she wants to come back to us when she's ready, Okay?'

Finn grunted, but he was not sure that the power of loving someone with all your heart was enough to keep them with you. He was learning the necessity of holding a piece of himself back, to guard against further hurt. He was learning that it was better not to ask questions, unless you could cope with an answer you did not want.

'Are we owning up about our greasy breakfast?' he asked Ben.

'Might have to, in case Delphi tries to fill us up with another.'

'Izzy's going to be mad at us for not taking her.'

'We'll deflect her with the adventure playground. Then, how about a picnic lunch at the beach house? It's such a great day . . .'

'Maybe we could surf in wetsuits . . .'

'We'll check the waves . . . Come on put a sprint on it, we need to look all macho and sweaty after a strenuous run . . .'

Ben set forth in an exaggerated, important fast walk up

the hill looking ridiculous. Finn, giggling, watched his father's powerful brown legs pistoling up the hill and loped after him.

They sat in a row on the sand, Hanna, Izzy, and Raza wrapped up in rugs and thick sweaters watching Ben and Finn surf in the icy, thunderous waves. Finn came in, exhausted and cold. Hanna wound him into a huge thick towel and made him go straight into a hot shower and change. When he came back to the beach Ben was still in the water. Finn sat between Hanna and Izzy and they watched Ben surf on, amazed that he found the strength to stay on in that winter sea so long.

It was late afternoon, the wind was beginning to drop and the waves to even out and lose their power, but still Ben stayed out on the water.

As the sea gentled, he could stand upright for longer and the watchers caught his euphoria as he judged the speed of a wave and sailed in with it.

Raza marvelled at the sheer power of the water crashing in. Hanna stared at Ben as he flew in on the crest of a wave, stared as if he was an unknown man, and not her husband. His strong body balanced on the board with long practised skill gave her an urgent sexual pull. She had always thought him almost physically perfect.

Up at the beach house, Delphi and Ian were making tea, glancing at the silhouette Ben made against the skyline. If they thought that there was something relentless about Ben's time in the water, they did not say so. The sea had always been Ben's escape.

Raza, shivering on the cold beach, had been stunned at how young Ben's father was. Zamir was Ian's age, a grandpa. Ben was even younger than Ajeet and Fakir, he was probably about the same age as Chinir. There was nothing frightening about him. Ben had greeted Raza with a smile. '*Salam alaikum*, Raza. Welcome.'

'*Wa alaykumu as-salam*, sir,' Raza had muttered, shy suddenly. Ben's amused face was not stern or moustached. He was dressed in old jeans and a sweater. He looked just like an older version of Finn.

'Call me Ben. Finn does,' he said. 'Finn says we have no chance of getting you into the water?'

'Indeed, no chance, sir, Mr Ben.' Raza grinned, but his voice was firm on the subject of the sea.

Delphi and Ian, carrying mugs of tea across the sand saw Ben raise his hand to indicate he was coming in. He caught one last glorious wave and stood upright, expertly sliding into shore with a satisfying swirl.

Delphi, watching Ben, thought, he is at the peak of fitness, pitting himself against the sea. Ian snapped him with his mobile camera, a last lone surfer framed against a pale gold horizon, as happy and absorbed by the elements as he had been as a teenager.

They sat around the old, scrubbed table in the kitchen heated by the even more ancient log fire. Chinir had joined them. He had dropped Raza off in Penzance, on his way to the hospital and was now picking him up. He stood talking to Ben. Both men were drinking beer. Raza saw the ease with which Chinir could either be very British, or very Pakistani when he needed to be with older members of Sarah's family.

Raza watched as the two men talked comfortably about 'damn politics', corruption of governments, and the need of a rigorous medical programme, both in Afghanistan and rural Pakistan. Then he was deflected by Izzy.

Izzy was enchanted by Raza. Uncharacteristically shy at first, she had collected tiny shells from the beach and brought them to Raza in a small pink bucket as he sat watching the surfers. She had carefully placed the most beautiful in his palms, crouching in front of him, staring up fascinated into his dazzling green eyes. Now sitting opposite him at the table she announced solemnly into a silence, 'I am going to marry you when I grow up.'

Startled, Raza gazed back at her earnest little face and was lost for words. He could see everyone else trying not to laugh. He must be careful not to hurt this little girl's feelings. He put his hand on his heart and said equally solemnly.

'I am honoured. I will keep these beautiful shells to me. Thank you.'

Chinir joked softly to Ben, 'No arranged marriage for Raza, it seems.'

Ben laughed. 'He might well beg for one . . .'

Finn whispered to Raza, 'Be afraid. Be very afraid . . .'

Hanna, watching Ben through sleepy eyes, ached for more sex with him.

Ian, noting Delphi's exhausted happiness in this last day with Ben, hurriedly searched for a tiny flaw in the moment with which to deflect a jealous god.

CHAPTER FORTY-SIX

When Finn and Raza went back to school after Christmas it was Raza who began to have nightmares.

'What is it?' Finn asked as night after night Raza reared up in his bed anxious and sweating. Raza was afraid to speak his fear out loud in case he made it happen. 'I am missing my father.' He whispered in the dark. 'I am just missing my Baba.'

Sudden homesickness had crept into him with the cold. His longing for Pakistan had begun to grow after the Christian festivities were over. The damp winter, the endless grey mists that covered sky and land made his heart heavy. No snow-capped mountains lightened the landscape here. Raza felt swamped by the sheets of constant rain. His bones ached for the warmth of the sun.

In London, where buildings and people dominated, he had been less aware of the greyness that now seemed to engulf his life. He longed for that particular depth of ink-blue sky that framed the Kashmiri mountains; for a particular light that turned the brown landscape silvery gold. Where a cold morning would shimmer with promise, before the sun flamed the land with harsh yellow warmth.

'But you always miss your father, Raz. Why is it suddenly worse? Have you heard something?' Finn sat beside Raza on the window seat of the empty dormitory. Outside a pigeon called from the tree on one long note.

Raza shook his head. 'No . . . but I . . .' His anxiety about Zamir formed into a pattern of dreams that always ended in the same way.

'Tell me, Raz. What is it?'

Raza stared at Finn with eyes so full of fear that Finn felt an answering flicker deep inside him. 'Every night,' Raza whispered, 'I am walking up the dry track to my village and up to the house I share with my father. I know this route by my heart. I can travel up and down it with blindfold. I walk past low stonewalls dividing our small fields planted with peas and vegetables. I can breathe all familiar smells and I can hear the goats and the voices of children. They are calling noisily one to another as they hide and jump from rock to rock. Even in dream I can see bright colours amongst the trees as small girls, they run laughing. I see clearly the older girls, they hold a length of veil between finger and thumb, to be ready to hide their faces . . .'

Raza closed his eyes and smiled to himself, feeling the joy of a homecoming. He wanted to let go, give into all that he really was, turn back into the 9-year-old Raza with no knowledge of leaving Baba or his home . . .

'But,' Raza said, opening his eyes and fixing them on Finn. 'As I draw near my house, my fear, it grow in me. My Baba, he is not sitting on old plastic chair outside the house watching the sunrise . . . In my dream I grab curtain that hang across the door and I burst into the house. The small room it is empty, my house it is deserted. Baba is not at his prayers. He is not inside waking to a new day. My Baba is nowhere. He is gone. Each night, Finn, my nightdream end in that empty room . . . My Baba, he is nowhere . . .'

Raza was distressed and trembling. Finn felt trapped with him in the empty landscape of the dream. He was caught in the cobweb of Raza's dread. He wondered if this dream meant Raza's Baba was indeed dead. He cast about for something comforting to say but was lost.

'It is only a nightdream, Raz,' he said finally. 'That's what you tell me, when I have nightmares. It's not real . . .'

Raza nodded. He was not really listening. He was looking out of the window at the sky. *He wants to be home in Pakistan*, Finn thought. *He does not want to be here, anymore, in an English school.* He stood up, feeling a rush of misery. 'Raz, I'll make you some toast before prep. Okay?' But Raza did not hear.

In class it became impossible for Raza to concentrate. He let his work slide, he could not complete assignments or prep. He rushed off to pray at inappropriate times. At night he began to wake not just Finn but Isa and Peter too.

Raza rang Sarah and begged her to find out from his uncles if his father was unwell. Sarah heard Raza's mounting anxiety with dismay. She did not tell Raza that the last time she had spoken to Maldi, he and Hanif had been worried, as they had not heard from Zamir for weeks. He had been unwell with a persistent cough and had not ventured down to Peshawar but sent a neighbour into town with produce or animals he wanted to sell. Sarah promised Raza she would contact both Maldi and Hanif and ring him as soon as she had news.

Ed Dominic was concerned at the sudden deterioration in Raza, both physically and mentally. He took him off for a chat and sent him to the school doctor for a physical check-up.

Ed wondered if they had all expected too much from this gifted boy who had had to adapt his life to fit into another culture in so short a time.

It took a week to trace Zamir. Seven days in which Raza languished, pale and shivery with unknown dread. He prayed five times a day but could find no relief from his overpowering anxiety. He was disturbing the other boys at night and Mercy decided to put him in sickbay where she could keep an eye on him. Finn was adamant that Raza should not be on his own at night and put in such a cogent plea to keep him company that Mercy and Ed Dominic relented.

In those seven days, Maldi travelled from Rawalpindi to Peshawar. Hanif took the bus from Peshawar to Zamir's village. There he gathered from neighbours that Zamir had been unwell. When Hanif arrived at Zamir's house he found it empty. The widow who cooked and washed Zamir's clothes did not know where he was. He had been ill. She had cared for him as best she could, but his cough was bad. He had gone down to the village about a week ago to see the doctor who held a roving clinic each month, but the doctor had never arrived. She thought Zamir must have seen sense and caught the bus to Peshawar to find antibiotics, for undoubtedly his chest was infected.

On the bus back to Peshawar Hanif heard that an old man had collapsed on the bus five days ago and had been taken away by ambulance to a hospital. By this time Maldi had arrived from Rawalpindi. With Hanif's sons they toured the state hospitals in Peshawar and eventually found Zamir, semi-conscious, lying on a dirty charpoy in a charity hospital corridor.

Maldi and Hanif touched their heads and held their hands to the sky in relief and frustration. Each month Sarah and Chinir sent money to the family for just such an emergency as this. Zamir knew this. Maldi had opened a bank account for Zamir, but his stubborn brother had steadfastly refused to spend any of Sarah's money on making his own life easier. He considered the money Raza's.

Sarah, when she heard, immediately instructed Maldi to get Zamir to a private clinic. Hanif's daughter-in-law knew the best one for him, in a wide tree-lined road in the suburbs. They transferred Zamir by private ambulance. Zamir had been given antibiotics for his chest infection but when the clinic X-rayed him, they found he had developed pneumonia and had a high fever. They doubted he would last the night.

However, in a cool, air-conditioned room Zamir's temperature dropped, although he had to be given oxygen to help him breathe. He was barely conscious and recognized no one.

Sarah and Chinir booked two tickets to Islamabad. Raza needed the chance to see his father before he died, but neither of them could leave their jobs at this time and Sarah was pregnant. It was decided Daniyal, who had a calming effect on Raza, and like Liyana, spoke Pashto, would travel with Raza.

Sarah and Chinir picked Raza up from school on Saturday morning. The flight to Pakistan was on Sunday evening. Chinir was going to drive Raza to Heathrow and deliver him to Daniyal.

'Facebook me, Raz,' Finn called as Raza climbed into the car. 'Let me know what's going on.' Raza nodded, his face ashen.

Mr Dominic called, 'We'll be thinking of you and your father, Raza. Take care, stay safe.'

As the car disappeared down the drive, Finn felt bereft. The school had emptied for the weekend, but he had wanted to keep Raza company until Sarah and Chinir picked him up. Isa had gone off into Truro with Peter Chan for the night. Finn sat on the school doorstep and stroked Norman, a town cat who regularly wandered up to the school kitchen. He buried his fingers into the cat's soft ginger fur and listened to him purr like a tractor.

Mr Dominic glared at the cat. 'Don't encourage him. He is in Mercy's bad books. He's just stolen a plate of chicken from the kitchen table.' Finn grinned. Norman was always in trouble. He ate everything, biscuits, toast and Marmite, crisps. The boys had learned this to their cost.

'By the way, your grandmother is on her way. Well done for the support you've given Raza, Finn.'

'He would have done the same for me.'

'Yes, he would.'

'Mr Dominic . . .' Finn stood up. 'Raza might not come back, might he?'

Ed Dominic looked down at Finn's anxious face. 'Let's hope that he will, Finn. He has so much potential, so much to achieve. But I don't think we can be sure that he will come back. I guess it depends on how he finds his father. He has been in a pretty bad way and consumed by home-sickness.'

Consumed was a good word, Finn thought, as he heard Delphi's car.

Raza had been consumed by fear for his father, consumed by longing for the familiar sights, smells, and sounds of Pakistan, for home. He had stopped trying to be a foreign Raz. He longed to be himself again. A Pakistani boy. Finn instinctively knew this and was overwhelmed by a gnawing loss.

In the car he said, 'Delphi, do you think Sarah and Chinir are frightened that Raza might stay in Pakistan, even though they are his guardians? If he didn't come back, would they go out to Pakistan and bring him back, do you think?'

Delphi thought about it. 'I don't think they would, Finn.

258

Sarah rang me this week. Raza's an intelligent boy. They feel they would have to accept Raza's wishes this time. Like you, darling, they're praying his father will recover and Raza will come back to us.'

'*Inshallah*,' Finn said.

'*Inshallah*, indeed,' Delphi said. 'Would fish and chips cheer you up?'

'It might,' Finn said.

CHAPTER FORTY-SEVEN

Peshawar, 2010

Daniyal did have a calming effect on Raza. He was waiting at the check-in desk with his luggage at Heathrow, unflappable and in command.

'Go, to my club. I've booked you a room for the night,' he told Chinir. 'Try not to worry, relax, maybe visit old friends? *Inshallah,* all will be well . . .'

Daniyal and Raza went together to the prayer room at Heathrow before they boarded the flight to Islamabad. Raza prayed for Zamir. Daniyal prayed for their safety. Exhausted by sleepless nights, Raza slept most of the flight. Uncle Maldi was at Islamabad airport to meet them and raised his hands in astonishment at the sight of the lanky youth that was Raza.

'Ahh! You leave a child and come home a man.'

He turned to Daniyal. 'I booked internal flights to Peshawar, but all local flights are grounded by the weather. We can try this evening, but I do not think there will be flights into Peshawar today . . .'

He saw Raza's anxious face. 'Be patient, Raza. We will

fly first thing in the morning. Meanwhile, your aunt Jalar has prepared food . . .'

They squeezed into an old taxi belonging to one of Maldi's many nephews and barged through the traffic with speed and panache. Daniyal closed his eyes. Raza breathed in the familiar smell of petrol fumes, sweat, and hot tarmac. He leant against the window gazing out at the motor scooters flashing past, at the familiar veiled women riding pillion, side saddle; small feet dangling in plastic sandals, holding babies with one hand while other children lay wedged between father and mother.

The overloaded, decorated buses rolled past billowing black smoke like ferries. Raza stared at the luminous, gold-edged veiled women with their kohled eyes and fingers bedecked with rings and bracelets. The manic traffic, the trucks full of soldiers, the swaying lorries and battered cars, all hooting, dodging, pushing, and shoving in an endless dance of death were like familiar music that throbbed to the beat of his heart.

He thought he might be forever changed by being away so long. He thought that the reality of being back in Pakistan would feel like a dream, but he was slipping back into a sweet, familiar rhythm of noise, bustle, and the language of his childhood. It was like tumbling back into warm water that soothed his troubled spirit. For a moment Raza wanted to close his eyes and weep, but he resisted, he needed to be strong and concentrate on reaching Baba.

Raza became aware that Daniyal and Uncle Maldi were talking in low voices, but the noise of the engine blurred their words. He thought of his brothers, Ajeet and dead Fakir. No one in the family ever spoke their names out loud these days, and it made him feel he could not bring them up in conversation either, but they were his brothers and he missed them at this moment. Baba was their father too.

Uncle Maldi's house felt small and cramped. Aunt Jalar also expressed astonishment at Raza's tall and filled-out frame. She seemed smaller and her wide grin of pleasure in seeing him showed up gaps in her teeth.

She had prepared food on a blue cloth on the floor and placed bright cushions for her guests to sit on. Daniyal sat awkwardly on the floor, apologizing for being unable to tuck his knees in.

'I am not as flexible as I used to be . . .' He smiled at Jalar. 'What wonderful food. Thank you . . .' They talked of family links and a long-ago wedding in Karachi when they had last met up. Daniyal noticed the small plastic table and chairs where Jalar and Maldi must sit when alone, which was probably not often, given the abundance of relations. He thought of his five-bedroom house back in England and felt guilty and humbled by Maldi and Jalar's generosity. Raza thought of Finn. Finn had hardly left his side for the last two weeks. He felt an ache, a flash of dislocation, then he gently placed his friend in a box and firmly closed the lid.

The biryani was the best Danyial had tasted for years and he told Jalar so. She laughed, delighted and said to Raza. 'Do you remember the last time you came to eat here, your Baba told you not to eat so fast?'

Raza grinned. 'He told me I was greedy and shaming him.'

'You were a little boy and very hungry,' Maldi said. 'How proud Zamir will be of you when he sees you now, Raza. Tall and strong, your bones filled out with flesh . . .'

'How is my Baba, Uncle?'

Maldi sighed. 'He is ill. Your father is a very obstinate man. He refused to go for treatment until he was too ill to travel. His suffering was unnecessary. Each month Sarah sends a sum of money to Zamir for his needs, for emergency.

Zamir will not use this money. He did not let us, his family, know he was ill, he just shut himself away with his herbs, when he needed antibiotics.'

'But he is better now he is in a hospital? Now he has these medicines,' Raza asked anxiously.

'He is comfortable. He is stable, but Raza, he is an old man with pneumonia and that is not a good thing to have at his age.'

'Fluid on the lungs,' Daniyal explained to Raza. 'This means difficulty in breathing. For someone old, it will take time to recover.'

Raza pushed his food away abruptly. 'I want be there, with him.'

'Tomorrow, *Inshallah,* you will see him. Your Baba is a strong man. Dr Shah tells me he is holding his own.'

Aunt Jalar brought out *shalwar kameez* she had brought in the market for both Daniyal and Raza. 'Wear these to travel to Peshawar. It is better. You stand out too much,' she said to Daniyal. 'Things have got worse in the last months. People are kidnapped all the time. You need to be careful.'

'You are flying with us to Peshawar, Maldi?' Daniyal asked.

'I did book a seat with you, but it is expensive. Now, after cancellation, I will follow you on the bus, Daniyal. It will be fine, Hanif will meet you at Peshawar airport.'

'Don't worry about the expense, Maldi, I would feel happier to have you travel with us. I have not been to Pakistan for over ten years. I am out of my comfort zone in terms of safety . . .'

There was an awkward pause while they waited for Jalar to engage Raza in conversation, then Maldi said quietly, 'Hanif and I have arranged armed security for you and Raza in Peshawar. Zamir has always been afraid that if

Raza returned home, Ajeet's Taliban group will grab him. This is why he never wanted Raza to come back for a visit, even though Sarah offered to pay for a trip.'

'Does Zamir have any basis to think Ajeet would still want to take Raza?'

Maldi shrugged. 'Neither brother ever forgave Zamir for spiriting him to the west. I do not know how real Zamir's fear still is, but there is a new Taliban group settled in the mountains less than fifty kilometres from my brother's village. Ajeet will be one of them. Fakir is not dead, by the way. He has grown into a bitter, disillusioned man who knows he has outlived his usefulness. Ajeet, on the other hand, remains powerful and dangerous . . .'

Daniyal absorbed this news. 'Is there a danger in becoming paranoid, Maldi? Who will really notice an ageing man and a boy visiting a hospital?'

Maldi snorted. 'Have your forgotten? To be Pakistani is to be paranoid. We see intrigue around every corner because usually there is. It is fatal to be complacent in this country, my friend. Every village and town here have paid spies . . .'

Daniyal thought of Liyana and the comfort and safety of home. Of the life Zamir had tried so hard to ensure for Raza. He hoped his sacrifice could be honoured, in death, as in life. He was a doctor, he knew it was unlikely this frail, malnourished old man would recover. Daniyal suddenly felt fearful and out of his depth. He had no idea how to keep Raza safe or how on earth he would persuade him back to England.

The private clinic Zamir had been taken to lay in the suburbs behind locked gates. Only cars with a pass and an appointment card were allowed to drive in and the security guard locked the gate quickly behind them.

At Reception they were asked to wait for a Doctor Shah

who was due any moment. The plastic seats were full of families. First wife, second wife, babies, grannies, aunties, and an array of servants to watch the children. Doctors and surgeons, doubling as government ministers by day, arrived late for their clinics. Appointments were a rough estimation. Everyone expected to wait.

After an hour Raza grew restless. Daniyal got up and went over to Reception. He was about to pull rank, give his name and medical qualifications and Sarah's, as she was paying the hospital bill, when he remembered he was supposed to be a poor relation. He explained politely that Zamir Ali's son had travelled a long way and was desperate to see Zamir. Could they go and sit with him until Dr Shah arrived?

The receptionist, a bored, laconic young man in a crumpled white shirt caught a passing doctor. She gave her permission but warned Daniyal that Zamir was heavily sedated and still needed oxygen. It was probable that he would be unaware of them as he drifted in and out of consciousness.

A young nurse led them down a corridor and into a small ward of four men. The smell of sweat, and worse, hit Raza, making him want to gag. All four patients in the ward were old and on drips or oxygen.

'Baba isn't here,' Raza said, frantically. 'My father isn't here . . .'

Daniyal looking around, realized he could not even remember Zamir's face. The nurse walked to the end bed. 'This is Zamir Ali.' She smiled at Raza. 'All men here are very ill; it makes them look different. *Inshallah*, your grandfather is responding to treatment. His breathing is a little easier . . .'

Raza stared in shock at the grey, sunken, and unrecognizable face of his sleeping father. His oxygen mask lay round his neck and he was breathing laboriously with his mouth open.

'Two days ago, your grandfather could not breathe without a mask, so you see he is doing well,' the nurse said kindly.

'He is my father,' Raza said angrily. 'He is my Baba.'

Uncle Maldi put an arm round his shoulders. 'Your Baba is indeed looking better, Raza. I saw how he was two days ago. Isn't that right, Hanif?'

Hanif sighed and nodded. There was a long way to go. His eldest brother had always seemed indestructible to him, indestructible and wise.

The nurse brought chairs and they sat around the bed talking softly, hoping Zamir would know they were there. Raza peered at his face trying to find features he would recognize. Without sheets of cloth wound round his head in a familiar turban, Zamir looked small and vulnerable. Raza touched one of his worn, misshapen hands. It felt clammy. He placed it between his own and bent and whispered prayers. Daniyal saw that death hovered in the shadows of Zamir's pinched face, in the laboured breathing, in the poor worn-out body.

Maldi remembered how hard life had been for Zamir, the eldest son. His brother had had to look after their widowed mother and after him and Hanif from the age of 14, not much older than Raza was now.

Zamir had lost wives and sons they all barely remembered. Ajeet and Fakir were lost to him. Only Samia and baby Raza had brought a rare, late joy to his life. All Zamia wanted was to break the chain of violence for his youngest son. Keep him safe. He had felt a burning pride in all Raza's achievements in England, but with it came a terrible loneliness. He had forgotten to look after himself. Maldi and Hanif both silently prayed to Allah that Raza would go back to England or Zamir's sacrifice would have been for nothing. They both suspected that, even if Zamir died, Raza might refuse to leave Pakistan again.

Daniyal was wondering how Sarah and Chinir would cope without Raza. How would he and Liyana feel without this boy in their lives? Was Sarah's late pregnancy going to be God's way of compensating their loss?

There were no hospital notes at the end of the bed. Daniyal leant and felt for Zamir's pulse. Zamir made small groaning noises and his head moved but his eyes remained firmly closed. Raza leant over the bed and whispered, 'Baba, I have so many wonderful things to tell you. You will be amazed. Being here with you is so much better than talking on a computer. I can see you clearly and hear you much better. I have missed you, Baba, but I am here now. I thank you for your wisdom in sending me away to learn for a while, but now I am back to take care of you . . .'

The old hand twitched in his. 'It will take me a long time to tell you of my life in England. I do not want to tire you. I need you to wake up, Baba. I need you to tell me I am talking too much, that I am giving you a headache. You know, like you used to when I was young and asked too many questions and you would send me back to the goats for some peace . . .'

Something passed across Zamir's face at Raza's flow of words and his lips twitched. 'Ah,' Maldi said, laughing. 'My brother smiles at the memory of your chatter. I think he can hear you, Raza.'

Raza silently thanked Allah. 'If you can hear me, Baba, squeeze my hand.'

Weakly, Zamir did so. Overjoyed, Raza whispered, 'Now I will be silent and let you rest. Now I know that you hear me.'

At that moment Dr Shah bustled into the room. His

white coat was reassuring to Raza. He pronounced Zamir's pulse stronger and his breathing definitely easier. 'He is malnourished. He needs to build up his strength. However, he must be a strong man to survive a serious chest infection. We can reduce his medication slowly. By tomorrow he should be more aware of his surroundings. Let him rest now, get a good night's sleep and return in the morning.'

'I would like to stay with my father. I can sleep on the floor. I will not get in the way . . .'

Dr Shah smiled. 'That is not possible, I'm afraid. This is an acute ward.'

'My father might get worse or die in the night and I will not be here for him.'

'*Inshallah*, your father will not get worse or die, but start to wake and recognize you. The hospital will contact your family if there is any change. Staying will serve no purpose. Return tomorrow and stay as long as you like . . .'

Raza had to be content. As they were ushered out Daniyal said, 'You have given your father a reason to fight and get better, Raza. He will rest easy now.'

From the clinic they drove straight to the mosque to pray. Raza knelt between his uncles. He listened to the call to prayer shimmering over the city. He felt the last rays of the sun touch and warm his arms on the prayer mat. He listened to the constant noise of traffic outside, the blaring horns, the screech of brakes. This life had gone on as if nothing had happened, as if he had never been away. With his head touching the prayer mat to hide his face, Raza wept to be back in Pakistan.

CHAPTER FORTY-EIGHT

Heathrow to Helsinki, 2010

Leaving Finn had been hard. In some ways his anger had been easier to deal with than his slow retreat from her. She had hurt him in such a fundamental way that she doubted he would ever trust her again. Retreat was his defence and Hanna knew she would never again experience unconditional love from Finn. Yet, she could not regret what she had done. In the months before she left Ben, Hanna had begun to feel an alarming fragmentation. She had watched herself from somewhere up on the ceiling. *Oh, look, there she goes, smiling, nodding, making the right responses, laughing at jokes she cannot understand, listening to gossip, comforting another lonely wife . . . There she is, Hanna Charles, fitting in to Ben's army life . . .*

But Hanna could not quite fit in. Women married to soldiers became friends, but she was constantly reminded she was an outsider by her difference. An outsider who startled senior ranks by speaking her mind; a woman who questioned the reasons behind military disciplines. Hanna felt she was forever looking in on a lighted room, unsure and impatient of the rules of hierarchy and rank. For someone uncompromising, she had had to learn, for Ben's sake, not to answer a polite query with brutal honesty. If Ben were to have a successful career in the army, she had to develop respect for rank and military precedence, even if she found it bewildering or inexplicable.

Hanna believed she had tried hard to bend herself into the role of a military wife, but in reality, she had always been resistant. Other officers' wives instinctively knew this and kept a little distance; there was a need to believe in and enter wholeheartedly into the life their men were invested in. It was a choice. Promotions could be lost by an errant wife. The army worked best when the unwritten military contract was adhered to. Wives worked with their husbands for the good of the regiment.

Izzy had wept when she had to say goodbye to Finn. She had clung to him until tears came to his eyes. Clung to Delphi too and wrapped her arms around Ian's legs. Ben had driven them to Heathrow. He was meeting the parents of one of his dead soldiers before he flew out from Brize Norton the following day.

At Heathrow Izzy had screamed to stay with Ben. Kicked out at Hanna and yelled that she did not want to leave, that she hated Helsinki. She had thrown herself at Ben and refused to let go. People stopped and stared at them. It had been horrific.

Ben had carried Izzy away from Hanna and disappeared into the crowds. She had no idea what he had said to her, but she came back calmer with a beige rabbit in a pink tutu to add to her collection. It was a rabbit with a small pink handbag that held a secret note from Ben and a little magic crystal inside.

Izzy had taken Hanna's hand, but she refused to look at her. Ben had said curtly, 'Hanna, sort yourself out before I get back home. I won't have my children made miserable and insecure by your indecision. If you want to stay in Finland, so be it, but you'll live there on your own. I won't give up either of my children. If you're not in the quarter when I get back from Afghanistan, I'll take it the marriage is over . . .'

He had leant towards her and pecked her cheek. 'I'm not a fool. Izzy mentioned Kai. No one receives all those Finnish texts unless they're having, or about to have an affair. You can't have it all. Kai and my children . . . Take care . . .' He had touched Izzy's head and turned and walked quickly away.

On the plane Izzy had sat clutching her rabbit, looking out of the window. She was very still, her small body turned away from Hanna. Hanna had felt sick. She was hurting both her children. She had become a selfish monster. Yet the familiar sick pull for Kai overwhelmed and stalled her.

When the plane revved up for take-off, Izzy had made a little animal noise of distress, craning her head to the window as if she might catch a glimpse of Ben. Then she placed her thumb in her mouth and rocked.

Hanna closed her eyes and leant back in her seat. All the wrong moves unfurling like a ribbon behind her . . .

She doubted that Ben had ever seriously considered her as an army wife. He was an ambitious career officer constantly on the move. She'd had a wonderful job in the middle of London and would eventually return to Helsinki. A relationship between them was never going to work. Hanna had known Ben's army friends were not keen on her. She could not take their war games seriously. She found most of the officers' girlfriends dull, clones of each other dressed in Boden, in practise for a life of conforming.

Hanna made no effort to get to know them at army functions. Why would she? She was only passing through, playing at being an army girlfriend. Hanna had got her kicks by using her novelty appeal as a sexy Scandinavian to make other women jealous. Her behaviour had made Ben uneasy, but he had been infatuated with her. Until she had been rude to his parents . . .

He had dropped her home at the end of that first, dreadful trip to Cornwall and turned down her request for them to be friends, even though she'd rung and explained about Kai.

Ben had never replied to her postcards, but on his return to London he rang and asked her and Annalisa to a party. It was there she learnt that he had nearly been killed. Later, he told her, 'I asked you to the party because I wanted to prove to myself that I was over you.'

The party had been a regimental, post-operation, let-your-hair-down party and a lot of drink was taken. Hanna and Ben had ended up in a small hotel in Notting Hill tearing at each other's clothes. In the morning they had stared at each other dismayed, for nothing had changed, their lives were not compatible, the relationship had nowhere to go. Yet Hanna had strangely felt more happy and secure, companionably lying in bed with Ben, than she had for months. Near to love, she thought as he held her. Near to love.

Ben had murmured into her hair, 'I've tried so bloody hard to get you out of my system . . .'

Hanna had pulled away. 'Don't love me, Ben. I'm not worth it. I hurt people. Someone once told me I have a shard of ice in my heart.'

'Who?'

'A boyfriend.'

'Kai?'

'Yes. I wrote to you while you were away because I was afraid you might get killed. Don't let's start this up again or we'll damage each other. You are off to Germany and my job is here.'

'There are trains and planes.'

'But no future, Ben. I would hate your life. You need to find a nice girl who will be a good army wife.' Ben had made a face and she had joked. 'Come and screw me whenever you are in London.'

'Hanna,' he had said softly. 'That is the difference between us. I have never screwed you or would just be interested in doing that.'

Six weeks later Hanna, remembering, with a sick thud, their weekend of unprotected sex, did a pregnancy test. It was positive. She could not believe her stupidity. Annalisa said, 'If you are going to have an abortion, it's going to be easier to have it in Finland, but you should talk to Ben, first, it's his child too.'

Hanna felt desperate and trapped. She loved her job. She was getting a lot of work and just beginning to earn good money. The last thing she wanted was a child, but she did not want to mess with her body. She knew women who had become infertile through abortion.

Kai sent the London office photographs of his new baby and loss of him and hormones kicked in.

'It isn't just your baby, Hanna,' Annalisa had said firmly. 'How can you morally justify not telling Ben?'

'I'm the one having this baby. Ben's career won't be ruined.'

'Neither will yours, for God's sake. Tons of women manage to have careers and babies, without your good fortune. You're earning good money; you can afford help with child-care.'

So, she had told Ben. He had flown back from Germany immediately. 'Please, Hanna, don't have an abortion. I'll help you financially. I'll support you . . .'

273

In the next few weeks London seemed to pall. It was a hot summer and Hanna felt tired and lonely. Annalisa had got engaged and was always out. She did not feel like partying. Her clients began to irritate her with their lack of taste and indecision. She hated her expanding waist and wilted with constant morning sickness.

She caught the plane one weekend for Frankfurt. She did not show yet and she wanted to see Ben. They stayed in a German Spa on Friday and Saturday. On Sunday there was a mess lunch after church that Ben had to attend. There, to her surprise, she found there were interesting young wives with small children, friendly and welcoming. Among them had been a lawyer, a doctor, and an Olympic rider. Hanna began to revise her judgement. Going back to the patch where the married families lived, she saw that the women happily helped with each other's children. The men were hands-on and involved with their families. Here, there seemed to be lives contentedly lived.

Hanna sat on a lawn holding someone's baby and realized with shock that she craved this same stability for her unborn child. She did not want to be a single mother alone in London. She felt isolated. Everyone seemed suddenly a couple.

Next to her Ben was talking work, but his eyes rested on her as she cradled the baby in her arms. As their eyes met Hanna felt a frisson of attraction and joy. She held Ben's eyes and mouthed, 'I think I love you.' She had watched his face light up as he laughed.

As the plane juddered and banked ready to land at Helsinki Airport. Hanna opened her eyes. Izzy was still asleep. She and Ben had been happy, once. Military life had been new and exciting at first. Lots of parties. Lots of attractive men in uniform. Lots of attention. Ben adored her. London was not far away. They would have two babies

274

close together. Then, when their children were older, Hanna could work part-time.

Hanna played army wives and the years slid by. They moved and moved and moved into different army quarters, that were all the same. Catterick, Dortmund, Shrivenham, Hanover, London, Frankfurt, Bulford . . . Irony of ironies. There were no more babies. Nothing happened. Hanna could not get pregnant again.

Hanna trod water, often alone, watching her young years spin away from her. Ben on active service. Iraq . . . with the special services, when she could not even know where he was. Iraq again . . . and finally, the endless, gruelling training for Afghanistan.

When Finn went off to boarding school, Annalisa, now married with two kids, had asked Hanna if she was interested in helping out, part-time, in the London office during term time. Excited, Hanna suddenly saw a future begin to open up for her. She enrolled on an interior design refresher course. She could combine a few weeks in London, with working from home, and being a hands-on army wife.

Then, Christmas came. Finn was home. Ben was home, safe and supportive. It was a celebration. She bought a stunning red dress and she and Ben partied. It was one of the best Christmases they had ever had. In January, after eight and a half years, Hanna found she was pregnant. Unfairly, she blamed Ben. She had wept hot, bitter tears at her treacherous body. She and Ben had given up contraception years ago . . .

With Helsinki glittering below them, Hanna had looked down at Izzy. How could she regret Izzy? She loved her. She had brought such a spark, laughter, and joy into their lives. But she had trapped Hanna.

Hanna looked out of the plane window as the wheels touched down. She could not forget Izzy's anguish at leaving

Ben and Finn. At saying goodbye to Delphi and Ian. She could not forget Finn stiff in her arms. Or Ben close to tears.

She thought of Kai's long fingers framing her face, his lips touching hers. 'You know, Hanna, our children did not ask to be brought into this world. If we do not love and guard them who will? I love you, but not at the expense of your children. I will always be here. We've fucked up our own lives, let's put our kids first now . . .'

Grief unbidden and powerful rose up in Hanna. *It's no good. I can't do it. I can't stay in Helsinki. I can't do this to Izzy and Finn. Kai is right, happiness is impossible at the expense of your children. I can't keep Izzy away from a father she idolizes. I can't leave my teenage son without me or his little sister. I cannot justify leaving a good man who has done nothing but love me. How strange, that I can't do it, after all. Take that last leap to be with a man I have loved all my life.*

CHAPTER FORTY-NINE

Cornwall, 2010

Delphi woke to find the day hidden in sea mist. Vicious rain lashed the windows from the east. The sea was a sullen gash between the rooftops; the world outside muffled by a Cornish grey blanket. The silence seemed ominous to Delphi and strangely oppressive.

It was a day you had to stride out into or moulder inside with the lights on, settling at nothing. Delphi lay warm in her bed and fought anxiety.

Each morning she felt the sharp bruise of fear before she stretched out to switch on the Radio Four news. There seemed hardly a day now when a soldier was not killed or injured. More insidiously, Afghan soldiers living and training in the British camps were abruptly turning into the enemy within. Blue on blue. 'Unnerving,' Ben told her. 'We sleep with our guns and one of us always stays awake and on guard.'

Each morning Delphi meditated and prayed for Ben's safety. For the safety of all soldiers. She knew that if anything happened to him, she could not be one of those mothers or wives who believed his death had been worth the sacrifice. She would be proud of his bravery without believing his death would make any difference to the war against the Taliban. They would re-form like a great wave once ISAF pulled their soldiers out of Afghanistan.

Yesterday, Ben had rung her to let her know he would be away from the base for a few days. He had sounded cheerful. He was looking forward to getting away from the noisy ops room for a while. He was off on patrol with his boys.

Delphi could hear Ian downstairs making tea. Finn had been subdued since Christmas. He missed Ben and Hanna more than he would admit. Finn was used to being with her and Ian during the term, but he looked forward to his half-terms and holidays on the patch in Germany, with his friends, with his own room, in his own house, with at least one of his parents.

Finn was no longer grounded in his own life. He needed the familiar environment of army life and service people around him. It was all he had known. It was his security. Most of Ben's regiment were out in Afghanistan. That brought the wives and children all closer together, helping one another through anxious days. However important she and Ian were to Finn, they could not give him this feeling of being part of a regimental family.

Only that close little bond of army families left behind in army quarters, knew what it was like to watch the news, day in, day out, while their men were away on the front line. Together, they counted the weeks, the days, the hours until the tour ended; when they could breathe again, sleep at night. Family officers were on hand to advise and comfort. Outings and entertainment were laid on to distract, to make sure there was fun to counteract constant anxiety. By leaving Germany, Hanna had placed Finn on the outside of a close military world that closed ranks to look after its own;

where there was a shorthand for grief and fear, because everyone understood.

Delphi heard Ian coming slowly up the stairs with her tea and sat up. Ian smiled. 'On a day like this the best thing to do is jump straight out of bed and do something, old thing, or depression will take hold.'

'Quite right, darling,' Delphi said. 'What are you planning? Shed?

'Shed.' He smiled. 'Making a new bird table, old one rotting away, as you know. What about you?'

'I'll meditate, then go off into town. There are a few things I need. I'll post my parcel to Ben and probably pop into the framers to see how he's doing. Shall we have breakfast together before you head for your shed?'

'Good idea. Beastly day.'

Finn, Peter, and Iso stood at the window gazing out at the rain-soaked landscape. The rain had stopped but the black sky was still full of it.

'The house match will be cancelled,' Peter said hopefully. 'Won't it?'

'Doubt it,' Finn said. 'There would have to be an earthquake or hurricane before Feathers would cancel a rugby match.'

'At least it's only a house match, not an away game and we haven't got to go to Redruth in this,' Peter said. 'We can be making toast in two hours, if we're lucky.'

'Let's get changed then.' Finn grinned to himself, thinking of Raza, who hated rugby, and the cold, with equal passion. 'At least Raz has got out of playing this match . . .' he said, wondering if Raza had found his father and if he was all right. The others sighed and agreed. 'Lucky Raz. Who wants to play rugby in a monsoon . . .'

It was not that Finn hated rugby, he was an average

279

player, quick on his feet, but his heart did not seem to be in anything this term. He had felt a restlessness in all he did since Christmas. A sense of waiting. For Hanna to come back. For Ben to return. To go home.

Hanna emailed and Skyped him regularly. Izzy seemed more settled. Hanna had stopped roaming around Finland visiting people, so Izzy was seeing more of her grandparents. Uki had made her a sledge with her name on it and she kept sending Finn photos of herself with the adopted ginger tom kitten who lived with their grandparents but, according to Izzy, really belonged to her. Izzy had imaginatively named him Tom.

She was making friends and picking up Finnish in a way Finn could not hope to do now. When he was born Hanna had wanted him to be bilingual, but it was such a difficult language and it excluded Ben, so she had given up after a few months. She also told him speaking her own language made her feel homesick.

The three boys trudged up to the playing fields under the dripping trees. Ahead of them they saw Chatto and his acolytes. As soon as Chatto realized Finn was behind him he started to take little mincing steps with one wrist bent as if he carried a handbag.

'Ignore him,' Peter warned Finn, as Chatto turned and danced jeeringly backwards to them to the laughter of his friends.

'Aw!' Chatto called. 'Aw, is Finny missing his little Taliban friend then? Oh dear, oh dear, what'll he do if the Paki never comes back but has run off to his band of brothers? Boo hoo! Boo hoo!'

He ran in silly little circles round Finn. Finn stopped walking and called out to Peter and Iso. 'Hey! Chatto is outing himself! How brave. I never suspected. I never realized . . . did you?'

280

Iso laughed and deftly stuck his foot out and Chatto went sprawling on to the sodden ground. Amidst the nervous laughter of his friends, Chatto hauled himself to his feet. Furious, he moved towards Iso but then saw Mr Feathers out of the corner of his eye. Instead, he leant toward Finn. 'My father says all Pakis are devious, corrupt, and untrustworthy . . .'

'My father says the same about politicians,' Finn retorted. 'Especially if they are called Chatto.' Even Chatto's friends smirked.

Mr Feathers drew level with the boys. 'Come on, boys, stop bickering. Keep it for the match.'

'You better watch it,' Peter said to Finn and Iso. 'Chatto isn't going to let that go. You made him look a prick.'

'He is a prick,' Finn said. 'What's his obsession with Raz, anyway? Raz has never done anything to him.'

'He doesn't like clever bastards like you or Raz. Or maybe he's just a racist.'

'Nice if we could beat Roskear, that would rile Chatto even more, but we won't, they're better players.'

'Chatto plays dirty. Hope Feathers is on the ball refereeing. We'll try and look out for you on the field.'

'I'm not afraid of that galumphing elephant,' Finn said. 'Chatto's got weight, but I've got speed.'

Chatto's House, Roskear, had a stronger team and it was a rough, dirty game. The rain started again halfway through the match in a drenching miserable mist. Finn thought of Ben. His dad was a tough rugby player. He could never hope to be as good or sporty as him at anything, except tennis. Yet Ben had never shown disappointment in him, only encouragement and pride.

Suddenly, in the rain, on a corner of the bitterly cold playing fields, Finn felt an abrupt stab of fear. The feeling was so acute that for a second he doubled over in pain.

None of the spectators shivering under umbrellas seemed to notice. Finn took a breath, straightened up and jogged across the field towards the action. He would email Ben straight after the game.

Peter threw the ball his way and Finn picked it up and ran weaving through bodies, adrenalin pumping, and scored a try to cheers. Even so, they lost the match.

Finn saw Mr Dominic answering his mobile as the boys filed off the field. Then he watched him moving fast, almost running back towards the school. Finn did not know why, but the unusual sight of his housemaster breaking into a run alarmed him. He was gripped by irrational panic and started to sprint after him. He shot under the avenue of trees, down the stone steps, hanging on to the rail and leaping down the slippery moss-strewn granite, as he watched his feet.

Mr Dominic was already out of sight and that meant he had been running at speed once he was out of sight of the boys. Finn felt sickness rise in his throat. He was frightened of turning the corner and seeing the school ahead, knowing, with every fibre of his being, that something dreadful was waiting for him there.

Delphi was posting Ben's parcel, filling in the Custom Declaration Form as she chatted to the woman behind the counter. Suddenly the urge to get home as quickly as possible overcame her. She paid for the parcel and hurried out of the post office, through the busy town and back through the park.

A thin opening in the clouds revealed a watery sun on a stretch of grey sea above the houses. Her house glinted white, still there. The same cars were still parked outside. Irrationally Delphi felt reassured. She hurried down the last few yards to the gate, out of breath, heart thumping, feeling foolish.

It was then that she noticed, behind a builder's van, a police car and a Royal Navy Land Rover parked at the bottom of the road by the post-box. She stood frozen, her hand on the gate. She knew what it meant. There was no army stationed in Cornwall. Naval officers had to bring bad news to families.

She clicked the gate open and saw Ian through the conservatory window talking to two officers in uniform. He had his mobile in his hand, and she thought, *He is about to ring me.*

Ian heard the gate and turned and hurried out to her. His face was grey with shock. He tried to say something, but Delphi had already moved past him, into the house, towards two young naval officers and an older policeman, whose face she recognized.

The men stared at her with that mixture of pity and dread. Delphi whispered, 'Is my son dead?'

They both shook their heads vehemently. 'No. No. Mrs Charles, Major Charles is not dead, but he has been injured. I'm so sorry. As with your husband, I am required to read out a formal statement to you, laying out the few details we have of what happened to your son . . .'

Delphi listened. *At 7.24 a.m. on the fourth of February, 2010 Major Charles was on an operation in a remote area of Helmand Province. We believe an IED was detonated directly on to the track the patrol were travelling. Your son and others in the patrol sustained serious injuries and were airlifted to the hospital at Camp Bastion where their injuries are currently being assessed . . .*

The officer lowered his roll of paper. 'We are very sorry, Mr and Mrs Charles, to have to bring you this news. I'm afraid we know very few details, as yet . . .'

Ian cleared his throat. 'You say serious injuries. Do you mean life-threatening?'

'I am afraid I don't have details at this time of your son's condition, but my colleague will give you some telephone numbers. We have already contacted Major Charles's wife, as his next of kin. I believe she is already on her way from Helsinki. She will be given a liaison officer as soon as she arrives. He will keep the family informed as soon as information is available. Your son's commanding officer will, of course, be contacting Major Charles's wife as soon as he can. There is obviously a news blackout at the moment . . .'

'Soldiers were killed as well as injured?' Delphi asked.

'I am afraid I have no details.'

'Are Ben's injuries likely to be severe?'

'I'm sorry, I have no details, Mrs Charles—'

'Finn!' Ian said suddenly. 'I must get to my grandson. He is in school here . . . Delphi?' Ian grabbed the car keys. 'Will you be all right on your own, while I go for Finn? You'll need to stay by the phone for news.'

Delphi nodded. 'Go, Ian. Drive carefully. Bring Finn back to us . . .' Then she saw Ian's hands were shaking, his face ashen. 'Darling, I don't think you are fit to drive. You're in shock.'

The police sergeant stepped forward. 'Come on, sir, I'll drive you. I think that's the best thing.'

One of the naval officers had written down a list of names with telephone numbers for Delphi. 'The welfare officers are here to help you, Mrs Charles. Just be patient, it might take a little while for you to get through on these lines. I'll leave my colleague with you . . .'

'Thank you so much,' Delphi said. 'But there is really no need. I will keep busy making phone calls.'

The officer looked at his watch anxiously. 'Are you sure, Mrs Charles? As soon as we have any news, we, or the family officer will be in touch.'

When they had gone the house seemed very still. Delphi

looked at her watch. Those kind naval officers had only been in the house an hour. It seemed like a lifetime.

She lit a candle in front of one of her Buddhas and prayed. Ben was alive. He had not been killed. He was strong. He was a fighter. Delphi hung onto this thought. She closed her eyes and listened to the wind outside and the cry of seagulls. Inside the silent house the French clock ticked like a heartbeat. She thought of Ben lying far from them all, struggling for his life in a field hospital. She could not bear it.

She went back into the kitchen and turned the telephone numbers between her fingers. She was terrified of knowing more; that Ben had died in hospital. That he could be so horrifically injured he might wish he had died. Delphi drew in her breath and gasped at this only too real possibility.

'My darling boy,' she whispered to the empty house where the air around her felt stifling, as if it had its own life. Was Ben lying in terrible pain? Was he conscious? Was he being operated on at this moment?

She reached out to dial a number and the phone rang. She grabbed it.

'Mrs Charles? James Bradshaw, Ben's CO. We met briefly once in Germany . . . I'm on Satellite . . . Can you hear me?'

'Yes. Yes, I can hear you. I remember you, James. Please, tell me what's happened . . .'

'Let me first reassure you that Ben was airlifted to Camp Bastion with great speed and he is getting the best medical attention possible . . . but I have to tell you his injuries are serious. He is in the operating theatre as we speak. We will know more in a few hours . . .'

'Did Ben remain conscious . . . after it happened?' Delphi felt a stab of fear.

'No.' James Bradshaw said quickly. 'I'm so sorry, Mrs

Charles, that I have to speak to you in these circumstances . . .'

'What are Ben's injuries?' Delphi asked quietly.

James Bradshaw hesitated. 'They are still being assessed . . .'

'Please be honest. I need to know if Ben might die in Camp Bastion.'

There was a pause. The CO's voice sounded unsteady. 'Ben has almost certainly lost his left leg . . .'

Delphi's feet went from under her. 'Are you there, Mrs Charles. I am so sorry. This must be such a shock. I cannot lie. Ben's injuries are severe. He caught the blast to his left side, and he's lost a lot of blood.'

'Thank you, James. This must be very hard for you and the rest of your men.'

'It is. My soldiers are in shock. We are a close regiment. An officer will contact you and Hanna as soon as there is more news of Ben's condition. I'm so sorry, Delphi, we are all praying for Ben. If anyone can pull through, Ben will.'

'James, have you spoken to Hanna?'

'I have. I didn't tell her the extent of Ben's injuries over the phone, but I warned her that he had been badly injured.'

'Good. I do appreciate you calling me. I realize I'm not officially next of kin, but because of the circumstances, I'd be so grateful if you, or someone in the regiment, could please make sure I'm kept up to date with what is happening to Ben. Hanna and I are in two different places at the moment, and my husband and I have Finn with us.'

'Of course, we'll try to keep you both in the loop. If Ben stabilizes, he will be flown back to Selly Oak in Birmingham as soon as possible. You will have a liaison officer appointed to the family.'

'Thank you, James. Please take care of yourself.'
'You too, Delphi. You too.'

Finn cut across the lawn, sliding and leaving slash marks as he ran towards the huge trunk of the fir hiding the entrance of Trevelyan House. He leapt down the last few steps onto the gravel and it was then he saw the police car with Ian, Mr Dominic, and a policeman standing beside it.

Finn felt the blood beat in his ears as he ran on gasping for breath. As the three figures turned towards him everything went into slow motion, like a reel of film unwinding. His legs seemed to slow as he ran, Mr Dominic was moving towards him, Ian was reaching out for him. He heard his own voice screaming, 'My dad? My dad . . . Is my dad dead?'

Mr Dominic caught and held him, steadying him. Ian repeated over and over, 'Ben is not dead. He is not dead, dear boy, but injured. He's been injured . . .'

'How? What happened? Was it an IED?' Finn's tongue stuck to the roof of his dry mouth.

'We don't know many details yet, Finn. We just know he's injured and been casevac'd to hospital in Camp Bastion . . .'

Finn began to shake and his teeth to chatter. 'Ben can't die. He can't die . . . he can't die . . .'

Mr Dominic shepherded him inside and Finn found himself wrapped in a blanket and propped in a chair by the fire. His dirty boots and socks had been taken off. Mercy tried to press a mug of hot tea into his hands, but Finn's fingers were shaking so much she put the mug down and began to warm his icy hands between her own.

Mercy kept up a gentle flow of comforting clichés as she tried to rub warmth into him. 'Finn . . . Finn, your father's a strong man . . . He will have the best care in the world.

Wonderful medical people in the hospitals out there, I was a nurse, so I know . . .'

Finn found her words comforting, but he wanted Hanna. Mercy turned to Ed. 'I'm going to run a bath; Finn needs to warm up. I don't want to use the boys' showers; they will be crowded after a match. Could you find him some dry clothes and bring them up?'

Finn let himself be led away. Mr Dominic got him into a hot bath and, free of mud, helped him pull clean clothes and a thick sweater over his head. He repeated over and over silently in his head. *Don't die, Ben. Don't die. Please don't die.*

His brain seemed unable to work properly or his legs or arms. He felt like a baby. He needed to concentrate on saying the words over and over, willing Ben not to die.

'You're in shock, Finn,' Mr Dominic said gently. 'You're going to be all right. The body sometimes shuts down when something traumatic happens. The brain needs time to accept what's happening . . .'

Ed Dominic shook him gently, tried to get Finn to meet his eyes. 'Try to keep breathing deeply. Your mother is on her way from Helsinki. Are you ready to go home to Delphi? Are you a feeling a little calmer now?'

Finn nodded and got to his feet. Ian took his arm as they walked downstairs. The policeman smiled at him. 'That's better, son. You look a lot warmer now. Have you ever been in a police car?'

Finn shook his head. 'Let's go home to Delphi,' Ian said, helping him into the back. Finn, sitting bolt upright in the police car, felt Raza's troubled presence beside him. He remembered Raza's intuition, his anguish, when he feared his father might be dead. Now, Finn understood Raza's terror and desperation. Now, he understood.

Ian was anxious to be home. He had rung Delphi. She

assured him that she was fine, that Finn was his priority, but Ian knew she had been on her own far too long. She must have had more news of Ben because there was something lifeless in her voice that filled him with dread.

CHAPTER FIFTY

Peshawar, 2010

Zamir was still frail but conscious the next day. The oxygen mask was once again over his face and his breathing remained laboured and painful to watch. He feasted his eyes on Raza in wonder and disbelief. Raza placed his hand over his heart with joy when he saw Zamir was awake and aware of him. He sat on the chair beside the bed and watched a flicker of pleasure pass across Zamir's face.

Baba was coming to the end of his life. Raza could tell, in the deeply etched lines of his face, and the sudden smallness of his body, that there was no more fight in him. His energy for life was depleted.

Raza leant forward to tell Baba about his life in England. Zamir's green eyes were still keen with curiosity as he focused on Raza, listening to every word. When he grew tired, he closed his eyes but folded his fingers around Raza's and pressed him to continue. Raza stopped talking only when he saw the old man had fallen asleep and was snoring gently with his mouth open.

Daniyal and Maldi were outside in the corridor, talking

to the security guard. Daniyal came into the room and looked down at Zamir. 'Let your father rest for a while. We will get something to eat and return shortly.' Something in Daniyal's tone made Raza get up and follow him out without a word.

Zamir heard his family leave the room. He sighed, content. There was a sweetness in his heart to glimpse Raza again. There were many things he wanted to ask him about his life in the west; to caution him before he died, but he was not sure he could find the strength.

He marvelled at this beloved son, tall now, his limbs filled out with good food. The boy was almost a man with a new maturity and strength and an easy ability to express himself. The bewildered little boy who left Pakistan was gone.

Zamir sighed. In the last few years, he had used a tiny amount of Sarah's money to employ a young village boy to help with his goats and fruit and vegetables. He had asked Hanif's daughter-in-law, Afia, to find him books and he sat outside his hut in the shade, reading of the world beyond Pakistan. Something he had never been able to do before.

The sense of inner peace and purpose he found in words that echoed his own sentiments eased his weary heart. He stopped doubting; he knew he had been right to send Raza away. History fascinated Zamir, for although it made him feel small and unimportant, it had a pattern he could see, and it brought his own life, and those of his family, into some sort of context. He did not believe that power, or real change could be facilitated by poor people like him, but he did believe it could be subtly altered by the educated men who wrote these books, who lived away from Pakistan. He liked to dream that Raza could be one of the next generation of Pakistanis who would work for and experience a different, more peaceful Pakistan. A Pakistan not continually at war with itself.

There was relief in the knowledge that many, outside his own small world, grasped the consequences for Pakistan, if the Mad Mullahs got their way and took Pakistan back to the Middle Ages.

Zamir wondered which of his brothers had summoned Raza to his deathbed. He would not have permitted it, if he had known. He felt anxious for Raza and Daniyal's safety. They had seen for themselves that he was well looked after, now they must return to England as soon as possible.

The young man he saw by his bed was not the child who had left him. Raza's new life, and all that he had become, had been influenced by others. Yet, regret that he had not been there to see his son turn from a child into a young man was far outweighed by his pride.

Zamir had thanked God for his goodness when Raza, with Liyana's help, with private tuition and English lessons, had won a scholarship to a new school far away from London. He had always known Raza had a quick brain, but to be proved right in all he had wanted for his son, was the only validation he needed.

The day Sarah told him that Raza had not only settled into the new school but had finally made a good friend and been accepted by other students, Zamir had gazed out at the distant snow-capped mountains and wept, knowing that life could not get better than this.

Zamir had no intention of dying just yet. He needed to make sure Raza went back to England. It was not going to be easy. Raza understood if he left Zamir now, they would never see each other again. Zamir closed his eyes and rested. The boy must be strong enough to recognize the need to return to his studies in England; to see there was nothing he could do for an old man at the end of his life, except fulfil his hopes of a better one.

If Raza stayed in Peshawar, the years in England would fade as if they had never been. Poverty would drive Raza into one direction or another, and Zamir knew which one Ajeet and Fakir would choose for Raza when he was dust.

He tried to sleep. His chest was painful just with the effort of breathing, of anxiety for Raza's safety. When he closed his eyes, he could feel the malign presence of his older sons edging nearer. He heard Raza come back and sit by the bed. Zamir moved his hand across the covers so he could feel the warmth coming from his son's fingers.

When Hanif arrived at the hospital at noon, he seemed jumpy. He and Maldi went out of the room and began talking in low voices. Daniyal watched them with growing unease. He felt safe within the hospital but not at Hanif's house. Hanif lived in a district of Peshawar that Daniyal would normally never dream of entering. He was beginning to feel dislocated, a stranger to himself in his cheap, creased *shalwar kameez*. He was weary with the heat and the need to be vigilant about his own safety and that of Raza's.

He would have liked to question the doctor about Zamir's condition and the level of his sedation. Zamir's chest pain, breathing, and colour indicated, Daniyal thought, lung cancer, a tumour, rather than pneumonia, but he could not be sure, and to question a diagnosis would reveal he was a doctor and put them at risk.

Daniyal longed for a cool, air-conditioned hotel room with a shower, a soft bed, and clean sheets. He felt ashamed of himself. He had forgotten this enervating heat that sapped all resolve and finer feelings. He had never known what it was to be a poor Pakistani. He did not think Zamir was going to die immediately or in this hospital, although he certainly wasn't long for this life.

He wished he knew what was going through Raza's mind. Would the boy insist on staying in Peshawar with Zamir or would he do the sensible thing and return to Sarah and Chinir with him?

After his medication, Zamir slept for the rest of the afternoon. Raza sat crouched near Zamir's bed. Every now and then Zamir would open his eyes to see if he was still there, give a half smile and doze again.

Daniyal told the old man of the happiness that Raza had brought into their lives in England. Raza was surprised. He knew that he had also caused trouble and sadness. He felt he was a disappointment to Sarah. Zamir's old crablike hand moved across the bed and patted Daniyal's arm, then he began to snore again, making Raza grin.

Zamir woke as the evening call to prayer issued from the mosque. He seemed anxious and lifted his arm on hearing Maldi and Hanif and beckoned them to come to his bed. Daniyal took Raza off to wash and pray at the back of the hospital, sensing Zamir wished to be alone with his brothers. Zamir reached out with a thin claw-like hand. Summoning all his strength, he begged his brothers to be vigilant, to keep Raza and Danyial close to them. 'They are not safe,' he kept saying in his cracked voice, and nothing Maldi or Hanif said seemed to reassure him.

Raza was, as always, reluctant to leave Zamir. 'Zamir is not going to die in the night, Raza,' Daniyal said firmly. 'He is gathering strength. He is tired, full of medication and needs to rest.'

Hanif's wife, Shiza, cooked supper for them. Hanif's son Ahsen and his wife, Afia, joined them. Daniyal found this welcome. Afia was a plain, cheerful woman, educated and certainly more intelligent than Hanif's son. The family were lucky to have her.

The two security guards had changed their uniforms for *shalwar kameez* away from the hospital, in order to be inconspicuous. In this area of Peshawar, the sight of armed security guards guarding poor men would make his neighbours suspicious. Hanif also insisted they ate inside tonight, in the tiny main room.

Daniyal considered it all a bit of a farce. If there were as many spies in Peshawar and surrounding villages as everyone said, Ajeet and his group of Taliban could certainly find and carry the two of them off without too much trouble. He did not have much faith in the thin and hungry young security guards.

It was as if his thoughts had conjured trouble. As they finished their meal two policemen turned up in Hanif's yard. They grinned as they stood in Hanif's doorway but greeted the family politely. '*Assalamu alaikum.*'

'*Wa alaykumu as-salam,*' Hanif murmured, looking dismayed. Maldi muttered something under his breath and the two security guards jumped to their feet. Raza stared, nervous. He did not like uniforms and the tension in the hot, little room was palpable.

'Will you not invite us in?' one of the policemen asked. Raza's head jerked up and he too leapt to his feet. He knew that voice. Fakir laughed. '*Salam alaikum*, little brother. I am very much alive. Did no one tell you? Do not fear, we are not policemen . . .'

Ajeet and Fakir took off their peaked hats. 'We did not want to be shot by your idiot security guards who do not know one end of a gun from the other . . .'

Ajeet turned to Maldi and Hanif. 'Fakir and I come only to see Raza.'

295

Raza was staring at Fakir as if he was a ghost. Fakir said, 'Come, outside in the yard where we can see you, little brother. This room is hot and crowded.'

The security guards followed them out into the yard fingering the guns in their belts anxiously. Raza felt a stab of excitement and fear that his brothers had come to find him. Fakir seemed much older and bent with some injury. He had burns to his face and one arm appeared to hang loose, but he was very much alive.

Ajeet, tall and gimlet-eyed, stood in the tiny yard, proud, still warrior-like and splendid, the same as he always was when he carried Raza on his shoulders.

Raza gazed at his brothers, startled by their sudden presence. All three regarded one another in silence. Daniyal watching, thought with surprise, *There is genuine affection here between these brothers.*

Ajeet and Fakir laughed suddenly and clapped Raza on the shoulders, held him away, teased him about his looks and youth and thicker limbs. Both men were in command, had a powerful presence in the compound. The guards remained poised but still. Shiza brought out a tray with small cups of Jasmine tea and the brothers squatted in Hanif's yard with their reluctant hosts.

'We have just visited Baba in hospital, Raza,' Fakir said.

'Was my brother awake? Did he know you were there?' Maldi asked, anxiously. 'He is very frail.'

'He knew,' Fakir said. 'But he chose not to open his eyes to talk to us.'

Hanif said angrily, 'Did you frighten him? Baba is ill. He must not be worried.'

'Uncle, we are Zamir's sons. We have a right to see our father.'

'Of course, you do,' Maldi said quickly. 'But you also know his greatest fear.'

'Yes. We do. God is good. In the end His will prevails. Raza is safely back in Pakistan.' Ajeet roared with laughter.

Raza felt himself sweating. Tension filled the yard. He had chosen to believe the security guards were there to protect Daniyal from kidnap, not him from his bothers. He sat beside Ajeet and Fakir, happy to see them alive but confused by his emotions. Ajeet's tone to his uncles made him uncomfortable. The words, innocent in themselves, were bullying, hectoring. Raza was reminded of Chatto and felt dismay.

Daniyal introduced himself to the two brothers, courteously, but with a certain authority. 'Raza returned to Pakistan to see his father, but he is in the middle of his studies in England. You should both be proud of him. He is doing well in his school.'

'You travelled with him?' Ajeet asked coldly.

'I did.'

'You hope to take him back with you?'

'Zamir wishes Raza to complete his studies in the UK before he returns to Pakistan.'

'Hmm,' Fakir said. 'All you western types, so frightened of being kidnapped; it seems to me it is you that does the kidnapping.'

'There was no kidnap. Zamir made the decision for Raza to live and be educated in England with my daughter.'

'The old man is dying,' Ajeet said. 'Raza will not leave him, will you Raza?'

Raza shook his head. Ajeet laughed again and got up. 'You see, Raza is not like you westernized Pakistanis, he is one of us. He is a *Pashtun*, not a Britisher.'

He ruffled Raza's head. 'We will be back. Don't fear. No one will force you to leave Pakistan again. This I swear.' The smile had gone. He stared at Daniyal pointedly, then turned to the watching family, savouring their fear.

297

No one moved. Ajeet stood, tall in the tiny yard enjoying the moment. He said softly, 'If family honour and loyalty is observed, no one need get hurt. My uncles, remember this . . .' He turned to Raza. 'Brother, we will be back.'

As they swung out of the yard and disappeared, Raza felt a dizzy and bewildering dislocation. Ajeet and Fakir's veiled threats were alarmingly clear. The sneering, bullying Chatto kept sliding into his mind as he stood in his uncle's yard. He felt conflicted. He thought, with a surge of loss, of Finn, who had always tried to protect him from that very horrible boy who wished to harm him.

He looked at Daniyal, who had been so good to him. It hurt him to hear him rudely dismissed, spoken to as if he was worthless. His chest felt tight and he realized he had been holding his breath. He let it out in a sigh of relief.

No one spoke. The security guards shifted their feet. Everyone in the room knew that these men would never have stood up to Talib commanders such as Ajeet and Fakir.

Daniyal thought wryly that at least he had proved a point to himself, security was farcical, and he would jolly well wear trousers tomorrow.

CHAPTER FIFTY-ONE

Cornwall, 2010

When Ian and Finn got back to Penzance, Delphi had lit a fire, the table was set, and the smell of supper filled the kitchen. Ian saw no sign of the shocked and frantic woman he had left earlier. For Finn, she was calm, the same as ever she was, and Ian saw the immediate effect it had on the boy and marvelled at Delphi's strength.

Delphi held Finn to her then sat him by the fire and handed him a ginger beer and Ian a whisky. She picked up her glass of wine and sat beside them. Finn watched her anxiously. 'Is Hanna coming?'

'Hanna is on her way. Mummo is travelling with her. Hanna did not want to leave Izzy in Finland.'

Finn took a deep, trembling breath and looked at Delphi. 'Ben? What about my dad?'

'I spoke to Ben's CO, James Bradshaw, earlier. Do you remember, I met him in Germany?'

'Yes. What did he say? Did he tell you what happened? Did he tell you how bad Ben is?'

Delphi hesitated and glanced at Ian. Finn said, his voice cracking, 'My dad's going to die, isn't he?'

Delphi looked at him. Nearly 13 years old. Thin as a whippet. Mature and brave because he's had had to be. She said quietly, 'Ben is badly injured, Finn. Surgeons are operating on him at Camp Bastion now. He will be receiving the best treatment in the world. They hope to fly him back to Selly Oak Hospital in Birmingham as soon as they can . . .'

'If he doesn't die.'

Delphi put her glass down and took Finn's hands between her own and shook them. 'We are not going to even think of Ben dying. You know how strong he is. We are going to will him to live with every fibre of our beings. We are going to will and pray so hard, Ben will feel the force of our combined love and strength. All negative thoughts are banned. Positive thoughts only. We are going to concentrate on having Ben safe home, Finn. We can do this. We can do this together, can't we?'

Finn looked at Delphi. Stared into her eyes. He could almost suppose she had the power to determine Ben's fate.

He nodded. 'Please, Delphi, I need to watch the evening news. Not to be morbid but because I need to believe it's true, what's happened to Ben.'

Delphi shook her head. 'No, darling, definitely not.'

'I would rather watch it with you and Ian than watch it later on my phone, on my own,' Finn said firmly. 'I have to know everything. I have to.'

Delphi wavered. She did not want Finn to see the news, but she needed to see it herself, as if it would somehow bring her closer to Ben. She glanced at Ian. He said, 'Finn, I don't think they will be releasing any details yet, but I do understand your need to watch it. However, I exercise the right to switch it off if immediately if I deem it necessary . . .'

300

Delphi kissed the top of Finn's head. 'Come on, we all need to eat . . .'

The flickering flames from the fire were reflected in the windows. Outside the rain lashed and the wind threw itself across the garden. Normally, Finn loved winter evenings tucked in with his grandparents, but the warmth and comfort of the room made what was happening to Ben feel nightmarish and unreal.

Ian asked Delphi, 'Did you speak to the family liaison officer?'

'Yes. Nice voice. He said he would be round tomorrow. I started to say there was really no need and that we were fine. Then, I thought, this is his job, this is what he does, how can I say, we don't need you to come around to comfort us when he is . . . the comfort officer.'

'Oh, my dear old thing,' Ian said, and they smiled at each other.

'Anyway,' Delphi added, 'how do we know what we might want to ask him tomorrow? A young officer called Simon, from Ben's regiment, also rang me. Basically, he's the one who keeps families informed. He will be attached to Hanna and look after her when she arrives. He was sweet, told me we could ring him day or night if we felt the need to talk or ask him anything. The military do seem to swing into action in an emergency.'

'When will Hanna ring us?' Finn asked.

'I'm sure she'll ring as soon as she lands. I spoke to your grandfather, Uki. Hanna was rushing to catch the first plane back to London, so I haven't spoken to her, but James managed to get hold of her. She will be kept informed as a priority . . .'

'It's nearly time for the news.'

'Finn, there's something you need to know . . .'

Finn whipped around his eyes wild. 'Don't say it, Delphi.

I'm doing as you said, willing whatever you heard not to be true. So please don't say it out loud . . . I'm not stupid, I know what IEDs do . . . but you said it, Dad's strong. He will be okay. He will . . . BE OKAY.'

'Finn . . .' Ian said. 'Seeing the news is just going to distress us all . . .'

'I know that, but the news will tell us something, even if it doesn't go into details. You will watch the late news when I've gone to bed, so it is not fair if you stop me . . .'

Watching the news was a surreal, out-of-body experience. Finn clutched a cushion and held it to his chest.

'*News is coming in of a serious bomb attack in Afghanistan. One solder has been killed and three badly injured in an attack outside a remote village in Helmand Province. The names of all the injured have not yet been released until families have been informed. We can however report that Corporal Sean Beaver was killed, and Major Ben Charles and Captain Andy Maynard suffered serious injuries. The third soldier injured is still unnamed, until his family, believed to be on holiday in New Zealand, can be contacted. Three Afghan civilians, two of them children were also airlifted to Camp Bastion for treatment . . . It is believed one child died before she could reach hospital.*

'*Colonel James Bradshaw, colonel of the regiment had this to say of his injured men . . .*

'"*We are all, naturally, in a state of shock at this horrific attack. We grieve the loss of Corporal Sean Beaver, an asset to the regiment and an extremely popular soldier. Tragically, Captain Andy Maynard died of his injuries earlier this evening . . .*"'

The Colonel swallowed. '"*He was a young officer with a great future in front of him . . . Our hearts go out to the families of these two brave men who lost their lives today . . . The regiment is a family, and we are hit very hard by this despicable and cowardly attack on our soldiers. Our thoughts and prayers are with Major Ben Charles and the other injured soldier and their families tonight. It is hoped they can be flown home as soon as possible to receive treatment and to be reunited with their loved ones. Thank you . . ."'*

The firelight flickered and the news moved on to more mundane things. The three of them sat in silence. Ben was alive. He had not lost his life in the dry Afghan dust like his poor corporal, or the young captain who had not made it home. Yet, trying not to dwell on the extent of Ben's injuries felt impossible. *Nothing feels real. It is like a sickening dream we cannot snap out of*, Delphi thought, struggling for calm, to keep her fears from Finn.

Finn closed his eyes. *Dear God, please listen to me. If you make Ben live, if you make him not too badly injured, I will not doubt you exist. I will do anything for the rest of my life. Please make him know we are praying to You for him to be okay. Please let him not wake up lonely without us. Please don't let him be in too much pain. Please don't let him die of his injuries. He is a good dad. Please God . . . Amen.*

Ian said gently, 'Bed, old thing. Sleep is what you need.'

Finn opened his eyes. He felt deathly tired.

'Go up, darling,' Delphi said. 'I'll bring you hot chocolate.'

Ian followed Finn upstairs, drew his bedroom curtains, turned the duvet back and found his pyjamas from the drawer. The room was warm and the stuffed animals on Izzy's bed comforting. Ian waited while Finn went to the bathroom and did his teeth. 'I know I'm going to drink hot chocolate but I'm too tired to get out of bed again,' Finn said wearily, climbing in.

Ian smiled and sat on the bed. 'I don't think one night is going to make your teeth fall out.'

They sat without saying anything, then Finn said in a small voice that took him by surprise, 'I want Hanna and Izzy to be here.'

'I know you do. Not long now. You've been the bravest of the brave today and I'm proud of you.'

'I don't feel brave. I feel scared.'

'I know. Try to sleep now. I've put your old iPod on the bedside table in case you want your music.'

'Thank you.' Finn held up his arms to hug Ian and Ian held him as he had when he had been small and kissed the top of his head.

'God bless, old thing. Night-night.'

'Night-night.'

Ian went downstairs. In the kitchen by the dying fire Delphi was weeping.

CHAPTER FIFTY-TWO

Peshawar, 2010

Raza woke early the following morning on a charpoy in the yard, scratching. It had taken him ages to fall asleep. His mind had been whirling after seeing Ajeet and Fakir after so many years. He felt hot and itchy. He missed being able to shower, to climb in a bath, to use shower gel and a thick towel. He sat up and as he lifted his *shalwar kameez* realized his whole body was covered in bites. He leapt off the charpoy with a yell and tore his top off and shook it. Maldi and Daniyal, sleeping under a lean-to near the curtained door, also shot up with a start.

'What is it, Raza?' they both called in alarm. 'What's the matter with you?'

'I've been bitten. I am covered in bites. All over me.'

The two men viewed Raza's body covered in raised red bites. 'Bed bugs,' Daniyal said immediately, beginning to itch himself.

Hanif and Shiza rushed out to see what the commotion was and Shiza stared mortified at the bitten boy. 'I borrowed your charpoy and covers from a neighbour. We are clean people; we wash our bed clothes and air our mattresses . . .'

'Of course,' Daniyal said hastily. 'This can happen anywhere, to anyone, Shiza. Raza, I will hose you under the tap. I have antiseptic and calamine in my bag and later we will go to the pharmacy . . . Hanif, take the mattress and covers out of your yard and burn them or all your family will be bitten . . .'

Shiza was already gathering the bedding and Hanif went and got a large piece of polythene and they threw the bedding in and tied it up and put it out of the yard.

Maldi held the hose while Daniyal subjected Raza to a gruelling and humiliating soaping.

'Sorry, Raza,' Daniyal said, 'but bugs lay eggs that cannot be seen.'

'Oh great!' Raza said, in English. 'Wonderful news.'

For some reason this made Daniyal and Maldi laugh heartily. Raza could see nothing funny in being under a cold tap in view of absolutely everyone because you had caught bed bugs . . .

Raza's clothes were thrown away and Shiza produced a spotless new *shalwar kameez* for him. Daniyal thanked her and took the opportunity he had been waiting for.

Since the episode of Ajeet and Fakir turning up dressed as policemen it was obvious the security guards were useless. Daniyal had lain awake and decided he was unwilling to go on being part of this farce. A morning with bed bugs had clinched his decision.

He turned to Hanif. 'I've no idea how long we are going to be here. Or how quickly Zamir will recover. I can't take advantage of your kindness in looking after us any longer, Hanif. You and Shiza have your work and you own family to look after. Raza and I will book into a hotel . . .'

He put his hands up at their protest. 'You can then stop

paying those useless security guards. Raza and I will be safe enough behind the barricade of a secure hotel. It makes sense. It will be more difficult for Raza's brothers to then dictate or control our situation. It is a pointless pretence to be anything other than what we are. I am a British Pakistani susceptible to ransom. Raza is the brother of Taliban commanders who want him to join them rather than return to the UK. This is the situation. Let's not pretend anything else. We are at risk, but let us have the dignity of being ourselves . . .'

Raza felt a great surge of relief and fondness for Daniyal. He felt like laughing. It was so simple, put like that. Pakistani lives seemed so unnecessarily complicated. Had it always been so? Did a love of intrigue occasionally make them exaggerate danger?

He saw in the faces of his uncles the battle between relief in Daniyal's wish to simplify their lives and a fear that if they accepted his decision family honour might be at stake. Raza also sensed their anxiety was for him. Would he stay with his father or return with Daniyal to England? Would Ajeet and Fakir try to keep him in Pakistan by force or abduction?

All Raza wanted at this moment was to be with his father. He would not leave him, but neither would he be forced by his brothers to go against Baba's wishes. He shut his mind to all other thoughts, except how good it would be to be in a clean hotel room with a bathroom and a bed without bugs. He scratched and wriggled and saw that the men had come to an amicable agreement at last. Daniyal stood up. 'Let's go to the pharmacy or you will scratch yourself raw . . .'

Maldi accompanied them. The security guards appeared to have vanished in the night. Daniyal, tired of feeling afraid, strode the streets of Peshawar as he had once as a student, for the first time feeling normal and a part of the life around him.

The traffic had ground to a halt. Maldi said, 'Something is going on. Demonstration maybe.' At that moment they saw a black Toyota Land Cruiser with blacked-out windows stop at the traffic lights. It flew a US flag on the bonnet. The car following behind also had smoked windows.

The lights changed as they walked past, and the cars drove over the junction towards the American Embassy. Suddenly, a lorry coming the other way veered across the carriageway and drove at speed straight into the Toyota. There was a rapid explosion and flames tore out of the lorry and started to engulf the Land Cruiser. Armed security guards leapt from both cars and dragged the passengers out of the smoke and flames. There was a moment's silence before the shouting, before people started running. Then sirens began to wail from all over the city as police and Rangers forced their way through traffic.

Maldi, Daniyal, and Raza were too far away to see if the Americans were alive or dead. They could see the tiny bodies of the street children lying in the road by the traffic lights, buckets of water and windscreen cleaner spewed with the garlands of frangipani they had been selling. A transvestite lay with his head blown off, his shabby *shalwar kameez* blowing about his body as if he still breathed.

CHAPTER FIFTY-THREE

Cornwall, 2010

Finn woke to winter sunlight. For a moment he was disorientated at not being in his room at school and then he remembered. Sick dread lurched through him. He could hear the murmur of Delphi and Ian's voices down in the kitchen. He thought of Ben lying wounded and unconscious. He thought of him in pain and turned in anguish and pressed his face into his pillow. He wished Raza was here. Raz, who always sensed when you were hurting, or things were bad. Raz, who would place his precious shawl over you if he could not find the right words.

He made himself think of Ben, safe in the huge RAF C17 Globe master. A flying hospital with an operating theatre inside with doctors and nurses who travelled with all the injured soldiers coming home for treatment. The plane was enormous. He had seen it on the television. Ben might actually be flying in it at this moment. He might be here already.

He sat up. Hanna must be in London by now. Had she rung?

Finn got out of bed and went out onto the landing. The first thing he saw through the open door of Delphi and Ian's room was Delphi's suitcase open and packed. He flew down the stairs and into the kitchen. Ian and Delphi sat at the table with a pot of coffee, talking softly. Delphi had a pen and paper in front of her. They both looked up quickly and seeing his face, Ian said quickly, 'It's all right, old thing. Ben is holding his own.'

Delphi got up and hugged him. 'I'll make you some breakfast darling. I'm glad you slept in, you were tossing and turning most of the night.'

'What's happening? Where are you going? Your case is packed.'

'I had an early phone call. The army are flying Ben back to Selly Oak Hospital in Birmingham to be treated . . .'

Finn gave a sigh of relief. 'Where's Hanna?'

'She's arrived at Heathrow with Mummo and Izzy. The regiment are organizing a flight on to Birmingham this morning . . .'

'I'm coming. I'm coming with you. I want to see Ben.'

Delphi put his mug of tea in front of him. 'Sit down, darling, there's something we have to tell you . . . I don't want to keep things from you.' Finn sat, his heart banging.

'Ben's injuries are severe, Finn. He needed to be flown home urgently because he will have to go through more operations . . .'

Finn noticed how bright the sun was on a bowl of blue hyacinths, on the bright cushions on the sofa. So garish was that yellow light that it made his eyes ache, it made him dizzy and sick. He knew. He knew what IEDs did. They blew men's limbs off.

His eyes stayed riveted on Delphi's sad face. Tears started to flow out of the sides of his eyes before she could tell him. But Delphi was unable to get out the words Finn dreaded. She could not say them out loud or make them real. It was Ian who said, quietly, 'Ben has lost his left leg, Finn. I'm afraid there is a possibility he might lose his right as well. I am so sorry, my boy, it is a terrible thing to hear.'

Delphi reached for him, but Finn backed away. He shook his head vehemently, weeping without sound. He ran upstairs, slamming his bedroom door shut. He threw himself on the bed. 'No!' He screamed. 'No . . . no . . . no . . . no . . . Not my dad. Please . . . please let it not be true . . . not my dad . . .' But Finn knew in that searing moment that there was no God to hear him. Because He did not exist. HE DID NOT EXIST.

Downstairs Delphi wept too. 'We had to warn him. We had to prepare him. What is the best thing to do, Ian? I wanted Finn to stay with you, then return to school to have some sort of normality with Ed Dominic keeping an eye on him, but I think he needs to see Hanna and Izzy. Be near Ben, even if he can't see him.'

Ian made an instant decision and picked up the phone. 'We'll all fly up to Birmingham together, Delphi. I can bring the children back with me if needs be. What's the number of the family officer? I am going to call in favours. We'll fly straight there and meet Hanna at the hospital. What time does Ben's flight get in?'

'They think around 6 p.m. Thank you, darling. It will be so good to have you with me.'

'Leave Finn be for a minute or two. It's a bloody hard thing for him to accept.'

'I'll make him toast, then I'll go up.' As if toast could make any difference, she thought.

'Delphi, however terrible this is for us all to take in. Ben is alive. Wounded, battling for his life, but alive . . .'

'I know. I know . . .' Delphi closed her eyes against the

day. 'If he lives, I can bear anything, Ian. If Ben lives, we can surmount anything.'

And we will, Ian thought. *Bless you, we will.*

Finn sat up on the side of his bed and reached for his iPhone. He wrote a message, ignoring the ones that pinged in for him. *Raz,* he wrote in anguish. *Raz.* Then he pressed send.

CHAPTER FIFTY-FOUR

Peshawar, 2010

Raza stood in the air-conditioned bathroom under the cold shower and let the water flow over him. His body, legs, and arms were full of bites. In his head he saw tiny, razor teeth chomping on his flesh. He shivered. Better than being dead. Better than being blown across the road into small parcels of torn fabric, blowing gold-edged, in the ensuing silence after the blast.

The American diplomats in their armoured vehicles had lived. It was the street children, beggars, innocent bystanders who had died. Pointless. Raza lifted his head and let the water flow over his face relishing the feeling of being cleansed, washed, clean. He thought abruptly of Finn. Finn had not emailed or messaged him; this was odd. He had not emailed Finn because . . . because it hurt too much. He might never see Finn again and he must be strong . . .

Daniyal put his head round the door. 'Are you all right?'

'Yes. I am okay.'

'Dry yourself and I will help you cover yourself in this

soothing ointment . . .' Daniyal looked tired, old, and sad. Raza said gently, 'You need to rest. You are not used to bombs. You have had a bad shock.'

Daniyal smiled. 'We both have. Many people have.'

'I am angry, so angry. You are a doctor and yet you could do nothing for those people. This is a terrible thing for you.'

'It was the most appalling and barbaric act. It was cowardly, without a thought for innocent people . . . children. To try to kill Americans on a public highway . . . what has it achieved? Nothing . . .'

'Rest, Daniyal. You can now sleep in the cool of a bedroom.'

'You will want to go to your father, shortly.'

'Uncle Maldi is coming back. In any case, I am sure I could find my own way . . .'

'Absolutely not. What are you thinking when the city is in turmoil?' Daniyal lapsed into English and Raza smiled.

'There,' Daniyal said, putting the cap on the ointment. 'You'll do. You'll just feel sticky as well as itchy.'

'In the light of this day these are small things.'

'Indeed,' Daniyal said.

Raza took another *shalwar kameez* out of his case and pulled the shirt over his head.

'Raza?' Daniyal said quietly. 'This is what the Taliban do. They kill and maim and bring misery to thousands of their own people in the name of God. Men like your brothers, Talib commanders, would like you to believe in the noble cause of *Jihad*, fighting against foreign invaders and Western Imperialists. There is nothing noble in what you saw today. Your father gave up his life with you, here in Pakistan, so that you could escape this endless, sickening violence. So that you could be educated; so that you could show men like Ajeet and Fakir that there are different and

314

political ways of working towards a goal; a more intellectual approach to Pakistani problems . . .'

Daniyal lay back on the bed with a sigh. 'Sorry. I did not mean to lecture you . . .' He closed his eyes. 'I cannot see you blowing people to smithereens with your brothers. What can you do here in Peshawar, Raza? What can you do?'

'I can take good care of my Baba.'

'You are a twelve-year old boy with a great future. Are you going to throw it all away?'

'I am nearly thirteen. It is my wish and my duty to care for my father in his old age. See what happens when he is not cared for? He grows ill and weak and there is no one to look after him . . .'

'I will say no more.' Daniyal held up his hands. 'I am too weary.' He longed, simply longed, to be home.

Zamir was sitting upright in the bed, eyes on the door, waiting for Raza. The oxygen mask was around his neck, but he was not using it and his eyes were brighter. He looked more like the father Raza remembered. 'He refuses to take any medication today,' one of the nurses told Maldi. She looked down at Raza. 'He is anxious. I think he wants to be clear-headed for you.'

She turned to Maldi. 'Two policemen visited him last night. They upset him. He needs to take his medication, or his lungs will fill up with fluid again. The doctor advised only a short visit this evening. Half an hour, no more, then he must rest.'

'*Assalamu alaikum*, Baba,' Raza said moving to the bed.

'*Wa alaykumu as-salam*, my son. *Assalamu alaikum*, Maldi.'

'*Wa alaykumu as-salam*, brother. You look more yourself today.'

315

Zamir lifted a thin hand. 'Drugs help the body but dull the mind . . . Raza, sit near me.'

Raza smiled. Here was Baba like he used to be, a little fierce, determined to speak his mind, determined Raza should listen.

'This attack on the Americans. We heard the explosion. Visitors here say women and children were killed and injured. I was afraid for you all, for my family . . . I hoped you would stay inside . . .'

'It was a bad day, today,' Maldi said. 'Zamir, don't worry about us. We have kept away from the centre of the city. Daniyal and Raza are now safely in a hotel this side of Peshawar. They will not return to Hanif's house.'

Zamir peered at him. 'There is a group of TTP Talibs formed in the mountains above our village. Ajeet and Fakir are with them . . .'

'We cannot know that they are responsible for this attack Baba,' Raza said quickly.

Zamir rested piercing green eyes on his son. 'I hear they have already accepted responsibility . . . I hear they are only sorry that no Americans died in their reinforced cars. This group of Talibs will regard their attack as a failure because only street people who matter little to them died . . .' He waved at the bed next to him. 'I heard it. Everyone was talking about what happened.'

He pulled the oxygen mask over his mouth and closed his eyes and breathed for a while. Maldi shifted uneasily, not wanting to cause Zamir any more anxiety. 'Ajeet and Fakir came to Hanif's house last night.'

'They came here too,' Zamir said tiredly, pulling down his mask. 'Dressed as policemen.'

'What did they say to you, brother?' Maldi asked.

Zamir smiled without humour. 'They came with anger

316

in their hearts and saw only an old man who is no threat to them. They still retain a little family honour that dictates they treat me with some respect and not too much contempt, while I live . . .'

He pulled the mask up again and breathed as if it hurt. 'Baba don't get tired . . .' Raza whispered.

Zamir lay so still that Maldi and Raza wondered if he had gone to sleep. Then Zamir took his mask off and said, with some strength, to Raza, 'Ajeet wants to mould you and indoctrinate you into his ways. This is not because he thinks you will be a fearless fighter for their cause, but because he considers you his property. He has always been obsessed by making you, his small brother, into his image. To take over when he becomes too old to command, but he will never trust you because of your time in the west. He will test you in terrible ways, Raza . . .'

Zamir took more oxygen but held up his hand because he wanted to say more.

'Fakir,' he continued, 'has been injured and suffers. He knows his time as a commander is coming to an end. His usefulness and ability to command respect is waning. Fakir cannot read written instructions or work a computer. He is ashamed to admit this to younger fighters . . .'

'Ajeet does not read or write either, Baba. This does not affect him. He has power still. I see it.'

'Ajeet's ruthlessness makes him strong. He is feared and admired. Other people will gladly do what he cannot. No doubt he will die a glorious death and be a legend and a martyr. Raza, if Ajeet once had a heart, he no longer remembers it. He would kill you, his brother, for his cause, as he would anyone that he believes has betrayed him, including me, if he could.'

'Baba,' Raza said, 'I have no intention of going off with

317

my brothers and joining the Talibs. I am no longer a child obsessed with guns. I stay in Pakistan only to take care of you.'

Zamir reached out to touch the fabric of Raza's *shalwar kameez*.

'My son, listen to me. I am trying to warn you. You will not be allowed to take care of me. You are no longer a child, but you are not yet a man. I will die, maybe in weeks, maybe in months, but I will die. Then what will you do here in Peshawar? Must my dreams and hopes for you die with me?'

Raza leant forward. 'Baba, I have changed. I no longer believe in violence as an answer. I have a British passport. When you are gone, then I can go back to England and resume my studies. Do not worry; my brothers would not harm me. Don't you remember how Ajeet carried me on his shoulders when I was small? He was always the one who protected me from other boys. I want only to take you back home to the mountains and care for you for the time you have. This is all I want, Baba. To be with you for a while, to make up for the time we have lost . . .'

Zamir gave a great sigh and closed his eyes. 'I am a poor man, but I hoped to die feeling proud that one of my sons might change the world a little, that I had done one good thing in my life. You betray me if you stay here in Peshawar, Raza . . .'

Raza leant towards him and whispered, 'Baba, I would betray you and myself if I do not stay and look after you.'

Zamir's hand shot out and held Raza's. 'Go now. Let me rest. You are not listening to me. Go away and think about my words . . .'

His eyes were bright with anger and fever. 'Death is nothing. How we live is everything . . .' Zamir firmly closed his eyes and lifted his oxygen mask to dismiss him.

On the way home Maldi felt frustrated with Raza. 'Don't

you understand? Your father only wants to recover enough to return to the house he has lived in all his life. He wishes to die facing the mountains and in peace. Why can you not give him that peace, Raza? Why can you not reassure him you will return to England with Daniyal?'

Raza said nothing. His mouth was set in a tight, obstinate line. Maldi said, 'So! How will you live, you and your father? You are used to a full belly now.'

Stung, Raza said, 'We have land. We have goats. We can live as we have always lived . . .'

'And starved when times were bad and seasons harsh. Why are you being so stupid? Do you think your brothers, the Talibs, will leave you alone if you do not do as they wish? You will be accused of being a spy for the west . . .'

'No more, Uncle. No more today . . . please.'

Maldi relented. 'It has indeed been a terrible day. I wish you had not witnessed such violence, Raza, but the reality is that we have an atrocity somewhere in Pakistan every single day of our lives . . .'

They passed the security guards and entered the hotel. Maldi went up in the hotel lift with Raza to see how Daniyal was. When Raza went to the bathroom, he said quickly, 'If you have any influence with that stubborn boy try to make him see sense. Zamir has all but begged him to return to Britain with you.'

Daniyal nodded and sighed. 'I intend to return home the day after tomorrow, Maldi. I've spoken to Liyana and Sarah, the bomb in Peshawar has been widely reported in Britain. They have been frantic with worry. I have booked two tickets, but I will leave with or without Raza. I have a duty to my own family.'

'Of course,' Maldi said. 'We all do. I too will go back to Islamabad in the next two days. Hanif will take Zamir home to his village when he is strong enough. That is all

319

he wishes, to end his days there with his books quietly and in peace. *Inshallah,* this happens.'

'*Inshallah*, Maldi. Goodnight.'

Maldi smiled. 'I hope not to be bitten!'

'Maldi, my dear chap. You are welcome to stay here . . .'

'You know that I cannot upset Shiza and insult my brother.'

'I know. Please thank them again for all they have done for us . . .'

Raza came out of the bathroom. 'Goodnight, Raza. I will see you tomorrow.'

'Take care, Uncle.'

While they had been at the hospital Daniyal had connected to the Internet. The bomb in Peshawar, small by some standards, but directed at Americans, had made the western news. Liyana had sounded shaky and begged him to return home. Daniyal knew he was neither street wise nor competent to do more than accompany Raza here in Pakistan. He could and would not force a 12-year-old onto a plane even though he held a British passport.

'I've got an Internet connection,' he said to Raza. 'It may not last. Do you want to check emails? Say hi to your friends?'

Raza hesitated. He had purposely tried to distance himself from his friends and school, put his English life at the end of a long tunnel so that it would seem unreal. He tried to resist Daniyal's laptop, but the draw was too strong. Casually he flipped to Facebook and trawled through rubbish messages and photos that seemed stupid and from another planet, after this violent day. There were no posts from Finn.

Raza cut to his emails and saw immediately there was a message from Finn at the top. He opened it. *Raz. Raz.*

Raza stared at the tiny word the English boys used for

him, stared at the three letters of his name. A great sweep of alarm and melancholy crept over him. His name was like a desolate, distant cry from another world, a world he had left, like a hand reaching out. Raza shivered and could not turn away from the words written small on the screen.

'What is it?' Daniyal came up behind him and stared at the screen.

'I don't know. Just my name.' He looked up at Daniyal. 'Something is wrong, Finn is in trouble.'

Raza typed, *Finn, what is it? What has happened? I am here*. And pressed send.

Daniyal put his hands gently on Raza's shoulders. 'Enough for today. You need to eat and sleep. There will be an answer in the morning. I'm going to order room service. Go and bathe. It always helps you.'

Raza did as he was told. Oh, how he loved deep warm baths and thick towels. Water healed. It was why Finn loved his wild Atlantic Sea.

Finn. He let his friend slowly slip back into his world.

Raza was woken in the night by the blip of an incoming email. He got out of bed and padded to the lighted screen on the desk by the window. He sat and flicked open his mail. Finn. *My dad has been blown up in Afghanistan. He might lose his legs, Raz, and I can't bear it. I can't bear it.*

Raza froze. Then gave a muffled cry and ran to the bathroom and threw water over himself. He knelt, rocked on his knees, head to floor, head to floor and prayed for Finn's baba, opened his hands and offered his prayers. He saw the sun setting in vivid reds and oranges over a grey winter sea. He saw Finn's Baba laughing as he stood high on his surfboard, strong as a lion, catching waves.

He got up and flicked to the world news. Two days ago, there had been an attack on British soldiers in Helmand Province. An IED had been detonated, killing two soldiers and badly injuring two more. Afghan children had died too.

Raza opened the curtains and looked down over Peshawar, a city he had known all his life. It seemed peaceful at night. Trees wavered against the dark skyline like the hands of dancers. Mountains rose darkly, framing the land and sheltering villages. He thought of his valley, thick with orchards of bitter almonds and apricots that tasted of heaven.

His village, his house, was as clear to Raza as if he had just walked down the track. He knew in that moment that he would never return there. All the beauty and wonder of his country was being laid to waste by violence. He did not want to be a part of this terrible, endless feast of killing.

Baba was right. If he stayed, he would get sucked into the circle of despair. Baba had given him this one chance to have a different life and he had come close to throwing it back in his face. Pakistan was his home, but for now he could do nothing to change it.

He thought of Finn. He thought of the injured father who would never ride the waves again. He felt very small in this violent, unpredictable world. He went to wake Daniyal. 'I want to go back to England,' he whispered urgently. 'I want to go back with you.'

Then he slowly began to text Finn, searching for the right words. *My heart it leap at your terrible words of your Baba's wounding. My heart it is breaking. Please, Finn, try not to despair, your Baba, he is strong, and he is young . . . I am sorry. I am very sorry.*

Raza stopped, overwhelmed by sadness. He could find no right words to give Finn comfort.

CHAPTER FIFTY-FIVE

Birmingham, 2010

The darkness is like soot, soft, smooth, and without sides. Ben wants to sink deep within its folds. Yet when he tries the pain sweeps over him in a sickening rush.

He is under a tree. Somehow a route has been cleared to him and he has been dragged to cover. A face appears in front of the sunlight sparkling through thin broad leaves. Cpl Parton, team medic. He tries to say, 'Dolly, what's going on?' But a strange sound comes out instead. Dolly is talking, reassuring him. 'You're okay, Boss, I've got tourniquets around both your legs . . . I'm just going to feel under your body armour for hidden wounds . . .' Ben screams and sees Dolly's eyes fly open as he finds the gaping wound in his abdomen. 'Okay, Boss, I'm going to get a field dressing on that now. We'll get you out of here as soon as its safe for the MERT to land . . .'

Ben has no idea of the passage of time. He floats. Morphine eases the pain. From a long way away, he can hear voices. 'Come on, Boss, stay with us. Come on . . . Come on, Boss . . . Stay with us . . .'

He feels the helplessness of Dolly beside him. They have three soaking field dressings over his stomach and a cannula has been fed into his right arm.

'This is the last one,' he hears another medic say. Dolly is desperately squeezing a bag of saline into his veins. Ben feels cold, bone-cold, feels his life begin to slip away.

'I'm going,' he whispers.

'Fuck off, Boss,' Dolly snaps. 'You aren't going anywhere till I say so. You owe me a round . . .'

The radio suddenly crackles with voices and the world erupts in gunfire. 'Here we go, Boss, we've suppressed that gun for a bit and it appears the MERT is being flown by another mad Cornishman from Culdrose who insists on risking his arse getting you out of here . . .'

He is bumped onto the folding stretcher, men at each corner . . . Painful, jerking movements as they run. He feels the hot breath of a chinook exhaust and its downdraught on his face as he is taken up the back ramp A glimpse of a nurse's face. Capable, assured hands cut away his clothes, insert needles. A tube is pushed into his throat to keep his airway open. He feels the tail of the aircraft lift and the noise of juddering engines, but he doesn't think he will make it home and the faces of the people he loves dance in front of him before blissful darkness descends . . . Then the whole thing begins again. The voices, the needles, the hands, the bleep of machines . . .

Okay, Ben. We're on the way back to Blighty now. We are taking you home . . . you are doing good . . . so good . . .'

But it wasn't good. Each time the sounds and voices became a little louder, a little nearer, the sweet, pain-free darkness began to lose its depth.

'Ben . . . You are back in the UK now. Safe home. Are you in pain?'

Ben fought not to swim upwards. Fear gripped him. Something bad was waiting for him up there, something terrifying, something worse than pain.

He felt gentle fingers remove his oxygen mask and the tube from his mouth. He fought panic but found he could breathe. Someone inserted a cannula into the back of his hand, lifted the covers to inspect his abdomen. Ben opened his eyes. There was a doctor in a white coat, a nurse in a blue uniform.

They both smiled. 'Hello, Ben. Welcome back. Do you know where you are?'

Ben shook his head. The doctor said, 'You're in Selly Oak Hospital, Birmingham, Ben. I'm Philip Dunstan, your consultant.' He hesitated then asked, 'Can you remember what happened to you?'

Ben shook his head again. 'You were injured in Helmand. You've been flown back to the UK . . .'

Remembrance swept over Ben. Sweat broke out all over his body. He turned his face away from them. The staff nurse touched his arm. 'Ben, we're going to keep you heavily sedated for a while. Please let us know if you are in pain. We can fix that. Try to relax. You're home now . . .'

Give me the darkness. *Ben prayed.* Don't let me remember. Let me sleep forever.

Hanna, Delphi, and Ian sat in a row in the family room watching the door. The staff at Selly Oak could not have been kinder or more thoughtful. Coffee, tea, and juice appeared at regular intervals. Finn sat on the floor with Izzy playing with toys from the box in the corner of the room. Hanna's mother, Eeva, had gone to the shops to buy the essentials she and Hanna had not had time to pack. Eeva had tried to take Izzy out of the hospital but she would not leave Hanna and Finn.

When the consultant came to tell them that Ben was

conscious, Delphi let out her breath in relief. Hanna sat bolt upright. She was so white that Ian thought she might faint. The consultant, a tired-looking man called Mr Dunstan, told them it was good news. Ben was still in the trauma ward, but the operation had gone well.

Finn stood up. 'Dad's not going to die?'

Mr Dunstan smiled at him. 'Your father is holding his own, thanks to the surgeons at Camp Bastion, but he has been badly injured, so we are going to have to keep a careful eye on him and keep him sedated for a while . . .'

He turned to Hanna. 'Your husband doesn't remember anything yet. He may never remember how he came to be injured, but the low point will come as he becomes aware of the extent of his injuries. It's tough, but Ben is not going to have to go through this alone.'

'Does he know he's back in England and in hospital?' Delphi asked.

'We've told him. I doubt he's taking much in at the moment. I know you are all desperate to see him, but he remains a sick man. Please be patient . . .'

He turned to Hanna. 'If you would like to come with me, Mrs Charles, I'm sure he would respond to hearing your voice. Just two minutes.'

Hanna, white with fatigue and shock, stared at him looking horrified.

'I . . . what about . . . Can Delphi, Ben's mother, come with me?'

Mr Dunstan looked surprised. 'I'm afraid it really must be a brief visit, for moral support, for him to know you are here.'

'Of course. I understand,' Delphi said, taking Hanna's arm. As they walked to the ICU unit Delphi felt Hanna trembling. It was the first time that she had ever appeared lost or vulnerable and Delphi held onto her.

Ben was lying on his back. The skin on his face was yellow and bruised. He lay awkwardly because of the injury to his left side. There was a bridge holding the weight of the sheet from his legs. He seemed to have lost bodyweight overnight. He looked smaller and ten years older. His eyes were closed and there were deep black shadows under his eyes. He was motionless and did not seem conscious. Hanna stood frozen, incapable of speech or of moving towards him on the bed.

Delphi released her hand from Hanna's and went to stand beside Ben.

'Hello, my darling. It's so good to have you home. Rest now and sleep. We are all here, just along the corridor. Hanna and Finn, Izzy and Ian. All willing you well and strong again, my darling . . .'

She turned to Hanna, but Hanna could not move. She was staring at Ben, imagining what lay under the bridge of sheets. She licked her dry lips but could not speak. Delphi bent and kissed Ben's forehead. 'God bless, my love. Hanna's here too. We're not allowed to stay, but we will be back when you've had some sleep . . .'

Hanna made herself move to the bed. Awkwardly, she touched Ben's bruised face with the back of her hand. 'Ben,' she whispered. 'Get better. Get better . . .' Then she turned and fled.

Ben moved slightly but did not open his eyes. Delphi looked down at him. The pain of seeing him struck down seared her. She felt light, without weight. Everything in her fought against having to walk away and leave him. 'Finn, Izzy, and Ian send their love. We will be back soon, very soon . . .' She placed her fingers where a needle with a drip had been inserted into the back of his hand. For a second Ben's fingers curled round hers then fell away.

When Delphi and Hanna left the room, Finn fought an

327

overwhelming urge to run after them, to cry out. He wanted to see Ben so badly, it hurt. Izzy let wooden bricks fall from her hands. 'I want to see Daddy. Why can't we go too?'

'Because Dad's not really awake yet, because too many people will make him tired.'

'We're not too many peoples, we're his chilren . . .'

Finn smiled and bent and hugged her. 'We'll see him as soon as he is a bit stronger, okay? Ian hasn't seen him either . . .'

'Us three will see him tomorrow?'

'Let's hope so, sweetie,' Ian said. 'Meanwhile we might have to do him some paintings, don't you think?'

They stood, Ian and Delphi in the park beneath the bare trees while Finn pushed Izzy on a swing. The sky was sullen, hostile, the ground cold and hard from the frost. They stamped their feet and kept moving in small circles waiting for dusk, for the lights to come on, for this day to end.

The army had housed them in accommodation for forces families near the hospital in a suburban house on a leafy road. There was a family room for Hanna and the children with a double bed and two singles. Ian had found a small hotel within walking distance for Eeva, Delphi, and himself.

When it became apparent that Hanna was in no state to look after the children, Delphi suggested that Eeva take her back to the hotel to rest while she and Ian stayed with Finn and Izzy in the family accommodation.

'I'm sorry,' Eeva said. 'I've never seen Hanna like this. She has always been very collected.'

'Shock,' Delphi said, quietly. 'Ben looked . . . so . . . damaged, Eeva.'

Eeva replied impatiently, 'Hanna might be traumatized, Delphi, but Ben and her children need her to be strong. What would have happened if you or I could not have been

328

here, and she'd fallen to pieces in front of the children? Look at my grandson, being so brave and grown up . . .'

'Don't be hard on her, Eeva. Shock affects us all differently. Ben's injuries are going to be life-changing. Hanna had to get straight on a plane. The poor girl has had no time to absorb the enormity of what's happened, and she's sleep-deprived.'

'Well, she certainly felt guilty to be in Finland when it happened,' Eeva said. The two women faced each other in the cold February afternoon. Neither of them said what they were really thinking: that Hanna's abject terror was for herself, that she would not be able to face Ben's injuries.

Ian called out to Finn, 'It's absolutely freezing. Let's go and find pizza and warm up.'

'Yes!' Izzy yelled. 'Stop the swing.'

'Oh, thank you!' Finn said to Ian. His teeth were chattering.

'We'll walk quickly to warm up,' Delphi said. Her mind was still at the hospital, at Ben's side. She wanted someone to be there when he woke. If she had been Hanna, she could not have left the hospital. She would not have left his side. Abrupt tears rose in her throat and she quickly took Izzy's hand and swung it. The leaden sky threatened snow and Delphi sang, 'My toes are cold, cold, cold . . .'

'It's my nose, nose, nose,' Finn replied.

'Nose and toes!' Izzy cried tremulously, and Ian copied her in a deep, sonorous voice, making her laugh.

United, they walked to the pizza restaurant.

'Tell me again, Delphi, did Ben know you and Hanna were there?' Finn asked when Izzy had finally fallen asleep in the small bed by the window.

'He was drowsy with morphine, darling, but I assured him we were all here.'

329

'Hanna looked awful when you came back. What did she say to Ben?' Finn asked abruptly.

'There was only time to whisper, "get better . . ."' Delphi's voice wavered, suddenly.

'You're exhausted, Delphi. You need to get to bed . . .' Ian called. He was making hot chocolate for them.

'Finn,' Delphi said gently, 'Ben knows we are all here.'

'I hope I can see him tomorrow, just for a moment, like you did?'

'Darling, let's see,' Delphi said wearily. 'I'm unsure whether you will be allowed to . . .'

She saw Finn fighting tears and she went and held him. 'Sweetheart, I honestly don't think Ben would want you to see him until he is a bit stronger.'

Ian interrupted firmly: 'Let's see how Ben is tomorrow and what the doctors say, Finn. We all need to go to bed now. Delphi, you are rocking on your feet . . .'

Finn turned to face them. 'I don't think Izzy should see Dad, she's too young, but I'm not . . .' He met Delphi's eyes. 'Delphi, Hanna won't be good at . . . she can't bear anyone ill. She is terrible around hospitals or injuries . . .'

Delphi suddenly wanted to snap, *This isn't about Hanna.* But she said, 'Let's turn the lights out and sleep. We'll talk in the morning. Please, try not to worry about everyone, Finn.'

In the dark Ben woke with a start. He slowly realized he was back in the UK, in hospital, but the dream or flashback had been terrifyingly real. He lay still getting his bearings. He listened to the hum of machines all around him and the footsteps and movements of the nurses constantly checking the equipment by every bed.

A staff nurse came to check his drip and saw he was awake. She smiled. 'Hello there. Good to see you're awake again. How are you feeling?'

His voice was strange and croaky. 'Horrible dream.'

'Morphine,' she said. 'Known for it, I'm afraid, but it does control the pain. Do you think you could manage a cup of tea?'

Ben nodded. That sounded good. The staff nurse turned and spoke to a nurse by the door and then came back to the bed. 'Are you in pain anywhere, Ben?'

'My side, but it's bearable.'

Mr Dunstan appeared by the bed. 'You're due more medication soon. Please don't suffer in silence. We don't want you to be in pain and the morphine will help, but I'm afraid it can make you hallucinatory. I'm going to check your wounds now you are awake, Okay? Let me know if it hurts . . .'

'In the dream I had lost my legs,' Ben mumbled. 'I was so relieved when I woke up and I could feel them both . . .'

The consultant's fingers stopped probing. The staff nurse was suddenly still. Mr Dunstan held Ben's eyes as he replaced the sheet over him.

'Ben, I'm sorry. You have lost your left leg. The good news is that we have managed to save your right leg. It's taken a complicated operation but it's all looking good at the moment . . .'

Ben stared at him, horrified, feeling sick and faint. 'I can feel my bloody legs. Both of them.'

The staff nurse said, 'I'm sorry, Ben. It's the nerve endings. I'm afraid this happens.'

Mr Dunstan put a hand on Ben's arm. 'I know it must seem like the end of the world, but I promise you, it isn't. It really isn't. We will be here to help you every step of the way . . .' His bleeper went and he said quietly, 'Ben, I'm sorry, another flight is coming in . . . I have to go . . .'

The staff nurse pulled a chair from behind the curtain and sat beside Ben. 'The orthopaedic surgeon at Camp

Bastion did a brilliant job. He was determined to save your right leg and he did. You got lucky. I know it doesn't feel that way right now, but you are a fit, strong guy and you are going to recover. You are going to be all right. Please believe that . . .'

Ben turned his face away from her and closed his eyes. The young nurse arrived back with his tea in a plastic cup with a lid and lip like Izzy used to use. 'I wasn't sure if you took sugar, so I've brought some packets from the canteen with me . . .' she said.

Ben opened his eyes and found her beaming at him. 'Thank you,' he said politely. 'No sugar.'

He lifted his head and sipped the tea which she held for him. It immediately made him want to retch and he pushed it away. The staff nurse began to check the drains in Ben's side and the dressings on both leg and stump.

She looked down at Ben's bruised face and battered body, careful to keep her feelings in check. She would never ever get used to this. Never. While she stood there, trying to find words of comfort, there was another flight of seriously injured soldiers being casaevac'd in . . .

She smiled at him. 'Pain relief, Major Charles?' Ben nodded.

'Ben, I'm sorry. I know it's a shock to hear and easy for me to say . . .'

Ben looked at her and tried to smile. 'I wouldn't think it was easy for you to say, Staff Nurse Haslet, however many times you have to say it . . . Perhaps, I already knew and chose to forget. I'm unsure. It doesn't really matter, does it?'

'What matters, Ben, is that you are alive and have a future.'

She moved away to get his medication and Ben lay in the dark waiting for the blessed needle that blocked out the

332

endless repeat of the screams of the injured, but not the smell and the terror and confusion which crept slowly back with the morphine.

CHAPTER FIFTY-SIX

Twenty-four hours later, Ian sat by Ben's bed reading Oscar Wilde while Ben slept. Ben had been moved out of the intensive care ward and was now in a side room on his own. Mr Dunstan had vetoed even a short family visit. Ben had woken with a temperature and he wanted to keep him away from any possible infection.

At four in the afternoon when the day was already dark and lights had sprung on in all the shop windows, Delphi had received a call from a staff nurse saying that Ben was anxious to see Ian and was obviously not going to settle until he had. If Delphi was hurt, she did not show it.

Ben was asleep when Ian arrived at the hospital. Ian had to close his eyes for a second when he saw Ben. How broken he looked, with his flushed face and poor, bruised body. The staff nurse on duty had told him Ben was probably struggling emotionally as he became aware of the extent of his injuries. 'To lose a limb is a devastating thing for anyone to accept. It takes time and a lot of support to help come to terms with these sorts of injuries.'

Ian's poetry book had inappropriately fallen open at 'Ave Imperatrix'. The poem was not one Ian wanted to read but it had been impossible to turn away from the words. For Ian it conjured a long-forgotten summer and Ben's strange fascination with this particular poem. At 15, Ben had a bad dose of glandular fever and he and Ian had spent weeks in the beach house together while Delphi worked for a big exhibition in Plymouth. Without television Ian had taken to reading aloud to Ben in the evenings. Ben had fallen in love with the rhythm of Wilde's poetry without necessarily understanding the meaning of all the poems.

The spears of crimson-suited war, The long white-crested waves of fight, And all the deadly fires which are The torches of the lords of Night . . .

Ian placed his finger on the page. He and Ben had been especially close that odd, suspended summer. With Delphi away in the Penzance house, painting for hours on end, Ian had felt protective of the languid and listless teenager laid low by a virus.

After a while in the quiet hospital room, Ian realized that Ben had opened his eyes. 'Hello old thing,' he said, closing the book.

'Ian, you came . . . Good to see you . . .'

After a minute Ben smiled. 'You're reading Wilde. You always read him when you're anxious.'

'Do I?' Ian asked, surprised.

'Yes. Do you remember how you used to read aloud to me when I had glandular fever?'

'I do.'

Ben closed his eyes tiredly. A wry smile hovered about his mouth. 'Are you reading "Ave Imperatrix"?'

Ian hesitated. 'I was. It fell open at that page.'

'It's the one we always read that summer. Read me a bit?'

'I would rather read another poem, old thing.'

'You know it has to be that one.'

335

Ian lifted the book to the light. As always, Ben found his soft highland lilt soothing.

'. . . *And many an Afghan chief who lies Beneath his cool pomegranate-trees . . . Clutches his sword in fierce surmise . . . The measured roll of English drums Beat at the gates of Kandahar . . .*'

Silence filled the room and Ian sat very still mentally wrapping Ben in a warm cocoon of love. 'If I don't open my eyes,' Ben murmured, 'I can almost believe we are back in the dusty beach house . . . I was determined to learn the whole thing by heart that summer . . . but now I can only remember snatches. Read on.'

'. . . *The gilded garden of the sun, Whence the long dusty caravan*

Brings cedar wood and vermilion: And that dread city of Cabool . . .'

'Enough for now, I think,' Ian said.

Ben whispered, 'Could I, in that long-ago summer have had a presentiment that I would end up here, like this, Ian? You know, I took the copy of Wilde that you gave me, to Lashkar Gah . . .'

He turned to Ian, his eyes burning. '*O loved ones lying far away, What word of love can dead lips send! O wasted dust! O senseless clay! Is this the end! Is this the end!*'

Ben clenched his eyes shut. 'I don't believe in any of it, Ian. I don't believe what we are doing out there will last. I wish I could go back. I wish I could go back to that summer in the beach house and be whole again . . .'

The room was in darkness. Outside in the lighted corridor the trundle of a drugs trolley could be heard rolling nearer. The voices of nurses called one to another as if from a different shore. The room seemed to Ian a small island wherein he was shipwrecked with his son, searching wildly for the right words of hope and comfort when he wanted to cry out like Wilde. *Ruin and wreck are at our side, Grim warders of the House of Pain.*

Ben said suddenly, opening his eyes, 'Last night I woke thinking I'd had a nightmare. I could feel my legs and I felt so relieved that I had just been dreaming. Then my consultant told me I'd lost my left leg. He said that you can still feel your legs even when they aren't there . . . At that moment, I wished I had died, Ian. All day I've fought an overwhelming wish just to be dead . . .'

Ian leant and put his hand over Ben's, and Ben grasped it tight. 'I know this is selfish, cowardly, and self-pitying . . . Two men died on patrol with me. I know soldiers who are triple amputees and here I am snivelling and whining when, thanks to a surgeon's skill, I've managed to keep my other leg. I'm bloody lucky, Ian, but I can't feel it . . . I can't bloody feel it. That word amputee . . . strikes terror into me. I don't want to be one. I want to be a normal man with two legs . . . I want to be me again . . .' Ben's voice cracked.

'Oh, my dear, dear boy,' Ian said. 'Don't fight this grief. You have a right to it. You have endured so much. You are not Superman. You can't be strong all the time. Weep. I am the only one here. You have cause to weep . . .' But Ben dare not let go.

A nurse came in with pills in a small dish. She checked his IV cannula and took his temperature. 'Mm, still a bit high.' She turned to Ian. 'Probably a good thing to let him try and sleep for a while.' She held the covers up and gave Ben a shot in his bottom.

'Beginning to look like a pin cushion,' she said cheerfully.

When she had gone, Ben said, 'Ian, I can't do this with Hanna, Delphi, or my children around. I don't want them to see me like this. I need to tackle the next few weeks on my own, here, in hospital where I'm in a military environment.

I need army banter to get me through. It's the only way I'm going to survive. I can't bear to see all the love and pity . . .

'I can't cope with anyone else's emotions. I can only cope with myself among other injured soldiers. I need a gallows humour to get through. If that sounds selfish, I'm sorry, but I'm begging you to take everyone away, back to Cornwall . . .' Ben lay back, sweating and breathing heavily.

Ian thought of Delphi and the children waiting, desperate to see him and felt anguished. But Ben's needs had to be paramount. 'I will try to explain to them all, gently, in ways they will understand, Ben, then we'll do as you ask and go back home, until you need us.'

'Thank you.' Ben gave a small sigh of relief.

Ian stood up. 'But, Ben, it's going to be very hard for Delphi and the children to leave here without having seen you. I think Finn and Izzy just need to see that you are home and safe. That you are going to be well cared for . . .'

'I don't want my children to see me like this, Ian. Izzy is much too young . . .'

'The one thing children hate to be is shut out. Their ability to cope is miraculous. Dear boy, will you see how you feel in the morning?' Ben nodded and Ian turned to go. 'Sleep now, you need to rest.'

'Thanks for coming, Ian. Will you leave your Oscar Wilde?'

Ian smiled. 'I can think of more cheerful books to leave you.'

'Yes, but at the moment it appeals to my sense of melancholy . . .'

He lifted his hand and Ian took it. 'How is the pain?'

'Bearable. The morphine shot is beginning to work . . . but I dream, I get muddled, forget . . .' Ben seemed to fall asleep holding Ian's hand, but he started mumbling. 'Opened fire . . . goats everywhere. Little boy . . . girl in a red dress lying in the road . . . dying . . . alone . . .'

Ben opened his eyes and looked at Ian, his words growing slurred.

'We . . . shot at a Taliban once . . . he came running at us from behind a building . . . his leg was shot clean off. Know what he did, Ian? He just turned and hopped away . . . that takes guts . . .'

Ian bent and whispered. 'Dear Boy, sleep now. Dream of the beach house. Dream of home. You will get through this and when you need us, we will be here, waiting. We will be with you every step of the way . . .'

Ian was not sure if Ben heard him. He felt overwhelmed by sorrow to see Ben suffering. He could do nothing. Absolutely nothing to help him at this moment.

He made his way out of the hospital into the dark. He did not know how he was going tell the expectant faces waiting for him that Ben did not want to see them. How could he explain that Ben needed to come to terms with his injuries on his own, that his recovery did not include his family at the moment? Ben might feel differently in the morning, but Ian did not think so.

Sleet blew sideways and chilled him to the bone. He felt older and sadder than he had ever felt in his life. For Ben to be so injured, in a war he did not believe in, was a terrible, terrible tragedy.

CHAPTER FIFTY-SEVEN

In the morning Ian had a message from the staff nurse on the ward to say Ben had a bad night, but he wanted to see his family before they returned to Cornwall. She said the visit must be brief. Ben was still very poorly.

Finn and Hanna went to the hospital to see Ben together. A Major Alex Brown was waiting for them. He was a friend of Ben's, a military doctor who had served in Germany with Ben. Both Hanna and Finn remembered him. He explained that Ben was still feverish and drugged with pain-killers, so they could only stay a few minutes. He suggested that he took Finn in to see Ben first, then Hanna could go in and have a private moment with Ben afterwards. Finn saw Hanna's dismay. He knew she would have preferred to go in with him, but he did not know what to say.

When he was shown into Ben's room, Finn felt a stab of raw shock at seeing Ben lying under a cage of blankets. He looked as if he was dying. He looked bruised and grey and terrible. He was trying to smile but Finn could see he was in pain.

'Hi, Finn. Don't take any notice of my ugly mug, only bruises, they look far worse than they are . . .'

Ben had tubes everywhere. Finn felt sick and shaky. Major Alex put his arm lightly round Finn's shoulder and Finn was glad of it. Watching Finn grow ashen, Ben muttered, 'I didn't want you to see me like this, Finn, but Ian told me that would have upset you more. Come here, . . . let me look at you . . .'

Tears poured out of Finn's eyes before he could stop them. He was furious with himself because he saw how it upset Ben. He went to the bed and Ben tried to hug him with one arm, and Finn tried to hug him back, terrified of hurting him. 'Get better, Dad. Please, please get better and be okay . . .'

'I will. I'm going to be fine. I promise you. It's just going to take me a while . . .' Ben's voice sounded weak and tired. 'What I need most, old thing, is for you to go back home now and help Ian look after the girls while I concentrate on getting better. Can you do that for me?'

Finn nodded. 'Good lad. We'll talk on the phone. I'll ring you often, I promise . . .' Ben closed his eyes. 'See you soon, my darling boy.'

Hanna was sitting on a chair in the corridor outside. Alex Brown told her that Ben was about to be given pain relief. 'I thought I would take you and Finn down to the canteen for coffee and breakfast . . .'

Hanna waved her coffee in a paper cup and declined. She wanted to wait there until she could see Ben, or she would lose her nerve.

In the canteen Finn found he could not eat anything either. Alex bought him a hot chocolate. 'Finn, might it help if I explain what will happen to your dad while he is here in Selly Oak?' Finn nodded.

'Well, Selly Oak has a mixture of military and civilian patients, as you can see, but military patients, like your dad, are kept together in the same wards. It's comforting for servicemen when they are still recovering to have staff in uniforms, and also each other.'

Alex Brown stopped for a minute, looking for the right words. 'It's going to take . . . some time for your dad to . . . adjust to what's happened to him, as well as physically heal, but believe me, he's in the very best place. He's going to be really well looked after here. When your dad is ready, Headley Court is the next stage in his recovery. It's where he will go for physio and rehab. As a family you'll be able to see for yourself what a wonderfully positive place it is when the time comes. There, they concentrate on getting servicemen over their injuries and back into uniform . . .' Major Alex paused. 'If it's at all possible.'

He smiled at Finn. 'Ben's as fit as a butcher's dog. They will get him on his feet again in no time . . .'

Finn stared at him and Alex Brown realized what he had said. 'You'll be amazed, Finn. All being well, your dad will be entirely mobile again by the time he leaves Headley Court . . .'

Finn did not believe a word of it. The regiment had fund-raised for Headley Court, it was a special place, but it was for injured soldiers who had been blown up and might never walk again. It was for soldiers who had life-changing injuries or were mentally injured or found it hard to cope with life out of uniform.

He didn't want to hear anymore. He wanted to close his eyes and put his hands over his ears and shut out Major Brown's meaningless words, meant to comfort him when there was no comfort. He knew Ben would never be the same again, ever.

Alex Brown was watching him. 'Your dad is going to need all your love and positive support in the coming months. You will all be a vital part of his recovery, Finn. At the moment he is still in shock and wants to be on his own, but I assure you this will change.'

Finn nodded, feeling wretched. He couldn't tell Major

Brown that he found it unbearable to see Ben lying there hurt and in pain. It terrified him. He wanted to run a hundred miles from this hospital and never come back. He wanted to go back in time and pretend Ben was still safe in Afghanistan and nothing had happened, that he was laughing, sending blueys. Or back at home in Germany, running with him in the woods where everything was just the same as it always was. Just. The. Same.

He looked at Major Brown. 'Will you be looking after my dad?' he asked.

'No. I'm not part of Ben's medical team, I'm just here for six months, learning more about PTSD. But your dad is a friend, and I want to support him, like many of his friends and colleagues. I thought you and Hanna could do with a friendly face this morning . . .'

He took out a card and underlined his mobile number. 'You can ring me anytime, Finn, if you are worried about your dad or feeling anxious. Okay?'

Finn nodded. Major Brown was all right. He didn't treat him like a child. As they walked back to find Hanna, Finn thought he would never forget that hospital canteen and the smell of bacon and Major Brown's voice telling him all the things Ben would have to go through and still never be like he was before.

As they walked back along the corridor, Finn's mobile bleeped. He dug his phone out of his pocket. It was Raza. *Finn, I am at Islamabad airport, catching flight back to UK. Soon I will ring you . . . Soon, I will be there . . .*

Raz was coming back. Finn stood motionless for a moment in the busy corridor. Raz was coming back. It was like a pinprick of light in a dark room. The prospect of school seemed suddenly less bleak.

Hanna was waiting for them in the family room looking pale and shaken. She said Ben had been drowsy from the morphine, so she had not stayed long. She looked at Major Brown. 'I have just had a phone call from the housing department. I have to go back to Germany to clarify my position with our quarter. It is illegal to leave a quarter empty without permission . . .' She smiled bleakly at Major Brown. 'Apparently I am in trouble.'

Major Brown was incredulous. 'Do they know what has happened to Ben?'

'I gather not. I did not tell them. They knew he was in Afghanistan . . .'

Finn knew Hanna could not have found the words to tell them.

'Crass bloody bureaucracy . . . I'll ring them, Hanna.' Alex Brown got out his mobile. 'Give me their number. Of course, you don't have to go back to Germany . . .'

Hanna held her hand up. 'Alex, I do need to go back. I'll clarify my position, officially, over the quarter, and collect the things I need from the house at the same time . . .'

'Are you sure?' Hanna nodded. 'Then I'll help you get a flight to Hanover . . .' Major Brown said. 'I assure you, Hanna, you won't be in trouble. I will ring the housing department and make sure of that . . .'

Finn was watching Hanna. He wondered what specifically Hanna needed from the quarter, and why now. Hanna turned to him. 'Finn, I am going to leave Izzy with Mummo. They can fly back to Helsinki together and I'll take a flight there from Hanover . . .'

Hanna saw Finn's face begin to close. 'If Ben changes his mind about wanting us around, I will fly straight back. Okay, darling? I will ring you every day, I promise . . .'

Finn turned away and Hanna said gently, 'Finn, I can get from Helsinki to Birmingham in almost the same time as it would take me from Cornwall. Izzy and I can't stay with Delphi and Ian. They are in bits and exhausted. Ian is eighty. I can't inflict a small noisy child on them. Do you see this?'

Finn did see. He wanted to say that she and Izzy could stay in the quarter and be comforted by their army friends until Ben needed her. But what was the point, he knew what she would say.

CHAPTER FIFTY-EIGHT

Cornwall, 2010

Finn's Diary

I'm back at school. Raz is back, too. He got a great welcome from everyone. I am really glad his father didn't die. Raz hasn't said much to me about what happened in Pakistan. Chinir told Delphi it was a terrible experience with lots of violence and that Daniyal had come back shaken.

Practically the first person I bumped into when I got back to school was bloody Chatto. He slid up to me before I had even seen Raz and hissed, like the creepy snake he is, 'You won't be so keen on your Taliban friend now, after what happened to your father, will you, Charles?' He did not even say he was sorry about my dad or anything, he is a total bastard. I wanted to punch him, but I knew I wasn't up for a fight at that moment.

It was horrible leaving Ben at Selly Oak by himself.

Delphi was really upset. She wasn't even trying to cheer everyone up like she usually does.

Izzy flew back to Helsinki with Mummo. I was amazed that she did not put up a fight, but Delphi took her in to see Ben for two minutes before we left and after that she seemed to accept it. Mummo had given her a new doll that wept and wet itself, that helped.

When Hanna phoned me from Germany, she said that the housing officer was very embarrassed when he discovered what had happened to Ben. Apparently, they are short of quarters at the moment so our next-door neighbours helped Hanna to pack our belongings away safely in the cellar so another army family can live there, temporarily, while they wait for their own quarter.

Mummo told me not to worry, Izzy would be fine. In Helsinki, Izzy has a pet cat, a pony she can ride and a nursery school she loves. She's beginning to have a new life. It makes me feel sad, like there's a hole in my stomach, even though I want her to be happy. Mummo hugged me and said she was only telling me to stop me worrying about Izzy. She said she was sure both Izzy and Hanna would be home as soon as Ben felt stronger and able to come to terms with what had happened to him. How can he come to terms with it? He can't ever. I can't bear to think about it. I have to close my brain.

Hanna told me she will commute between Birmingham and Helsinki until she knows how Ben's treatment is going. She is thinking of renting a house near to the hospital, so we have somewhere to stay when we visit him. Her voice sounds sort of dead when she talks to me on the phone. It's like I catch *her mood. I used to feel the same in the quarter in Germany sometimes, the feeling that Hanna was somewhere else. Someplace Izzy and I could never quite reach.*

CHAPTER FIFTY-NINE

Ed Dominic, walking up the drive one Saturday morning, saw Raza and Finn sitting on the front step of Trevelyan House, munching toast in the early spring sunshine. The steadfastness of the boys' friendship always touched him. He was, however, worried about Finn.

Last year, although they were only in Year 8, Ed had placed both boys in the high ability stream, believing they were capable of taking some of their GCSEs a year early. But this was before Ben had been injured or Raza had been whisked off to see his sick father in Pakistan. Raza's work ethic had recovered. Finn's had deteriorated alarmingly.

Finn had so far resisted all attempts to talk about Ben, either with Ed, Mercy, the school counsellor, or his friends. Ed knew from Delphi that it was the same when he went home for the weekends. Finn refused to face Ben's injuries. He backed away, shut himself off. It was obvious that he had closed down emotionally in order to cope, but as Delphi said, at some point, Finn would have to come to terms with the fact that Ben had lost a leg.

*

Raza sat finishing his toast and wondering how to reach Finn. He had returned to school to find a different Finn. Finn did not want to talk about what happened to his Baba, but neither could he think of much else. Raza knew this. Knew the fear that grew in your heart so large you had to hide it from yourself. Worst of all, Finn was neglecting his studies and did not seem to care. Mr Dominic had conveyed his concern to Raza. Asked him if Finn had spoken to him about his father's injuries.

'No,' Raza had told him. 'There are some things too hard to talk about, but I watch for him . . .'

Mr Dominic had smiled. 'I know you do, Raza, but we are all concerned about him. He has stopped working . . . this is a worry . . .'

Raza had looked at his shoes. He did not want to be disloyal and talk about his friend.

Mr Dominic said, 'I am only asking because you are Finn's friend, Raza, and you probably have more insight than anyone, on how he is feeling . . .'

Raza was silent. He did not have insight. For him studying had been an escape and he did not understand how Finn could give up studying when he most needed to make his Baba proud and not give his family worry.

'I know life has been tough for you too, Raza,' Mr Dominic had said. 'Leaving your father all over again must have been very hard . . .'

Raza had met Mr Dominic's eyes. 'Yes, it is hard for me, sir, because I am not with my father, but no one has hurt him. I do not have to sleep each night knowing that my father is suffering, knowing that his suffering will be for many a long time. Finn, he cannot be the same person he was, sir, when this bad thing has happened.'

Mr Dominic agreed. 'No, of course, he can't. But his grandparents are concerned, because Finn won't talk about the nature of his father's injury, the fact that he has lost a leg. It's important that he does accept this, Raza. His father is coming home for the first time at Easter.'

Raza had felt worried at this, but he said more confidently than he felt, 'Finn, he talk often to his father on the phone. Each day he writes of his thoughts into his journal. *Inshallah*, when his father is back home, Finn will see he is the same man as ever he was. He will clearly see this.'

Mr Dominic had led him to the door. 'I'm glad you are his friend, Raza.'

'I too am glad for this friendship, sir . . .'

'What are you thinking?' Finn asked, putting his empty plate on top of Raza's.

Raza said in a rush, 'I am worrying why you have stopped working, Finn, it is not good.'

Finn looked at him and shrugged. 'Can't see the point,' he said dismissively.

Raza stared at him. 'The point, it is not to fail exams. The point it is not to get left behind and get bad marks, Finn.'

Finn shrugged again and got to his feet. 'Who cares, Raz? Come on, let's get Saturday morning lessons over . . .'

Raza got to his feet too. He said quietly, 'Your father will care. Delphi and Ian will care. Your mother will care. I care. Everyone cares for what happens to you, Finn.'

For a terrible moment Raza thought he had made Finn cry. Tears came to his eyes, then he turned and walked away to the dormitory to collect his books, but not so fast that Raza could not catch up with him.

Raza said miserably, 'I am sorry. I want to help . . . but I do not know how . . .'

Finn said abruptly, sitting on his bed, 'You can't help, Raz.'

351

Raza sat on his bed opposite him. 'When I have to leave my father for second time, I think my heart it will break. He is very old, Finn, not like your Baba, more like grandfather, Ian. I come back to UK because all my father want in life is for me to study and be educated. I come back for this education to make him happy. To work and make him proud, but I will not ever see my Baba again. He is sick and he is old, and he will die before long . . . I know little bit of what is in your heart . . .'

Finn stared at him. In the distance came the clatter of footsteps and laughter, as from a world that still went on turning, when his world had stopped in its tracks.

'How can you bear it?' he whispered to Raza. 'To leave your home and your father, forever?'

'Because he wish it. Because that not the whole truth. I see terrible atrocities in my country when I go home. I see with different eyes. It shock me . . . I know if I stay, I will not escape it and I do not want to be part of endless violence . . .'

Raza shook his head as if to banish an image from his mind. He smiled at Finn. 'I have become a little British and spoiled. In Pakistan I miss this school. I miss my friends. It is why I do not email or text you while I am away, Finn. I know that if I stay in Pakistan, I will never see you again so I must put you out of my mind or it too hard for me . . .'

Finn swallowed. He saw, from the pain in Raza's eyes, that it was not easy for Raza to tell him things he would rather not talk about. He was doing it in the hope that he would do the same. But Finn could not. He could not articulate his horror. Could not explain his dread. He did not even understand it himself. Delphi and Ian kept telling him that Ben was out of danger; that he was making incredible progress. Really doing well. But all he could feel was a great blanket of hopelessness. Despair sometimes. Because life was never going to go back to how it was.

He could not concentrate. Could not work. Could not think. All he could do was take himself back to the place and the time he was last happy, when they were a family together, on the patch. A world he knew with soldiers everywhere with packs on their backs, and Ben was one of them. Where all the dads wore combats to work and the guard at the gate of the barracks saluted Ben and his office smelt of Labrador because all the other officers seemed to have one . . . Finn squeezed his eyes tight shut. His world. All he wanted was to go back to a place where Ben was whole. Where Ben was safe . . . Where they were all four together. There were no words for his fantasy. There were no words to explain to Raz. No words, when trust in your world is gone.

Raza sat motionless. Finn's distress was so tangible it reached across the space between them like icy sea fret. Raza shivered, recognizing the desperate, muffled howl in the dark fighting to get out. He had felt it on the plane from Islamabad. He had felt it in his first days in London. Indeed, he thought he would die of grief.

He leant towards Finn. 'I am here,' he whispered. 'Words do not matter. I am here, same as ever, Finn.'

CHAPTER SIXTY

Finn's Diary

I've started to go to Raza's house at the weekends. It was his 13th birthday on Saturday. I've got to wait until May. Sarah made the biggest chocolate cake I've ever seen. Raz isn't into parties. He told me he and his father did not celebrate birthdays; that lots of people in his village did not even know when they were born. It was also the day his mother died so I can see they would not celebrate.

We play computer games on Chinir's huge Apple computer. It's cool, we can just hang out, no one keeps asking me if I am okay all the time. Chinir and Sarah are mostly at the hospital working, though Sarah is home more as she is pregnant and getting quite big. Don't envy Raz when the baby comes. Babies cry a lot.

Raz spends more time than me studying for our exams. I've stopped worrying. We've got ages before our GCSEs. Don't see the point of killing myself, even though Mr Dominic has warned me that my grades are slipping. Ben rings me every week, we don't talk long because he gets tired. Sometimes he Skypes, if I am home with Delphi and Ian, but I think he prefers phone calls when we can't see if he is really cheerful or just pretending. His bruises have faded, and he looks better, but he has black circles under his eyes. He tells us that he is really well looked after, and army friends pop in to see him all the time. He told Delphi that the physiotherapists at Selly Oak are awesome and he hopes to start a proper regime as soon as the wound in his side is healed. But sometimes I can hear in his voice that he is exhausted and depressed, even though he tries to hide it.

Delphi and Ian travel up to see him every other week. Hanna says she and Izzy Skype him. Mary and Fergus rang me last week to say they had surprised him with a visit. They said he was doing brilliantly, and they had made him laugh. Well, Mary can make anyone laugh. I think they phoned me because I have not been to visit Ben yet. I know he is ready to see us now. Mr Dominic told me I can have a long weekend, anytime, to go up with Delphi and Ian. But I'm trying to shut it all out. It's easier to be with my friends. When I'm at school I can pretend nothing has happened to Ben. I can get through the days. I'm afraid of going to see him. That my feelings will show. I don't want to see Ben in pain. I don't want to see other wounded soldiers like my dad. I can't bear it.

Ben said on the phone, when I was making excuses, 'Of course, you are busy with exams. I'm not going anywhere. Be lovely to see you. But only when you are ready . . .'

I know I must go. I want to go. I will go soon.

Raza had set off for his usual Wednesday afternoon run when Finn spotted Chatto and friends in their running gear setting off after him. Knowing that meant trouble, Finn ran to get Peter Chan and Isa out of the Games Hall.

They raced to the creek and saw Chatto and four of his acolytes following Raza along the muddy creek path. Peter said, puffing as they ran, 'We should have gone for more help, Finn. We are going to be outnumbered.'

'There wasn't time,' Finn shouted, feeling anxious.

As they got nearer, they saw Chatto and the other boys had circled Raza by the pond, where the path diverted up into the woods. Raza stood facing them as they jeered. 'Taliban, Taliban . . . Taliban . . .'

Chatto started poking him with a stick and yelling, 'Murdering people . . . blowing up soldiers like Finn's dad. You deserve a lesson . . . you Paki . . . bastard. Your father should have died a horrible death and you should have stayed where you belong in Pakistan . . .'

Where did all the hate in Chatto come from? Finn wondered, shocked. He was revving the others up to fight Raza, but before Finn could shout to Raza, he had launched himself at Chatto so fast that Chatto was caught off guard and went down like an elephant.

Finn had never seen Raza lose it before. He had his hands round Chatto's throat and was using all his strength to bang Chatto's head into the muddy ground. Chatto's friends stood watching with their mouths open but they did not go to help him. Chatto's face started to go an odd colour. Isa, Peter, and Finn yelled at Raza to stop as they ran to pull him away. Raza was so mad he wouldn't let go and Finn, Peter, and Iso had to drag him off. Chatto lay on the ground clutching his neck and gasping, purple in the face, as they held onto Raza.

Chatto's friends stood there looking down at Chatto in

shock. After a minute Finn saw with relief that Chatto was going to be okay. His friends helped him up and he limped away without another word. Raza began to shake until his teeth chattered.

'It's okay,' Finn said. 'It's okay, Raz.'

Peter and Isa kept telling him, 'You didn't start it . . . It wasn't your fault . . .'

'No,' Raza whispered over and over. 'Violence is not okay. Is not okay.'

The three of them got Raza back to the house and pushed him into a hot shower. When Peter and Isa had gone ahead to supper, Finn sat with Raza on his bed looking out at the big fir. 'I will go to pray,' Raza said, but he did not move. After a long silence, without taking his eyes off the tree, he said, 'When I was in Peshawar, a car full of explosives was driven at some American diplomats in big armoured car. All Americans, they were okay, because it was reinforced car, but so many beggars and children, they were blown up by the roadside. It was terrible to see . . .'

He took a deep breath and Finn shivered, thinking of Ben, waiting to understand the connection to Chatto. 'Chatto, he say my father should die horrible death and I am so angry. My father, he send me to England to get away from violent things like this bomb, but also he send me away from my two brothers . . .'

Raz turned away from the window to look at Finn. 'When I first come to England, I miss my brothers, I look up to them. When I go back to Peshawar, they come to find me. I am glad to see them after much time, but I do not like the way they talk to my uncles and Daniyal. I notice how their voices always hold threat. They like to make fear and they laugh with pride at the power they hold. I see, suddenly, that my brothers, they remind me of that horrible English boy, Chatto . . .'

'They are bullies.'

'Yes. I see they are bullies for the first time. Since I first come to this school always Chatto is there saying something bad in my ear about me or my country, about my family, and he says bad things to you, my friend. This is why I lose it . . . I wish to hurt him, but he is right to whisper in your ear like snake, Finn. My brothers are indeed Talibs. They would kill all invaders of Afghanistan. They would kill and injure soldiers like your father, and for a minute I too wished for that boy, Chatto, to die at my hands. I am worse than him. I am no better than my brothers . . .'

Finn did not know what to say. He watched the fir tree and the red and black sky growing behind it. He was not sure how long they sat in silence before Raza whispered, 'I understand if you can no longer be my friend.'

The charcoal clouds merged with the scarlet and spread like a stain outward; it was like blood seeping into the sky.

After a bit, Finn said, 'Do you remember, I emailed you when my dad got blown up?'

'Yes. I was in Peshawar hotel room after that explosion.'

'I knew you would understand something terrible had happened without me telling you . . . and you did.'

Finn nudged Raza with his elbow. 'Come on, Raz, don't be dramatic. You caught Chatto off guard, but you would never have killed the fat idiot . . . Whatever your brothers are, you are no more Taliban than . . . Mr Dominic.'

That thought made both boys laugh. 'Thank you, Finn,' Raza said. 'Mr Dominic, he may not agree with you. I will have to go speak with him. There will be trouble.'

There was trouble. Chatto's father, the MP, threatened to bring charges. He wanted Raza expelled, but it was Raza who had the school's support. Both teachers and students spoke up for Raz. They told Mr Dominic what he already knew, that Chatto was trouble and had been picking on Raza since the day he arrived.

Mr Dominic was not going to be intimidated by Chatto's father. He declared that he would not tolerate racism or bullying in his school and the boys heard rumours that he told Chatto's father that if anyone should leave the school, it should be Chatto.

Chatto's father, it was said, backed off then. There was a rumour that Chatto had been expelled from his last school. To Finn's bitter disappointment, Chatto wasn't banished. Mr Dominic decided to give him another chance.

'He's still in school, skulking, trying to big it out,' Finn told Delphi. 'But he avoids Raz. He's scared of him, now. It's ironic really . . .'

Raza had to take his punishment though. He got grounded, lost privileges, and did a lot of detentions. In the process he became a bit of a hero for ending Chatto's reign of misery . . .

Delphi said, 'Finn, have you ever considered that Chatto must be a very unhappy and damaged boy?'

'No,' Finn told her, 'I haven't. All I know is school is a better place. It's called poetic justice. Good result.'

CHAPTER SIXTY-ONE

Ben lay asleep on the day bed on the veranda of the beach house.

Delphi had put a thick rug over him. He had been reading a book, but it had dropped from his fingers onto the floor. The pages blew in the wind. Finn saw it was a book on Buddhism.

A watery sun lit the sea turning the dog walkers into silver silhouettes. Finn reached out to touch Ben's hand in case he was cold, but the hand felt warm. He knelt on the dusty floorboards and looked into Ben's sleeping face. It was thinner, the skin drawn tight and yellowish. The darkness under his eyes made his face seem in constant shadow. *He doesn't look like Ben anymore*, Finn mourned. *He's shrunk into someone smaller.*

Ian had explained to Finn that once Ben got to Headley Court there would be a gruelling fitness regime of physiotherapy. Ben would slowly rebuild muscle tone and body weight and his bulk would come back. They would get him out of the wheelchair and onto his feet.

Finn sat cross-legged watching Ben sleep. The strong painkillers made him sleep a lot. When his eyes were open, his pupils reflected pain, like he was one big bruise. Finn edged closer. The rug over Ben smelled of seaweed and summer, of the beach house and musty sand. Finn looked at Ben's legs, stared at the foot at the bottom of the blanket. Ben was wearing one thick sock. Under that rug there was only one leg.

Shakily, Finn stretched out his hand to where Ben's other leg should have been. He touched the emptiness. He felt the space in the bed. His fingers roamed over the prickly rug seeking a miracle, but there was none. There was no leg. He slowly bent his head to that empty space, circled his arms around the place Ben's leg should have been and silently wept.

Ben stirred, reached blindly out with closed eyes 'Finn? God, you're cold, come under the rug.' Ben lifted the rug and Finn crept under it. They lay side by side on the musty cushions facing the sea. Ben was wearing an old discoloured fisherman's sweater of Ian's and tracksuit bottoms. The warmth emanating from him was comforting.

After a while Ben said softly, almost as if he was talking to himself, 'You know, Finn, every time we lost one of our soldiers in Helmand, we placed them in a little room with candles. All his mates in camp would go to say goodbye, take turns to keep watch over the dead soldier. We did this until we could fly him home to be met at the door of the plane and repatriated in a military ceremony. You have seen people lining the streets of Wootton Basset to honour the coffin of soldiers as they pass through. Every single soldier we lose is like a member of our family . . .'

Ben stopped for a minute, gazing out at the unsettled light on the sea. 'It is the worst, the very worst thing, to have to tell families that their sons or their husbands have been killed or badly injured . . . I used to find it astonishing that most families of soldiers with life-changing injuries just gave thanks he was alive. In my ignorance, I sometimes wondered if it would have been better if some of those men had died. I thought that their families could not possibly realize what lay ahead for them all. Now, it's happened to me, I understand how precious life is. I will heal. I'm alive, unlike two of my team. I am here, watching the sun rise and set. I am here at the beach house with you. Do you see how lucky I am?'

Finn was silent; he did not know what to say. Ben said softly. 'Losing a leg won't stop me living my life, Finn, it just makes it a bit harder. My God, I've seen what soldiers with far more serious injuries can achieve . . .'

The thought shot through Finn's mind before he could stop it. *It's like Ben's convincing himself.* Ben turned and caught the flash of pity in Finn's eyes. It hurt and made him angry. 'I'm still the same person, Finn,' Ben said, holding Finn's gaze. 'I am still the same man . . .'

Finn heard the sound of Ian's truck bouncing over the track to the beach house bringing back provisions. He heard Mary and Delphi's voices coming nearer as they walked across the sand. He pushed the rug from his knees, got slowly off the day bed and walked away to switch the kitchen lights on for them.

Ben is not the same person. His leg has been blown off. He has stomach wounds that make him hunch over. He used to be fit and strong and run for miles. He used to hold a sword and march on the parade ground. He is not the same man he once was. To pretend is . . . is . . . just being glad to be alive. Ben is kidding himself . . .

Finn stood in the doorway framed by the light and glared at the wheelchair in the corner. Then, abruptly his anger subsided and he hated himself. An unbearable sadness filled the void. He wanted to rush out and tell Ben he loved him, that he knew what Ben meant, *that he was the same person*

362

inside. But he knew that could not be true either. It broke him up, made him want to kick something, to run away, because *Ben had to kid himself. What else could he do?*

Delphi and Ian came out onto the veranda carrying trays. 'Is it warm enough to have drinks out here, do you think?' she asked.

'Of course, it is,' Ben said. 'This is the best part of the day, watching the sun go down.'

Mary jumped up to take the tray from Delphi. 'It's wonderful out here. I can smell summer around the corner, and we've got plenty of rugs . . .'

'Darling,' Delphi said to Finn, 'I've made you a hot chocolate and left it on the kitchen table, it was too hot to carry . . . While you're in there, have a quick look at the mermaid paintings I've been doing for Izzy. Tell me what you think because you're the story-teller . . .'

The sun was slanting through the bars of the veranda and the sea was turning a mellow sepia. Finn turned to glance behind him as they lifted their glasses to toast each other. Ben was back in his wheelchair. Mary and Fergus were sitting on large cushions. Ian was in the old leather chair looking weary. Delphi was busy filling bowls with crisps and nuts. Finn saw that her hair was turning abruptly white.

It was nice to have the soft sound of laughter and familiar voices rising and falling, rising and falling against the sound of the sea. It felt both comforting and sad in a way Finn did not understand. A yearning for something that no longer existed. Not for a shabby, safe army quarter, but for everything loved and held within its walls . . . Izzy and Hanna and Ben. But the old Ben. Finn wanted the strong, happy Ben in uniform, always late for supper, calling, 'Hi guys, I'm home! Where is everybody!'

This was the dream he dreamed at night and woke to in the mornings. He could not bear the truth. He could not bear the wheelchair, the crutches, the empty trouser leg dangling. Most of all he hated this . . . this . . . everyone pretending that everything was going to be fine. Grown-ups yak-yak-yakking and telling lies. When it could never be fine. Not ever.

He looked down at Delphi's paintings on the kitchen table. He knew she was trying to involve him, and the little paintings were hauntingly beautiful. Silvery mermaids with long red hair riding golden sea horses through frothy white waves. Izzy would love them.

He lifted the paintings and felt a pang of longing for Hanna. For her green, grey eyes, for her beautiful shiny copper hair, for the spicy scent of her . . .

Ben used to call her his mermaid. Those days seemed so long ago. Finn often found he was unable to sustain his anger with Hanna for being the way she was. He just wished she was here, with him, in England. He missed her. He missed her so badly sometimes he doubled up with the thought of her gone forever. Izzy had a bad cold and Hanna had not wanted to book a flight until she was better.

He carried his hot chocolate to his room. It scared him seeing Delphi and Ian growing old. How terrible if they died. The very thought made him shiver. Life seemed to be constantly tilting and shifting under his feet. There was nothing safe to hold onto anymore.

At night, Finn tossed and turned into the sleepless dark. He knew he was going home with Raz more and more to escape Delphi and Ian's undercurrent of grief that was wrapped in a cheerful stoicism. He knew the cheerfulness was for him, and an effort for them to maintain.

This would be the first Easter he had ever had without Hanna. No searching for eggs with Izzy this year. Finn looked up. Ian was standing in the doorway nursing a glass of whisky and holding a small bowl of crisps. 'All well, old thing?'

'Yeah, thanks. Think I might just stay here and read my book for a bit.'

Ian came a little way into the room. 'Good idea, bit noisy out there . . .'

He put the bowl of crisps on the small table by the bunk bed. 'You know where we all are, if you change your mind . . .'

Finn nodded. 'Tell Delphi the mermaids are great . . .'

Ian smiled. 'I will. You have a peaceful read. See you later.' Then he went slowly back outside leaving Finn feeling comforted. He heard Ben laugh and felt himself smiling. It was a good sound. It was good hearing Ben here, just outside.

Finn fell asleep over his book and woke with his bedside light still on. On the floor beside the bed there was a glass of milk with a saucer on top, and a sandwich. Finn grinned. Delphi, just in case he might starve in the night. His watch said 1 a.m. The house creaked but was otherwise silent.

Finn got out of bed and changed into his pyjamas. He ate the sandwich and drank the milk. Underneath the glass was a sheet of paper. Delphi had written, *Fabulous surprise! Izzy is better, Hanna has got them on a flight and they'll be here tomorrow. A lovely family Easter will be had by all. Isn't that perfect, darling! xx*

Finn lay in the dark listening to the sea. This time tomorrow Izzy and Hanna would be here at the beach house. He let hope and a cautious contentment creep towards him as waves broke, in small, soporific slaps. Thinking he heard something, he got up and walked out onto the veranda and into Ben's room. Ben was asleep in the new bed Ian had had fitted to replace the old saggy one that dipped in the middle. He slept on his back; the hated wheelchair next to the bed.

Finn watched Ben for a moment, taken aback by the protective wave of love and pride that rose up inside him. Would Hanna sleep here with Ben, or with Mary and Fergus in the chalet next door? She was coming over for Easter, so it was possible that she was missing them and thinking of coming home. He looked out at the black sea that rippled and swelled in the dark, at the half-moon that scudded between thick black clouds lighting the night in shafts of pale, yellow light. Then he padded back to bed.

CHAPTER SIXTY-TWO

Finn went with Mary and Fergus to meet Hanna's plane at Newquay Airport. Finn stayed inside arrivals, but Mary and Fergus stood outside in a cold wind and watched the small plane land. Fergus said bleakly, 'To see Ben felled like this, without Hanna's love and support . . . Whatever Ben said about doing this on his own, Hanna should have stayed in England near him. The army would have supported her, you know, given her temporary housing . . . Not sure I can ever forgive her . . .'

Mary, watching the passengers coming down the plane steps, saw Hanna emerge, clutching Izzy's hand. 'We're not here to judge Han, Fergus, but to support them both. They're our oldest friends and they are both going through hell. I'm sure Hanna has had time to see how fragile life is, that Ben and the children desperately need her to be here . . .'

Fergus stared at her and even as the words passed Mary's lips, she realized she did not believe them.

As she watched Hanna and Izzy cross the tarmac in the dark, Mary imagined Fergus struck down like Ben, imagined herself walking away from him and gasped at the inconceivability of it.

367

Izzy launched herself at Finn and he caught her, held her to him as she clutched his neck in a fierce embrace.

As Mary hugged Hanna, she could feel the sharpness of ribs under her fingers. When Hanna moved to hug Finn, he remained stiff in her arms, as if unsure how to be with her, what to hope for, how to trust. Mary and Fergus stood watching, stunned by sadness.

Delphi and Ian greeted Hanna as warmly as they always did. Izzy started to hurtle towards Ben in his wheelchair. Fergus managed to grab her before she could throw herself at him. Ben's stomach wound was still healing, and Ben had admitted to Fergus it was more painful than his leg at the moment.

Fergus lifted her up to Ben and she threw her arms tight round his neck. Ben made strangling noises and kissed her hair loudly making her laugh, then she wriggled to the ground and ran to Delphi.

Ben smiled *hello* at Hanna from across the room. Despite Izzy radiating excitement and noise, Hanna's arrival felt awkward and Finn felt a rush of conflicting emotions. Happiness Hanna was here. A fierce protectiveness, and resentment that she could make his heart ache.

As they sat around the old, scrubbed table for supper, Delphi and Mary found themselves overcompensating for any uneasy silences. Even Izzy's chatter ceased as she caught the tension emanating from her mother, and the uncertainty in the room.

Delphi saw that Finn was watching Hanna. Hanna sat, wary of them all, like a cat placing her paws carefully, unsure of firm ground. Delphi sighed. The poor girl was, despite all their efforts to be normal, the elephant in the room, the woman who had deserted her post, gone absent without leave.

Ben and Fergus were bantering funny stories of hospital

life and vague, hopeful plans for the summer that hovered ahead of them. Hanna sat, still and contained at the edge of them all, trying not to show the resistance she always felt when surrounded by Ben's family.

Ben found it hard to bear her discomfort. It was not that Delphi or Ian were being anything but warm; it was that Hanna no longer felt one of them. Watching her, Ben wondered if Hanna had ever really allowed herself to feel one of them. Delphi and Ian's old-fashioned courtesy had always irritated Hanna. The very Englishness of their lives seemed to set Hanna's teeth on edge.

Ben made an effort to bring her into the conversation. He asked her about Mummo and Uki, and Izzy chipped in excitedly with stories of the kitten and the pony she some-times rode. Finn, not wanting to hear of Izzy's new life, abruptly left the table on the pretext of getting another glass of water.

By the time Hanna got Izzy into pyjamas and she was sitting by Ben, expectantly waiting for a story, everyone was exhausted and ready for bed.

Ben looked at Hanna and laughed. 'Dear Lord, shouldn't this child be on her knees by now?'

Hanna smiled back. 'She'll go out like a light, any moment.' And she did. Finn carried her into the bottom bunk, glad of an excuse to get into his bunk and shut the door. He climbed into his own bed and played games on his iPhone.

Promising they would make sure Ben was safe in bed, Mary and Fergus sent Delphi and Ian to bed and cleared away the supper things.

Ben felt exhausted. 'I need to go to bed, too. Hanna, get some sleep, you look all in. Mary's made you up a bed next door. I'll see you in the morning.'

Hanna's relief was palpable as Ben turned his wheelchair

and moved down the veranda. 'Do you need any help, Ben?' she called after him, praying that he did not.

'No. Thank you, I'm sure Fergus will put his head round the door before he leaves. Night, night, Hanna.'

Something in his voice seared Hanna. 'Goodnight, Ben, I hope you sleep . . .' *Oh God,* she thought, *this is hard. Somehow, I have to get through Easter.* Hanna knew she had done the right thing in coming, for Finn and Izzy, but it was quite the wrong thing for her and Ben.

As Ben wheeled himself along the veranda towards his room, he suspected Delphi would not go to sleep until she had seen for herself that he was safe in bed and had everything he needed. There was already a washbasin in Ben's room but Delphi had found a small chemical loo which she had put in a corner and screened off so Ben could pee in the night without worrying about disturbing anyone. He much preferred his crutches to the wheelchair, but the wound in his side still caused him pain. He hated his dependence on the wheelchair, but his balance was still not good, either. Ben had been grateful that Fergus had helped him into the shower that morning. He was grateful to Fergus for many things.

Fergus felt inclined to take Ben a whisky but thought better of it. Ben was still wobbly on his crutches and he might need to get out of bed in the night. He took him a cup of tea instead. Ben raised his eyes at it. 'Bugger that, Fergus, exchange it for a proper drink.'

'You sure?'

'Of course, I'm sure. If I doubt my ability to lower myself into my wheelchair to go and pee, I'll buzz you on the phone . . .'

Fergus went away and poured two whiskies and they raised their glasses to each other. Ben hoped Fergus would not get maudlin and ask him how he was doing. He had noticed a lot of frantic wine-drinking during supper. They sat in companionable silence for a while and then to his dismay Ben found himself asking. 'How do you think Hanna looks?'

'Tired, thin, and miserable.' Fergus answered.

'The awful thing is, I haven't really thought about how it is for Hanna at all. I've just been selfishly focusing on myself, on getting back on my feet . . .'

'Foot,' Fergus said, grinning.

Ben looked at him and they both snorted. Ben took a deep drink and loved Fergus for not avoiding the subject of his leg. It was why he liked Selly Oak; he needed a particular brutal forces humour to stop him feeling sorry for himself.

'Thanks, Fergus,' he said, 'for bringing me down to Cornwall, for spending Easter with us, when I know you'd really rather be with your two.'

'No, I wouldn't,' Fergus lied. 'They are experiencing the wilds of Derry with Mary's parents, who have no Internet . . .'

Ben made a horrified face. 'They will never forgive you.'

'Ah,' Fergus said. 'My parents-in-law are ferocious poker players, so we are expecting that boredom will have turned our two into gambling addicts by the end of the holiday.'

Ben laughed. 'I mean it, Fergus. It's so good to have you and Mary here . . .'

'If it was the other way around you would do the same for me.'

'If it was the other way around, Mary wouldn't have left your side for one single second,' Ben said quietly, and Fergus kicked himself.

'I'm sorry, Ben, I'm so bloody sorry. Maybe . . .'

'Don't, Fergus, it's not going to happen. A legless veteran

is hardly going to entice Hanna back, is it? I don't want her pity. It's the last thing I need.'

'Is that why you sent the family away, Ben, so Hanna would not feel so bad?'

'I sent my family away because I could only cope with my own trauma and pain . . . I did not want to see it reflected every day in those I love . . .'

Ben looked Fergus in the eye. 'It would be a lie if I said that I did not hope, with a tiny, unrealistic part of me, that Hanna would insist . . . would want to stay in Birmingham with me, but my wife's horror was palpable as soon as she walked into my hospital room . . .' Ben gave a raw laugh. 'As I knew in my heart it would be.'

Fergus felt grief. 'Give her a time to adjust, Ben. She's here. She came for Easter. Don't second-guess her feelings. Hanna nearly lost you, the shock of it will have made her revaluate . . .'

'Fergus, we both know, even if things had been right between us, this . . .' Ben indicated the space in the bed where his left leg should have been, 'would have killed it dead. My beautiful wife loves perfect things. Always has. I am a man with a stump that will become raw and bloody once I start to walk on it. She would never cope with the blood and guts, the pain and depression, the suicidal doubts of who the hell I am now, or why the fuck I'm still here . . .'

Hope was not something Ben could dare let in, so he stamped on it. 'Hanna married an illusion,' he said quietly. 'She married into an institution that she has come to see as snatching away all her freedoms. And maybe it has. She liked the idea of love because she was carrying Finn. Fondness only carries you so far . . . that is the truth, my friend . . .'

Ben looked away, out of the window to hide his misery. Fergus wanted to bawl. It caught him, like a blow between the ribs. He couldn't speak. He longed for Mary's Irish gift of magic words that would be apposite and wise, but he did not have that gift. Eventually, he asked quietly, 'Ben, have you talked to anyone about PTSD or depression?'

Ben was silent and then he said, 'It's all right, Fergus, I'm not about to do anything stupid. I have my children and Delphi and Ian to think of. I couldn't do that to them, but it's crystal clear that I'm better in Selly Oak then here at home. I can't cope with all this emotion swirling around, not my wife's or my son's or my mother's. I can only concentrate on the next moment, on getting fit, on walking again. On the next day and the one after that. I don't want anything at the moment, pity or love. . . I don't have the capacity to reassure anyone. I know it's selfish, but I just need to be in a totally clinical environment . . . to get on with . . . finding . . . what's left of me . . .'

Ben paused and leant back and closed his eyes. His voice was so soft that Fergus had to lean forward to hear. 'At Selly Oak, there is a corporal from the Welsh Guards . . . Taffy. He lost both legs and one arm in Lashkar Gah two weeks before me. He has a poster up by his bed charting his planned climb up Ben Nevis with Prince Harry. He'll do it too. He spent most of his childhood in children's homes. He joined the army at sixteen because they turf you out of care and onto the street as soon as you are deemed an adult . . .'

Ben opened his eyes and looked at Fergus. 'That's only three years older than Finn . . . Taffy told me, that for him, the army was like coming home. It became his family. For the first time in his life, he had excitement, plenty of food, money, and good mates. People who cared whether he lived or died. He was part of team who looked out for each other, part of something that mattered. He was a natural leader, duck to water, trusted and loved by his men.

Ferociously brave in battle. He risked his own life getting his soldiers to safety. He's twenty-four, Fergus and I've heard him cry with pain, but I've never once heard a word of self-pity or "why me" . . .'

Ben drained his glass. 'So, when I'm in pain or sorry for myself, I clamp down hard and I think of Taffy . . .'

'Depression doesn't work like that, Ben. Your feelings are just as valid as someone with worse injuries. Don't clamp down on your anger, or pain, it isn't healthy . . .' He looked at Ben's grey face. 'You're in pain now. Have you taken your painkillers?'

Ben nodded. 'I have. I'm talking too much . . .'

'Always keep talking to me, Ben . . .' Fergus picked up both glasses, remembering the harrowing tours of Bosnia and Iraq they had shared together. He was glad he was out of the army, away on his boats, where a moment's indecision did not cost a life. Where responsibility hinged on inanimate objects and instruments, with little to fear but the weather and irresponsible skippers.

'Good night, Ben,' he said. 'Sleep well.' At the door he turned back. 'You and Hanna had loads of happy times, you know. Mary and I shared a lot of them with you.'

Ben opened his eyes. 'I know. Really, I do. I'm okay. Stop worrying about me and get to bed.'

'Ring me on your mobile if you need anything.'

'I will. Now bugger off.'

'Buggering off,' Fergus said, weaving off into the night to Mary.

In the dark Ben could feel the painkillers beginning to work. The whisky helped. The sea rippled and slapped against the sand. Clouds raced over a half moon. The wooden beach house creaked as it cooled down in the familiar, comforting sounds of his childhood. Ben thought of Finn and Izzy next door. Of Delphi and Ian in the big

374

wooden bed that took up most of the room. All those he loved under the same roof, almost. His heart ached, then hardened, as it must. His thoughts rested on his mono-syllabic, moody, teenage son who was also hardening his heart, to endure, to survive, to go forward. He and Hanna could no longer be relied on to be either united, or to make Finn feel safe or secure. It was a harsh growing up.

Ian had fallen asleep almost before he had said goodnight to her. Delphi lay beside him, soothed by the warmth he gave out. So many suppressed feelings in this house tonight, hiding hope and expectation. Politeness that hid grief, hers. Confused, passive aggression, Finn's. Guilt and fear for what the future held, Hanna. Pain and loss and buried hope, Ben's.

Thank God, Delphi thought, for Ian, Mary, and Fergus who provided a quiet steady normality.

In the dark of her own room Delphi tried to banish her anguish. It was a miracle that Ben was home, sharing Easter with them all. How dare she mourn for a Ben whole and happy, standing tall and fearless on a surfboard, laughing, lucky, chasing his children; running, running, on those beau-tiful strong legs, his healthy body unmarked, his eyes unclouded by pain.

Delphi knew what lay ahead for him: months and months of rehabilitation as he clawed his way back to a semblance of a normal life. And it looked as if he was going to have to do it without his wife. Delphi wept in the dark, silently, as she had learnt to do. Her tears were hot and stung the creases of her eyes. But it was a relief, a searing relief to let go, to give in to her sense of impotence, of secret outrage towards the politicians distanced from danger. For the MOD who could not even make sure their forces had the right equipment to keep their soldiers safe. Was it worth it, this lasting damage wrought to a generation of men sent to fight thousands of miles from home? Would it make an iota of lasting difference?

Ben, like so many others, had gone out to Afghanistan whole, and come back mutilated. It was not just his physical wholeness Delphi wept for. It was what lay behind his eyes. That casual, joyous ease with which he had seemed to slide effortlessly through life had been abruptly replaced by something darker. Delphi did not think it would ever entirely come back. He would never be quite as he had before. Never so light-hearted, or care-free, or trusting or sure again.

Her clock said 4 a.m. Outside the sea roared. There was weather coming in. Delphi turned on her side. *Oh, for goodness sake,* always the dreaded hour before dawn, when all is as bad as it can possibly be. She willed herself to happy thoughts. She would pick daffodils for the table tomorrow. They would all hide Easter eggs for Izzy. Dear little cheerful soul. Izzy's exuberance was just what they all needed. Tomorrow would be easier; everyone had been tired tonight. It was unfair to blame Hanna for abandoning Ben, wounded, when she had already left him. Hanna had put her own needs before those of her family, but her misery in doing so was apparent. Hanna was Hanna and she had ventured bravely back into Ben's family lair for Easter and that took courage. Delphi admired her for it, but Hanna needed to build bridges with Finn. She needed to be open and honest with him, even if it hurt.

CHAPTER SIXTY-THREE

The next morning a cold wind had whipped up in the night. Slanting rain buffeted the beach house soaking the balcony round the house and making everyone miserably cold. Delphi and Ian decided on an immediate evacuation back to the Penzance House for Easter lunch. They packed up the food and put Izzy in the car in her pyjamas with Hanna, leaving Finn to help Fergus with Ben's wheelchair.

Delphi was worried about getting Ben down the steep steps by the gate and into the house, but Fergus, helped by Mary and Finn, managed to lift the chair down the steps without any trouble.

At the front door Ben stood leaning on Fergus and one crutch, while Finn hovered nervously holding an umbrella over him. Mary and Ian got the wheelchair over the threshold and into the house and Fergus hoisted Ben up, over the steps and back into the wheelchair. Ben was pale and shaking by the time he had been wheeled to the kitchen and placed by the Aga.

Delphi anxiously tucked a rug around him. 'This will help you warm up, darling.'

'Just to complete the paraplegic look,' Ben muttered

crossly, but the short journey and the effort of getting in and out of Fergus's truck and into the house had exhausted him. They could all see how frail he still was. Even Izzy, who stood in her pyjamas holding one of his hands to her cheek.

Ben smiled at her. 'I'm fine, sweetie, I'm just cold and need my coffee. Why don't you go and get into your best Easter bonnet, ready for the egg hunt?'

Izzy laughed. 'I haven't got a bonnet, silly . . . I got a best red dress.'

'Wow! Can't wait to see.'

'Come on, Mumma,' Izzy called. 'Help me with my dress. Then we've got the egg hunt . . .' She turned worriedly to Delphi. 'You didn't leave all the eggs in the beach house?'

'I certainly did not! Go on, darling, get dressed, then your breakfast will be ready . . .'

Hanna took Izzy upstairs and Ian went to light the fire in the sitting room. 'Right, coffee for that officer . . .' Mary said, as Delphi beat eggs into a bowl. Ben took a painkiller with his coffee and felt himself slowly begin to relax as the pain dulled and receded. He felt lulled by Mary and Delphi's companionable chatter and amused by watching Finn happily flitting round the house hiding small chocolate eggs in inaccessible places for Izzy. Finn had, it seemed, temporarily given up being teenage cool and disdainful. Ben smiled, carefully storing the feeling of contentment in these small things, the smell of home, the old kitchen clock ticking, the sound of Ian scrunching paper for the fire. The rise and fall of muffled conversation and giggles coming from around the house . . .

'Would you like a quick shave and a wash, Ben?' Ian asked, quietly coming into the kitchen. Ben nodded gratefully and Ian wheeled Ben out of the kitchen and along the passage to the downstairs shower room. The wheelchair passed straight in. Ian smiled, pleased. 'When we decided to put a shower in the downstairs loo, I persuaded your mother to have a wet room and a wide door for my impending decrepitude . . .'

Ben looked around at what had been the old cloakroom. 'Delphi said you'd had a shower put in here . . . You're as tough as old boots, Ian, you'll see us all out . . .'

He manoeuvred himself to the basin. 'I can't tell you the relief at not having to heave myself out of this chair again . . .'

Ian closed the cloakroom door. 'I can see you're in pain, Ben. Is it your leg or stomach wound?'

'Stomach wound.'

'May I take a look?'

Ben pulled up his shirt reluctantly, not wanting Ian to confirm what he already suspected. 'Sorry, Ben, but can you stand upright for a second, so I can see properly . . . Hold on to the towel rail . . .'

Ben pulled himself up, groaning under his breath. Ian washed his hands and examined the wound with gentle fingers. 'Okay. Sit back, old thing.' Ian eased Ben back into the chair.

Ben ran water into the basin and pulled out his wash bag. He knew what Ian was going to say. 'Your wound is infected, Ben. I'm going to get a dressing to keep it clean but you're going to need antibiotics. I'm retired, so I can't prescribe, but I'm going to ring my doctor, who's also a friend. The sooner you take it, the better. Do you know what antibiotic you were on at Selly Oak?'

Ben told him. Ian nodded. 'Okay. I'll be back in a moment.'

'Ian, don't tell Delphi, she'll fuss and worry, and I don't want Easter spoilt.'

'I won't say a thing. I'm going to make a phone call, dress the wound, then try to slip out on a pretext . . .'

When Ian had dressed his wound, Ben shaved and washed and changed his shirt and felt better. He looked in the mirror. God, he looked a hundred. What had happened to his eyes, they seemed to have receded into black holes. He felt strangely outside himself, as if he was watching himself behind glass. He had sometimes felt like this as a child when he had a temperature. It was odd.

Delphi was outside, hovering. 'Are you okay, Ben?' she asked, peering at him. Ben smiled. 'I'm absolutely fine, Mum.'

Delphi looked at his flushed face and felt a surge of fear. He was not absolutely fine. He had called her Mum. He was feeling rock bottom low.

'It will be hugely tiring being out of hospital for the first time, darling.'

'It is, but I'm fine. Come on, I can hear my impatient daughter, let's have breakfast, then she can egg-hunt . . .'

After breakfast Ian slipped out of the house for the prescription and Izzy thundered around the house finding the eggs, guided by Finn. Ben wheeled himself to the sitting room out of the way and sat by the fire with the papers. Fergus joined him and they sat reading out headlines to each other.

Ian came back with antibiotics and a huge bottle of sparkling water as an excuse for going out. He poured a glass and took the pills in to Ben. Ben took them with another painkiller. Fergus felt uneasy. He could see Ben was in pain and it was one hell of a long drive back to Birmingham tonight. Getting home for Easter had been a goal for Ben, although his medical team had warned him this might not be realistic. In the end they decided that the morale boost for him overrode the risk of travelling so far.

Fergus and Mary had driven to Cornwall overnight so Ben could sleep in the huge back seat of the Discovery.

Looking at Ben's grey face now, Fergus had doubts about how sensible this trip had been. He saw the physical and emotional toll it had taken on Ben. Being with his family, seeing Hanna again, had drained him.

Fergus took Ian aside. 'What is it, Ian? My back seat's like an armchair, but is Ben going to be up to the long drive back to Selly Oak?'

'I took a look at Ben's stomach wound, it's infected. He has a temperature and he's in some discomfort. He needs to be back in hospital, Fergus. At least you're driving overnight and hopefully the antibiotics will have kicked in and with painkillers, Ben should sleep.'

'Okay, but I think Mary and I will head off earlier than planned. After lunch, if you don't mind, Ian.'

'Of course not, I think you should. We're so grateful to you, Fergus. You and Mary have done a wonderful thing bringing Ben all this way to see us.'

'Pretty small undertaking in the scheme of things,' Fergus said as he went off to find Mary.

Hanna found Finn in his bedroom. She came straight to the point.

'Finn, we need to talk about your grades, they are terrible. What is going on?' Finn shrugged without looking up from his mobile.

'Please put your phone away and look at me.' Finn sighed heavily and threw his phone on the bed. Hanna sat beside him.

'So, are you deliberately setting yourself to fail your GCSEs on top of everything else?'

Finn shrugged again and muttered, 'No. Just don't see the point in killing myself over exams.'

Hanna said, exasperated, 'For goodness' sake, Finn, I've got one toddler to deal with, I don't need two.'

Finn glared at her. 'You've hardly got me to deal with, have you?'

Hanna watched him. 'Is that the problem?'

Finn flushed.

Hanna said more gently, 'I don't want to fight with you. I am sorry if you feel I have abandoned you, Finn. I know how hard it must be, especially after what has happened to Ben . . .'

'So, come back then. You should be here for him.' *You should be here for me,* he thought silently and looked at her. 'I don't think you are sorry at all . . .'

Hanna sighed. 'Finn, you have been in boarding school without living with me in term time for four years. There is no difference between my being in Germany or Finland, when you are in school, except what you make of it. Wherever I am, I love you, and I am always here for you, that will never change . . .'

'That's rubbish . . .' Finn spat the words out. 'Germany is where our home is . . . or was, before you left our quarter empty.'

Hanna was silent, shocked by his aggression, miserable about the truth of it. She could not spell out the bare facts to him. Her absence from their quarter made not an iota of difference. Everything changed in a flash, the moment Ben was blown up by an IED. Their lives, their home in Germany, Ben's livelihood. For it was, most likely, the end of Ben's army career.

Finn continued swinging his feet against the side of the bed, 'You told me we would rent a house near the hospital so we could visit Ben easily. Are you going to?'

'Finn, Ben is still at Selly Oak and wants to go through his treatment on his own, as you well know. We have to wait until he is ready to be transferred to Headley Court, then we can talk about it.'

Hanna paused, then said, 'Don't you think Ben has enough to contend with, without you deliberately sabotaging your exams? It is one thing to make me pay for hurting you, Finn, but you know how upset Ben would be if he knew you had stopped working . . .'

Izzy yelled up the stairs, 'LUNCH IS READY. Delphi says you MUST all come now . . .'

Finn leapt to his feet. 'I'm not making anyone pay. I don't care what you do, but I care about my dad. I care about Izzy.'

Hanna stood up and faced him. 'So, you are not glad to see me, not glad I came to spend Easter with you?'

Finn looked away. 'I didn't say that,' he muttered miserably, looking at the floor. Hanna slowly and carefully wrapped her arms around his stiff and angry body. Finn did not move away.

'Good,' she whispered, feeling him relax ever so slightly against her. 'Because I am so happy to see you, even if you are like an angry croc who might bite my head off any second . . .'

Finn tried not to smile. Hanna smelled spicy and warm and he breathed her in. She kissed the top of his head. 'Wherever I am, wherever you are, I love you. Please don't stop working. I love that clever mind of yours . . .'

Finn dared not ask the question. Hanna did not lie. They left it at that and went downstairs together.

Delphi, with Izzy's help, had decorated the lunch table with small yellow chickens and bunches of creamy primroses. There was roast leg of lamb and apple crumble. How did she do it? Mary wondered, seeing Ben and Finn's face light up when they saw the table, watched Izzy's excitement as she was allowed to help light the candles. Mary understood suddenly that for Delphi, keeping all the little family traditions going, as if nothing had changed, was how she coped, how she kept a continuity and order for the people she loved.

Outside the day was dark and rain and wind hit the long casement windows making them rattle. But here in the big warm kitchen Delphi had drawn her disparate family together for Easter lunch. Around the table, there was a pause, a lull, a cessation, of all but a sweet contentment in being together and eating food prepared with love.

A meal can slide past, unnoticed, Mary thought, when often it stands, like a flash of a camera, into a sacred memory, a time and a place in the life and in the breaking up of a family.

After lunch Ben wheeled himself away from the heat and noise of the kitchen back into the sitting room. He sat looking out of the window to a grey sea beyond the garden. Waves flung themselves over the railings in great, white angry sprays. Voices and laughter in the kitchen came to him in little bursts. At lunch, a sweet happiness had crept over him as he glanced around the table. He knew how lucky he was to be here with his parents, his children, and his closest friends. His pain had receded, and he felt a strange soporific detachment, as if he was viewing everything from the wrong end of a telescope.

'Ben?' Hanna came up behind him. He turned from the window.

'Hello, darling,' he said, from habit. 'Too many people? Feeling the strain?'

She smiled. 'A bit. How are you doing, Ben?'

'I'm fine,' he said. 'My treatment's going well. Thanks for coming. It's made the children's Easter . . . and mine,' he added.

Hanna watched him. He looked awful. She could feel

her heart thumping as she asked. 'Ben . . . would you like me to come back to England?'

Ben stared at her. 'For Finn, or for me?'

'Both of you, of course.'

Did Hanna think he could ever forget her reaction when she first saw him in Selly Oak? 'Is this sudden pity, duty, or lurve?' He had not meant to sound cynical, but it came out that way.

'Ben, whatever you think, I care about you.'

Ben took a deep breath. 'I know you do, Han, but it's a commitment I don't think you can make. I saw the horror on your face when you first saw me, and you haven't experienced my worst days. Days when my stump bleeds and I have to stay in bed with the bloody mess that was once my leg uncovered under a cage. Days when my stomach wound is so painful, I am delirious with pain. Days when my physio makes me scream . . .'

'Oh Ben . . .' Hanna stood, pale and stricken.

'I've got months and months of rehab . . . do you honestly believe you could constantly look at me at my lowest . . . legless and all, without turning away from the sight of me, because that would be so much worse than not having you at all . . .'

Ben scanned her pale and beautiful face. 'Han, you did not want to be with me when I was fit and whole, what makes you think you could cope with life with me now that I am an amputee?'

Hanna flinched. 'Don't say that . . .' Her mother's angry voice reverberated in her head. *Hanna, this is not about you, or what you want or feel. It is about Ben. It is about being there for him so he can get through the shock and horror and pain and face the future. It is about Finn and Izzy, who need each other. It is about being together as a family and helping each other through a tragedy. If ever Ben and Finn need you, it is now . . .*

Her friends seemed to think she was a monster. Even Kai had turned away, shocked that she could get on a plane and leave Ben . . .

'It's the truth,' Ben said. 'Even if you do not want to hear it. It's what I am. What I will always be. You can't dip in and out of our lives, hedging your bets, Hanna. Don't come back to me because your life is not working out in Helsinki. Don't come back because you are worried about Finn. Only come back if you are strong enough to want to spend the rest of your life with a damaged man at the end of his career . . . and I don't think you are.'

Hanna stared at Ben. It also required the power of a love she did not have for him. 'You make it sound so bleak . . . You cannot know yet whether it is the end of your career . . .'

'Hanna,' Ben said, more gently. 'Please don't feel guilty. Plenty of people can't cope with injuries like mine.' *And lots cope with far worse.*

He closed his eyes, feeling exhausted.

Hanna stood there, frozen in misery as the moments ticked; faced herself with brutal honesty for the first time. How well Ben knew her. She had come for Easter, but not for all the right reasons. Her future in Helsinki was far from sure. She had wanted to see Finn, see how Ben was doing, but it was Kai's rejection that had propelled her here, to see if there was any way back. There wasn't. Ben deserved more than she could ever give him. Hanna stood seeing pain etched on his face, where once there had been love. A shadow of the man he had once been. She closed her eyes, swamped by sorrow for the strength of a love she had squandered. She owed Ben honesty. She owed him that. She could not leave him with any hope, because she could not do this. She could not be his nurse and comforter, whatever the outcome for her.

She whispered, 'You're right. I would be no use to you. I'm so sorry, Ben.'

Ben opened his eyes and nodded. 'You made your choice some time ago. My being like this doesn't change anything. Now be honest with Finn. He has conflicting loyalties, and you are confusing him. He needs to know exactly where he is with you. It is the not knowing that hurts him, Hanna, the false hope. Can you, please, tell him, as gently as you can, that you are not coming back?'

Hanna nodded. 'Not here, not today. I need to time it, carefully, for his sake, Ben. Finn and I have an uneasy Easter truce, but I will . . .'

Hanna was silently crying. From relief or guilt, Ben did not know.

'I came to try to do the right thing . . .'

Ben held his hand up. He could not take much more. 'Doing the right thing is not enough, for either of us . . .'

'I know.' Hanna bent and pressed her mouth to Ben's forehead and left the room.

Ben turned his wheelchair back to the window and shivered at the vicious, grey winter sea that thundered up the sea wall sending plumes of white spray and brown seaweed sailing up over the rail and onto the prom. Even in that final moment of letting Hanna go, he had thought how beautiful she still was.

'Hi, Raz, how're you doing?'

'Hi, Finn, I am sick with too much chocolate.'

Finn snorted. 'Tell me about it!'

'I hope you have good Easter. I hope your father, he is growing stronger?'

'Yeah, thanks, he's just left to go back to hospital in Birmingham. Some friends are driving him.'

387

'It is good that you can spend celebration together,' Raza said carefully, catching something in the tone of Finn's voice.

Finn said, 'My mother suddenly arrived for Easter with my little sister. I wasn't expecting her. It was a surprise.'

'That is good. You have your whole family together for festive holiday.'

'Yeah, it was good,' Finn said. 'It made my dad happy.'

'Of course, and it must make you happy, also, Finn.' It was not quite a question, but Raza spoke with an upward inflection as if he was unsure.

'Yeah. My mother told me off for not working.'

'She is right. You are not working.'

'I know . . .' There was a silence.

'Is your mother still with you?'

'No, she and my little sister caught the sleeper to Paddington. Izzy was very excited about it . . .'

'Now you are missing everyone.'

'Actually, it's my dad I'm feeling a bit weird about . . .' Finn stopped.

'Weird?'

'Yeah, like . . .' Finn searched for words. 'I dunno, my dad's much better. I can see he's getting stronger, but when he was leaving, like, when he was in the car and they were all driving away, I got, like this stupid panic, that he was disappearing forever and I'd never see him again . . . and the feeling won't go away . . .'

Finn did not tell Raza that he had run after the car calling out as it pulled away from the kerb. Fergus had braked sharply, and Finn had wrenched the back door open and climbed into the back where Ben was lying against a barrage of pillows and cushions and wrapped in rugs. He had leaned towards Ben and said fiercely, 'Love you, Dad.'

Startled, Ben had whispered back, smiling, 'Love you back, old thing . . .'

Ben had looked feverish, lying against all the cushions, his eyes too bright. Finn had felt a cold clutch of fear. Seeing it, Ben had said gently, 'I've just got a bit of a temperature. I get minor infections because my immune system is low. The hospital will sort it. See you soon . . . I'll Skype you . . .' He had shivered in the cold air coming from the open door.

'See you, soon,' Finn had repeated, backing out of the car and shutting his father into the warmth and letting Fergus drive off into the late afternoon . . .

Raza knew that Finn was waiting for him to give reassurance. The responsibility felt awesome. He thought carefully before he spoke.

'I think perhaps you are sad. Both your parents, they leave you after happy day. And your father, he was very injured. You nearly lose him. Although he is now stronger, it is natural, I think, that you are afraid still of something happening to him . . .'

'What if the horrible sinking feeling is a premonition, Raz?'

'It is not premonition, it is fear. The same fear I have for my Baba. You must banish this fear from your mind and pray for your father and think only good thoughts for him, Finn.'

Finn was silent, then he said, 'Yeah, I know. Thanks, Raz . . . Better go, Delphi is calling me . . .'

'See you Sunday, Finn.'

'See you Sunday, Raz.'

By the time Fergus and Mary got Ben back to Selly Oak, he had a full-blown fever and was rambling. He was rushed straight back into ICU where he could be under close supervision. Fergus felt the slow crawl of dread as Ben was wheeled away from them.

'I better ring Ian,' he said to Mary, as they fell, drained, onto the bed in a Travelodge near the hospital. Ian answered immediately as if he had been waiting for their call.

'Ben has been taken back into intensive care,' Fergus told him.

'I rather thought he would be,' Ian said, sounding brisk. Fergus realized Delphi must be in earshot. 'They need to move fast to find the cause and inhibit the spread of infection . . .'

'Of course, they do. It's just a little setback . . .'

'Indeed, it is. Fergus, Delphi and I can't thank you and Mary enough for your kindness this Easter. Without you, Ben would not have been with us all.'

'I just hope it wasn't too much for him, Ian.'

'He would have been fighting this infection before he left Selly Oak, Fergus. It is just very bad luck. We'll ring the hospital in the morning. You must both be exhausted . . . go and have a large drink, sleep well and thank you both again . . .'

Mary was pouring the contents of a miniature whisky bottle into a tooth glass. She handed it to Fergus. 'Should we let Hanna know? She'll still be in London. She's not flying back to Finland until tomorrow night.'

'No,' Fergus said. 'That is up to Delphi and Ian.'

CHAPTER SIXTY-FOUR

Delphi had known that Ben was in pain on Easter morning. She had heard Ian ring the doctor and knew he must be going out for a prescription. At lunch, Ben had sat slightly removed from them all, smiling, enjoying his children and trying to disguise the fact he was eating little. At the end of the meal, she had watched him wheel himself quietly away from the noise to the peace of the sitting room.

Delphi had wanted to run after him and beg him to stay in the warmth of this house and rest. It was madness to do a horrendous long drive back to Birmingham. But she also knew Ben could not make it up the steep stairs to a bed and their old saggy sofa was no place for him to sleep.

The call from Selly Oak to tell them Ben was gravely ill came at 5.30 a.m. the next morning. After Fergus's telephone call, fearing the worst, Ian had decided to book Delphi on an early morning flight to Birmingham.

They drove to Newquay in shocked silence. Ian stood in a cold wind watching Delphi walk across the tarmac to the small plane, climb the steps and disappear. He felt overwhelmed by dread and powerlessness. He had decided he must stay in Cornwall for Finn. If the worst happened, he needed to be here, near him. But Ian was conflicted with wanting to be with Ben, with the professional urge to know exactly what his medical team were doing to combat the infection. It was not easy to stop being a doctor. He wished he did not know the danger. Ben's weary body was going to need huge reserves of strength and will and luck to fight this infection.

Ian turned and walked back to his car. He had sensed that Ben had had enough. He did not have any more fight or will or mental strength left in him. Ben had reached the first goal he'd been striving for. He had spent Easter with his family, against the odds. But what now?

A long, painful rehab, a life without Hanna and, Ian suspected, without a military career. Ian knew Ben would eschew any attempt at therapy or counselling. This damned infection had come at the most vulnerable and dangerous time for Ben.

Ian thought about driving to the school and preparing Finn, just in case. He decided against it. There was a need to be honest and warn the boy, but not yet. All might be well and what good would frightening Finn do? Hanna was in the air, flying home to Finland. He would ring her tonight.

CHAPTER SIXTY-FIVE

Birmingham, 2010

When Delphi arrived at the ICU at Selly Oak, Ben was heavily sedated, his body full of tubes with instruments constantly bleeping by the bed. Ben's consultant told Delphi that the next few days were crucial as Ben slipped in and out of consciousness.

Delphi had found a guest house where she could walk through the park to the hospital. She spent each day meditating, praying for him to pull through. She was only allowed moments by his side. She and Ian had decided not to tell Finn how ill Ben was. They disliked keeping things from him, but they did not want to set him back or frighten him. According to Ed Dominic, Finn was working again and seemed more like his old self.

Although he was sedated, Ben tossed and turned and cried out in his sleep. Walking through the corridors, Delphi had been shocked to see how many seriously injured soldiers were still being flown in from Afghanistan. Beds were urgently needed in the high dependency unit, and Ben was moved into a nearby side ward although he was still being carefully monitored.

Delphi could now spend more time with him. She sat through the long hours while he slept, sketching the nurses coming and going.

She drew the view outside the window; a view she knew she would never forget. She drew Ben's long fingers lying on top of the covers and his flushed and troubled face sleeping. She did not know if he was conscious of her there, but she began to read softly to him in the hushed afternoons. Snatches from books he loved, books of his childhood, tales of adventure influenced by Ian, in the years that mattered, the years she had missed. *Jeeves, The Thirty-Nine Steps, Flashman, The Jungle Book.*

Sometimes she dozed beside him listening to his breathing. She let her breath flow in and out to slow the painful thud of her heart. Always to the same refrain. *Please, God, Please God, Please God, do not let this good man die.*

For Ben was a good man. He had, even as a child, felt he must stay strong for everyone else. Even when she left him. Even when Hanna left him; even when wounded and casaevac'd home. But at what cost? Ben would never allow himself to crumple, to be vulnerable, to hurt. Delphi paced helplessly up and down the stuffy little room grieving for him. So damaged, so wounded, not just by the lasting impact of an IED, but by a wife who no longer loved him, who could walk away when he needed her most.

Delphi was torn and seared by memories of the little boy he had been. Of all the times she had been absent, the times she had neglected him, the times when he was ill or unhappy at school. All those lost years he never once blamed her for. Ben growing up loyal, steadfast, and secure, because of Ian. When he was small, he had delved deep for that nugget of hope and contentment in small things, and grasped

394

it, held it triumphantly, aloft, so that something gentle in him could survive.

Delphi had always marvelled and been humbled by Ben's capacity for happiness, for wanting the people he loved to be at ease, even if they were behaving badly. Ben and Ian did not share the same blood, but they were alike in their ability to accept and love people as they were. She pondered what it cost loyal men to suppress judgement, to squash that little voice of truth in order to go on loving.

She wondered if it was possible that Ben had fallen for Hanna because she was as self-centred as she herself had been in his childhood. If Ben had been drawn to a pattern of love that he was familiar with.

Delphi sat through the long dark days reading tales Ben loved in the fall of afternoon light. Words that had made him laugh or comforted him or he had fallen asleep to. She sensed, and hoped, in the concentrated stillness of his body, that the familiar words fell like distant sunlight over his tired heart and weak body. She wanted to warm and woo him back to a world that could and would be good again. She wanted him to hang on and believe that this pain would eventually pass. That other loves and lives would move into the spaces left bare. Nothing could be the same, but if she could help him through this, Ben would find the strength for another way of living his life. All Delphi had was the power of her love. She concentrated with all of her being on his still form in the bed, willing him back to them all.

CHAPTER SIXTY-SIX

Cornwall, 2010

When Ian picked Finn up for the weekend, he did not seem his usual reassuring self. Finn had been told that Ben had an infection to his wound and that Delphi had gone up to Birmingham for a few days to cheer him up. Finn, remembering how ill Ben had looked in the car and how scared he had felt, suspected Delphi and Ian were not telling him the whole truth.

He had tried to reassure himself that if it was really serious Delphi and Ian would tell him. They were always honest with him and had never treated him like a child.

When Delphi rang him from the hospital to explain Ben was too tired to talk to him for a few days, she had assured him that all his energy was going into fighting his infection. She would have told him if she thought Ben was going to . . . She would have told him . . .

Finn felt cold dread all over again. What if it was so bad Ian was afraid to tell him Ben might die? There was something in Ian's eyes Finn had never seen before and it frightened him. He could not bear to make Ian say the words that would break them both.

Ian took Finn fishing on Sunday morning. He made a picnic, but neither of them were hungry. They didn't talk much. Fishing meant you did not have to talk. Finn wondered if this was why Ian had bought him up to the reservoir. He got the distinct feeling Ian wanted to say something to him. That he was perhaps waiting for Finn to ask if Ben was going to die, and then he would tell him, gently, how ill Ben was, and that, yes, he might die. Neither of them could think of anything else. Finn was sure of this.

They sat side by side in the cold, waiting for non-existent fish to bite. Finn suddenly yanked his rod out of the water and threw it onto the grass.

Ian turned, startled. 'There are no stupid fish here,' Finn told him angrily.

Ian said, 'Doesn't seem so, does it, old thing. Shall we go home?'

In the car Finn said, 'I don't believe in God anymore.'

'That often happens around your age,' Ian said as if he was not surprised.

'If there was a God, he wouldn't let people, like my dad, suffer . . .'

'Would it make you feel any better if it was someone else's dad, suffering?' Ian said as he turned the car into the drive of Salubrious House. He turned to look at Finn. 'I think I am too weary to have a theological discussion on whether there is a benign God, Finn. But war and the result of war, are man-made tragedies. I do not believe God saved Ben's life but chose to let the two soldiers either side of him die, but—'

'That was just good and bad luck and where the bomb went off.'

'But,' Ian said firmly, 'neither do I believe God was absent, Finn. Did you know men pray to God and their mothers in battle? You can choose what you believe, but personally

397

I find it more comforting to believe in a God, than random luck. Less bleak, don't you think?'

Ian never got angry or argued or suggested you were a prat even when you wanted an argument, but Finn knew he had a way of ending it. He got out of the car and Finn saw suddenly how bent and old and sad he seemed. He could have been sitting reading the papers by the fire if he hadn't had Finn home for the weekend. He was tired of Finn. Finn was tired of himself. He felt terrible.

'I'm sorry,' he said gruffly. 'I know I'm in a bad mood. I'll go back to school early. Will you drop me off at the train station?'

Ian looked at Finn, relieved. 'Are you sure?'

Finn nodded. As Ian put him onto the train back to Truro he said quietly, 'God is watching over Ben and I have enough belief for both of us . . . all will be well, my dear old thing . . .'

Tears came to Finn's eyes. He could not say anything. He nodded and got onto the train. He kept looking out of the window, watching Ian getting smaller and smaller, then he sat back in the silent empty Sunday train.

CHAPTER SIXTY-SEVEN

Birmingham, 2010

Through the strange, long days of fever, Ben became aware of Delphi sitting by his bed. He did not want to surface, he wanted to go on floating in a drug-induced nether world forever. He craved this no man's land, this confused dream-like state, this absence of pain, this quiet giving in.

Yet it was impossible to stay submerged. The drugs wore off. People floated back. He became aware of his surroundings, to have periods of lucidity. Ben kept his eyes closed. With lucidity came something new to him; a creeping, suffocating hopelessness, a reluctance to remember, an encompassing lethargy that was enveloping and frightening.

All his life Ben had had an aim, an ambition, a goal. He loved his life, his job, his role in the British Army. He adored his family, his children, his wife. In one hideous flash it had disappeared. All certainty gone.

How do I re-invent myself? Where do I start? Worst of all, that insidious, persistent little voice in his head. *What's the point? I'm better dead.*

Just leave me alone, he thought, irritably, when hands

399

painfully turned him, changed his drip, dressed his wounds, jabbed his bottom . . . *for God's sake, just let me die* . . .

Delphi's voice started to penetrate the fog. Ben would listen to her reading for a while, before his brain took off again, resisting reality for a little longer. Despite fighting it, he became more and more aware of his mother's presence in the chair beside him, listened to her heavy sleeping breath as she dosed, heard the soft sound of her pencil on the sketch pad, the words she read, a familiar tale unfolding. And despite his resistance, the world drew him slowly and reluctantly back. Back to Delphi's voice, her strength, to her single-minded, determined will that he live. Ben knew his crisis was over but could not summon the energy to care.

As soon as he was back in his own room the nursing staff had him up and out of bed. Imperative, they told him. 'We must get you moving and back into physio.' Ben's body felt weak and unresponsive, his limbs heavy and as reluctant to move as he was. He ignored his protein drinks and pushed his food about his plate, escaped into music played on his headphones, desperate to block out the hours, the long dreary days.

Ben's plummet into depression was horrifying to Delphi. She had never seen him like this, and, for the first time in her life, she could find no way of reaching him.

Ben's consultant tried to reassure her. 'The reality of his situation is probably just hitting home. It's hard for fit, healthy men at the top of their game to be struck down like this. Having a major infection has been a big setback, like recovering from flu, when your body is low, depression sets in. PTSD is always going to be an enormous, hidden issue for combatants. It can sweep in suddenly or take years to manifest. Mending bodies is far simpler than treating minds. We can help Ben, but I can't force him to seek help.

Most of all it's vital to get him back into a strict routine of physio and exercise. His stomach wound is healing well, thanks to the antibiotics. Now we need to work on his mobility, on getting Ben fit again, concentrating on what he *can* change will boost his morale and get him back on track . . .'

Predictably, Ben refused to talk to anyone: therapist, regimental padre or concerned colleagues. 'Go home, Delphi,' he told her irritably. 'I'm not, after all, going to die, there is nothing more you can do here.'

'So, are you just going to give up and wallow, Ben?' Delphi snapped, suddenly angry. She opened her mouth to remind him of Finn and Izzy.

'Don't you dare tell me that my children need me,' Ben snapped back. Then seeing her face, he said more gently, holding out his hand to her: 'I'm sorry. Go home to Ian, Delphi, please. This is not helping, you seeing me like this. I need to get on with this on my own . . . in my own way.'

The staff nurse on the ward was of the same mind and advised Delphi to go back to her family and get some rest. 'Try not to worry, Ben's entitled to a bit of anger without worrying that he's hurting those he loves . . .' She smiled. 'He can swear at us – it's water off a duck's back . . .'

Delphi had welcomed Ben's flash of anger; it gave her hope. She rang Ian and he flew up to Birmingham to see Ben, and to take her home.

The following morning, early, a cheerful physio Ben had not seen before turned up at his bedside with a wheelchair. 'Hi, I'm Lucy Adams,' she said in an Aussie accent. 'I hear you've had a bit of a setback. Sorry about that. I'm here to make an assessment, so we can start to get a programme of gentle physio going. We need to concentrate on that good leg to get you standing and walking again.'

Before Ben knew it, she had him into the wheelchair and down in the lift and into the physio department. He was shocked at how weak he had become in ten days. He needed help in getting up onto the massage table and he was so stiff that even the most basic exercises now hurt. He lay back and let the physio manipulate his limbs with expert fingers.

'Yell, if it hurts,' she told him, concentrating. 'And it will hurt. It's really important you move as much as possible now you're better and keep your circulation going, but you know that . . .'

Ben did not answer. 'I've read your notes. You were doing great before you got sick and there's no reason for you not to get back your strength and muscle mass quickly . . . Can you turn on your left side? Does it hurt? Okay, I'll go really easy near your wound site . . .'

Ben could feel her deft fingers gently probing his stiff muscles, back, arms, leg, neck. When he flinched or jumped, she would go back and massage the muscle until it relaxed. It felt a little as if he was being warmed back to life. At the end of the treatment, he saw she was exhausted and closed his eyes in gratitude. 'Thank you,' he said. 'That does feel better.'

'My job,' she replied, and Ben heard the smile in her voice and opened his eyes. 'I feel almost human again,' he said, smiling back.

'Good . . .' She helped him off the table and back into his wheelchair and began wheeling him back down the corridor.

A male physio was wheeling a double amputee towards them. He was a small wiry man strapped into his chair. He beamed at Lucy.

'Hi, Tommy!' she said. 'I'll be back down in five . . .'

Tommy winked at Ben. 'Getting me new legs fitted,' he

said. 'I've ordered them longer than my old pair on account of my missus being taller than me before . . .'

Ben laughed. 'Good idea! Good luck . . .'

Lucy Adams wheeled him into the empty lift and pressed the button to go up. 'Good to see Tommy joking again,' she said. 'He's had one setback after another. He was in a real dark place . . . But dark places do pass, with help. It's hard not to dwell on all you've lost, rather than all you can and will achieve . . .'

She paused, looking down at him. 'In the end, it's a straight choice, Ben, we can work together as a team to get our patients back to having a fulfilling life. It won't be the same life they had before, but that doesn't mean it can't be a bloody good life, full of new, exciting challenges . . . You were doing really well. It would be a crying shame if you let this blip in your recovery affect all the hard work you've been doing for months, don't you think?'

Ben stared back at her, amused by her strong Aussie accent, impressed by her straightforwardness. 'Please don't start singing from *The Sound of Music* or break into a rendition of "Waltzing Matilda" to get me motivated, Lucy . . .'

Lucy threw back her head and laughed as the lift door opened.

'I'll keep it as a threat . . . Major Charles.'

'And I strongly suspect meeting Tommy was timed to go with your little pep talk . . .'

Lucy smiled. 'It wasn't, but we could take it as a sign . . .'

They passed a woman carrying a bunch of narcissi as they walked back to the ward, the smell was pungent in the stuffy corridor. Ben thought of home, of the Cornish daffodil fields, of the hedges alive with spring.

Someone had placed his post on his bed. There were letters from Hanna and paintings from Izzy. There was a rare card from Finn and a beautiful hand-painted card from Delphi. All pulling him back to the world he still had.

His mind had suddenly become this flaky thing that could not be trusted. He had never before experienced black, destructive depression that descended like a heavy grey blanket from all corners of the room, but he had seen it in Hanna. He must not let it take hold. He loathed self-pity, it was a self-indulgence that sucked the hope and will out of you. He would fight it, accept help, take pills if necessary . . .

He lay back on the bed, holding onto his letters, aware of his newly relaxed muscles, of his damaged body tingling, slowly coming to life again. Lucy Adams, physio, extraordinaire, was right. It was a straight choice.

CHAPTER SIXTY-EIGHT

Cornwall, 2010

Zamir died on the 25th of May, the same day that Sarah's baby was born, a girl they named Samia, after Raza's mother. Zamir's last letter to Raza reached him the same afternoon. The synchronicity of these three things soothed Raza, as if Zamir had planned it.

Daniyal heard the news from Hanif and immediately rang Chinir. Chinir left Sarah and his new baby at the hospital and drove straight to the school to tell Raza. Mr Dominic called him out from breakfast. Raza's first thought on seeing Chinir's grave face was that something had happened to Sarah, and he called out her name in alarm.

Chinir reassured him that Sarah was fine. He told him, as gently as he could, that Hanif had rung to say that Zamir had died in the night.

'Did my Baba die peacefully?' Raza whispered, knowing that Chinir would, of course, affirm it, but needing to hear the words.

'Truly, it was a peaceful death, Raza. Your father died in his sleep in his own house . . .'

'It was what he wanted,' Raza said, bereft.

'It was what he wanted, but I'm sorry to bring you this news, Raza. Even when you know death is coming, it is very hard to hear.'

Raza stared at Chinir, unable to absorb the enormity of a world without Baba. He wanted to turn and run, to be on his own. Instead, he asked politely, 'How is Sarah?'

Chinir, unable to hide his joy, smiled. 'Sarah gave birth to a little girl in the night. Both are well and sleeping.'

'This is good news.' Raza touched Chinir's arm. 'I am happy for you and Sarah, Chinir. Allah gives and he takes away. This is how it is . . .'

'We are naming her Samia, after your Ami, Raza . . .'

How small and polite and desolate, he looked, Chinir thought.

'Raza, Mr Dominic has agreed that the best thing for you is to come home with me. Sarah will be out of hospital tomorrow. Liyana is already here. Daniyal is driving down to see the baby at the weekend . . . We will all be together to mourn your Baba, Raza.'

'Chinir, thanks, but it is much better for me to stay in school and work. Truly, I prefer to be busy. Tomorrow, it is Finn's birthday. I should be with him. I will come home, maybe at the weekend. Please . . . you must go back to Sarah and your new baby. Chinir, I will be okay. I promise.'

Chinir looked at him anxiously. 'Are you sure? Raza, I wish . . .'

'I am sure. I must go now, or I will be late for class . . . Please tell Sarah that I am so happy for her, for you both . . .' Raza bolted.

Mr Dominic, who had been hovering, watering the pots by the front door, assured Chinir that they would keep an eye on him. As Chinir left the school he felt guilty that the exhilaration and joy of being a father swamped all other considerations at this moment. He and Sarah would have to take care that the birth of their baby, and the death of Zamir, did not make Raza feel replaced and displaced too.

Raza, out of breath from running, tucked himself into the shade of trees bent crooked by the wind and looked out at the creek. The tide was out, and waders picked their way through the mud. The fluting call of curlews hovered like a prayer over the water.

Despite the horrible incident with Chatto, Raza still loved this creek. He came most days for the peace. It was where he felt nearest to Zamir. He would tell Baba of the old herons standing like spooky old men in the branches of the small trees that lined the creek. He would describe the white egrets and oystercatchers picking their way over the shingle. He would close his eyes and lift his head to the faint mewing *pi-pi* of a buzzard, hovering above him in the vivid blue sky.

Raza felt at one with this ancient and mysterious place. He loved the water gleaming and undulating at full tide, the banks rustling with the sounds of unseen animals and birds. It filled a need in him for wild, untamed places.

Raza delved into his pocket for Zamir's letter and smoothed his fingers over the scrawled Pashto writing. The words were his father's, but the writing was not always in his hand. Zamir, must, at times, have dictated this long rambling letter from his sickbed.

The letter was in the form of a diary, which Zamir must have started after Raza returned to England. He wrote of the melting snows and of spring and the Indian sparrow hawk he had spotted hunting for food near the newborn lambs. It had nested in the cracks of the mountain, near the cave the sheep used in bad weather.

Zamir spoke of the valleys coming alive with wildflowers, of the planting of crops in the stony fields and of his prayers to Allah for a good season. He wrote of the young boys who helped guard his goats and sheep, and his gratitude to Sarah and Chinir for the medicines that made his life easier.

He catalogued, like a threnody, the flow of his end of days, of what he saw between sunrise and sunset as he sat in the shade outside his tiny stone house. The rhythm of these days was no different from all the days of Raza's childhood, but there was a new contentment in his father, an ease and peace in his old age.

Raza wondered if Zamir's long descriptions of the life they had once lived together was carefully written so that his son would never forget his roots or where he began his life.

Raza yearned to reassure Baba that his childhood, his village, his home, all lived on inside him. They were visited each morning he woke, and they were left behind each night before he slept. Their life together could never be torn from his heart.

As Zamir grew frailer and sensed his own end, his writing had grown more anxious and scrawled and others had taken his pen.

Raza smiled at the thought of Zamir lying back like an old Pasha dictating his thoughts in this last, long, rambling letter. It was obvious that he had not trusted anyone to post it after his death; but made sure it had been posted and registered before he died.

His last entry had shown no fear of death, only a weary sadness in leaving Raza to an unpredictable world. He expressed gratitude for all that Sarah and Chinir had done and been to them all, for taking Raza as their son. He was joyful that Sarah was at last to have a child. Allah was indeed good and rewarded the blessed.

Lastly, for he was an unsentimental Pashtun, he tried to tell Raza how proud he had made him.

Anyone can hold a gun, he wrote, *but you have battled your fears and forged a life in another country and proved yourself beyond all my hopes and dreams with scholarships and prizes.*

I trust you to always be a good Muslim and to turn your back on all that is without honour and to take with gratitude all that you know to be good.

Don't forget our life together, here in Pakistan, for it will fade like the dream of another man. Do not return until you are sure of the part you can play in the future of our country. Never think that you are just one man who cannot change anything, but one of many who can. Do not feel alone. I travel with you . . .

The light was fading. The tide slipped in over the mudflats. The sky beyond the trees glowed orange. Raza sat on, his heart far away in the mountains with Baba. In his house no more than a shack, smaller than Finn's beach house. He did not want to leave the comfort of it. If he admitted to himself that Baba was no longer there, he would have no anchor to ground him. Baba had been the heart of his life. Baba was home. Baba was Pakistan. Where would he turn now? The life he once had, the boy he once was, were gone. Sarah and Chinir now had their own child. Who would Raza Ali be? Raza felt an aching loneliness, floating adrift in a world and a culture not his own. Without Baba he would blow away in a cold English wind . . .

Raza heard someone walking through the trees towards him. He knew those footsteps well. Finn sat beside him without speaking. They watched the incoming tide creep in over the mudflats. They listened to the last ripple of scuttering birds in the dusk as the sun dropped, tingeing the edges of clouds golden. Then, in silence, they walked back to school, together.

CHAPTER SIXTY-NINE

Raza could not sleep. He tossed and turned for hours and then got out of bed and went to the window. The night was cold and clear and there was a mass of stars. He shivered and his stomach rumbled. He had gone to pray and missed supper. He heard Finn get out of bed. Isa and Peter were dead to the world.

'You cannot sleep either?' Raza asked.

Finn sighed. 'No, not with you tossing and turning and flumping about with your pillow. How those two can lie there snoring is a mystery.'

'Sorry,' Raz said bleakly, and his stomach growled again.

'You need toast,' Finn said. 'You missed supper. Come on, I'll make you some.'

'We are not allowed in the kitchen at night.'

'We'll shut the door and be quiet. Come on . . .'

Finn pulled his dressing gown from the door and threw Raza his. They opened the bedroom door and moved down the corridor past the bottom of the stairs. There was always a lamp, left on at night, on the hall table. They slid the kitchen door open and shut it behind them before switching the light on. Finn got two pieces of bread and put them in the toaster. He switched the kettle on and found the hot chocolate. Raza could not relax, he had a healthy respect for not breaking rules, but he was also extremely hungry.

They sat on bar stools drinking hot chocolate and eating toast and peanut butter and Raza immediately began to feel better. Finn said, with his mouth full, 'Maybe you should have gone home with Chinir, Raz . . .'

'No.' Raza shook his head. 'I am better here, at school, working. My family, they are all together for the new baby, also they would talk, talk, talk to me about my feelings, and I just want quiet to remember my Baba. My childhood was my own. I did not share it with them. There is my life before UK and there is my life now.'

Finn was silent. Life before and life now. Before Hanna left them. Before Ben's accident. And after. After, stretches on and on with one frightening thing happening after another. Ben could still be snatched away at any moment. The thought stopped Finn's breath.

He looked at Raza. 'Which is more shadowy and unreal, the life you had in Pakistan or the life you have here?'

Raza ate his toast and thought about it. His brothers were totally shadowy and unreal to him now. He had tried never to think about the terrible day when Baba would be gone from this earth. The life his father had forced upon him in England, had become a place where he thrived. His life had been transformed by education in a way that never could have happened if he had stayed with his father. Yet, with Zamir's death came a feeling deep inside him that he would always be a Pakistani boy in a foreign country. No education or documents or success or friendship would ever change that basic fundamental fact. A cultural cavern suddenly loomed up at him from a dark place of grief and he had no words for this knowledge. It made him feel so lonely that he shivered.

Finn watched him, troubled. Raza stared back; it was the first time he had been unable to voice his thoughts to Finn, because mostly they did not need words. Raza had watched Finn change in the last few months, withdraw from people and into himself. Raza understood. When the worst happens, you need to seal your heart away to survive.

Eventually, he said, 'Before, my life in Pakistan is a small but happy life, or I think it is. When my father sends me away from him to England, I believe my heart is broken. I am angry and confused at this immodest life my father has sent me to endure. Then slowly, through my new family, I find books and good people, and I understand that my daydreams on the mountain, when I made my father angry by neglecting the goats, was my boredom. My brain, it had nowhere to go. I do not know who I would be if I had stayed in Pakistan, I know only the person I am now, Finn. My father he was my Pakistan and now he is gone it feels as if I have lost my country also.'

'England is your country and your home now, Raz, with Sarah and Chinir and with all of us, your friends . . . It has been for a long time; you know it has. It is just the shock of your father dying, that you feel scared you have lost everything . . . I'm scared all the time that my father might still die . . .'

Raza nodded. It was true. Finn was afraid. 'Thank you. But I will never truly be an Englishman here, Finn, and if I ever go back to Pakistan, I will never truly be a Pakistani—'

The door was pushed open and Mrs Dominic put her distinctive pink head round the door. She looked at the two boys and said quietly, trying not to laugh as they jumped, 'As the kitchen is out of bounds at night, I am assuming this is a dire emergency?'

Both boys nodded vigorously. Mercy Dominic edged into

412

the kitchen wearing a beautifully patterned kimono. She leant against the door.

'I'm afraid I couldn't help overhearing the last bit of your conversation . . . You know, boys, there are no certainties in this life. We are many people in one lifetime. There really is no such thing as a perfect time and place. It's just an illusion. Wishing we were back somewhere in the past stops us being able to explore the place we are now, or the people we've become. None of us stay the same. We can't halt time. Life moves on whether we want it to or not . . .'

The two boys sat with their eyes fixed on her and Mercy Dominic hesitated. 'Grief and the loss of happy times is tough. Growing up and letting go of a safe and secure time of childhood is tough. But I can assure you both that talking about life at four o'clock in the morning is absolutely the worst time to do it . . .'

She ushered them to the door. 'You might not believe it at this moment, but you guys just need to hang in there. There will be a million more good and exciting times coming for you both . . .'

Finn and Raza nodded silently, mildly embarrassed at her arms round their shoulders. At the door, Mrs Dominic said, 'So, given that school rules have been broken, was there a definitive emergency that I can enter into the Night Book?'

Raza looked slightly alarmed, but Finn hid a grin. 'Yeah, definite emergency, Mrs Dominic . . .'

'Some sort of toast emergency, Finn?

'Exactly, Mrs Dominic. Exactly. Raz went to pray and missed supper and his stomach was rumbling horribly so . . .'

'You took pity and did the kind thing?

'I did the only thing I could in the circumstances, Mrs Dominic. Make toast.'

Raza was anxiously trying to follow this exchange, unable to discern whether it was peculiar British humour again or they were in trouble.

'If you disappear this instant and don't start a precedent, I will forget I have ever seen either of you . . . Goodnight . . . and go to sleep!'

'Goodnight, Mrs Dominic, thanks.' Both boys scooted back to their room. Mercy Dominic smiled and washed up their mugs and plates and made herself a cup of tea. She was now wide awake. She thought about being 13 and shivered. That awful hybrid state when you were neither child nor adult nor seemed to fit anywhere. A world where you suddenly realized the adults did not have the answers, did not always make the right moves and sometimes hid the truth . . . Making forbidden toast in the middle of the night seemed a pretty mild rebellion, Mercy thought, as she went back upstairs to Ed.

CHAPTER SEVENTY

Ben nursed his beer and watched the two sea-blown boys at the table. He was sitting by the veranda rail with his leg up on a stool. Raza had been staying with them since school broke up for the summer. He had jumped at Delphi's invitation to stay as long as he liked. His father had just died, and Ben noticed he spent a lot of time praying and going off on his own while Finn surfed.

Raza had, under pressure, learnt to swim in the school pool, but Finn could not get him out into surf. Raza still seemed in slight awe of Ben and, scrupulously polite, would keep on calling him 'sir'.

'I'm Ben,' Ben told him, smiling. But Raza had then called him, 'Ben . . . sir.'

'Well,' Delphi said laughing, 'better than Sir Ben!'

Ben was intrigued by the dynamics of the friendship between the two boys. Raza seemed devoid of any jealousy or possessiveness. When the weather was right, Finn surfed relentlessly with the legions of surfers who descended on the beach each day, but Raza seemed contentedly happy with his own company. He helped Delphi, fished with Ian, and walked or read on the beach. He lay on the veranda devouring novels by both English and Pakistani writers and Ben noticed that he liked modern history and Pakistani politics, mostly written by American Pakistanis.

When Finn had exhausted himself in the water, the boys would lie side by side on rugs on the sand, reading or showing each other things on their phones. Their voices would waft up to Ben resting in the afternoons at the far end of the veranda. He saw that in some undefinable way the two independent boys needed simply to be around each other.

The closeness he had always had with Finn seemed to have vanished. Ben knew it was an inevitable part of Finn growing up and going through the grunting teenage stage, but in the long dark nights, on bad days, when he felt overwhelmed by the future, the thought came to him that if he had died, he could have remained a hero to Finn.

Ben understood that losing his leg had traumatized Finn in a way he probably could not explain. Finn was young and fit with his life before him, the very thought of losing a limb would have freaked him out.

Ben longed to show him all that was possible, what other soldiers with far worse injuries had achieved. But Finn did not want to talk about Ben's injuries or be involved with his treatment at Headley Court. He was helpful, breezily affectionate, but somehow detached, and he avoided being alone with Ben. It hurt, and Ben wished he was man enough not to let it. Of course, Finn wanted to escape and surf all summer with his mates. His safe little life had been knocked from under his feet. Hanna had promised to speak to Finn. Had she? Ben hadn't had the strength to ask her, and Finn had given him no chance to get near the subject of Hanna.

Delphi voiced her own worries about Finn to Ian. 'I miss the old, kind, happy Finn. I can't seem to get near the boy he's become.'

'Give him time and let him be,' Ian said. 'Finn will come to realize that his world hasn't ended, and Ben most certainly isn't going to be defined for the rest of his life by losing a leg . . . But you can't expect things to just slide back into place this summer as if nothing has happened, Delphi. Ben is recovering from serious injury and Hanna is absent.'

Ian picked up his fishing rods. 'The boy he's growing into will become easier with time,' he said, kissing the top of her head. 'Now, I am going fishing on the headland with another lost boy . . .'

Delphi watched him walk away with Raza towards the headland and wondered what she would do without him.

Hanna was due to fly in from Helsinki, leaving Izzy at the beach house for a few days while she worked on a design commission with Annalisa in London. Ben hoped to be off his crutches for Izzy before they arrived. He had been fitted with his first prosthesis, but he was struggling with the pain.

When Lucy Adams, his physio, rang Ben one morning to find out how he was getting on, Ben admitted to her he was frustrated. If he misjudged the amount of time he spent on the prosthesis, he rubbed his leg raw and was in agony. He felt a surge of relief when she told him she was in North Cornwall on holiday with friends and offered to drive over and look at his leg the following day.

At Headley Court Ben felt safe and anchored, his treatment safely managed and monitored. At home, he felt more vulnerable, and terrified of falling. He could not trust his body yet, nor was he sure when he was pushing too hard and should rest. At night, the pain kept him awake and his imagination would take over and wander into the unknown realms of the future and what it might hold for a man confined to a wheelchair.

In the early hours of one morning, when Ben was lying sleepless, he saw Raza carry his prayer mat out onto the veranda to pray. He watched from the open door of his room that opened onto the veranda. The boy wore the baggy *shalwar kameez* that he slept in. It made him look smaller than he was, touchingly frail, and a long way from home. Familiar flashback exploded in his head. Terrified children, the blood and tattered remnants of a little red dress. So many boys like Raza hanging about isolated villages, tending flocks of goats. Decoys for the Taliban, recruited, their childhoods vanished by the time they were eight.

When Raza finished praying, he sat still facing the sea. What amazing things this young boy had achieved in three years, Ben thought.

It took him a moment to realize that Raza was silently crying. He pulled himself upright and the movement startled Raza and he jumped up and looked into the dark room.

'Raza?' Ben whispered. 'Come and talk to me.'

Raza got up. 'Did I wake you, sir?'

'No, you didn't wake me. I've been awake for hours. Come in.'

Raza pushed the swing doors open and came cautiously into the room. 'Is there something I can get you, sir . . . Ben?'

Ben smiled. 'Nothing, thank you. Just come and sit with me for a while. The night is endless.'

Raza silently lowered himself onto the wooden floor beside the bed and sat facing Ben cross-legged in the dark. His ability to be still was alarming. Cautiously, Ben said, 'You must miss your father very much, Raza. Especially at night, when we all feel alone.'

He heard Raza swallow and then he said in a voice not quite steady, 'I do, sir. Tonight, I dream my Baba is still

418

alive. When I wake, I know it is only a dream and I am very sad.'

'Your father must have been very proud of you. If you were my son I would burst with pride.'

Raza's face was a white blur in the dark. He sniffed. 'Thank you.'

'You know that Delphi doesn't allow anyone to be sad or lonely in her house, so we'll have to do it in the dark when she isn't looking.'

Raza smiled. 'Indeed, this is true . . .' He shuffled a little nearer to see Ben's face. 'I am sorry that you too are sad and lonely in this long night.'

'Well,' Ben said. 'I feel better already for your company.'

After a small silence, Raza said, 'S . . . Ben . . . there is something I must tell you. After this you might not seek my company.'

'I think that's unlikely. What is it?'

Raza stood up and moved to the bed where Ben could see him.

'I am sorry for your injuries and I am very troubled when I hear. I come from small village in the mountains above Peshawar. It is very poor place. My father, he send me to England, so I do not join Taliban. My brothers, they are both Talibs, sir. They fight in Pakistan, but I know they go over border with PK Talib groups. They hate all western invaders. They angry about American drones. Men like my brothers, they are responsible for terrible injuries to ISAF soldiers, like you, sir. This my blood . . . this is where I come from . . .'

Ben stared at him. A brave little Pashtun who was not telling him anything he did not know. 'Raza,' he said gently. 'I already know that you come from the Swat Valley, from the Tribal Areas. It's Taliban country. It was realistic to suppose that some of your family would be Taliban. That does not make you one. Or your father, does it?'

Raza shook his head. 'I do not agree with Talib methods, but I do not agree with American and British methods to invade other countries. It makes worse violence.'

'I agree, it often does . . .'

Raza looked shocked. 'But you are British soldier.'

'I am a British soldier, but I am not convinced that even with the best intentions, foreign soldiers can have any lasting benefit for Afghanistan or its people, Raza . . .'

'You can say this? You are allowed, sir?'

Ben closed his eyes. 'Probably not.' Though, as he would probably never wear a uniform again, he was not sure his opinion mattered much, except to the families of those who had been killed or were maimed and injured.

Ben felt pretty sure that new political leaders would grow weary of the financial cost and gruesome death toll in Afghanistan. American and British forces would eventually be withdrawn. All the ground taken from the Taliban, all the 'safe places', would almost certainly be violently taken back. The training and recruitment of fiercely brave Afghan soldiers went on, but the Afghan Army needed more organization, discipline, and years of support to face the Taliban on their own.

Ben realized he was mourning the loss of a role he had tried to do well, where he had tried to make a difference. 'I've never spoken my conflicting thoughts out loud and I probably won't again, Raza. So, you see we both have secrets, and it makes us friends, doesn't it?'

His leg throbbed and Ben pulled himself up in the bed to change position. Raza smiled back. 'Yes.'

'Look, the sun's coming up,' Ben said. 'I'd like to watch it from the veranda. Can you see my crutches?'

'Lean on me,' Raza said.

'I'm too heavy.'

'I am strong. More than I look,' Raza said. He was too.

Ben leant and hopped to the veranda rail with Raza's arm firmly round him taking his weight. Together they leaned over the rail and watched the flushed skyline rise into a golden orb that edged upwards and turned the black sea gold. The beauty of the new day, the warmth of Raza's strong arm and the ending of another endless night made Ben grateful.

'My father, Zamir, and me, we would watch the sun come up over the mountain when I was small boy . . .' Raza whispered. 'My father, he would send me off to the goats with chapatti and earnest words not to daydream and let the goats stray. Those times seem long ago, but the sun, it is still the same sun rising all over the worlds and making our hearts full of wonder, for we will never know what it is that is coming next . . .'

'And that, my wise young friend,' Ben said, smiling, 'is the very thing that makes life both exciting and frightening.'

CHAPTER SEVENTY-ONE

Finn and Raza were fishing on the rocks at the far end of the beach. Ian had gone back to the beach house for lunch, reminding them to watch the tide. Neither boy had caught anything, and they sat munching on pasties, holding slack lines and wondering if they should call it a day.

They had brought books and provisions out with them. The beach house was bursting with people visiting Ben, and a physio from Headley Court had turned up.

Finn glanced at Raza. Ben and Raza seemed to spend a lot of time together when he was surfing. He had been surprised at how easy they seemed in each other's company. They swapped books, Taliban poets for Siegfried Sassoon. Mohammed Hanif for Bruce Chatwin.

Finn had listened to Ben telling Raza about an exercise on the Afghan/Pakistani border, before he was posted to Afghanistan. He told Raza he had been struck by the contrast of the stark beauty of those mountains and the harshness of lives lived amongst them. Finn realized that Ben understood far better than he could the life Raza had led with Zamir, before he came to the UK.

Finn hadn't heard the story of that trip, and he felt a stab of jealousy that Raza was hearing it. He knew it was his own fault. As soon as the summer holidays started, he had felt the dread of uncertainty gnaw at him and retreated. Hanna and Izzy were not here. He dreaded hearing Ben was no longer in the army. It was all he had ever known. Everything felt unreal. He could not bear to watch Ben learn to walk again, felt panic at the sight of the empty trouser leg.

The only respite was in the water, battling the elements, judging the waves, riding in on the crest of them. Finn was aware he had boxed himself in, but the more miserable he made himself, the harder it was to respond to his family, to get out of the box.

The only thing he was absolutely sure of was that anything could happen in the blink of an eye, to anyone, and there was not one single thing you could do to safeguard against that. Surfing was his escape, his retreat, his sanctuary.

The tide began to turn, and the two boys reeled in their rods, clambered back down the rocks to the beach and threw themselves on the rugs Ian had left. It was a heavy, sultry day without sun and Finn was hoping there would be clean surf later. He did not want to go back to the beach house full of adults.

Raza got out his book but did not open it. He was fidgety, anxious about Finn. For the first time in their friendship, Raza was aware of something coming between him and Finn. He was bewildered by it, for Finn had asked him here and Raza knew, deep in his heart, Finn needed him in some way.

He sieved sand through his fingers. Then he said, in a little rush, 'Finn, why it is you do not want to spend time with your father?'

Finn's head jerked upwards. 'What do you mean? I'm with him every day.'

'You fetch things for your Baba. You will make him tea and coffee and get the paper for him. You will discuss with him about the surf. You sit at meals with your family, but you are never really . . . there. You will always be leaving to go to another place. You do not give time to him . . .'

Finn stared at Raza, taken aback. 'Rubbish. I'm around all the time . . .' His face closed. 'Anyway, you are always talking to him about books and stuff.'

'I enjoy to talk to your father, but it is to you, his son, he would like to spend time with . . .'

Finn turned away and chucked a stone towards the sea in a small angry gesture. Raza watched him, troubled. He had been trying hard to understand Finn. His Baba's injuries had been very terrible, but he was alive, he was healing, he was going to walk again. He tried always to be cheerful. He never complained about his pain. How could Finn not honour and support his father? Raza could see Finn was hurting and how concerned his family were by his behaviour. It made him hurt too; he wanted to help. He had never before felt unable to talk to Finn.

The afternoon was oppressive. The sun pressed against a grey blanket of cloud and weighed down on both boys. 'Finn . . .' Raza said miserably. 'I know it cannot be that you feel . . . shame of your father because he has lost a leg, but I worry that this is what your father might think when he is feeling sad . . . He is very brave man . . .'

Finn swung round, furious. 'Don't be stupid!'

Raza flinched but held Finn's eyes. 'In my country many men and children lose their limbs by bombs. There are no hospitals or money for doctor and nurses like here, where they can make limbs work with computers. All this your father can have. I see he fights hard in much pain to walk again. If he were my Baba, I would be very proud . . . I would be . . .'

424

Finn jumped to his feet. 'Well, he's not your bloody Baba, is he, Raz? So, stop butting in and talking about things you know nothing about.'

Raza's piercing green eyes flashed as he too jumped to his feet. 'If he were my father, I would be joyful. I would give thanks to Allah each morning that he is still alive. It is all that matters . . .'

Raza bent and gathered his things together, picked up his rod and walked away, straight-backed, looking small and alone as the great expanse of white beach swallowed him. The anger drained out of Finn. He opened his mouth to shout, *Raz, Come back!* But no sound came. *What just happened?* It was the first time he and Raz had ever had an argument.

Delphi found Raza packing up his few possessions from the bottom bunk and putting them in his rucksack. 'Darling, are you leaving us?'

Raza straightened and placed his hands together and gave her his little bow. 'I return home to Sarah and Chinir to see little Samia, Delphi.'

'Of course,' Delphi watched his face. He was not looking at her and misery emanated from his small frame. 'Is everything all right, Raza?'

Raza nodded. 'Finn's mother and little sister, they arrive soon. You have many visitors. I am one more person.'

'There is always room for you, Raza. We think of you as family. We have two beach houses for the summer. Lucy, the physio, is only visiting for the day. Hanna is only staying one night. She's just dropping Izzy off.'

Raza was silent. Finn never spoke of his parents not being together, even though Ben was back from Afghanistan, even though he was injured. This must also be hurting Finn, making him sad. Raza sighed. He did not know how to

425

deal with the new Finn. He wanted his friend back. He said cautiously, 'Thank you, but I think it better Finn spend time with you on his own. I will go back to my home now.'

'Okay.' Delphi smiled. 'As long as this is what you'd like to do and you're not leaving because you think you're in the way.'

Raza smiled back but the smile did not reach his eyes.

There was a burst of laughter from the veranda where Ben was showing Lucy Adams his progress. 'Please will you say goodbye to Ben. I will not interrupt,' Raza said, heaving the rucksack on his back.

He had been going to ring Chinir or Sarah to ask if they would pick him up, but suddenly he wanted to be gone. 'Darling, what's the rush? It's miles to the main road. There are no buses. You can't walk to town . . .' Delphi trailed off as she saw Raza's raw misery.

Ian stood in the doorway. 'Delphi, I've suddenly realized I've got to go into town to pick up some more wine and barbecue stuff. Can I give you a lift, Raza? Be glad of the company.'

Raza let out his breath in relief. 'Thank you. Yes please, sir. I will come with you now . . .'

'Good, throw your bag in the back of the truck and I'll get my keys . . .'

'Have you really got to go to town?' Delphi asked under her breath.

'No,' Ian said, and she saw he was angry. 'Will you go and see what Finn has to say about this, Delphi? I won't have anyone made to feel unwelcome while they are under our roof.'

Finn was aimlessly throwing pebbles at a small cairn of rocks he had built. If he heard Delphi, he gave no sign of it. She sat down beside him.

'Raza wanted to go home. Ian is giving him a lift. Would you like to tell me what happened?'

Finn sniffed, shot another stone at the mound, but was silent.

Delphi said, 'You know, Finn, the trouble with feeling miserable is that you make the people around you equally miserable. Pushing everyone away is not the answer. None of us can help you when you're like this . . .'

Delphi paused. 'I don't often see Ian angry. Raza has been a part of this family since the first day we met him. He's lost his father and he's adrift. That's why he loves spending time with Ben. He's lonely, Finn, and Ben enjoys his company. Sarah and Chinir are immersed in their new child. You surf to the exclusion of all else, and, when you are out of the water, you are monosyllabic. I relied on the fact that Raza felt happy, included, and settled with us and he understood that we all love having him around the place. Suddenly, he's packing his things, anxious to go home and I'd like to know why.'

'I didn't ask him to go. It was his decision,' Finn muttered. Then added under his breath, 'He went too far. I got mad.'

'Raza?' Delphi sounded incredulous 'About what?'

'Ben.'

'What did he say?'

Finn was silent. Delphi waited. When she eventually spoke, Finn heard her weariness. 'I know how hard this last year has been on you, Finn. So much has happened, and Ian and I have been distracted and anxious over Ben, but he needs us all, darling. He needs every bit of love and support we can give him . . .'

Delphi paused, watching Finn's closed and unhappy face. 'I do understand how unbearable it is to see him vulnerable and injured when he's always been so fit and tough. But I don't understand why you, the kindest of boys, are finding

427

it so hard to show Ben that you love him and are just as proud of him as you ever were?'

Finn slumped, covered his eyes. He did not know. He did not know why or where his anger was coming from, and he hated himself. He could not bear to see Ben struggling to walk. He could not bear to watch him hiding his pain. Delphi rubbed his back for a while, too tired to engage anymore.

As she trudged back across the sand to the beach house, she saw that Ben was standing hanging onto the veranda rail with one hand, and holding onto Lucy, the physio, with the other. He was wearing his prosthesis and taking small steps and Lucy was whooping encouragement. Ben was gritting his teeth but smiling at the same time. Then he collapsed onto a chair and the girl bent and said something and Ben burst out laughing, threw back his head and roared. It was so long since Delphi had heard that infectious, throaty laugh that her spirits lifted in a small joyous moment. The sound of his belly laugh had got lost, somehow, down the years, in his tricky marriage to Hanna, in the turn life had taken. Ben, Delphi saw suddenly, was going to be fine. He had rarely let anything defeat him and he wasn't going to let it now.

CHAPTER SEVENTY-TWO

'Hi,' Lucy said to Finn as he hosed down his surfboard at the back of the house. 'Your dad mentioned you might have a spare board I could use in the morning, if the surf's up? Delphi has kindly asked me to supper so I'm going to stay over in the chalet next door tonight. I'd really like to get in the water in the morning. Too good an opportunity to miss . . .'

Finn turned the outside tap off and looked at her. She was tall with masses of streaky blonde hair and creamy coffee tanned skin. She had an open, smiley face as if she was always happy. Perhaps she was. She seemed to make Ben laugh anyway.

'Yeah, plenty of boards here. Bit old though, not the lightest. How good are you?'

She pretended to look offended. 'I'm an Aussie! I surfed before I could walk.' She wiggled an eyebrow at him. 'Blinking good.'

Finn grinned. 'Okay . . .'

'Got a wetsuit?' she asked hopefully.

'Well . . .' Finn felt himself turn pink as he sized her up. 'I think the only one that will fit you will be Ben's. All the others are quite small . . . I mean it will be a bit big in places . . . not that you are big, of course, just that all the wetsuits are . . .'

Lucy swivelled her wrist at him. 'Keep digging, Finn, the hole is getting pretty damn deep. You're saying my charlies are so big I can only fit into a six-foot man's wetsuit, right?'

Finn, shocked, went pinker and giggled, trying to avert his eyes from her creamy bosoms in a tight yellow top. 'No! No! You're not . . . I mean . . .'

He gave up and they grinned at each other. 'No worries,' she said as they went into the house. 'I'll wear whatever's going. If you wake early and the surf's up, come and bang on my door?'

'Sure,' Finn said. 'I'll go to the café and catch the surf channel to see what the weather's doing tomorrow . . .'

'They have Wi-Fi?'

'Yeah.'

'Mind if I grab my laptop and tag along? I want to check something out.'

Lucy Adams sat with a beer in the crowded café looking completely at home. The weather forecast was not good. The surf was going to be messy the following day. Finn watched her, nursing a Coke. She was funny and bantered easily with the surfers in the café. She was also quite pretty.

She fired up her laptop, concentrating against the background noise. When she found what she wanted, she got out her mobile and plugged it in her ear and started talking to someone as she scrolled for something online. She gave a whoop as she found what she wanted and pulled her earphones out.

'Hey!' she said to Finn. 'Come and take a look. This will interest you.'

Finn moved chairs so that he could see the screen. Prosthetics. Artificial legs. He blanched. Wanted to run.

430

'Now,' Lucy said. 'This is what I'm after . . . I've just spoken to Ben's prosthetist, because your dad's in a bit of pain . . . When he's back at Headley Court we'll try this one, see . . . really light . . . Watch this video, Finn. Eat your heart out, Blade Runner . . . Isn't it amazing? See how fast that guy's moving? Now, for every day, there is . . . this one. Light but solid . . .'

'What? You mean Ben could have more than one?'

'Yep! Your dad will probably end up with about four different legs for different things . . . watch . . . you see, swimming, surfing, running, playing football. Everything is computerized and tailor-made these days and technology is improving all the time . . .'

She turned to look at him. 'Your dad's leg will change with time as he builds muscle, so we have to check regularly. It's a question of re-balancing his body and building confidence, but there is virtually nothing he won't be able to do. He might have a slight limp, especially when he's tired, but no one will even know he has a prosthesis. Fantastic, technology, isn't it?'

'Yeah.' Finn kept his eyes on the screen, fascinated. 'Do you mean Ben might run again? He was an ace runner. He always beat me.'

'Sure. These legs aren't just for Olympians. Most servicemen are fit and sporty, so they have a head start. It won't be the same, Finn, your dad will get exhausted and ache and get sore, but his injuries won't dominate his life, plus he's not the sort of guy who would let them. Ben will find ways of doing the sports he loves.'

She seemed so sure, so positive. Finn looked at her as she closed down her laptop. For a second he wondered if she had engineered getting him to look at the website with her, but he didn't think so. Lucy glanced at her watch. 'Hey, we better get back. We mustn't be late for your gran's supper.'

As they walked back to the beach house she asked, 'Can I ask why you call your dad Ben?'

'I always have,' Finn said. 'I call my mother Hanna, too.'

Lucy grinned. 'Okay. Confirms my opinion the Brits are a bit weird . . .'

Finn laughed. Delphi, hearing him laugh, looked up, surprised.

Good Lord, that girl can make anyone laugh, she thought.

432

CHAPTER SEVENTY-THREE

The rain woke Finn, hitting the roof like bullets. He could hear the surf crashing down on the beach in great bursts like thunder. He lay on his back unable to sleep, feeling the emptiness of the bunk underneath him. Raz had been sleeping there on and off for nearly three weeks.

He thought about Hanna and Izzy, who were arriving tomorrow. At least he would have Izzy in the bottom bunk. He thought about how no one really talked about Hanna when she wasn't here. Sometimes it seemed like she'd died or something. Like they were all stuck waiting to see what she was going to do. Frozen, like when the music stops in musical chairs.

When Hanna first left, Finn had thought it was Germany, and being alone so much, that made her unhappy. He told himself that when Ben came back from Afghanistan and they were posted somewhere else, things would be okay again and they would all live in an English quarter together, somewhere.

He knew they would never go back to the quarter in Germany, where their things lay packed in the creepy cellar, where some other family ate, and slept and played in their house. But in his head, all the rooms remained exactly as they were, full of their things.

No one talked about what was going to happen next. Finn knew that Ben would have to be medically assessed at some point and a decision reached on whether he would be fit enough to stay on in the army. Ben must think about it all the time he was learning to walk again. The army had been his whole life and he loved it. Finn had heard Ian telling Delphi that whatever decision a military board made, Ben's days of active service were over. Ben wouldn't be able to bear it. He would hate sitting at a desk all day.

Hanna wasn't going to come back. Finn was pretty sure of that now. If she wasn't here in England with them when Ben was in hospital and rehab, she would never come back. Hanna had turned her back and walked away from them and taken Izzy with her. Just like that.

He missed Raz here in the dark, talking about the shadows of kites wheeling over his house in the evenings . . . of apricots lying like small yellow clouds in the fields; of the great swathes of swirling snow on the mountains in winter that blocked all roads and cut his village off from the world.

Of how, in summer, he ran wild in forests full of butterflies with shafts of sunlight slanting like golden blades upon soft brown pine needles under his feet . . .

Raz had told Finn his secrets, whispered about the gun factories in a valley near Peshawar, that his brothers used to take him to. He had a photograph he kept hidden. He was sitting between his brothers. They had fierce faces, and turbans and beards and guns. Raz also had a turban, and he peered out with an eager pride, as he sat between his brothers. It was another life. A life Raz had lost . . .

Finn squeezed his eyes shut in an agony of remorse. He

434

had yelled at Raz and he kept seeing the look in his eyes. He had destroyed the absolute, unspoken trust between them. His raised voice had been a form of betrayal. Finn groaned. He would do anything to have yesterday afternoon back; to expunge the words he had yelled. Raz was only trying to understand what he didn't understand himself. He had never meant for him to go away.

Finn climbed out of his bunk and dropped to the floor. The rain was easing. He pulled a sweater over the *shalwar kameez* Sarah had given him and switched his bedside light on. There, just under the bottom bunk lay Raza's prayer mat. Finn pulled it out and held it. Then he walked out into the corridor and opened the door to the veranda.

At the far end he saw the covered glow of Ben's bedside light. Finn crept carefully to where Raza always prayed and put the mat down. Then he remembered he must wash before he prayed so he went back to the bathroom and splashed water over himself in the way Raza did.

Finn knelt on the prayer mat and bowed his head to the floor wondering if, as an infidel, he would be struck down. *Please Allah, let Raza know I'm sorry. Please let him come back. Thank you, Allah.* He swayed and bowed his forehead repeatedly to the floor and found the rhythm somehow soothing. Kneeling on the little Afghan rug in his *shalwar kameez,* Finn felt as if his body and heart were slowly moulding and shimmering into Raza's thin form. As if he was slowly metamorphosing into his friend. As if he could breathe into himself the spiritual essence of Raza. Raza and all his goodness.

The rain eased, but the crash of waves thundered on as he knelt. Finn thought of Delphi's shrine to Buddha at the other end of the veranda. He thought that all the gods were probably the same and maybe it didn't matter whom you prayed to as long as you believed in something. And mostly he did believe God existed, because, as Ian said, the alternative seemed too bleak to contemplate. Like now.

Finn got to his feet and turned to the glow of Ben's room. He pushed open the swing doors and moved quietly to the bed and watched Ben sleeping. He looked younger when he was asleep. Finn felt love squeezing his heart. Ben could have died. He and Delphi and Ian could have buried him, and he would have spent all this summer knowing he could never, ever speak to his dad again. Like Raz. This is how it felt for Raz.

Ben suddenly put out his hand to Finn and opened his eyes as if he had known he was there. 'Finn,' he said sleepily. 'Bad night?'

Finn nodded. 'Feel like talking?' Ben asked, trying to wake up.

Finn nodded again. Ben threw him a pillow. 'Climb into the bottom of the bed where I can see you.'

Finn climbed onto the end of the bed, carefully. 'I was horrible to Raz,' he said, in a rush. 'But I never meant him to go home.'

'Have you rung him?'

'No. I don't know what to say. I . . . don't . . . know who I am or what I'm doing anymore . . .'

Ben pulled himself upright. 'In what way, old thing?'

Finn tried to find the right words. 'Like . . . I'm scared most of the time, waiting for another bad thing to happen, to you or Delphi or Ian or Izzy. It makes me want to run . . . to escape, so I don't have to talk or think or feel anything . . . the only way I can stop my brain is when I'm surfing . . .'

'Oh, Finn . . .' Ben said wretchedly. 'I'm so sorry . . .'

'No!' Finn said. 'It's not your fault; it's me. I get angry. I got angry with Raz because what he said is true . . .' Ben waited. 'He asked me why I didn't spend more time with

436

you. He couldn't understand why I disappear all the time surfing.'

'Do you think you could be angry with Hanna and me, as well as life in general?' Ben asked carefully. 'With Hanna for leaving and with me for getting myself blown up? You have quite a lot to feel angry about.'

Finn stared at Ben. All of a sudden, he realized that deep down inside him was a great bellyful of anger. He got off the bed and paced about. 'You lied, Dad. You told me you were safe. You told me that you would mostly be in the ops room and hardly ever go out on patrols. That's what you said, when you knew it wasn't true. I bet you got bored and went out on that patrol and got yourself blown up . . .'

Finn stopped, his voice shaking. 'Come here, Finn,' Ben said. He patted the bed beside him. 'What I told you was true. I was the OC and my job was planning operations from headquarters in Lash, but the morale of the men and women under my command is also my responsibility. I try to prepare my team for a war zone, but the reality is that some find it hard to cope with the constant stress of combat and the death of comrades. I was out with the boys that day because it was not just a routine patrol, but a tricky operation in harsh terrain . . .'

Ben felt himself pulled back into that morning, tricky did not even begin to cover it. He felt again the headiness, the strange alertness filling his veins with adrenaline as they stepped into danger. Somewhere, up there above him, in the low range of muddy compounds, on a skyline lit by the rising sun was 'Objective Zulu', a twenty-three-year-old bombmaker. Scattered for a kilometre all around the small village was his squadron, quietly moving into position. His earpiece softly hummed as his troops confirmed they were ready. A cut-off group in the narrow ditch to the north, a fire support group in the clump of trees to the east. The voice of the ops officer confirming the target was on station above him. Ben listened to the barely heard tick of a helicopter gunship in the sky above him. In front of him his soldiers steadily walked, clearing a route with a metal detector swinging from side to side. They were now amongst low walls and stunted trees. The small, dusty road felt horribly remote. It was quiet, too quiet. An image of Hanna suddenly flew into Ben's head and he shook it away.

At that moment, across the track, a small boy appeared. A dicker? They all kept their eyes on him as they moved along the track. The Taliban used children to watch the infidels and trigger attacks. The boy had startling green eyes, like Raza, and was watching them intently. Ben heard Andy's intake of breath as a small girl with a herd of goats appeared from a belt of trees. A distraction? The interpreter issued a sharp warning.

Ben did not see the little boy wave his stick in the air. There was a sudden flash and thump of explosive from the wall beside him. The air was filled with dust and he was somewhere on his back. When the dust cleared, he could hear the dull, steady explosive crack of a Russian-made heavy machine gun and the answering rattle as his squadron responded . . . then . . . then, as the life blood pumped out of him . . . Dolly beside him . . .

Ben shivered and came back to the beach house. His face must have reflected something of the horror he longed to forget, because Finn was watching him with tears in his eyes.

'Finn, this could have happened to me at any time and in any place in Afghanistan. It's the luck of the draw, I'm afraid . . . You will have to accept that I'm left with these injuries. I've lost my left leg. My stomach wound has slowed my rehabilitation, but my right leg is going to be fine, thanks to a surgeon's skill. Things are never going to be quite the same again, but as you know, I'm horribly competitive and love a challenge . . . In a year or so, I hope to be able to do many of the things I did before, it's just going to be harder to achieve . . .'

Ben smiled. 'Just let me say this, my dearest boy, never feel bad if you feel embarrassed by my prosthesis or that I'm an amputee . . . these are totally normal feelings to have . . . It will take time for you to get used to me this way . . . that's all it is . . .'

'I'm not ashamed, I'm not embarrassed, Dad . . .' Finn cried, trying to stem the guilty tears welling up inside him, but they poured out of the sides of his eyes in a great soundless flow.

'Come here . . .' Finn could feel Ben's heart pumping with emotion as he held him. He rubbed Finn's back, laid his cheek against Finn's head. 'It's okay,' he whispered to him. 'It's all going to be okay. You'll be utterly amazed at how okay life is going to be . . .' He said, laughing gently. 'Different, but okay.'

Finn smiled, sniffed, and sat up. He should be the one doing the comforting. 'It's what Raza asked . . . if I was ashamed of you losing your leg. That's why I got mad at him and called him stupid. He said that if you were his father, he would be proud, and just thank Allah that you were alive. I shouted that you weren't his bloody father. I forgot his father had just died . . . I feel terrible . . . I'm not a good person anymore . . . I hurt people.'

'You, Finn Charles, have always been one of the nicest people I know.' Ben smiled. 'Have we cleared some air tonight? Do you feel a bit better about things?'

Finn nodded and Ben said, 'You need to make it right with Raza, Finn. Don't leave it. Ring him or go see him tomorrow.'

'Yeah, I know. I will.'

'Any chance of a cup of tea?'

Finn grinned. 'You're going to turn into a teabag soon.' At the door he said, 'Dad, you know Lucy?'

'I do.' Ben looked amused.

'Last night, she showed me this website where there's all these different artificial legs you can have as you progress. All for different things, like a blade for running and a really light one for swimming or walking. You could have, like, four different legs so you can do lots of different things . . . She said there is no reason you can't surf, but you won't be as good as her.'

'Did she indeed?' Ben grinned. 'We'll see about that.'

In the kitchen Delphi already had the kettle on. 'Hello, darling, we all seem to be awake tonight. It's like Clapham Junction.'

Finn laughed and went over and hugged her. 'I'm sorry,' he said. 'I'm sorry. I'll make it right with Raz.'

'Good,' she said, kissing his forehead. 'Nice to have Finn back!'

As she poured hot water into the mugs, Finn said, 'Delphi, do you think Hanna will ever come back to live in England? Or do you think they will get a divorce?'

Delphi put the kettle down and decided to be truthful. 'Sweetheart, I don't know, but I think it's doubtful. Too much has happened. If Hanna wanted to be with your dad, she would be here with him now, wouldn't she?'

Finn nodded, realizing that, somehow, through all the long, miserable weeks he had spent being angry, he had already accepted this. It had already become a reality. Almost. 'I was going to ask Ben, but I didn't want to make him sad.'

'I think Ben has accepted that Hanna will always be part of your life, but she will go on living in Finland. But it's time they both talked to you. Not knowing leaves a little opening for hope and that's unfair. Do let's try to make sure your parents explain what's going on between them, darling, then you can tell me . . .'

Finn grinned, loving her. 'Come on,' she said, 'let's take this tea in to Ben . . .'

The three of them sat in Ben's room in companionable silence, listening to the rain. Ben wondered if he would ever sleep for eight hours again. Then he smiled, thinking of Lucy sleeping next door. It was a nice thought. Some women were born happy and liked to make others happy. And some were not.

Delphi thought, *We have weathered some of the worst moments of Ben's life and I think we are coming through.*

Finn eyed Raza's prayer mat still lying in the corner of the veranda. He missed him with such an overpowering sense of loneliness that he doubled over.

CHAPTER SEVENTY-FOUR

Finn arrived at Raza's house early the next morning, even though he had only slept for a few hours. Lucy offered him a lift. She was leaving early to go back to her friends in Padstow as there was no surf. She dropped Finn outside Raza's front door and waited until Sarah opened the door.

Sarah beamed, surprised to see him. She told him that Raza and Chinir were out, checking a mosque in Carnon Downs, because the one in Truro was going to shut. She said they should be back any minute and took him into the kitchen.

She was feeding the baby, Samia, in a little chair. The baby had grown lots of wild dark hair. 'She's grown bigger,' Finn said. Sarah laughed. 'Babies tend to do that, sweetie.'

Finn liked Sarah. When he came to stay with Raz she always seemed pleased to see him. Their house was immaculate, very modern, and always a bit hot, unlike the beach house or Salubrious House. The curtains and blinds were heavy and dark to shut out the sunlight. At Delphi and Ian's house they hardly ever closed the curtains, so everything was faded by the sun.

Finn loved the paintings in Sarah and Chinir's house.

They were by a Pakistani friend of Sarah's in Karachi. They were full of colour and vibrancy and depicted another world. Large photographs of the lakes and mountains of Skardu in north Pakistan hung in the hall and in Raza's room. There was one of a busy market in Peshawar. Finn knew it was where Raza used to go with his father. One of Raza's uncles had a stall there. To Finn, these places now seemed familiar because of the stories Raza had told him. He loved to gaze at the photos. They seemed full of mystery and made Finn want to go there one day. The *shalwar kameez* Raza and Sarah had given him had come from that market.

Finn bent to talk to the baby and she suddenly opened her mouth in a big gummy smile. 'She's cute,' Finn said, laughing. He was suddenly back in their first German quarter with Hanna and baby Izzy.

Sarah was watching him. 'Bet you haven't had breakfast. I'm going to make you a hot drink and toast. I've never known toast to fail as a pick-me-up.'

Finn sat on one of the high stools by the granite island where they ate breakfast. Sarah asked him how Ben was doing, and Finn told her about Lucy the physiotherapist and how she had told him that Ben was doing great. Sarah said she thought it was inspirational how much Ben had achieved in a few months. She said it must have been hell for them all to watch Ben struggling and in pain. Finn had never been on his own with Sarah before. He liked the way she talked about Ben so easily.

Finn watched her as she buttered toast and the baby gurgled in the hot kitchen. Her hair was incredibly dark and shiny. 'In my job and Chinir's,' she told him, 'we see difficult and tragic things happen. The first reaction of relatives to someone badly injured is often disbelief. An absolute refusal to accept that this huge, life-changing,

443

incident has swept their old life away. If they don't accept it, it hasn't happened . . .'

She poured boiling water into a teapot and turned to him. 'But you know, Finn, when we talk to people a few months later it is so different. The injured person has faced challenges he never dreamt he was capable of overcoming. The families have met other families like themselves, battling to get the best support for their injured loved ones. This will sound trite, but many accident victims do not become beaten by the vast change to their lives, but enriched . . .'

Sarah put tea and toast in front of Finn. 'In the west you like neat and happy endings and although I've lived nearly all of my life in the UK, I remain a Pakistani and Muslim in mindset and spirit. I believe life is one continuous loop. Wonderful and terrible things happen, but there is never an ending, just the beginning of the next part of our lives . . .'

Sarah bent and picked Samia out of her chair and wrinkled her nose. 'Eat your toast while I go and change this little madam.'

She went to the door, then came back. 'Finn, I wonder if you realize that you and your family have changed Raza's life? He was a very different and unhappy boy before we came to Cornwall. I had begun to think I had done the wrong thing in bringing him to the UK. When he met you, everything changed in an instant, or that's how it seemed. I misjudged so many things. My choice of school for him, my ability to spend enough time with him. Raza's anger with his father, with me, for whisking him out of Pakistan . . . It was an enormous culture shock for a little boy from the mountains. He was overwhelmed by homesickness, Finn. He really did have a hard time . . .'

Finn said, 'Raz is part of our family now. It's not me that's changed his life. It's because Raz has a brain the size of a planet. In school here, he doesn't have to hide his cleverness. Everyone likes Raz . . .'

Sarah smiled. 'You were his first true and constant friend, Finn. Raza's a Pashtun, fiercely loyal. He will be your friend unto death . . .' She laughed. 'In Pakistan there is a saying. "My home is your home. My family is your family." For Raza you have made this a reality.'

Finn grinned. 'Delphi sometimes worries that you and Chinir might think we have kidnapped him . . .'

Sarah laughed again. 'I don't feel remotely jealous that he loves being with you, Finn. Just so grateful that he is settled and happy. I love Raza. It makes me sad that we never truly bonded in the way I hoped. Maybe it was his age or that he felt I took him away from his father. It could be that he grew up in a totally male environment and is more comfortable with men. He is closer to Chinir and Daniyal, than to me, although he adores my mother, Liyana. She was there for him at the beginning and I was not . . .'

They heard car doors slamming outside. Chinir and Raza were back. Sarah winked at Finn. 'Raza is going to be startled to see you eating toast in my kitchen.'

When they came through the door Raza's face lit up when he saw Finn. 'You better not have eaten all the toast,' he said, grinning widely.

CHAPTER SEVENTY-FIVE

Hanna and Ben sat on the veranda in late afternoon sunshine watching Finn and Raza play with Izzy in the sea. 'Izzy's in heaven,' Hanna said. 'She's got you and two boy slaves all in one package!' She turned to look at Ben. 'You're looking so much better. You've made unbelievable progress, Ben. I'm so glad.'

Ben smiled. 'Getting there.' Hanna's relief was palpable. 'You're looking good too, Hanna.'

'Working again always makes me feel good. I've been looking forward to being back in London for a couple of weeks and catching up with Annalisa . . .'

There was an awkward silence. In the background the fridge hummed. Delphi and Ian had taken themselves off to Penzance for the night. 'We need to talk to Finn, Hanna. Not surprisingly, he's been pretty screwed up this summer.'

Hanna sighed. 'Yes, I have gathered that.'

'I haven't talked to him about the future because he's had enough to cope with, but practical decisions have to be made. I don't know what you've said to him, but we need to be clear and consistent about what we are going to do.'

446

'I was going to talk to him,' Hanna said quickly, 'but you got sick and Ed Dominic told me Finn was working again. I was so relieved, I decided to leave it for a while . . . It's been difficult, Ben, I try to phone Finn. I try to Skype and email him regularly, but he rarely answers. But you're right, we must talk to him . . .'

Hanna leant forward. 'Please, don't think this has been easy . . . that I can just walk away from our marriage without regret. I wish . . . I regret many things . . .'

For the first time Hanna looked directly at him. 'In Germany, I felt as if I was trapped in a dark place behind a glass wall. I was on one side of it and everyone else seemed to be on the other . . . It is impossible to explain, to even try until you start to come out of it . . . It's only the last two months I've begun to feel in control . . . and I've had a lot of help . . .'

Ben watched her thin hands fluttering in her effort to make him understand. 'Leaving you injured, going back to Helsinki, made me a pariah at home with my friends, with my family, even with Kai, who has known me all my life . . . No one seemed to understand how I could . . . I was made to feel like a monster, Ben . . . It was my father who made me look for help. I have therapy. I take pills. But I am slowly becoming myself again . . .'

Ben stared into the beautiful face that had once entranced him. Hanna always managed to make other people's tragedy about her, but for the first time in his life Ben understood what being trapped behind a glass wall felt like. It was a terrible, hopeless place from which you needed help to escape. From which, he suspected, you could never entirely escape. Hanna had suffered depression or been deeply unhappy for years and he had never comprehended its grip or power. Or had not wanted to. He understood it now, and it helped him accept Hanna's flight from him and from army life. But he could not forgive her for the timing. Walking out as he left for Afghanistan. When Finn needed her most.

As if Hanna knew what he was thinking, she smiled. 'Being back to myself, does not change my intrinsic character, Ben, but therapy has helped me to take responsibility for my actions . . .'

'I'm glad you're getting treatment, Hanna. I'm hardly blameless. I was too preoccupied to realize you needed help. Or perhaps, I just didn't know what I could do about it . . .' Ben said wearily. 'I didn't even understand what depression felt like until I was injured . . .'

'I'm sorry, Ben . . .'

'Not your fault,' Ben said quickly. 'My depression was caused by my injuries. Got it well under control . . .'

He got up and leant over the veranda rail, so Hanna could not see his face. Hanna closed her eyes, felt wretched. There were so many things she could say. Ben could say. But neither had the will. It was all too late. She had slowly started to work again, to pick up the pieces of her old life. She sensed that Ben too had turned his thoughts away from her towards whatever his future held.

In the distance they both watched Izzy and the two boys running in small waves, their laughter rippling into the windless morning.

Ben said, 'Our marriage is over, Hanna, but how are you going to make it right with your son?'

'I can't,' Hanna said quietly. 'I can never make it right with Finn.'

Her pragmatism caught Ben by surprise, and he turned to face her again.

'I've abandoned him at the worst time, when he is caught between childhood and becoming an adult. He will never forgive me. It will never be the same between Finn and I . . .'

448

Ben heard rawness in her voice, real pain and regret. 'Not necessarily,' he said gently, 'but you do need to convince him that you can still have a relationship with him, wherever you are. That you will always love and care for him, that will never change.'

Hanna said in a sudden defensive little burst, 'I am told that I am a selfish woman and perhaps I am. I know you and I would never have married if I had not got pregnant with Finn. I always planned to keep working, have a career. I am no good at just being just a mother. It bores me. All those endless years of army life when I watched you pursue the career you wanted, knowing I could never catch up or be financially independent. I was stuck, sitting alone in an army quarter waiting for you to come home, waiting for the next posting . . . praying it might be London so I could have some sort of life of my own . . .'

Ben stared at her. Hanna was describing thirteen years of their life together. Hanna got up and paced the veranda. 'Do you have any idea how many army wives felt like me, Ben? Women with degrees and abandoned careers and hopes . . . all of us thrown randomly together and having to like each other and get on, in a vacuum . . . Years of our young, productive lives we can never get back. For what? Our husband's promotion? When one bad report from an incompetent or jealous senior officer can kill your army career dead, no matter how hard you work . . . No matter how many of you die or are injured, the army will spit you out or make you redundant or try to cheat you of your pension. And, wives, they have to just sit on the side-lines watching, knowing they no longer have the ability to earn a decent wage that might influence their passed-over-for-promotion husband to leave the army and find a life outside . . .'

Hanna ran out of breath. Ben stood, stunned by the force

449

of her anger and resentment. Of course, he had known she was fed up with Germany, with not being able to work, with him constantly away, with having a small child again after six years. But he had absolutely no idea she had loathed the army and their life so much.

'And there was me thinking there were good times,' he said quietly. 'Skiing, lovely holidays, a decent wage, two lovely kids, a happy social life . . .'

'Oh God!' Hanna said. 'I did not mean to say any of that, Ben. Of course, there were good times, especially in the early days. We had fun . . . It is the life you chose and love. I'm sorry.'

'Don't apologize,' Ben said. 'It's how you feel, Hanna. But what a pity you never said any of this to me as explicitly while we were married . . .'

He had one eye on the children, hoping they could finish this conversation before they wandered back.

Hanna stood by the rail beside him. 'I tried. Ben, I tried, but neither of us was good at facing the truth about our relationship, were we? You are right, our marriage is over, but I want things to work between us. I think we could try a new way of living. I have regular work in Helsinki, but I have arranged to be in the London office regularly to help Annalisa. Izzy is small still, so she needs to stay with me, but I will bring her to England whenever you want. Izzy can spend holidays with you. When she is older, if you wish her to go to boarding school in England and she is happy to go, then that is fine, but I want her to be bilingual and to know her Finnish roots . . .'

She turned to look at the children in the sea. 'I would love Finn to come out to Finland regularly, to get to know his grandparents better and spend time with me in my own country . . . something we have never had time to do . . . I know it is going to take time for him to get used to us being apart, but as he gets older, I hope he will become curious about his Finnish roots . . .'

Hanna sat down suddenly. 'Most of all, I would like to be friends with you, Ben, good friends, because we have two children together and we have had happy times too . . .' The truth, she thought, is never the whole truth. Until his accident, she had never stopped wanting Ben. Found him physically pretty perfect. The long separations added excitement to sex when he came home. She loved Ben in dress uniform. Loved it when they were both partying, the beautiful couple, the centre of attention. None of it was enough, but it had kept Hanna in her marriage. It kept them both from talking, it kept them from facing the cracks when the sex was so good, and love was not quite enough . . .

The children were out of the sea and wrapping themselves in towels. In a moment they would begin to make their way up to the beach house.

Ben turned from the sea to look at Hanna. 'One day,' he said, 'everything you say will make perfect sense, Hanna, but I haven't quite reached that point yet. I've lost my career, my health, and my family in one fell swoop, so forgive me if I haven't quite worked up to the happy ever after bit . . .'

Izzy was waving and yelling 'Daaddy!' Ben turned and waved back. Finn was carrying her on his shoulders.

'I will never blame you, Hanna,' he said, watching the little procession come up the beach. 'You may not have liked the army, but you were an amazingly good and supportive army wife for years, and you were on your own for a fair chunk of our married life . . .'

He turned and smiled at her. 'So, don't be hard on yourself. I'm sorry that I was so happy and self-absorbed in my own career that I miscalculated the effect of army life on you. If I had my time again, I would try to be different and more understanding. But please . . . just make sure you explain everything to Finn before you leave tomorrow. Be honest, tell him what you've told me. How you felt, how you feel. Treat him like an adult. I think you'll find he'll respond . . .'

Hanna came and stood by the rail beside him. The children were silhouettes, almost shadows as the day slowly faded.

'Thank you,' Hanna said. 'You have always been a lovely man. It makes this much harder. Shall we talk to Finn tonight, after supper?'

Ben nodded. Despite everything, he felt relief. Relief in not having to try to please Hanna and failing anymore. Of accepting the ending of one life and the slow reaching out for another.

CHAPTER SEVENTY-SIX

Delphi and Ian had driven back to Penzance for the night, leaving Ben and Hanna in the beach house with Finn and Izzy. In the night Finn thought he heard a noise and he got up to check on Ben. He found Izzy had crept into Ben's bed and was taking up all the room. Ben was worried about squashing her. Finn lifted her up and carried her back to Delphi and Ian's bed where Hanna was sleeping for the night. Izzy did not wake when he placed her back beside Hanna and neither did Hanna. His mother looked small in the great big old wooden bed. Finn had forgotten how much he loved her hair, glossy as conkers.

Hanna and Ben had talked to him that evening. Hanna was going to base her life in Finland, but she would come back to the UK regularly for work. Izzy would come to Ben for half-terms and holidays. It was not a shock. Finn was expecting it. Hanna had left them ages ago. He had had to get used to a life without her.

Finn had noticed a difference in Hanna. She seemed happier, calmer. As if she had gathered enough strength to finally tell him she was staying in Helsinki for good.

Just a different way of living, she said to Finn. Hanna

sounded so upbeat that she made it sound perfectly reasonable and possible. Finn could see Ben was worried about how he would take it, but when he saw that Finn was not going to react, he looked relieved. For Finn, hearing Hanna say out loud that she was not coming back to England to live, felt like a door closing. He felt both pain, relief, and a hardening of his heart. He would never let Hanna hurt him again. He wanted to move on with Ben, with Delphi and Ian. His pain was for the loss of Izzy. As he looked down at his sleeping sister, Finn did not think he could ever forgive Hanna for taking Izzy away from them.

Finn's Diary

Hanna has gone to London, leaving Izzy, who insists on sleeping in a camp bed in Ben's room. 'Oh, heaven help me!' Ben said happily.

Raz is back in the bottom bunk. I showed him the web page from the hospital about the bionic legs and stuff that Lucy showed me. He was fascinated. He is going to show it to Chinir. I think Chinir would be interested, being an orthopaedic surgeon, it's pretty revolutionary. Chinir told Raza that army surgeons are advising civilian doctors on how to save limbs because they have learnt so much from being on the front line in Afghanistan.

I've been thinking about what Sarah said about when bad things happen and life changes, but not necessarily for the worse. I sort of know what she means. Sometimes, it was like Ben and Hanna drained the air of oxygen when they were in a room together. Every small thing seemed such a big deal some days. I'd forgotten how Hanna used to leave me for hours babysitting Izzy. I'd forgotten how I came to dread the holidays because they were always snapping at each other. Ben said that bickering is a habit married people get into, after a while you don't even know you are doing it. I was always dreading them telling me they were going to get a divorce long before Hanna decided to leave. That's why Delphi gave me this diary. That day seems so long ago, now. I don't want to go back to how it was. Like I was a different person in another world. I didn't even KNOW Raz then. That's so weird.

It's like, ever since Hanna left, I've been making

our life in Germany perfect in my head, but it wasn't. A lot of it was happy and lot of it was not. Hanna did not want to be an army wife anymore. You can't make people happy if they don't want to be there anymore.

Hanna said that sometimes people still love each other but are better living apart and being good friends. I told Ben that it was just something parents said to their children when they wanted to feel better themselves. Ben smiled and lifted his eyebrows. 'Well, it's true that some people are better living apart. But being good friends . . . that takes a while to get there.'

He was looking at Izzy and he sounded sad. Every time we see Izzy, she is a little bit bigger. As the months in Helsinki go by, we will lose the funny little in between bits of her. Izzy will change and grow up and not be so funny anymore . . .

CHAPTER SEVENTY-SEVEN

Ben sat in the shadow of the veranda staring at one of Delphi's paintings stacked up ready for her next exhibition. Blood red. A violent slash of sunset bleeding out into the sky, darkening into molten liquid as it fell into a bottomless depth of sea. To fall in would be to sink, to drown with hands raised.

This was a painting of Delphi's fear, an explosion of grief, a silent mourning for his physical wholeness; for him cut so randomly down.

She had captured all the horror and feeling of helplessness; captured her battle with despair. It was all there on the vast canvas. But so was the essence of Delphi, a spiritual light that transcended the darkness. Ben found hope, as he stared into that vivid world of Delphi's imagination. It was there in the curl of gold sunrise edging up the painting. It was there in the ghostly suggestion of a figure riding the waves and heading for a safer shore. Ben closed his eyes. He thought of the emotional cost it must have taken to create such a painting.

In her head Delphi was a Buddhist who should accept what life gave. But she was his mother and her guilt, that she grieved for all he had once been, was reflected in this searing work. Here was the extraordinary wonder of life set in a landscape that sustained them all. No one gazing at it could doubt the anguish and rage, for there was a darker, inner landscape here, too. This painting mapped a progress of the human spirit: hers, his, the whole family. It charted the pace of a long, sad summer that had brought them through to something deep and precious.

A certainty lay in the work. An inner realization that none of them could go back to the people they had been. Delphi had captured the indefinable sense of purpose that loss sometimes brings.

Gazing at it, Ben realized he did not want to be the man he once was. It would be stupid to say he was glad he had been injured or lost a leg, but in losing that leg he had gained insight and courage and strength from strangers. He had stopped seeking or hoping for the unobtainable; that all would be well. He had learnt to let go of what he never really had. Let go of Hanna.

Ben lifted his head and looked around him. This, here, now, was what he had. Settling for that meant he could reach out with unsteady but curious hands for what lay ahead.

He looked away from Delphi's painting, out to the sea ever moving beyond the beach house. Sun flickered in a wide arc to his right like silver fireflies caught in the waves, but further out to sea the sky was purple. Weather coming in.

Finn was surfing. Crashing and gliding in on thunderous waves. For a second Ben felt a raw stab of envy, a longing for his son's strong limbs. Then it was gone.

Raza stood on the edge of the sea, watching, as Finn flew into shore in the dazzling path of the setting sun. Finn dropped his board on the sand and wriggled out of his wetsuit and towelled himself dry before pulling on his faded *shalwar kameez* with a sweater on top. He sat beside Raza and they let the water lap over their toes. The shirt tails of their *shalwar kameez* flapped in a brisk little breeze as they munched on crisps.

Summer was nearly over. Delphi and Ian were beginning to pack up the beach house. Soon Ben would go back to Headley Court for more rehab. Selly Oak was closing, and the new Queen Elizabeth hospital was replacing it. Lucy had chosen to transfer to Headley Court, so she could continue treating Ben, and other injured soldiers, through rehab. That had made Ben happy. Finn liked Lucy. She made Ben laugh and she was a brilliant physio with awards and stuff . . .

Raza was thinking that if Ben was going to surf next summer, *Inshallah*, he would have no excuse not to go into the water. It would be shameful to be afraid. Watching Finn in the sea had made him want to stand on a board and fly into shore in the path of the setting sun too.

'I think I will learn to surf next year, Finn,' Raza said.

Finn grinned at him. 'That's only because Ben is determined to surf next summer, and you might feel a wuss.'

'This is true,' Raza said equably.

'Funny,' Finn said, 'I don't really mind going back to school next week . . .'

Hanna and Izzy were back in Helsinki. Delphi had a big exhibition coming up. Ian was going up to Scotland to fish. Ben was going to rehab. Everyone had somewhere to go.

'I do not mind either,' Raza said. 'We have exams coming up and I must work hard. I do not want to fail.'

'You won't fail,' Finn said. 'I am the one who has to work to catch up.'

'You will,' Raza said solemnly. 'I know this.'

Finn watched sea and sky merge. As soon as the sun slid

down the horizon the cold would bite. He stood up. 'I think I know what I want to be when I grow up,' he said. 'A journalist, or maybe a foreign correspondent. Delphi's right, when you write things down, they make more sense than when you're trying to say them. Sometimes, you don't even know what you're thinking or feeling until your fingers start writing . . . I'd like to travel to countries I know nothing about . . .'

'I think I will do medicine,' Raza said, jumping up and pulling a sweatshirt over his head. 'Maybe become surgeon. It would be good thing to have skill to mend people, to put limbs together again . . .'

Finn turned to look at him as they walked along the edge of the sea. He thought, with a little lurch, Raz is thinking of how he can help his own people. He will go back to Pakistan to mend limbs. He won't stay here. He will leave us . . .

Raza was saying, 'Seeing Ben, it change me, how I think. Also, Chinir, he influence me . . .'

He turned and caught Finn's expression. He said quickly. 'But who knows what we will do, how we will feel in a few years' time . . .'

Raza leant towards his friend and both their heads were caught in the slanting rays of the dying day. 'Finn, I must one day return to Pakistan, but wherever I am in the world, wherever you are, we will be friends until death. We can always travel to find each other. You know this.'

Finn nodded. He did. 'My family is your family. When you have no family, we are your family.' He nudged Raza. 'Isn't that what you say in Pakistan?'

Raza grinned. 'It is.'

Raza and Finn were still down there, walking on the shoreline in the last hazy light. The two small figures seemed to shimmer as they moved against the sparking swell of the sea. What would they have done without each other this last year? Ben wished it was in his power to protect them both from an uncertain world, but it was not. It seemed to him, watching the blurred, dancing images of the two boys walking close together, disappearing into the dusk, that all their lives were no more than a speck on the landscape, no more than breath on a mirror.

AUTHOR'S NOTE

I wrote *The Long Road from Kandahar* before the tragic fall of Afghanistan in August 2021.

In 2009, I was lucky to have the opportunity to live in Pakistan for a year. It opened my eyes to a country and a culture I knew little about, and to so many freedoms we all take for granted.

On my first nervous flight to Karachi, I looked down at the stark, red mountains of Afghanistan and wondered how anyone could live in that barren landscape. I imagined British soldiers a long way from home, dying and being severely injured fighting the Taliban. I thought of my son who had been posted to Lashkar Gah.

In Karachi, I lived in a safe apartment within a guarded hotel. My life was severely restricted, but somehow full of curiosity and wonder. The hospitality and kindness of the Pakistani people who protectively tucked me under their wings gave me a glimpse of a world fraught with difficulties, but full of joy. I made lasting friends, devoured Pakistani writers, observed like a sponge, and wrote by a pool.

Bored, young waiters from North Pakistan would come over in the long afternoons to tell me about their lives.

One, a young Pashtun called Naseem with startling green eyes, would bring me an apricot on a white plate with a linen napkin. He would talk wistfully of home and of the beautiful orchards his family had left behind in the Swat Valley. I did not know it then, but he would become the inspiration for Raza.

One trip up to the golden Kashmiri mountains certainly influenced my book. Ill-advisedly, but weary of the heat of Karachi, we headed for Bhurban. It was a stunningly beautiful drive on the cliff road from Rawalpindi. Once, these wild resorts were alive with climbers and walkers, but terrorism changed the fortunes of North Pakistan and now the poverty was clear to see.

A landslide forced our driver to divert inland through one of the isolated villages. There was a frightening abundance of fierce-looking men striding about, but not a woman or a girl to be seen. When I look back at photos of that trip, I can still experience the ethereal beauty of the Kashmiri mountains, but I can also remember the guards with guns that sprang out of the cool forest as we walked, confirming that danger lay everywhere and was not a figment of our imagination. It was still unsafe and foolhardy for foreigners to travel alone; we should have listened to our friends. In Karachi we were cocooned, but the other face of Pakistan was of hardship and poverty: a wild, indifferent Pakistan. I saw how fertile a recruiting place it must be for the Taliban.

Back home in the UK, with Afghanistan constantly in the news and my own son sending blueys from Lashkar Gah, I began to think about the children of soldiers fighting away from home. Finn and Raza sprang into life, organically, clear and fully fledged.

There are a generation of soldiers like Ben who have fought in more than their fair share of conflicts: Bosnia,

Kosovo, Sierra Leone, Somalia, Iraq, Afghanistan. War takes its toll and scars are hidden. Ben, fighting in Lashkar Gah, becomes disillusioned by what can be achieved in Afghanistan. Raza states that invading armies might try to do good, but that they eventually leave those countries to their fate . . .

In August 2021, with my book finished and delivered to my publisher, I watched the fall of Afghanistan with horror, and wept. The speed of it was surreal. I could never have predicted such a bleak abandonment and ending. I wanted *The Long Road from Kandahar* to be about the power of the human spirit to endure, the strength of friendship and love, and the ability to find joy in each other and to move forward with hope.

ACKNOWLEDGEMENTS

My love and thanks to my son, Toby, for reading early drafts and for guidance with military protocols, as well as a chilling understanding of the procedures in the aftermath of an IED. Any military errors in this book are entirely mine.

Thanks as always to Lynne Drew, for listening and involving me on the lovely cover of this book; to Lucy Stewart for her endless patience; and to all the team at HarperCollins who work so hard to bring a book to life.

Thanks as ever to my agent, Broo Doherty, for unconditional support.

I am also grateful to the late Toby Eady, who loved the very first draft of this book. His encouraging telephone calls gave me the strength to persevere.

It was a joy to work with Celine Kelly, my editor for *The Long Road from Kandahar*. I am so grateful for her observations and insight, which were invaluable, and I much enjoyed our lockdown WhatsApp editing calls from Canada.

I am deeply indebted to the poet, Paul Henry, and his publisher Mick Felton, for allowing me to quote from his beautiful poem 'The Breath of Sleeping Boys' from *The*

Brittle Sea: New and Selected Poems (published by Seren 2010). I had this haunting poem in front of me while my son was in Afghanistan and the rhythm and emotion of the words have been at the heart of my writing. To have it at the beginning of my book means everything. I am delighted that Paul's new book, *As If to Sing*, is out at the same time as this, and is again published by Seren.

Lastly, but definitely not least, love and thanks to my son, James, in New Zealand for his long calls that close the distance between us, and to all my lovely, supportive family. To my friends, neighbours and dog walkers, bless you for simply being there.

I am donating some of the proceeds of this book to Help4Heroes and to Afghan Red Crescent.

READING GROUP QUESTIONS

Zamir has to make a difficult decision at the start of the novel in order to change Raza's future. What do you think of his decision? Could you have done the same thing?

Raza is shocked by many aspects of life in Britain, and there's a huge cultural divide between his life there and his life with Zamir. What do you think you would notice if you were viewing British culture for the first time through Raza's eyes?

Raza and Finn form an unlikely friendship and ultimately an alternative family of sorts. What do you think draws them together?

Hanna struggles within the confines of her role as mother and wife. What do you think of her decisions throughout the novel? Could you relate to her point of view?

Ben goes through an incredibly tough, life-changing event. How do you think you would react if you were in his position?

Delphi and Ian have to watch their son lose so much, while also comforting their grandchildren. What would it be like to be in their shoes? Did they handle everything as you would have done?

Raza's essay 'Vanished Lives' gives us a brief history of his home country and the way people have been mistreated. How did this make you feel as you were reading it?

What did you think of the contrast between Ben – a soldier fighting in Afghanistan – and Raza – a child surrounded by the consequences of war?

What does the novel teach us about the way people are treated if they are from different backgrounds? Do you think you learnt anything?

Which part of the novel has really stayed with you? What would you say if you were recommending it to a friend?